The Assassin's Mark

The Tudor Rose Murders Series

Book Four

G J Williams

The Book Social, 51 Gower Street, London, WC1E 6HJ
info@legendtimesgroup.co.uk | www.thebooksocial.co.uk

Contents © G J Williams 2026
The right of the above author to be identified as the author of this work has been asserted in accordance with the Copyright, Designs and Patents Act 1988. British Library Cataloguing in Publication Data available.

Print ISBN 9781917163040
Ebook ISBN 9781917163057
Set in Times.
Cover design by Sarah Whittaker | www.whittakerbookdesign.com

All characters, other than those clearly in the public domain, and place names, other than those well-established such as towns and cities, are fictitious and any resemblance is purely coincidental.

All rights reserved. No part of this publication may be reproduced, stored in or introduced into a retrieval system, or transmitted, in any form, or by any means electronic, mechanical, photocopying, recording or otherwise, without the prior permission of the publisher. Any person who commits any unauthorised act in relation to this publication may be liable to criminal prosecution and civil claims for damages.

Dr G J Williams, like John Dee, is Welsh but raised in England. After an idyllic childhood in Somerset, where history, story-telling and adventure were part of life, a career of psychology, first in academia and then international consulting, beckoned. It was some years before the love of writing returned to the forefront of life.

G J Williams now lives between Somerset and London and is often found writing on the train next to a grumpy cat and a cup of tea.

When not writing, life is a muddle of researching, travelling to historic sites or plotting while sailing the blue seas on the beloved boat bequeathed by a father who always taught that history gives the gift of prediction.

The first book in The Tudor Rose Murders series, *The Conjuror's Apprentice*, was published by Legend Press in 2023. The second book, *The Wolf's Shadow*, was published in 2024, and the third book, *The Cygnet Prince*, was published in 2025.

Follow G J on Twitter
@gjwilliams92

and Instagram
@gjwilliams92

Visit
www.gjwilliamsauthor.com

When I was nine years old a wonderful teacher asked, 'What do you want to be?'

'A writer,' I said.

'Go on then – you can do it,' were the words that never left me.

Five decades later he stood at my side when my first book was published. Every day his kind encouragement all those years ago inspires me to keep going.

This book is dedicated to Mr Gerry Williams – the best teacher I ever had. Also to his wife Joyce – another wonderful teacher and good woman.

Cast of Characters

Mortlake

Doctor John Dee – the Queen's philosopher
Margaretta Morgan – apprentice
Katherine Dee – wife of John Dee
Thomas Digges – student of John Dee
Bela – servant

Court and The Strand

Elizabeth I – Queen
Blanche ap Harri – chief gentlewoman
Robert Dudley – Earl of Leicester
Sir William Cecil – Elizabeth's chief advisor
Lady Mildred Cecil and Robert – Cecil's wife and son
Francis Walsingham – Spymaster
Alice Burton – beggar and witness

All Hallows and St John's Priory

Josef Mabelain – mender of the cloths of All Hallows Church, mender at the revels yard
Vicar Richard Tyrwhit – vicar of All Hallows Church

The Tower of London

The Duke of Norfolk

Tutbury Castle

Mary Queen of Scots – prisoner queen
Mary Seton – lady in waiting to Mary Queen of Scots
Lady, Bess of Shrewsbury – guardian gaoler of Mary Queen of Scots
The Earl of Shrewsbury – guardian gaoler of Mary Queen of Scots
Lord Huntingdon – investigator of the Shrewsburys
Winnie – kitchen servant

France

Catherine de Medici – Queen Mother of France
Duc d'Anjou – third son of Catherine de Medici
Cardinal of Lorraine – Uncle to Mary Queen of Scots
Henry Norris – English Ambassador

The Tovey Household

Sam – wherryman and manager of the Tovey boatyard
Master Tovey
Goodwife Tovey – his wife
Tillie – their adopted daughter

The McFadden Household

Angus – vintner
Susan – Margaretta's sister and Angus's wife
Jack and Maria – their children

The Constable Business

Siôn Jenkins – owner and manager
Huw Morgan – Margaretta's brother
Grace – Huw's wife

Prologue

The beggar woman cowered back into the shadow, her stomach churning in terror. She clamped filthy hands across her mouth to stifle the scream and prayed that the beast would not smell her fear.

Blood still dripped from the dead man's throat as the knife sliced open his tunic. The figure leaned over, sniffed, licked the saliva from smiling lips and sighed satisfaction. The horns growing from a head bent low and held close to the body, shone in the flicker of pitch torches.

Then the glint of a talon on a crooked index finger, and the white skin of the victim was scored with a diamond-droplet shape. Finally, a slit just above the heart, and a tightly folded cloth pushed inside. A needle, and seven neat stiches before a spray of brown spittle spattered the paling face.

The horned figure rose, turned to stare at the beggar woman, incanted dark words, and strode away, cloven hooves pressing into the soft mud of the alley.

Through the mist one word was whispered.

'Baphomet.'

Part One

Mortlake and London

Chapter One

March, 1570. Mortlake

The hammering thundered through the dark household. Margaretta slipped the horoscope she was drawing under a cloth, snatched up her candle and went to the entry hall, shouting towards the back rooms at the maid, Bela, to open her ears and do some work. She turned the heavy key and the door opened with a creak of unoiled hinges. 'Earl Robert. What brings you to Mortlake so early? We were not expecting—'

Robert Dudley stepped over the threshold and made his usual perusal of her breasts. 'Where is Dee? And what is that stink?'

'In his laboratory. The smell is his latest alchemic venture. I will get him.' Margaretta pointed to the large room off the hallway. 'If you would like to wait in—'

'No time. We have a devil among us.' He walked past her and down the dim corridor towards the oak door carved with, NO ENTRY. Margaretta ran after him, his agitation coming into her senses and the inner voice started.

I am not sure I need my special gifts to hear what you do not say, sir. You are rigid with fear. You think of a devil. Your gut churns. Now the image of Elizabeth, our Queen. Your chest tightens and you recall the sight of . . . 'Oh, my God.'

Dudley glanced back at her cry, frowned his confusion, then pushed open the door with a clatter. The room was bright with candles. In the far corner, Dee was hunched over a desk, magnifying glass in hand, scrawling notes into a book. The air was thick with fumes and the smell of dung. He did not look round. 'Damn it, Margaretta. You break my concentration with your infernal noise. Who was at the door?'

'Me. And I need you to stop and listen,' growled Dudley.

Dee spun round on his wooden stool, a smile spreading across his face until he saw the stance and face of the other man. 'Robert. What brings you from Court? From your face I would guess—'

'Trouble. Deep trouble.' Dudley squared his shoulders and jutted his chin. 'And it is now six years since I was made an Earl. You should call me Leicester.'

Dee raised one eyebrow and sniffed. 'You forget that I used to get you by the lugs, pull you from your playing, and make you sit at a study desk. It is my tutoring that made you so useful and interesting to the Queen who has so honoured you. You were Robert then and are Robert now – no earldom changes your name.' He pointed at a seat by his desk. 'Sit in Student Digges' chair and unburden yourself.' He nodded at Margaretta to bring paper and pen.

Robert Dudley, Earl of Leicester, and still assumed the Queen's lover as well as favourite, huffed his irritation but held his tongue. He brushed the seat to take away the dust which would take the perfect sheen off his black velvet breeches and doublet, richly embroidered with thread of gold, glinting in the candlelight; then raised the pomander hanging on his belt to mask the smell. 'The Devil has been witnessed in the alleys around Whitehall Palace and his evil left as a warning. Elizabeth is in great danger.'

Dee frowned and glanced at Margaretta. 'Are you taking notes?'

'Yes, Doctor.' *I have been taking your damn notes for seventeen years and have never missed a word, and still you ask.*

Dee looked back to Leicester. 'Go on.'

'A body was found at dawn this morning near the eastern gate of the palace. One of the guards.' The Earl took a deep breath. 'Dear God, it takes true evil to do that to a man. His throat was slit and the body carved with a strange symbol. Drawings have been sent to Cecil and Walsingham. Then, worse, a message was sewn into his—'

Margaretta's hand began to shake as the images came into her mind. *Slit skin. Flesh sewn. The smell of blood. A woman screams of the Devil; that she has seen the cloven-hoofed one. I feel panic.*

Suddenly, Dee's finger tapped on her paper. He had seen the shaking. 'Wine, Margaretta. Tell Bela to bring a flagon and three glasses. I feel we will need it. I will write the description of the wounds.'

Margaretta breathed relief and went to the kitchen. 'Bela. Wine and glasses for three, and be quick.'

A fair-haired girl looked up, eyes narrowing in spite and her face more sour than normal. 'Mistress Katherine wants me to keep her company while she—'

'And Goodwife Dee knows that her husband's work is important – especially so when the Earl of Leicester is sitting in the laboratory waiting for wine.'

There was a squawk from behind Bela, and Katherine Dee, formerly Katherine Constable, barrelled out of the dairy room, her face reddening with excitement. 'My John has the Earl in his office?' She began pressing her hair into her coif and arranging her skirts. 'We must make him welcome.' Her voice was rising in agitation and perspiration pearled on her brow. 'Get the best Gascon wine, Bela. And the glasses gifted by the Earl for our wedding. Make sure they are washed and polished. Oh, and sweetmeats. We must provide sweetmeats.'

Margaretta raised a hand. 'Just wine, Mistress. I think the visit will be short. And I think the doctor will be leaving with him. Me too.' She turned and went back to the laboratory, leaving Katherine to fuss.

Leicester had completed his description of the wounds

and slumped in his seat. Margaretta took back the paper and the pen, whispering to Dee in the Welsh that bonded their ancestry, '*Gofynwch am y wraig.*' Ask about the woman. Dee made a tiny nod and looked Leicester straight in the eye. 'I sense a woman in this tale.' He smiled at the other man's declaration of his brilliance.

Margaretta bit her lip. *And ever it will be. My feelings. My sensing of words unsaid. My mind seeing the truth... and you taking all the praise and wonderment. You old scut. Will you ever tell the truth of me?*

Leicester paused while Bela, lips pursed in resentment, clattered in with a tray. As she banged the door shut, Leicester reached for a glass and nodded. 'Yes, a woman witness and not mad, just poor. She was evading the night watchman by hiding behind a door left against the palace walls. They found her raving in the streets this morning, terrified and begging for a priest. Claims she saw the Devil – horns, claws, hooves, everything.' He took a gulp of wine. 'She insists the Devil is among us. And I tell you, good Doctor, only Satan could carve a man like that.'

Chapter Two

Dee, Leicester and Margaretta entered the great yards of Whitehall Palace in the Earl's carriage. He had insisted they came through Charing Cross and not the great Holbein Gate where people tarried hoping to get a glimpse of royalty. Margaretta was seated by the driver to stop the bile rising. Even after years of travelling with Dee, her stomach had never learned the rhythm of wheels. She was clutching her master's bag full of paper, quills, a full ink horn and also the velum with Dee's latest method for alchemising base metal into gold. He had insisted on bringing it despite Leicester snapping that this was, 'not a time for begging money from Sir Cecil'. Of course, Dee had ignored him in his fervour to be the winner in this pursuit of the Philosopher's Stone.

As they clambered down, Leicester barked at a scowling servant to 'hide this carriage and do not tarry'.

Oh, Robert Dudley, Earl of Leicester. Your arrogance is despised. I feel it more now than eight years ago when they called you a killer. You are puffed up with pomp. But beneath the confidence you cower in fear.

Leicester pointed towards the river. 'He is in the sheds at the top of Preny Bridge steps. Easier to move him unseen from there. Say nothing until we are inside. I want this kept from flapping ears.'

They moved in silent procession through two yards and

between the Thameside buildings of the palace and onto the wooden boards of Preny Bridge. An icy March wind blew off the river and rain-threatening clouds gathered above. Margaretta looked out across the water, thronging with swans and wherries, taking a deep breath before facing the horror. Sensing her slowing, Dee raised a finger towards her face. 'No withering away, girl. It is but a body. It will read like a book.'

Damn you. You know how death sickens and frightens me. Yet you have never shown any sympathy.

Leicester pulled open the door and clamped a hand over his mouth as a swarm of black flies buzzed into their faces. Margaretta let out a cry. Dee batted his hands and stepped inside. Leicester followed. Then the bark from Dee. 'Step inside, Margaretta. No time for whimpering.'

Leicester stiffened. 'Be kind, Doctor. She is but a woman. Her humours are weak in the face of such horror.'

Damn you both. One torments my fear of death and the other torments my strength.

Margaretta stepped into the dark of the shed, clamping nails into her palms to stop the shaking. 'Just taking a breath, Doctor. I have no fear.' She turned to the body on the table. 'Oh, dear God.'

The man had once been tall and strong with a broad chest, but his body had already started to shrink and seep. Yellow skin stretched across the face, and the lips pulled back across broken teeth made a terrible grimace, as if the pain of death was still in him. Dull eyes stared at the ceiling. Dee stepped forward and prodded at the neck. 'A deep cut. The main vessels of life cut through.' He frowned. 'But little blood. Strange.' He lifted the hands, turning them. One was missing a thumb and the index finger, but it was an old wound, well healed. Dee then looked back to the face. 'Very yellow. Looks like he was a drinker. No scuffs to the hands and no bruising. And the right hand is all but useless. This man did not fight his attacker.'

Leicester muffled a groan and nodded at the body. 'Open his tunic.'

Dee beckoned to Margaretta. 'Step forward. No dithering. I need you to draw what you see.' He pulled the tunic aside and gasped. 'Dear God. He has been carved.' He picked up a piece of straw from the floor and traced the ragged line of the symbol etched into the yellow-white skin of the dead man's chest.

As Margaretta pulled out paper and ink to draw, Dee folded the tunic back further and revealed another wound over the man's heart. 'What is this? There is thread in the skin.'

Leicester shuddered. 'The other sign I told you about. It was sewn into him.'

'And why was this removed before I was called?'

'We did not think.'

Dee growled and turned back to the body, bending over to peer at the wound. 'Seven stitches. All even. Describe this sign.'

'A piece of cloth embroidered with a star and B in the middle.'

'Where is it?'

'Cecil's office. Out of sight.'

Dee growled again. 'Bad practice. You should have waited for me. What do we know about this man?'

'All I know is that he is a palace guard. Cecil is getting information on him.'

Silence fell as Dee stared at the body. Then, 'Take me to where he was found.'

Two guards were ordered to stand at each end of the alley, facing out, with stern orders to let no one pass. Dee stopped where the body was found, looking up and down the path. 'Dark. No windows overlooking and so no witnesses. Only feet from the King's Gate but out of sight.'

Leicester nodded. 'And no scream was heard by the King's Gate guards.'

Dee made a cynical smile and looked down. 'A slit throat is silent, Robert. Are you sure he was found exactly here?'

'Yes. Why?'

Dee pointed at the ground. 'No blood. If his throat was slit here, it would be everywhere – even up the walls. But nothing.' He turned and looked up the alley. 'Track marks where his heels scraped across the ground. Come.'

The scrapes led to the end house. Dee pushed the door and reeled back as the stench of blood, vomit and human mess came out of the pitch black. 'Our killing place.'

Leicester stepped inside. 'Dear God, it stinks like a slaughterhouse.' They could make out the shape of a table with a candle towards the back of the room. He walked over, felt around for a flint. As the flame flared, Margaretta cried out and pointed at the back wall. Written in large uneven letters was a message.

Dee took the light and held it to the wall. 'It's written in his blood.'

'What does it say?' asked Margaretta, her voice shaking.

'*D'abord la terreur, puis la mort.* First terror, then death,' whispered Dee. Next to him, Leicester began to shake and reeled away towards the door, saying he needed air.

Dee handed the candle to Margaretta, telling her to hold it high. In the corner, a bed with rumpled covers and a box. A table, clean and clear. In the far corner, a smaller table with papers. But the rushes on the floor were black with dried blood and stains splattered up the walls and over furniture. The only sign of a struggle was a three-legged stool, broken in two, and in the corner a bucket had tipped over, spilling vomit. There was also the terrible stench of an unemptied privy bucket, full to the brim and buzzing with flies. He went back to the door. 'The lock is unbroken. Seems the killer was let in.' He perused the buckets. 'A flux of both bowels and stomach. Could be poison. Look for food.'

A shelf behind the table held part of a loaf and a slice of cheese wrapped in cloth. Also a bottle, corked and full.

Margaretta picked up the bread. 'This bread is soft and it has been eaten by mice.' She lowered the candle and gazed around the floor. 'No dead mice. So, unlikely it is tainted.'

'You are thinking well. Put it in the bag anyway. The bottle too. We will test it at home.'

She did as he bid, bracing herself against the table and fighting the waves of nausea heaving through her. 'I need to get out, Doctor. I feel sick.'

Dee took her arm. 'Not yet. We need you to feel this place. Think of the dead man. What comes through into your mind?'

Do you have a heart in that breast of yours? Can you not see how affected I am? No. 'I sense evil. There was terrible pain. Unable to stand. Stomach cramping and everything going black. Confusion. Fear. Then hope. Then a hot slice across his throat. Oh, God. I feel— Please. Let me go outside.'

'So, terror before death.' Dee reached out and took her shoulders. 'Be brave. Keep feeling. We must get answers before Leicester comes back in.'

'I feel more than the fear of the dead man. I think of the ground and feel satisfaction. Something left behind. Delight.'

Her master looked around. 'There are only blood-soaked rushes here.' He took Margaretta's arm and tugged her out of the door where Leicester was leaning against the wall gulping air. He pointed up the lane. 'I want to check the ground again.'

They looked around in silence and Dee muttered, 'Just a muddle of mud and footprints. The damn fools have trampled all the evidence. Too dark to see anything with all the overhangs from houses.' He called up the alley to the guard. 'You, man. Get a torch.' He handed the delivered flames to Margaretta, commanding in Welsh, 'Try to feel the killer. What gave delight?'

She lowered it to the ground and swept it around in an arc. *What were you feeling? I feel satisfaction.* 'There.'

In the soft detritus of the lane was a perfect impression of a huge cloven hoof. Dee stared and looked to Leicester. 'You said a woman saw the Devil. God help us.'

Chapter Three

The woman had evidently been begging for years. Her ragged clothes stank with grime and the mess she had made when terror had ultimately liquified her bowels. A once pretty face was sunken and lined. Dry lips curled over toothless gums. When they entered the cell, she shrank back, turned her face to the wall, and wailed her distress. 'I have done no wrong, sirs. I had no place to rest my head so hid in the shadows from the watchman. I did no harm.' She started to weep and beg for mercy.

Leicester grimaced his disgust and looked to the guard. 'Do we have to abide this stench? Are there no clean clothes?' The only response was a shrug.

Dee lowered his voice to that of a kind father. 'Do not weep, goodwife. We only want the truth.' But the woman kept her face to the wall and started to pull at her hair. He looked to Margaretta, bewildered.

I feel your shame. You poor woman. You fear these men – terrified they will take you to the Bedlam with the other vagrant women who have no shelter other than a dark alley. 'My Earl Leicester, can you command a pail of water, some rags, a lemon, a comb and a simple dress? Her distress is because of shame.' She looked to Dee. 'Leave her with me.'

The two men gone, the woman calmed and faced

Margaretta. 'My name is Alice Burton. I have not always been this way, miss.'

Margaretta smiled. 'None of us are born to begging. What brought you to this?'

Alice bowed her head. 'They took our land for the sheep. My man said the only way for us to eat was to come to the streets of London. But it were so hard. We had only skill for farming. He found a little work but not enough for two, and then I found I was with child.' Tears tumbled down her sallow cheeks.

I see two men. You are crying, begging. Money changes hands. 'He sold you?'

Alice nodded. 'I was bought as a servant and... and to keep a man's bed warm. But when he saw I was with a babe he threw me to the streets. My little one was born dead. God's blessing, I told myself.'

The door opened and the guard dumped a pail of water with a lemon floating in it, cloths, a comb and a brown smock, then slammed the door. Margaretta stood. 'Come, Mistress. Take off those rags. The water is cold, but clean.'

Twenty minutes later, Alice Burton was sitting in a clean dress, combing lemon juice through her hair and squashing the falling lice. 'Now you are a woman again, Alice. I need you to be brave and tell me what you saw last night.'

The woman whimpered and put her hands over her eyes. 'It was the Devil himself. I hid behind an old broken door propped up in the alley when I heard the footsteps. Chink, chink, chink. I believed it to be the night watch and feared I would be gathered up. But when I looked out it were not him. Instead, the Devil knocked on the door of the house.'

'How did you know it was the Devil?'

Alice frowned. 'Well, I did not just then. He was all covered in a long coat, a cloak and a hood. I saw no face. All black.'

'Was he let in?'

'Yes. The man within greeted him. But he were groaning.

Then the door closed and all was quiet. A minute later, the door opened, and God save me, the Devil emerged. Huge he was and dragging that man.' Alice let out a wail. 'God save my soul. He looked my way.'

'Describe every bit of what you saw, Alice.'

The woman wiped the sniffle dripping from her nose. 'Tall. Taller than a man. I could see the horns on his head as he dragged that poor soul along the alley. Then the claw... a huge claw. He cut the tunic away and I did see him scratching at the chest. He were sniffing the body. Then he were sewing him.' She started to rock. 'He stood, looked my way, and said strange words.'

'Can you repeat anything at all?'

'No. It were not English. But it began with a B.'

'Did you see his face?'

'All black. No face.' Alice grasped Margaretta's arm. 'Is my soul doomed?'

Margaretta took her hand. 'No, Alice. I think the good Lord was using you to see the evil so that you could tell us and help my master keep our Queen safe.' She smiled. 'I think you were blessed for once in your life. Now let me keep you safe.'

She found Dee and Leicester waiting outside. 'I would keep her protected here in case she recalls more.'

Leicester nodded and gave curt instructions to the guard. 'Ensure she is fed and warm, or it will be the worse for you.'

Dee was already walking back to the carriage. 'To Cecil. I want to see the other evidence. Margaretta, you can tell us all on the way to The Strand.'

Chapter Four

The carriage trundled up The Strand to Sir Cecil's London house. Margaretta had been here a few times in the past ten years, but each time its loveliness grew as more features were added. As they turned into the courtyard, Margaretta looked up at the red brick turrets topped with domes and whispered, 'beautiful.' The carriage driver chuckled, 'He do call it his "rude cottage".'

Seeing Leicester, the servants jumped to open the great oak door and bowed as the party went through into the receiving chamber. Thomas Bellott, the household steward, came forward and bowed. 'My Earl of Leicester. Doctor Dee. Sir Cecil awaits you in his office.' He turned a disdainful eye on Margaretta. 'Your servant to the kitchens this time, sir?'

'She comes with me, as usual, to scribe.' Dee ignored the raised eyebrow.

Margaretta bobbed her head and smiled. 'Good day, sir.' *You can glower all you like. My master cannot do this without my gifts and if that upsets your sensibilities about rank, I care not.*

They were led through an inner courtyard into a loggia walk with marble pillars looking out over perfectly manicured gardens full of shrubs and walking lawns. Margaretta stared at the life-size statues of Roman emperors, counting five in the courtyard alone. Beyond were the Covent Gardens, laid out with vegetable patches and fruit trees. Dee pointed to the right, towards a low building with the shouts of men coming from it. 'The bowling alley is lively today.'

'The wards are enjoying some sport between their lessons,' replied Bellott.

The office door opened onto a scene of quiet work. Cecil was seated at a desk below a window onto the gardens, papers piled in front of him. An oil lamp glowed in the dullness of a March morning. Behind him, the walls were lined with books, and in every corner was some treasure or other – a clock, porcelain bowls, another statue of a Roman emperor, a cabinet of golden coins. In the corner, his son was head bent to a paper on a smaller desk.

Sir Cecil, this work for our Majesty has made you rich but it has aged you. The once pink skin of your face has paled to grey, as has your hair. Those hooded eyes seem to sink further, and lines are deepening. Your visage has thinned, making those three moles on your right cheek even more prominent. But I suppose we are all very different to the people who first gathered in 1555. My copper curls are also fading and people call me mistress when I used to be called girl. The only one who does not seem to show the growing of age is my master. John Dee is as fresh-faced as ever.

Cecil looked up and nodded curtly at Leicester before greeting John Dee.

I feel anger. It rose when you looked at my Earl of Leicester. And your eyes narrow. You recall fear. I think he threatened you. Distrust.

Cecil called over to young Robert to go and see his mother and watched with a kind smile as the boy gathered his pens, gave a lopsided bow to the guests and lolloped out, his twisted little back bending him sideways.

Oh, you poor man. You have such love for that little child, but you worry and fret for him every day. I hear his mother's voice, whispering low that he will be burdened all his life with a bent body. She weeps when you both speak of it. 'Is Lady Mildred well, sir?'

Cecil jerked out of his thoughts. 'Yes, Margaretta. She will be pleased to see you.' He winked. 'She is working in the upper library and will trust *you* to look at the books knowing they will be safe.' John Dee seemed oblivious to this barb about his magpie behaviour with anything written.

Cecil bid them sit. 'We have dark deeds to discuss.' He shot a look at Leicester. 'Yet more dark deeds that threaten the peace of our realm.'

Leicester glowered back and barked, 'I have only ever put Elizabeth and peace first, Sir Cecil.'

My, there is anger in you, Sir Cecil. You dislike and distrust this arrogant earl. He has tried to harm you.

Cecil ignored Leicester and spoke to John Dee. 'Tell me about this killing. When the sergeant of the guards reported to me, he was shaking, saying nothing he had seen on a battlefield was such evil as he saw this morning.'

'It was designed to create fear alright. The victim has every sign of being poisoned – evidence of a double flux, yellow skin. But he was despatched with a slit to the throat. Seems he knew his killer, and there was no bruising or signs of a fight. Just a toppled stool and pail. Do we have any information about his acquaintances or how he lived?'

Cecil nodded. 'According to the sergeant, Pierre Perotin has lived in London for some years and became a guard when his hand was injured in a loom, meaning he could no longer weave. He lived alone having lost his wife in the last outbreak of plague. He is – was – quiet, hard-working, well liked, trusted, did not frequent taverns nor the doxy-houses. A pious man, keeping to his Huguenot faith but never pressing it upon others. Concern was raised when he did not arrive at work yesterday, but when someone went to check, he was heard groaning with the flux.'

'Did no one enter to help him?'

Cecil shook his head and looked grim. 'There has been an

outbreak of sweating sickness in the east of the city. People are afeared, John. They think the miasma moves from one person to another. They called through the door, heard he was alive, and left.'

'So, the killer was unafraid of the miasma,' murmured Dee. 'Are any other palace guards affected by a flux?'

Cecil shook his head. 'Pierre ate in the guard's kitchen the night before last. They are all healthy and well.'

'So, he was poisoned elsewhere. We have his bread. It will be tested this evening in Mortlake.'

Cecil sat forward. 'What put such terror into the sergeant?'

Dee stood and went to the wooden side table to pour himself a goblet of wine. 'The killer was leaving a series of messages. The first is on the wall. The words, *D'abord la terreur, puis la mort* have been daubed in the victim's blood.'

Cecil's face paled as his brows made little winces.

Those words alarm you, Sir Cecil. You pinch the bridge of your nose. A sure sign of your worry. I try to alert my master, but he is staring out of the window.

Dee continued. 'He was then dragged along the alley and the desecrations done in the light of the palace pitch-lights. It is at this point the beggar woman claims the visitor had turned into the Devil – taller than a man, hooved and horned. Whoever or whatever dragged Pierre Perotin was strong, for he was a big man and would be heavy in death. He was carved with a symbol. Margaretta, give me the drawing.' When it was handed to him, he spread it on Cecil's desk. 'But this mark is like nothing I have seen. It is not a mathematical or astronomical sign. There is no letter in the Greek or Hebrew alphabets that fits.' He looked at Cecil. 'But this is only half the evidence. I understand there was something within the other wound – the sewn wound.'

Cecil opened his desk and took out a folded square of oilcloth. Inside was a piece of fine silk, blood-stained, with a symbol embroidered into it. 'This was sewn into the skin.'

Dee pulled it close and peered. 'A pentacle with a B in the centre. Neatly sewn.'

Leicester looked over his shoulder. 'What the hell does that mean?'

Dee raised a hand to silence him and traced the shape in the silk. 'The pentacle is seen as a protective symbol against evil spirits. It represents the five wounds of Christ. But this is upside down and has B in the centre. Then there are the words on the wall.' He looked up at Cecil. 'Are you making the same connections as me?'

Cecil groaned and shut his eyes. Leicester banged the desk. 'For the love of God, tell me what you are fucking seeing.'

John Dee crossed the room to pour more wine, snapping at Leicester to keep calm. Then he sat and took a deep breath. 'Until 1308, the greatest defenders of the Catholic faith were the Knights Templar. Their methods made them the most feared religious order in the world and people still tremble at their name. The pentacle of the five wounds was their emblem. But they were accused of increasing their power by worshipping an evil pagan deity in the shape of a horned goat. The name of that deity was—' He looked to Cecil and they both said together, 'Baphomet.'

Cecil continued the story. 'When the Templars were brought to their knees with accusation of pagan rituals, and other great sins, the last blow was the burning of their grand master, Jacques de Molay. As the flames rose, he screamed a curse on those who had condemned him.'

Leicester gulped and whispered, 'First terror, then death?'

Dee nodded. 'Exactly. And the two men who had condemned the Templars were dead within months. Pope Clement went through the agonies of a growing cancer and King Philip of France fell while hunting boar and was gored to death by his own quarry.'

Leicester started pacing and smacking his hands against his thighs in agitation. 'My God. The hoof prints. The terror before death. The calling card of the linen. Are you telling me that the pagan goat-deity of the Templars is roaming the streets outside the palace?' He looked up, eyes wild with fear, shouting. 'Is this linked to—?'

Cecil slumped back in his chair and pinched the bridge of his nose again. 'This is what we have been dreading.'

These two men are recalling something written. A secret. Cecil does not know whether to speak it. Doctor Dee is looking between them and not at me. I must risk. 'Lord Cecil, was this forewarned?'

Cecil shot her a stern look and then frowned. 'Seeing into my mind again, Margaretta? Be careful, mistress.' He looked to Dee. 'You must keep secret what I tell you.'

Dee bridled. 'There should be no secrets. How can I investigate if I am not given all the information.'

Cecil picked up a bell on his desk and rang it. In seconds the door opened, and Bellott looked in. Cecil beckoned him forward and opened a box on the desk, took out a key, and handed it over. 'Go to the iron chest and bring the package from Rome.' As the man left, Cecil shifted, looked to Margaretta. 'When the package is brought in, you should leave.'

It was Dee's turn to snap. 'Unfair, William. Your secrets and the dark deeds of others have been well guarded by Margaretta. She is my assistant and will stay.'

Sometimes I do like you. You are loyal. Not always kind. But loyal.

Cecil glared but nodded assent. Then they waited in tense silence until Bellott returned, handed over the rolled and ribbon-tied package, and retreated.

Cecil spread the paper out, weighting it down with candlesticks. 'This was signed by the Pope on February 25th. It arrived in England last week. We are trying to supress all knowledge of it.'

Dee walked around to read over Cecil's shoulder. 'This is a Papal Bull.' He started to read and made a sharp intake of breath. 'The pretended King of England, the serpent of wickedness... we declare the foresaid Elizabeth to be a heretic and favourer of heretics... A servant of wickedness... she has filled the nobility with heretics... to be cut off from the unity of the body of Christ... declare her to be deprived of her pretended title to the kingdom aforesaid, and of all dominion, dignity and privilege... we charge and command all and singular the nobles, subjects, peoples and others aforesaid that they do not dare obey her orders, mandates and laws... those who shall act to the contrary we include in the like sentence of excommunication.' He stood straight and turned to the window to stare across the lawns. 'So not only is Elizabeth excommunicated, but every Catholic is charged with going against her on pain of excommunication if they do not.'

'Precisely,' muttered Cecil. 'This is an order to kill our Queen. And just days after it arrives on my desk, a man – a Protestant man who guards her – is slaughtered by the palace walls. I fear these are connected.'

'Oh, indeed it is,' whispered Dee. 'Elizabeth, and the Huguenots she shelters, are called heretics by the Catholic Church. Given courage by the Papal Bull, someone has invoked the greatest guardians of that faith – the Knights Templar and their pagan deity. They are sending the old curse to Elizabeth. First terror, then death. But where does this killer come from?'

Cecil opened his desk and pulled out a letter. 'Maybe afar. Henry Norris, our ambassador in France, has been writing for months claiming that the Guise family, and also Catherine de Medici, plot against Elizabeth and seek to support Mary Queen of Scots. But early in March, this arrived.' He handed the paper to Dee.

'He says that he has been given word that a man with one eye and a cut face boarded a ship last month with intent to do harm to Elizabeth. Do we know who this man is?'

Cecil shook his head. 'No. Walsingham has a list of people newly arriving in London, but we cannot find anyone of that description. That said, if Norris is right, then this person arrived here about the same time as the Papal Bull.'

Leicester put his head in his hands. 'Are you saying the French have invoked and sent a pagan devil? Are we facing a creature from hell?'

Dee shook his head. 'No, Robert. We are facing an assassin. And he goes by the name of Baphomet.'

Chapter Five

Lady Mildred Cecil was sitting at a desk, head bent and quill in hand when Bellott opened the door to announce Margaretta. She looked up and smiled. 'Margaretta, my dear.' She put her finger to her mouth in a sign to say nothing and pointed to a seat. 'Come sit. The wind outside is bitter.' Then the sound of a throat being cleared in the corner. Margaretta turned to see young Robert with a book. He rose to make a little crooked bow, and his chest twisted to the side.

Oh, you poor mite. You always fear I will be sickened by your twisted body. You have had much sadness. I hear the name crookback. Pygmy. I hear voices of young men taunting you in low voices. I hear you shout at someone. You run away. I hear the name, Edward. 'Hello, Master Robert. Do your studies go well?'

The boy grinned. 'Yes, mistress. Was that the great conjuror downstairs?'

'Yes. But he is no conjuror. He is a man of learning – just like your father and your mother too. He has a mind as big as the planets he studies.'

'May I come visit? I hear he can make gold. I heard my father speak of it.' He grinned. 'I am seven years old and can understand things.'

Mildred laughed and patted her son's head. 'And you have much more to understand, my sweet. You may stop your studies for an hour while I talk to Margaretta and show her our books. I saw one of the wards, Peregrine Willoughby, in the gardens talking to your little sister. Go and see him and Lizzie.'

The child lolloped to the door, waving as he went. Mildred sighed and looked at Margaretta. 'I know of the killing but want Robert shielded from such deeds. I asked to see you in order to speak of him. He has been quiet lately but will not say why. What do you feel when you look at my boy?'

'That he is a sweet-natured child and lucky to be your son.' *But I also feel he will not stay that way. His twisted body will harden that childish innocence.*

Mildred went to the window to look down on Robert, now walking slowly with another boy towards a structure in the corner of the garden which wound in a spiral like a shell. 'Robbie likes playing king of the castle on the snail mount. Peregrine is a kind boy. I ask again – what do you feel?'

The sounds came again. 'Many voices. One above the others, calling him crookback and pygmy. Edward.'

Mildred Cecil took in a sharp intake of breath and turned away but not fast enough to hide the tears gathering in her eyes. 'The wards. Damn them. But Edward de Vere is twenty years old and not a child… at least in years.'

I have a growing feeling of foreboding. 'Trust your instincts, my lady. Keep him away from Robbie. He will turn his sweet nature to bitter.'

'So said, John Dee,' whispered Mildred, then shook her head. 'Listen to me fretting. You are my guest and I burden you with my fears. Now tell me how John is progressing with his alchemic experiments.'

Thirty minutes later there was a knock at the door and Bellott stepped inside to say that Doctor Dee was impatient to leave and asking for Margaretta. With a sigh, she rose and bade farewell to her friend.

As she reached the door, Mildred called out. 'I forgot to tell you, my dear. Your brother-in-law, Angus McFadden, is our vintner.'

Margaretta tensed. 'I'm afraid he is indeed my brother-in-law. Has he done something to cause offence? I am sorry…'

'No, no, dear. It is just we have not had a bill from him in four months. We do not like to be in debt.'

A clench in my gut. Angus would dig a penny from a midden. There is something wrong. Oh, God. That means I have to visit them when I have avoided it these five years. 'I will pay a visit and see what the delay is, my lady.'

Damn, damn, damn. I feel my fist clench with just the thought of seeing my sister's face.

From the bottom of the stairs was an angry call from John Dee. 'Hell and damnation, Margaretta. You are gossiping while there is work to be done. We have a murder to solve and a queen to protect.'

Margaretta ran down the stairs. 'What is happening now?'

'Cecil will charge Walsingham to make a list of Catholics, and Leicester is going to the palace to increase vigilance in every corridor and corner. You and I are digging deeper.'

'Where are we going?'

'Back to the killing place. I have questions.'

'Why are you so angry?'

A shrug. 'Cecil refuses to talk of my alchemic progress until Baphomet is found.'

Chapter Six

A guard had been positioned outside the house and stepped in front of the door when Dee and Margaretta approached. 'No entry. Move along.'

Dee bridled. 'Do you know who I am, sirrah? The Queen's philosopher.'

The guard stared ahead. No response.

And here we go – that furious indignation when someone does not recognise you. In a minute you will start ranting about all your works, your writing, and how you defined the day of the coronation. Then you will go on to how you are called to Court to advise the Privy Chamber. Let's not go down that road. 'Excuse me, goodman. This is Doctor Dee on business for Sir Cecil and my Earl of Leicester. We were here earlier today.'

The guard's eyes moved between the two and then a flicker of recognition before a silent step to the side. Dee huffed and pushed the door open with a bang, leaving Margaretta to give their thanks. Inside was dark and the air still thick with stench and flies. Margaretta covered her nose and went to light the candle. Dee growled through the gloom. 'Why do you show courtesy to the ignorant, Margaretta? That churl should be—'

'What, Doctor? Whipped for doing his job? His eyes gouged for not recognising the great Doctor Dee? If you were a little more pleasant, you would get further with people.'

Dee glowered. 'Katherine says I am a man of perfect manners.'

'Katherine thinks the sun shines out of your nether regions and has done so since the day she met you. She spent nine long years pining for your attention before her husband was kind enough to die in a tavern and leave her free to flutter her widow's eyelashes at you.'

'Katherine was a good wife to Master Constable.'

'She was indeed. It was goodly of her to mourn him – even if it was only the five days to the burial.'

'You are becoming a snip-tongue, Margaretta. And you forget your position. Apprentice.'

'Apprentice? Sixteen years must be the longest apprenticeship in England. I manage your library, I work on your mad experiments to conjure gold from base metal, I do all the horoscopes which bring in your income, and I still moon-wash your damned crystals. Then, when you are called to investigate dark deeds, it is me who scries and talks to the angels until I am sick to my stomach. When does this apprenticeship end?'

Dee wagged his hand to shush her. 'Keep your voice down. People will hear.'

'That you cannot work without me? Maybe they should know.'

Dee rounded on her. 'What has eaten into you, woman? You were like a feral cat all the way here in the carriage and now you show impertinence to your master and friend.'

Margaretta slumped. 'Lady Mildred told me that Angus McFadden has not sent her a bill in months. There must be something wrong. I have to go to Susan's house and see what it is.'

Dee softened. 'Ah. The evil sister. When did you last see her?'

'Five years ago, when I went to see their new home near The Vintry. But my brother, Huw, and I were sent away by Angus, still resenting the fact we had wrested back the papers for Huw's land in Wales.' Margaretta looked pointedly at

John Dee. 'Helped by Mr Will Fleetwood who you still see as a competitor.'

Dee ignored her last sentence. 'It is a long time to stay away.'

'You mean it's a long time to be banished. But she is still my sister. Mam and Dada in Heaven would expect me to go.'

Dee softened his voice to that of a friend. 'Go in the morning and get it over. We will investigate here and go back to Mortlake. Tomorrow you can take the best horse to Susan's.'

From harsh to kind in a blink of your eye. Maybe that's why I stay your apprentice... no, your partner in crime.

Dee pointed to the wooden box at the foot of the bed. Margaretta lifted the lid and pulled out clothes, all folded with sprigs of rosemary and wormwood to keep out fleas. Nothing strange. She put them back. In the far corner the small table held a few scraps of paper and a quill pen next to an ink horn. Dee lifted each parchment. 'No writing. But he must have been educated to have the implements. Look around for books.'

Margaretta shot a hard look. 'Which we will leave here. You cannot steal from a dead man – again.'

Dee ignored her and looked along the shelves but found only a few pots and a pan which would be used to cook over the central fire, now a pile of cold ashes. 'Do you sense anything here?'

'Well, he was a careful man. Look at how he kept his clothes. If he had anything of value, he would put it very safe.' She looked under the bed, the pillows, felt along the walls for a hidden cupboard. *Nothing. Help me. Let me sense you. Come through the veil and guide me, Pierre Perotin. There it is. That inner hum. I have honed this skill for the past fifteen years. I have to trust it. I keep thinking of the clothing box.* 'The box has a cross painted on the top. It is a strange thing.'

Dee came to her side. 'The Huguenot Cross. Based on the Lily of France, it is full of symbolism. The four petals represent the four gospels, the little roundels at the tips of the petals are the eight Beatitudes. Then fleur-de-lys lies between the four petals, each with three petals. That makes another four petals for the twelve apostles.'

'Beautiful,' whispered Margaretta. She lifted the lid and pulled out the clothing again. Wafts of the bitter herbs were a welcome relief from the mess in the corner. She slid her hands across the smooth polished wood of the base. Something shifted very slightly. She pushed harder and the base moved. 'A false bottom. Get a knife.'

Dee slid the blade around the edge until he found a chiselled hole. With a flick it lifted. There was a single Bible, bound in leather. 'Of course. Huguenot's have so long been persecuted for believing they can reach God directly, without the channelling of a priest, that they have long learned to hide their tools.' Inside was written the name Pierre Perotin and the name of two churches. One had been scored out – ~~Church of the Huguenots, Threadneedle~~ – and under it, All Hallows, Barking.

Margaretta frowned. 'Barking is ten miles to the east. Why would he go all that way to a church?'

Dee shook his head. 'This is the great church by the Tower. It once belonged to Barking Abbey before old King Henry dissolved and plundered the monasteries in order to marry our Queen's mother, Anne Boleyn.' He looked around. 'There is nothing here to tell us anything except Pierre was a simple, careful, God-fearing man.'

'So, who wanted to kill him and why? Do you really think it was Baphomet himself?' Margaretta gripped her hands together to stop the shaking.

'No – a man of flesh and blood, who wanted to use Pierre's body to strike terror into our streets and our Queen.'

'I am frightened, Doctor.'

Dee shook his head, still looking around. 'So am I, Margaretta. Frightened for Queen, country and all who live in it. But the only way out of fear is evidence. So far, we only have a body, symbols, a strange link to an old curse, one witness maddened by fear and a cloven hoof print. Someone must have seen something. Come.'

Chapter Seven

A wide-eyed child opened the door of the adjoining house. 'Is your mother here, little one?' asked Margaretta. The child shouted back into the dark room, and soon came the sound of shuffling. The woman was wide, round-faced, and would have been pretty if it were not for the deep pock-marks across her nose and cheeks.

You are frightened. The alley full of soldiers all day, people saying nothing, rumours of your neighbour killed by a devil, a wailing woman hauled away at dawn. 'Good afternoon, mistress. This is Doctor Dee, and I am Margaretta. We seek information about your neighbour, Pierre Perotin.'

The woman shrugged. 'We knew little of him. He kept to himself, and we are not long living here. They say he is dead at the hands of a devil.'

'Did you see or hear him yesterday?' asked Dee.

A flash of shame swept her face. 'Heard him groaning through the wall and, in the afternoon, calling out to God. But my husband said I was to stay away from sickness to protect our own and the other guards. They have the Sweat in the East you know.'

Dee nodded. 'Your husband is also a guard?'

'Yes. Only a week in his new job, and one of his kind is dead in the alley. Shook him up proper it has.'

'Did you hear a visitor arrive at the house last night?'

Another flash of shame. 'We were not here. The child was abed and my husband said we should go for refreshment to celebrate his new job – though I do not know if he is so happy now.'

Dee growled. 'You went to a tavern leaving your child in the house?'

Shame turned to indignation. 'We are hard working. We need a little rest.'

Dee started barking his questions. 'What time did you leave for your *rest*? And was your neighbour still groaning?'

'It were early evening, as dark fell… and, yes, he was.'

'And when you came back?

She gulped. 'Silence. I thought he were sleeping. A fair guess as it were after eleven of the clock.'

'And did you see anyone or anything in the lane?'

'No one. Nothing.' She pointed along the lane towards the river. 'We came from that direction, so did not pass Pierre's house, or his body if it were in the lane.'

Dee huffed his frustration and turned to walk back down the alley, snapping at Margaretta to follow. He paused on the way to look again at the cloven hoof in the mud. He leaned down and measured it against his hand and sighed, 'What evil has come here?'

Then a call from the end of the alley. 'Doctor Dee. You are summoned.'

They looked up. It was a guard, fully armed and beckoning for them to approach. 'Mistress Blanche says you must come into the palace for audience.'

Dee's chest puffed with delight. 'Indeed, I will. But how did Cousin Blanche know I was here?'

The guard gave a wry smile. 'Mistress Blanche knows all, sir. Every move and muttering.'

Chapter Eight

Dee almost trotted down the tapestried corridor in his excitement. At the end, standing before a huge carved oak door, was Blanche ap Harri, dressed in austere black with a white collar and coif, just a simple but large brooch as a nod to her wealth and status. She nodded at Dee and then smiled warmly at Margaretta. '*P'nawn da, Margaretta. Wyt ti'n iawn?*' Good afternoon, Margaretta. Are you well?

'*Ydw, meistres. A chithau?*' Yes, Mistress. And you?

A nod and a small wink before Blanche turned back to Dee, her face hardening. 'What have you discovered? The guards have prattled and Court is humming with talk of devils. Now we endure those foolish girls twittering around the cent table.' She tutted and shook her head. 'Why Elizabeth insists on being surrounded by empty headed beauties is a mystery.'

Dee nodded, seeing an opportunity to please the woman he wanted to call cousin but who had refuted his kinship every time. 'Indeed, Mistress Blanche. She needs wisdom not a wittering.'

Blanche narrowed her eyes, 'Then ensure you do not witter.' She turned, beckoned over her shoulder, nodded to the guard who jumped to open the door and they were led into the presence chamber. A group of young women seated on cushions, each stitching a linen, stopped when Dee passed by and the quick movements of needles through silk were replaced with hands moving to hide whispered comments and knowing looks. Only one was bold enough to speak.

'Doctor Dee?'

He stopped with the smile, usual when he was recognised at Court, and seemed to not hear Blanche's hissed command to hurry along.

'I am indeed, Doctor John Dee. Her Majesty's philosopher.'

The woman was tall, beautiful, red haired, and pale of complexion. Dark eyes looked Dee up and down and she put her head on one side like a coquette. 'I understand you can tell me of my destiny, sir.'

Blanche stepped in. 'The only thing certain in your future is an unfinished embroidery... for which Elizabeth waits.' She turned the stare on Dee. 'Come.'

He bowed to the group of women, now looking wide-eyed at the chastised lady in waiting. 'I can be reached at Mortlake.' Then he jumped as Blanche snapped at him like a disobedient puppy to follow.

Oh, there is a story here. Blanche feels fury when she looks at this pretty lady. And you, pretty lady, feel passion mixed with fear mixed with desperate hope. You think of Robert Dudley. Blanche looked at me and frowned. A sign to say nothing.

Dee beamed when he realised he was being led into the Privy chamber – the inner and secret sanctum of Court. Another door was pulled open on Blanche's command and they walked into a smaller room, lit by many candles making everything gleam, even the rich tapestries. A smaller group of women were playing cent in the corner. All around were tables of trinkets and treasures. On the wall a huge spiralled horn. Margaretta stopped to look at it and Blanche turned back to hurry her, but the voice was gentle. 'They say it was taken from a unicorn and brings with it the protection of Heaven.' She raised her eyes to the ceiling and shook her head. 'Anything for Elizabeth's favour.'

Dee looked to the throne, raised on a dais in the middle of the room. 'Where is Her Majesty?'

Blanche pointed to a smaller door at the far end of the Privy Chamber. 'This interview is to be secret, Doctor Dee. You will have audience in the Bed Chamber.' And John Dee grew another few inches with delight.

Inside, Elizabeth was pacing and passing a curved animal horn from hand to hand. She turned and reached out for Dee's hand. 'Tell me the truth. My ladies say the Devil is just outside the castle walls. There is murder.' Then she looked to Margaretta. 'What is going to happen to me?'

You poor woman. You are racked with fear. '*Peidiwch â phoeni, Eich Mawrhydi. Mae'r doctor yn gofalu amdanoch.*' Do not worry, Your Majesty. The doctor is looking after you.

Dee smiled, nodded and gripped Elizabeth's hand in his. 'It is true. We will not allow harm to enter your chamber.'

Elizabeth seemed to sink, clutching John Dee and staring at the floor, her hands trembling. 'I pray you speak true.'

All this finery and yet, in your fear, you are no different to a woman in the fields. This room is like a dream. A bed made of shell, larger than the dwelling of a poor man. Walls hung with silk tapestries and every table holds a hundred little treasures. Boxes inlaid with mother of pearl, golden cups, leather bound books shone to a gleam, silver dishes of sweetmeats and sugared plums. I remember these to be your favourite. And you in the middle, like a fragile, painted doll. Your skin shining white with ground pearl, lips painted berry red, and a head of crimson hair curled and primped and puffed out with a hairpiece. Those long, slender hands heavy with rings. One larger than the others. They say inside that bauble is a tiny painting of your mother, Anne Boleyn. Your dress is a work of art in silk and adorned with pearls and gold. You have everything for your body but not peace of your mind. You poor woman. Something else. A pain. Your leg. You think of your father. Fear again.

Suddenly, Elizabeth collected herself and stood straight.

'You know, Doctor, the great kings – and the one queen – of Europe call my kingdom the Devil's Land. Yet they will bring every kind of hell to any poor soul who does not share their mind for popery. Is that Christ's teaching, Doctor? To look into the heart of a man and slice it out if you do not like the way it beats?'

The Queen started to pace again, pulling the pearl-topped pins from her hair, throwing them to the ground as her voice became shrill. 'They say my cousin, Mary Queen of Scots – the woman who I have given safe haven – is planning my death. Cecil claims she sits in Tutbury Castle, like a spider spinning a web, thinking she will trap me like a fly and take my throne. He says she has charmed her captors.' She sank onto a cushion, pulled another pin and threw it across the floor, shouting, 'Why do my people hate me? Am I so reviled that they would replace me with a women raised in France and never known in our land; who is accused of blowing her own husband to Kingdom come; who can barely speak a word of English and who is a puppet to those princes who would take all that we have into the grip of the Pope? Would they cast me aside for her?' She put her hands up to her face and began to weep.

Blanche stepped forward and took her by the shoulders, like a mother calming a child. 'Hush, now. *Mae'r bobl yn eich caru chi.* The people love you. You cannot falter because of a few fools.' She pulled a linen from her sleeve and dabbed at Elizabeth's eyes.

The Queen sniffed, nodded and whispered in Welsh. 'I am frightened. You must stay with me. All day. All night.'

Dee stepped forward. 'I calculated your coronation day to start a long and prosperous reign. Your destiny is foretold by the planets and not by greedy men.'

'But they say the Devil is walking the streets around the castle. What if he enters?' She stood and began to pace again.

'The Devil is spirit, my lady. Not flesh and blood. If the

Devil truly walked the palace walls, he would walk through them and you would know by now.'

'Pah,' snapped Elizabeth. 'I have seen many a man filled with evil, Doctor. Satan can enter a man and walk through that very door.' She put trembling hands to her face again.

'No,' said Blanche. 'In the last hour Cecil and Leicester have put every guard on high alert. No one enters unless they are known and trusted. Every morsel of your food is tasted before it reaches your rooms and every part of your clothing is rubbed on a maid's arm before it touches your skin.' She looked round at Dee. 'We have asked Cecil to demand a calming draft from his apothecary as well as a salve.'

Oh, how the doctor bridles. He likes to think himself our Queen's physician as well as her philosopher.

Elizabeth looked to the horn still in her hand and held it out to Dee. 'Will this magic work? They say that this horn will sound if poison is put in my dish.'

Dee made a kind smile. 'I think that claim is fantastical. Trust your tasters and not the horn of a field beast.'

Behind them, the door opened and Robert, Earl of Leicester, stepped inside. Blanche stepped across to greet him and there were a few whispers between them. Margaretta heard the words: 'Douglas… stop her nonsense… unkind.' *I feel anger from you, Blanche ap Harri. And from you, my Earl of Leicester, guilt, discomfort, irritation. You nod and step around Blanche and almost run to Elizabeth. She looks up, red-eyed. Then her head falls to your chest.*

'Does my Two Eyes see my demise?'

Dudley took her shoulders and stepped back to look her in the face. 'No. They see a glorious sight. You have, all around, those who will protect you. I have gathered Cecil, Walsingham and my old tutor, Doctor Dee, here. We have protected you before and we will again. You must rest quiet, my love.'

Oh, how you take the glory, Robert Dudley. But when our Queen looks at you, though she smiles, there is sadness, hurt. I sense the love between you still, but it is tired. Not the passion I witnessed eight years ago. When Blanche said the word Douglas, you felt guilt, worry. What is happening? Whatever it is, you do not want Elizabeth to know.

Elizabeth turned to Dee with a weak smile. 'Good doctor, go and do your work. Root out this evil and send this devil back into the flames from which he stepped. May you be our salvation from wickedness, 007.'

The number he writes on his letters to Cecil. So, it does mean something and it does relate to his relationship to our Queen. The old rogue. I've asked him over and over about it and every time he avoids an answer.

Dee bowed low and assured Elizabeth that nothing – not even his quest to turn metal to gold to fill her coffers – would detract him from her safety. He took the offered hand, kissed it and made to leave. As they walked backwards across the polished floor, Elizabeth called to Margaretta. 'Speak with Blanche. *Bydd yn onest*. Be honest.'

Did she flash her eyes towards Dudley and wink? 'Yes, Your Majesty.'

Chapter Nine

Outside the door, Blanche gave a deep sigh. 'She is like a frightened kitten. The empty heads are saying the man was carved up and sewn; that his body was covered in strange satanic symbols that herald Elizabeth's death.'

Dee growled his irritation. 'Why do women turn a molehill into a mountain?' The sharp intake of breath from Blanche stopped him and he mumbled an apology. 'I mean some woolly-headed women.'

'Likely because they are told tall tales by woolly-headed men who like to see them squeak and swoon,' snapped Blanche. 'Now what is the truth?'

'The man was poisoned then his throat slit for a quick end. There was indeed a strange symbol carved into the man's chest, and also an embroidered linen with a pentacle centred with the letter B sewn into his skin above the heart. We found the mark of a cloven hoof in the mud. There was also a bloody message on the wall. That and the pentacle leads us to think there is a link to the Templars. We think the killer is invoking Baphomet.'

Blanche swayed and reached for the wall, but batted Dee away when he reached out to steady her. 'So there really was a devil. Dear God. How do I protect Elizabeth?'

'I do not think it a spirit, Mistress Blanche. No. This is a man of flesh and blood, using the old symbols and curses of the Templars – a Catholic assassin invoking Baphomet to create terror.'

Blanche shuddered again. 'These symbols. Do you understand them?'

Dee shook his head. 'No. But Walsingham is adept with cyphers.'

A sharp nod. 'A rather forward-speaking young man. Elizabeth has already named him a Moor for his swarthy looks and gruffness. He needs to watch his manners in her presence.'

'I will tell him so, Mistress.'

Blanche went suddenly quiet. 'If this is a Catholic threat, is there a link to the letters?'

Dee raised his hands in question and started to trot as Blanche barked a command to follow and marched off down the corridor, making servants and guards jump aside to let her through.

My word, how your standing has risen, Mistress Parry. The death of that fool, Kat Astley, five years ago has propelled you into the standing in Court you were promised as a young woman. And look how you rise to it. It is like watching Moses parting the Red Sea.

They arrived at a door on heavy hinges and barred across in iron. Blanche pulled a ring of keys hanging on a silk rope from her waist. Both locks opened, she beckoned them in and nodded to two chairs as she lit a row of candles at a desk. The room was well furnished with leather bound chairs, walls of books, glittering glasses and decanters of wine. On the large desk were ledgers and writing quills with silver inkhorns, also a large magnifying glass. 'This is my office where I keep records of all books, jewels, gifts, letters – everything that comes into Elizabeth's life which is not on legs.' Another key opened an iron box and she pulled out a sheaf of papers. 'William has been getting letters from Henry Norris, our ambassador in France, speaking about plots and one-eyed men. But all these have been sent directly to Elizabeth in the past three months. They are in order.'

Dee opened the first and read it through. 'This is from Mary Queen of Scots. Her written word is poor, but as expected, she says she had no part in the rising of the Northern Lords last year. She ends with a plea to "allow a true prince to follow the path of destiny to the throne". So, while claiming no link to the treacherous Lords, she forwards their demands.'

Blanche nodded and handed over the second letter and Dee read again. 'From Catherine de Medici. The former Mother-in-law, as Mary of the Scots was married to the Dauphin.'

Blanche huffed. 'She could not wait to rid herself of this arrogant princess as soon as the Dauphin – by then the king – died of earache. It is said she celebrated for days when Mary embarked to Scotland.'

'But in this letter, she is now supporting Mary. She demands her release.'

Blanche leaned over and tapped the bottom of the page. 'Read the last line.'

'If you refuse the destiny of allegiance through a prince of the blood, then allow the rightful destiny of a prince to your throne.' Dee looked up. 'Similar words.'

'Exactly. And a change of strategy. Catherine de Medici is tired of pushing for marriage between Elizabeth and her weakling second son, Charles, now King of France.'

'What are you saying, Mistress?'

Blanche sniffed. 'That vile little ambassador of France, Mothe-Fénélon, has hinted that the French Queen will, instead, offer her third son, the Duc d'Anjou.' She picked up a decanter and poured three glasses of wine, anger making her spill on the desk. 'A dreadful man-child with the morals and dress of a Southwark doxy.'

Below the line of sight, Dee wagged his hand in a signal to Margaretta to ask no questions. 'Well, there is little hope of such an offer being accepted. But why her change of attitude to Mary? Show me the third letter.'

Dee frowned as soon as he saw the name of the sender and looked at Margaretta for a second. 'Sent by Mothe-Fénélon himself. He demands an audience to present terms for the release of Mary Queen of Scots to follow her destiny as a prince of the blood and natural successor of Elizabeth. He claims to be representing the wishes of Queen Catherine and Mary's blood family.' Dee looked up. 'The Guise faction? But they are busy fighting the holy war against the Huguenots and they are not allies of Catherine de Medici as she sees them as a threat to her sons.'

'And with good cause. The Guise men are handsome and charming and so loved by the people. Her sons are lacking in wit and twisted of body or twisted of soul. But then we had this from Cecil's trading spy.' She handed over a scrappy parchment, many times folded.

Dee carefully unfolded the paper and frowned. 'A letter from a Thomas Martinfield to a Lord Conway? Who are they?'

Blanche looked surprised. 'I thought you were in the circle. Never mind. Give it back.' She held out her hand. 'Give.'

'But this warns of a Medici-Guise plot to poison Elizabeth. It speaks of conjuring and horoscopes showing that an attack is imminent. Who the hell is Martinfield?'

Blanche stood. 'You need to speak to William Cecil. If you are working for him, he needs to appraise you.' She nodded to the door, ignoring Dee's rising colour as indignation and fury filled him. 'Wait in the outer hall while I speak with Margaretta.'

As the door shut, she moved to their mother tongue of Welsh. 'I fear I have opened a hornet's nest. I assumed William would tell him of this rising threat from Europe. But I have other concerns.' She reached over and turned Margaretta's hand upwards to trace the lines across her palm. 'These wisdom lines of the druids run deep in both of us. Now speak true about Elizabeth.'

I feel you, Blanche. Frightened, worried, concerned. Like a mother helpless to protect her child. Yet in here there is also satisfaction, even a tinge of revenge. 'Her fear is deep and she also feels great hurt – especially when she speaks of Queen Mary.'

Blanche nodded. 'Mary Queen of the Scots, overseen by Lady Bess and the Earl of Shrewsbury at Tutbury. Yes, she schemes and plots to take the throne and will not relent in her belief she is our rightful queen. They say she is working on getting the support of her captors. Damn her.'

'But I also felt fear when she said "one queen" in Europe.'

'Catherine de Medici, called the Serpent Queen, due to her nasty reputation for poisoning foes. Elizabeth has certainly offended her by prevaricating over King Charles. As for the Guise, Mary's blood family, they will attack anyone that is not papist.' Blanche dropped Margaretta's hand. 'Enough of mad queens. Tell me of Robert.'

'I heard you say a man's name. Douglas. He felt guilt. Our Queen feels hurt.'

'And the woman who asked for a horoscope?'

'Passion. Hope. Desperation. She thinks of Robert Dudley. But how can these be linked?'

'The woman is called Douglas after her father. She is a widow – a merry one at that – and has set her sights on Robert.'

'Then he has set his sights right back at her. Seems he likes copper hair and a pretty face.'

'Indeed. If you were higher born, you might be Lady Leicester by now,' laughed Blanche.

I smile though that is like a dagger to my heart. I have loved twice. The first, Sam, who I pushed to a friend in the belief that my life was one of caring for my mother and brother. The second, Christopher, was stolen by a fat fustilugs then God. All I ever wanted was someone to love and love me back. A chance to have a child and hold it close. Just a simple natural thing and yet so precious. Sometimes, when all is quiet, I speak to God and ask why he forgot me when he handed out the passion in the world. I ask why I give to so many only to be passed by and never noticed. But I am in my thirty-third year now and this face is that of a woman past her prime. Oh Lord. I forgot we share this ability. You are looking at my face and see right into my heart. 'I think Her Majesty is much hurt by Lady Douglas.'

Blanche nodded. 'Robert has waited twelve years to be made king, so when Elizabeth suggested he marry Mary Queen of Scots, hope turned to anger. Since then, his head is easily turned.'

She took Margaretta's hand again and folded her fingers back over her palm before studying the creases created by the bend of her little finger. 'One great love, late in life.' She winked.

Before Margaretta could ask any questions, there was a knock at the door and a servant entered. 'Her Majesty calls for your return, Mistress Blanche. She is upset and says her leg needs attending.'

Blanche rose. 'I must go.'

Margaretta checked the servant had closed the door. 'I felt that pain. She thought of her father.'

Blanche sighed. 'Indeed, she would. An ulcer on her leg gives her much discomfort. She fears it is the start of the stinking ailment that afflicted her father in his last years. But Cecil has asked his apothecary to work on something. I will even have that tested.' She tapped her chest. 'This mother cat will not let any foolery affect her kitten.'

Margaretta laughed. 'I think you refer to Kat Astley, may she rest in peace.'

Blanche nodded. 'The day that fool died, my true purpose started. Elizabeth oft says that Anne Boleyn gave her life while Kat Astley gave her love. But now it is my role. I rocked her cradle. Now, in the dark of the night, when she is riven with fears, I rock her in my arms.'

I see tears in those eyes. Kat Astley took your position and the hurt remains. 'I think God set things right that day, Mistress.'

Blanche smiled, and patted Margaretta's shoulder. 'Indeed.

I am blessed – but also riven with fear. Now, go and rally John Dee and use your skills to make my Elizabeth safe again. You can think of loneliness another time.'

So, you did feel my thoughts.

Margaretta nodded and stood to leave. 'There is a woman called Alice in the palace cells who has been brave in telling what she saw. A poor thing with only the rags on her back. Could she have water to wash each day and maybe some warm clothes, shoes and a little kindness?'

'It will be done.'

Chapter Ten

Evening was setting in as they reached Mortlake and still Dee was raging about a Thomas Martinfield sending information about conjuring and horoscopes. 'This is my area of expertise, Margaretta. I should be informed.' Margaretta's attempts to mollify by suggesting that Sir Cecil would not want to mention such letters in front of Leicester fell on deaf ears. She tried to turn the conversation to Elizabeth's ulcer, but he was further incensed that Cecil's apothecary was better trusted. She thanked God when they turned into the yard.

Katherine Dee was out of the front door like a rabbit from a trap and Dee was given his usual effusive greeting, kisses on his cheek, and the barrage of questions about his day. He was kind, affectionate, and answered everything, yet told her nothing; then guided her in saying all he wanted was a glass of good wine and a seat by the fire with his wife. Her face fell. 'Your mother insists she sits with us tonight. She says her rooms are drafty. I did say that I would have a fire built up for her, but you know how she snaps at me.'

Dee sighed and turned to Margaretta. 'See if you can keep mother quiet for one night. And put Pierre Perotin's bread in the corner of the stable. If we have dead rats in the morning we know where he was poisoned.'

Margaretta handed the bag of papers to her master and went to place the bread in the stable, high on a shelf above the reach of the dogs, then went to the very comfortable cottage of Mother Dee, across the yard. They had arrived here five years ago, after Master Constable, Dee's landlord had died in the middle of a wine-fuelled game of cent in a quayside tavern and Catherine woke up a widow. She had neither the money nor the inclination to keep the house in St Dunstans, and Dee faced the prospect of moving all his books and equipment to another home. Mother Dee had made her move and offered him the run of her house in Mortlake, plus funds to buy adjacent cottages for converting to a separate house and a laboratory. She made great plans for 'My John' to return to his mother's nest. But she had not reckoned on John Dee, in the intervening weeks, marrying his former landlady and arriving with a wife. The atmosphere had never risen above frosty.

As she knocked on the door, Bela, her lemon-bleached hair coiled under a coif and her waist pulled tight into a new dress stepped out of the shadows, head cocked to the side with a smirk.

And here it starts – out of earshot and so the venom will flow. Doctor Dee told me that 'bela' is the Hebrew word for destruction. He laughed, not knowing what truth he told. You are dreadful.

'So, you are going for a dark evening with the old Witch of Mortlake, Margaretta.' A sickly smile. 'Katherine said she would prefer my company this evening anyway.'

She has said no such thing, but she is flattered at your fluttering and lies of how ladylike and graceful she is. Because Katherine doesn't know that you laugh behind her back. You are like a rotten egg, Bela. Smooth, pale and perfect on the outside with a putrid heart inside. I smile. You hate that because you cannot know what I am thinking.

Mother Dee was sitting at her table, counting pennies. She looked up with a glower which softened when she saw Margaretta. 'Good. It's you. I thought it might be her.'

Margaretta sat at the table and dropped her voice to coaxing. 'Another argument with Katherine?'

'She wants to kill me. Says I should stay here in this drafty hovel and shiver my way through the tempest of a March night. She is…'

'She is your son's wife, Mother Dee, and very loving of him. She wants them to spend time together. And they have made you a lovely home in this cottage. Warm too if you would bank the fire.'

The old woman sniffed. 'She is too old for romancing my boy. She must be ten years his senior.' She banged a penny down on the table. 'And she spends too much.'

'I think it is more that your son does not earn enough and then buys too much. If it were not for all the horoscopes I do, which he passes as his own work, we would be hand to mouth. But he is so consumed by turning iron into gold that he spends all day distilling everything he can find to see if it leads him to The Philosopher's Stone.'

Mother Dee sighed and nodded. 'Like his father. Money ran through his fingers like water too.'

Not quite true. He made a fortune and lost it through foolery. 'Well, let's hope the doctor can make gold instead of losing it.'

The old woman tutted. 'What was the stink last week? It was terrible. It still makes my pillow smell.'

'Pig shit, horse dung, marigold flowers and the feathers of a goldfinch. It didn't work. The iron just smelled.' The two women laughed and Margaretta poured them each a beaker of the spiced wine keeping warm on the grate. She banked up the fire and put a blanket around the old woman's shoulders. 'Come, Mother Dee. We would all be the happier if you could accept Katherine. She loves your son just as you do.'

There was a huff and Jane Dee changed the subject, asking about the day. Margaretta told snippets – about visiting Cecil to work on a secret mission, being entrusted with the Queen's business – everything that would please the woman but none of the killings that would alarm her.

Mother Dee was soon bored and swivelled the conversation. 'That pupil of John's arrived back from Kent today. Thomas Digges. First person he asked after was you.'

'He probably wanted me to sort his notes. Do not get ideas.'

'A good catch.'

'I am nearly thirty-four and he is twenty-four. Ten years difference.'

'No matter.'

'So why does it matter that Katherine is ten years older than your son?'

A sniff. Then silence.

Some hours later, Margaretta crossed the courtyard and entered the main house. She could see the light under the door at the end of the corridor – the sign that John Dee was still hard at work. She stepped inside his office to find him staring at the table, his brow furrowed. Without looking up, he muttered, 'At last. Mother has talked long tonight.'

'She is lonely, Doctor. If you visited her more often, she might be better minded to accept Katherine.'

Dee gave a low growl. 'I cannot bear another lecture on how I am like my father.' He looked back at the desk. 'Anyway, I had more important things this evening. Look at the cards.'

Margaretta pulled up a stool. Amid the papers and equipment strewn across his working area was the casket he used to hide his tarot cards and, in front of that, three cards. 'The Hierophant, Judgement, and the Knight of Pentacles. What question did you ask and what was the order?'

'I asked what was behind the death of Pierre Perotin. I spread the whole deck face down and used the crystal pendulum while thinking of the body.'

'That's a new technique.'

'Yes – combining the mind's image with the crystal. An experiment. But it worked. The stone kept swinging clockwise on every card until it was held above these three. Then it immediately started swinging left-right.' Dee tapped on the Hierophant card. 'This one first, then Judgement, then the Knight of Pentacles.'

'The Hierophant appears to be a religious figure. Maybe the Pope who has passed judgement on Elizabeth.' She picked up the Judgement card. 'An angel with wings of fire and a tempest around his shoulders, he holds the flag of England while heralding judgement onto naked people below. They implore the angel while floating in coffins on a choppy sea. Look at their colour – grey like dead bodies.'

Dee nodded. 'Only one is female, the rest male. These are the men Elizabeth has put around her whom the Pope despises.'

Margaretta picked up the third card. 'The Knight of Pentacles, carrying his symbol – but the right way up. Indicating good.'

Dee chuckled. 'Do not be too literal Margaretta. When I had these cards painted, I did not want them full of symbols that would hold that evil. The only card in the whole deck with an inverted pentacle is the Devil card.'

'Knights always mean action and pursuit. Is this the killer carrying out the Papal Bull for the Pope?'

Dee sighed deeply as he reached into his bag and pulled out the bloodied linen with the embroidered pentacle and B. 'You are thinking well. Maybe Baphomet is an assassin using the Templar curse to bring terror then death, believing he is delivering the wrath of the Catholic Church. But who is he? The only hint we have is talk of a one-eyed, scarred man boarding a boat in Calais?'

Margaretta reached over to the casket. 'Another question. Is there anyone else?' She shuffled the cards, muttering the question under her breath, her eyes closed as she spread the cards in an arc across the desk. She moved her hand along it, asking the question. The candle flickered and she stopped. 'This one makes my hand tingle.' She turned it over and Dee gave a yelp.

'The Queen of Pentacles, looking down at the symbol in her hand. She looks kind but what is *she* seeing?'

'To her, the pentacle is upside down. She is looking at evil. But who is she? Blanche has letters from both Mary Queen of Scots and the Queen of France. Is it one of them?'

Dee gathered up the deck and placed it in front of Margaretta. 'It could be. In which case we are facing a Catholic plot to kill Elizabeth and put Mary on the throne.'

'That is what Thomas Martinfield wrote of in his letter. He also spoke of poisoning.'

Dee grimaced. 'One more question. What is their aim? Now put your hand on the deck, ask the question and cut the cards.'

Margaretta closed her eyes, and asked the question, then slid her fingers down the side and split the deck. As she raised it there was a sudden loud crack of breaking glass. One of the alchemical flasks had shattered on the far desk and was spilling a foul-smelling liquid over the bench. She turned back to Dee who was staring, ashen faced, at the card.

'The Wheel of Fortune, reversed. It means the world will turn towards the dark. Light will go and evil will rise. Freedom gives way to restriction. The players in this story are trying to change the fate of this country.' He looked up, eyes full of worry. 'And if we do not find out who they are, we cannot protect Elizabeth from their plotting. The assassin, Baphomet, is bringing first terror with the intention of then achieving the death of Elizabeth and, with her death, he kills our freedom. If Mary of the Scots is put on the throne, we will be at the mercy of Catholic Europe.'

Chapter Eleven

A hard rain was falling at dawn. Margaretta rose, lit a candle, tried to get the dream images of her sister, Susan, out of her mind as she dressed quickly, then slipped out of the back door to the stables. The bread was half eaten – not a dead rat in sight. She went to the kitchens to warm herself. Only cold ashes. 'Damn that girl.' In seconds, she was hammering on the door of Bela's room. 'Get up, slugabed.'

'An angry face peered out. 'Katherine said I…'

'I give not a damn. Move your backside and do your work. And you call her "Mistress Dee", not Katherine.'

'You just hate it that I am better friends with the mistress.'

'If your feet were as fast as your forked tongue, you might be a better maid. Now move.' Margaretta walked out and stamped along the corridor to her master's laboratory. From the smell coming under the door, he was distilling again.

She entered into a fug of steam with a stink worse than a midden. 'Dear God, Doctor. What are you brewing now?'

'Sheep droppings. Stronger than horse dung.'

'And how will sheep shit make gold?'

He looked up. 'I just need to make a solution so strong it changes the properties of metal.' He adjusted the flame below the glass container and stood back with a satisfied smile. 'Thomas will observe and monitor the process while we are investigating.'

'We have no dead rats. Pierre's bread is not poisoned so we need to add where he was poisoned to the mystery. What is today's plan?'

'First, All Hallows, to see what we can find of the dead man. Then on to Cecil to inform him of our... intuition. I will send a message saying to expect us and to have Walsingham there too.'

'Don't mention the cards. You know how jumpy he gets.'

'Fie. William is as interested in the occult as I am. He just pretends to be offended by them, as he fears what others might say.'

Dear Lord. For a man who can see the future, the stars, the power of crystals and cards, you are blind to what is in front of your eyes. 'I will visit Susan first.'

Dee turned, eyes wide. 'Are you serious, girl? You have not seen your damned sister for five years and now you want to visit her ahead of our work?'

'But yesterday you said I should go this morning.'

Dee shrugged. 'That was before we scried the cards and saw the threat. No. We go to All Hallows by mid-morning. To Cecil by midday for the list of Catholics and to tell him to stop his damned secreting. That gives us the afternoon to plan our next move and maybe interrogate someone.' He turned away.

Oh, God. I have to go. 'I have to see Susan. I dream of her. Something is wrong.'

'No.'

'If I am bothered by Susan, I will not be able to feel.' She raised her chin. 'If you need my skills then you need to give me freedom for a few hours.'

Dee reddened in irritation. 'The years have made you stubborn, Margaretta.'

Margaretta turned to the door, calling over her shoulder. 'Years of serving *you* have made me stubborn, Doctor. It is not age – it is survival. I will meet you at All Hallows at eleven of the clock.' She shut the door on his roar of indignation and nearly barrelled into a wide-eyed Thomas Digges. 'Good morning, Master Digges. Be careful with your calculations today. The old scut is in foul mood.'

The student stepped in front of her, clutching his books and papers to his chest. 'May I speak with you later, Mistress Morgan?'

'About what Mr Digges?'

'An idea. A proposal.'

Hell's teeth. A clench in my gut. Why are you blushing? Unease. 'Much later, Mr Digges.' She did not wait for his reply but strode up the corridor, collected a warm cape from the pegs on the wall and went out into the rain.

Chapter Twelve

Margaretta was standing in the covered portico, looking up at fading limewash and patches of wood-rot, when a wary maid opened the door. 'Yes, Mistress.'

'I am here to see my sister.'

The woman frowned. 'What is her job here?'

'Being vile, spending money, ignoring her husband's awfulness and raising two children who have the misfortune to have their parent's blood in their veins.'

The woman gulped. 'You want to see Mistress Susan?'

'Ah, we understand each other.' Margaretta winked and stepped through the door. She looked around. *Dust, damp, and the painting of our Queen is gone. What goes on here?* She set off down a dark corridor – the maid on her heels, pleading that to arrive unannounced was not a good idea – and opened the door. It was as cold as a cellar, with one candle burning on the table, and measly fire of one damp log. Sitting before it, wrapped in a blanket, was Susan. In the corner her two children. Maria was wrapped in a cloak and Little Jack, who was now a young lad of fifteen was also wrapped but holding a wooden toy and rocking. He did not look up. For a second, Susan's face showed relief before shifting to anger. 'What are you doing here?'

'I dreamt of you. Either there is something wrong or your

spirit had found a soul and was calling me. I knew it could not be the latter. So, what is wrong?'

Susan looked away and almost spat. 'There is nothing wrong.'

'Do not lie, sister. Your house is in disrepair, no stable lad came to take my horse, and you are sitting in a dark, cold, silent house wrapped in a blanket. Now spill the truth.'

Susan stood, her face contorting with fury and raised an arm to Margaretta. 'Witch. You cursed us with ruin. You did this.' In the corner, Jack rocked harder and began to slap at his own head.

Margaretta stepped back. 'Are you turned to madness?'

Susan kept wagging her finger, eyes wild, and her mouth pulled down as she struggled with the words. When they came, it was a shriek. 'You cursed us... swayed your evil... weeks later it started. I will tell of your spells. I will...'

Margaretta raised her hand, 'Stop your bile. I have done no such thing.' She turned to the children. Maria was cowering. Jack was slapping harder and harder and letting out animal moans. Approach only made them pull back as if being attacked. Margaretta turned to Susan. 'What the hell is happening here? How long has Jack been this way?'

'Since the day you cursed us. You turned our life into one of misery and decline.' Susan gripped the back of a wooden chair and pulled her head up, her voice lowering to cold fury. 'Before you, we were rising. You could not bear to see us prosper.'

'Fie, sister. The only thing I could not bear was your husband's vile attempt to rise by stealing our brother's inheritance.' The noise from Jack was loudening and he slapped harder. Susan did not even look at him. Margaretta grabbed his hands before crouching to look at his face. 'Stop this, Jack. Be still or I will stare into your eyes until you look back.' The boy went still and dropped his head, eyes closed, breathing hard. 'Will you be quiet if I let you go?' Just a nod.

Slowly, his aunt released his hands and leaned over to pat Maria who was weeping silent tears.

She looked to Susan and quietly commanded, 'Call the servant to get your children clean and dressed, and to bring us a beaker of warm wine. No matter it is early. You need to tell me what is happening here.'

Susan jutted her chin. 'I do not need the help of a witch.'

'But I think you need a sister, Susan. By the look of this place, you have no other friend.'

The room was silent as the servant shut the door. Susan had hunched in her chair, making no move towards either child. Minutes later the wine arrived.

Margaretta sat at the scratched table, picked up her beaker and pushed the other towards her sister. 'Drink, Susan. The honey might sweeten you.' Then a sigh. 'Let us stop this harshness. Tell me what is happening. I know Angus has not been sending out his bills. Maria is like a frightened kitten and Jack is...'

'... cursed by you.' Susan pointed at the desk in the corner. 'You stood next to that and cursed us.'

'That is foolery, Susan. I made no curse. I only wanted to make you do the right thing by signing a letter. Good thing I did, for I prevented you being truly cursed by God. I put you on a path to honesty even though your dreadful husband schemed and lied.'

Susan shook her head but would not look up. 'You cursed Jack and...'

Margaretta banged her fist on the table making her sister jump and yelp. 'If... IF... I had the ability to curse, I would not curse Jack – a child I love as if he were my own. I would have cursed your damn husband for his gluttony for money – Huw's money. Now spill your misery.'

Susan gulped. 'Some time after your curse, my husband began to change. His sweet nature turned to anger...' She glowered at Margaretta's 'Pah' of derision and continued.

'Then the terrible headaches. He had to take wine to sooth the pain. Now he is not the man I married.'

My God. Usually when I am in your company all I feel is your spite and venom. But this is different. Your fear makes me tremble. I hear harsh words, raving. A man paces and screams. I sense you looking at someone in terror. You try to shield your children. But you are so very tired.

Susan narrowed her eyes. 'Do not look at me like that. I do not need your pity.'

Margaretta leaned forward. 'Sister, five years ago, I walked into a new house of wealth and comfort… now cold and misery seeps from the very walls. Your children are suffering, and from the dark circles under your eyes and the pallor of your skin, so are you. Is Angus at The Vintry?'

Susan shook her head and fat tears began to gather in her eyes. 'He has been unable to go for many months, maybe a year. His stumbles when he walks and his eyes are full of pain. He has asked the yard manager to run the business until he recovers.'

Margaretta groaned. 'Not the long lanky lad who was around when Huw was working there?' Susan nodded. 'Well, his brains are in his breaches and not on the good selling of your barrels. When did he last deliver you money?'

'Every week, but less and less. He says business is slow at the moment.'

'Fie. Business is thriving and the rich would sell their servants for a cask of sack-wine – as you know.' Margaretta stood, and looked down on her sister, her voice kind. 'Take me to Angus.'

Susan's hands trembled as she opened the door to the sleeping chamber. Inside the air was thick and stale with the smell of a man long unwashed. Margaretta held in a gasp as she looked through the gloom at her brother-in-law, lying in the bed, a goblet of burgundy wine in his hand which had slopped on the cover. A dark dribble of the same flowed from the side of his mouth. He raised his head and peered through red-rimmed eyes. As the light of Susan's candle illuminated his face, Margaretta let out a small cry. His face and neck were covered in purple-red lumps, like the buboes of the plague. His head swayed as he tried to focus. 'Wife?'

'Yes, Angus. I bring a visitor.'

Angus grunted and slowly turned to Margaretta. 'Who are you?'

Dear God, what has happened to you? You may have the heart of a devil but you were once a handsome man. Now you look as if you have been living in the gutter for years. You stink. I was waiting for the usual peering at my person, then saucy words. But you just wince your confusion like a child. 'I am the one you call Little Sister, Angus. Have you forgotten my face?'

Angus stared, his face blank, then a slight shake before he looked to Susan. 'Who is this?' His face clouded and he pulled himself up but wobbled like a deer taking its first steps. 'You bring people to steal from me. Damn you.'

Susan made a little whimper and made a desperate glance to Margaretta. 'No, my love. This is Margaretta. My sister. You remember Margaretta and Huw?'

Angus scowled and rocked his snarl side to side, revealing a row of blackened teeth. 'Bring wine.'

I have seen enough. 'Susan, let us go.'

Chapter Thirteen

'You look like a wretch. A sodden cloak, wet hair, and misery on your face,' snapped Dee. 'You need to shake yourself to better mind if we are going to meet the vicar of All Hallows. At this rate he will think I have brought you for the last rites.'

Margaretta ignored him, twisting away when he stretched over to tap her shoulder to make his point. *Hell's teeth. You know how seeing Susan brings me down. But you cannot see the worry in me. No. You think only of what you need from me.*

'What ails you, Margaretta? I need you alert and feeling.' Dee sighed as Margaretta shrugged. 'I suppose if my Katherine were here, she would ask what has upset you – what your sister said.'

'Because your good wife has more wit for people's feelings in her little finger than you have in your whole being.'

Dee glowered. 'You wax and wane like the moon, Margaretta. Only last week you were calling Katherine a dalcop for liking Bela.'

His companion raised her brows. 'That is true too. Bela and her yellowed hair, forked tongue, and greedy eyes, plays your wife like a drum. Tickling her when she wants something and hitting her behind her back. You should throw her out.'

Dee wagged his hand in exasperation. 'Servants are Katherine's domain. Mine is the mind and our mission. Now tell me quickly of Susan. We need to go.'

'I found her sitting in a cold house, her husband sick and raving through his drink in a bed, and my nephew and niece like frightened animals. Angus is being cheated. Do you remember the lanky boy in the yard?'

'Vaguely. But it is a long time ago. Tell me of Angus.'

'Raving. No memory of me. Dark lumps on his face. Unable to sit without rocking – as if he were on a swaying ship. His words were harsh. I felt Susan's fear of him.'

Dee groaned. 'And I recall you going to Clarissa the herb woman to get a remedy for the French Pox. It must be…'

'… twelve years ago. Yes. It worked. Susan recovered.'

'But Angus did not take the medicine, did he?'

Margaretta shook her head.

'When we go to Cecil's house, ask to go to the library and find a book by Girolamo Fracastoro. Look for a poem about a shepherd meeting a Greek king.'

Margaretta tutted. 'I want a remedy not poetic words, Doctor.'

Dee growled. 'That snip tongue again, girl. Fracastoro was a genius and set out the stages of the French Pox – which he called Syphilis – in the poem. If it describes Angus, you know what you are dealing with. But, for the love of God, do not let Lady Cecil see what you are reading. We want no taint against our name.'

'My sister is not a taint.'

'Oh, yes. She is. She has tainted your life and nearly your brother's too.' Dee lifted a hand to stop the train of conversation. 'We must go to All Hallows. I will speak, and you sit in a pew in pretence of praying. You can tell me all you feel when we leave. He must think you just a simple servant.'

'Very well.' *Damn you.*

All Hallows Church was quiet but for the sweeping of an old woman at the far end. John Dee marched up and asked for the name of the vicar.

'Richard Tyrwhit, sir. A godly man if ever there was.'

Dee smiled his most charming smile. 'Please ask Vicar Tyrwhit to speak with me.'

As she scuttled off towards the vestry, Margaretta looked around. The ceiling was high and vaulted in oak. The seats gleamed and the air perfumed by the beeswax that shone them. Tapestries and banners hung on the wall.

Footsteps heralded the vicar walking quickly up the aisle. 'I am Richard Tyrwhit. You seek me, sir? Do you need prayer? He looked at Margaretta. 'Is there trouble with the girl?'

'No trouble, father.'

The churchman reached them, stopped and blanched. 'You are John Dee. I did not see your face in the shadow, sir.'

Dee bridled. 'Yes. Doctor Dee – priest, and philosopher to Her Majesty. Not the hugger-mugger and conjuror which the weak and unwise of mind continue to believe. We are investigating the murder of one Pierre Perotin. I understand he is a congregant of yours.'

The priest gulped, shock making his Adam's apple bob like a ball on a fountain. 'Murder? Dear God.'

Real fear. Confusion. A true shock to you. You are a good man. Honest. But you think of a woman.

'Tell us everything you know of him.'

'A quiet, pious man. Arrived here to escape attacks on Huguenots in France many years ago, then the poor fellow lost his income when his hand was damaged. Not long after his family were taken by the plague. But he was never one to beg or complain and so secured a job as a royal palace guard. A good one too, I am sure, for he was tall and strong, honest and never one to imbibe.'

'This church is a long way from his dwelling in Westminster. And why come here when Huguenots have their own church?'

The priest nodded. 'He came with others from the Huguenot Church in Threadneedle Street. I have a small French flock of that faith now – considered part of our congregation even though foreigners.'

'But why come to *this* church?' snapped Dee.

The vicar looked perplexed. 'No bad event, Doctor Dee. They simply followed another Huguenot – our clothe mender. A goodly friend to all in this place.'

'His name?'

'Josef Mabelain. A weaver, mender and merchant.'

'Is he here?'

'Indeed. He is in the vestry with our sacristan mending an altar cloth. I will get him.' The vicar turned.

'Wait. When was the last time you saw Pierre Perotin?'

The vicar halted mid-stride and turned, looking abashed by Dee's tone. 'Last Sunday, when he took communion.'

'Any sign of sickness?'

Tyrwhit frowned. 'None at all. We are blessed.'

You tremble. You think of a woman again. You do not want trouble.

Dee grunted and nodded to the back in a silent command to get Mabelain. As the other man disappeared, he whispered to Margaretta. 'What do you feel?'

'Confusion – not guilt. But he keeps thinking of a woman.'

'I will ask. And let us see what the other brings.'

Soon the sound of footsteps echoed down the church. Shuffling along next to the priest was a man dressed in black, so short he reached only the shoulder of the priest. With each step he lurched to the side on a leg that was shorter than the other and twisted, the foot so crippled that it turned inwards and he could only use his toes. As he came into the light of the candles, Margaretta had to supress a gasp and force herself to show no shock. As if the twisting of his leg were not affliction enough, this man had a face so ugly she had to make herself to look at him. One eye was dark and peering. The other was turned to the right. The skin on his face was covered in small scars and a wide, flattened nose spread above a bulbous mouth, shining with spittle. His hair, black and tufted, was cut close to his head. He said nothing when the priest introduced him but stared at John Dee with his one good eye.

Dee made a small bow. 'Mr Mabelain, I understand you are a clothe mender here.'

A small nod was the only answer.

You are very worried. Look how you ball your hands to hide the tremble.

'Has Vicar Tyrwhit told you of the demise of Pierre Perotin?'

The straight eye widened and he looked to the minister before answering, 'Yes, sir. I am most shocked. He is... was... a good man – a Huguenot like me.' The voice was quite high with a slight French accent. He put a hand to his mouth, looked down and shook his head. '*Mon dieu.*' As his sleeve fell down his arm, Margaretta could see many small scabs reddening his skin.

'Tell us all you know of him.'

'He came from a small village in Brittany. His father was murdered for his faith and so he fled to England, for your gracious Queen has always been a friend to our people. A year or two ago, there was an accident, and he was not able to weave. He became a guard.'

'Is that all you know?'

The Frenchman nodded, his good eye starting to blink rapidly.

Dee persisted. 'But Vicar Tyrwhit told us he followed you here from the Huguenot Church in Threadneedle Street.'

The man nodded again and stuttered. 'When the Huguenot Church became too full to pray in comfort, the welcome I had here was spoken of and several followed me.'

Why are you thinking of Sir Cecil and another man? I hear the name Walsingham.

'And they were welcomed,' cut in the priest as if to defend.

'Did Pierre have enemies?'

A rapid shaking of the head. 'I doubt it. He was a quiet man. Rarely spoke of anything but the Bible and his work.'

'So, you do not know who would slit his throat and carve his body with strange symbols?'

The smaller man let out a small shriek before stumbling sideways and grabbing at a pew end to steady himself. He clasped a hand over his mouth as if to stop any further noise escaping. Tyrwhit reached out to steady him and murmured words of comfort.

Strange. You feel fear and worry but not horror. I feel that coming from the vicar, but not you.

Dee turned to Margaretta who gave a small nod to show she had picked up the feelings. '*Merch*,' she whispered.

He turned back to the priest. 'I heard a woman of your congregation died recently.'

Tyrwhit gulped and looked briefly at Mabelain, who was looking up at the ceiling as if in prayer. 'Lucille. Yes. But she was old.'

'What happened?'

Mabelain answered. 'They found her dead at her home on Wednesday last week. The neighbours sent for me, and I was asked to run here immediately and ask for burial.'

'Where is her family? I will speak with them.'

'She lived alone. In the alms-houses in Bethnal Green. But there can be no connection,' insisted the vicar.

'Lucille is a French name is it not?' Dee paused as the holy man paled.

It was Mabelain who answered, his voice shaking. 'She was one of us. Huguenot. But she was old. Very old.'

Why do you keep wincing? And why am I picking up alarm?

'Was Lucille a friend to you, Master Mabelain?'

The small man turned as if surprised she had spoken. 'No madam. The women of her neighbourhood cared for her. Not the men. That would be unseemly.'

You wince again. There is more to this.

Dee jutted his chin and assumed his arrogant voice. 'You are not to speak of Pierre Perotin. If word of this terrible deed reaches the streets, I know it will have started here.' He turned to Margaretta. 'Come girl.'

As they walked up the aisle, there was a call from the Frenchman and he limped and scraped after them. 'Doctor Dee. Forgive my reserve. We Huguenots have learned to lie low. If there is anything I can do to assist your enquiries, please let me know.' He made a small bow which twisted with his leg.

Dee grunted a thanks and made for the door.

Outside, they mounted their horses and set off in the direction of The Strand. At the end of Seething Lane, Dee turned to Margaretta. 'Well?'

'The priest is horrified and frightened. The Frenchman is worried and anxious. But I did not feel horror from him. And he thinks of Cecil and Walsingham.'

Dee's eyes widened. 'Does he indeed'

'I have never met this man Walsingham. Why are Cecil and Leicester pulling him into this mystery?'

'New to Cecil's circle. Sharp mind, speaks French, good with money and knows a huge number of London merchants through the business he inherited through his first wife. Abroad he is connected to Protestants as he fled there for his education when Bloody Mary Tudor ascended to the throne. On top of that he has a love of decoding cyphers. Cecil has great plans for him.'

And I do not need to feel your thoughts to see the envy in your face.

Dee tutted and changed the subject. 'Anything else in the church?'

'There is discomfort over the old lady. Mabelain winces.'

Chapter Fourteen

Mildred Cecil wafted into the room, breaking into a smile. 'My dear John. How do you fare?' She turned to tell a servant to bring wine and when the door was closed continued, 'I hear William is keeping you busy on this terrible business of the palace guard.'

Dee nodded. 'He is. And I am glad to be of service to our Queen.'

Mildred smiled, gestured to a chair and poured a good goblet of wine. 'How is your good lady wife?'

Dee made a tight smile – the sign he was not interested in small talk. 'She lights my every day. I thank you for asking. Is William available?'

'Alas, no. My Lord Pembroke lies dying in Hampton Court. He has requested William's presence to finalise his will and testament.'

Dee jerked as if he had been shot. 'Dying? But I did not know.' He sat heavily and looked away.

Mildred patted his arm. 'I think you have a long history with him, John.'

'Indeed, yes. He was my first patron. Took me in to calculate horoscopes for all his family and friends. He introduced me to Court as a young man.' Dee pressed his lips together as if trying to crush the rising emotion and bowed his head.

Well maybe I can never feel you, but I see sorrow going

through you in waves and you cannot hold back the tears. All I recall is a rough-tongued man with his stinking cur-dog as he snarled at you in the Tower all those years ago. He was the man who told you to go to Bishop Bonner and remember the number 007. I think he was saving your life that day in 1555, but you have never spoken of it again. Lady Mildred just looks at you, not knowing what to say. But I have a way of breaking this brittle atmosphere. 'My Lady, Doctor Dee says you have a book of medicine which might be good reading. The Doctor's reputation as a physician is growing and I can help if I know more.'

Mildred turned in relief. 'What book do you seek, my dear?'

'It is by Fracastoro, an Italian doctor who wrote poetry.' Margaretta flicked her eyes to John Dee in a signal to leave him alone.

Mildred gave a nod and patted Dee's shoulder. 'Rest awhile with your memories, John. Call a servant if you need more wine.' She beckoned to Margaretta and the two women left for the upper library.

Inside, Margaretta inhaled the perfumes of leather, paper, ink and the beeswax of polish and candles. It was a heaven of learning and wisdom. Shelves which covered every one of the four walls, full of tomes of science, medicine, philosophy, languages. All the thinking and wit of great men – and now a few women – enveloped her. The sound of Lady Mildred putting a book on the polished table in front of her brought her back to her senses. She stepped forward and opened it. *Oh, God. It is all in Latin. What do I do?* 'Might I have a sheet of paper and a pen, my lady?'

Mildred raised her brow and tapped the book. 'This is the first of three volumes my dear. And why are you seeking to learn a poem about the French Pox? I doubt the imps of Mortlake come with such a malady.'

I am caught. She looks at me with those knowing eyes. I cannot lie. She will know. 'I just thought... um.'

'That I would not notice or question? Fie, Margaretta, I live in a court of powerful men and scheming women. My job is to see everything and make sure it reaches my husband's ears if it has not reached his own eyes.' She took Margaretta's arm and turned her. 'Are you in trouble, my dear?'

Hells teeth. She thinks I have the pox. 'No, indeed, madam.' *I can feel my face reddening. How do I get out of this?*

Mildred held her gaze. 'I thought not. Then someone close enough that you risk my suspicion.'

I cannot hold in the tears. I hate my sister, but I love her too. She is my kin. Don't cry. Don't cry. 'Yes.' *My voice sounds like a mouse.*

Mildred pulled down another book and patted the seat next to her. '*Medicina* by Johannes Fernelius. There are four stages. The first is pustules around the mouth or the regions below clothes – you know what I mean.'

Margaretta nodded. *Those are the pustules I found on my sister's mouth twelve years ago. Clarissa healed her. Maybe I can get Angus healed too.*

'The second stage is a rash with swelling around the upper legs and armpits. Often terrible weariness. The third stage has no signs – as if the malady has left the body. But then the final stages come and these are desperate. Buboes on the skin, madness, unsteady legs and eyes that cannot see. Once at this stage there is no cure.' She turned to Margaretta. 'From the look on your face, I have just taken away all your hopes.'

'Yes.' *That voice of a mouse again.*

A pat on her arm. 'Then all you can give is kindness, my dear. My advice is to go to Clarissa, the herb woman in Southwark, and see if she can relieve the worst of it.'

'Doctor Dee said I was not to admit we knew anyone with this disease, madam. He will be angry.'

Mildred let out a hard laugh. 'Ah, our John is an innocent, is he not? My dear, half the men of Court are riddled with this foul disease. They take their purses to Southwark or the stews of the battlefield and come back with a life-long gift.' She stood and walked to the window. 'But those who really suffer are the wives who must live with their husbands' bad choices.'

'But those women are helpless, madam. What can they do?'

Mildred face hardened. 'Choose a man for his goodness rather than his gold.'

You think of your husband. Always faithful. There is never a sniff of him even speaking to another woman unless you know of it. 'Not all women are as lucky as you, my lady. They do not make their own choices.'

'You challenge me well, Margaretta.'

'Oh, I did not mean to offend... I...'

Mildred raised her hand. 'No need. Wit is better honed if sharpened by debate. You are right. I look down from a pedestal of good fortune and good choice. If you meet a man, you think about that, Margaretta.'

Oh, how that hurts. My heart has never truly mended. I watch the doctor's love for Katherine and rejoice in their happiness. Then I close the door and go to a cold bed alone. And I think it will always be so. Lady Mildred is looking at me with eyes of pity. I must sit up and smile. 'Indeed, my lady. If ever I am so lucky I will remember your words.'

Downstairs, John Dee was still staring out of the window. The decanter was empty. He turned his head slowly. 'I think I will go back to Katherine.'

Back at Mortlake, Dee was helped down from his horse, no one mentioning his unsteady legs and slurred speech. Katherine Dee ran out as usual and stopped; then took in his face and gently put her arms around him. And John Dee wept.

Chapter Fifteen

It was gone eight of the clock and Margaretta was finishing her last horoscope. Requests were frequent and no customer ever knew that the neat lines, numbers and well written explanations were the hand of John Dee's apprentice. She slumped back with a sigh.

Why do I feel such foreboding? My sister, Susan, is locked to a man who is descending into madness. My nephew and niece are suffering. So is she. I do not want to care about her. But I do. Somewhere out there is a madman who will slice, slit and sew a poor innocent who seems to have done no wrong in this world. Doctor Dee is wracked with grief for a man who was only ever harsh to him. I have to daily suffer the forked tongue of that vile maid. I feel so alone in all this. I don't even have the strange comfort of my brother anymore. It is good that he has found love with little Grace. But I miss his smile, his seeing of colours, his magical mind. Now there is only me. No one to hold my hand and say 'all will be well, and all will be well', as my Dada used to do.

The door opened and Thomas Digges entered. Margaretta smiled to cover her irritation. 'Good evening, Master Digges.'

He strode over. A round-faced man with a mass of close-cut, golden curls and a wispy beard of copper and blonde. Large eyes under heavy brows and a long straight nose gave an air of higher birth. The voice matched – a little twang of disdain so often heard in those born with fewer worries. 'Where is the doctor? I have a letter from Tycho. I think it will interest him.'

'He is with Mistress Katherine having had bad news, Thomas. I think your letter must wait.'

There was a moment of perplexed staring and then a smile. 'Then I shall tell you about it. You are quite intelligent. Tycho is working on the effective combination of Copernicus' heliocentrism with the Ptolemaic system to create his very own system, to be named after himself. I think the doctor and I should leave with haste to meet with him, for he is also looking at elements of science which might lead us to the Philosopher's Stone, and wealth and great profit. Yes, I will plead with the doctor to...' He looked up. 'Why are you sitting with your arms folded and your eyes closed?'

'Because you speak of things that have no meaning to me.'
And worse, I sense from you a desire to impress. I often hear you talk of a girl called Ann St Leger. So why impress me? But you usually leak. So, I will just stay silent and wait.

Digges looked bemused, then sat up with a small smile as if a light had shone on reason. 'But if I educate you, then you can be of use, keep the papers, work on some calculations. Read my papers for errors and sense.'

'I already do that for Doctor Dee, while sitting in the most infernal stench in Christendom created by your mad pursuit of eternal life and endless gold. How you think that the gold God puts in the ground can be bubbled up in a glass flask?'

Digges gulped in alarm and indignation. 'Mistress Margaretta, you are bold-tongued... not good in a wife.'

'Wife?'

'Yes. I have considered the matter. You would be an asset to my career. That is my idea... proposal.'

Margaretta raised an eyebrow and jutted her chin. 'An asset?'

'Er, yes... I... I need a wife who can... um... help my work.' He paused. 'Ah. Of course, you wish to be loved. Well, yes... I find you to be pretty despite your years.'

'How very kind.'

Digges made a faltering smile. 'So can I consider you…'

'An under-educated asset?' She stood, snatched up the horoscope and stamped to the door ignoring his protestations that he was misunderstood. Outside she leaned on the wall and breathed deep.

'Oooh. So, you are getting uppity with Master Digges. That will not go well for you. You know how the master likes him.' It was Bela, standing in the shadows, a smirk on her face.

'If your ears are as sharp as your tongue, Bela, how do you always manage to be deaf to any command?'

The smirk deepened. 'The mistress says she will see me raised in the household because I am a better maid to her than you have ever been. She says you have been around the house too long. Some of the scholars say you are only here because no man would have you.'

Damn you. Your usual game. Taking a few snippets of fact and mixing them into a bowl of bile. Katherine said I have been with her a long time. One of the scholars teased me that I needed to stay away from the stink if I wanted to get myself a good man. But you, Bela, with your love of spite, weave those into a story to turn the knife. You are dreadful. Margaretta forced a knowing smile and turned away to walk down the corridor to the yard door.

'Where are you going?'

'To sit with Mother Dee. For all her seventy years she has a sweeter face than yours – and she does not have a soul that will sour the wine.'

'Two old maids together then.'

Bitch. I will have you.

Chapter Sixteen

Margaretta opened her eyes on a cold, damp Saturday morning and groaned. Why had she not refused Mother Dee's flagon? The old woman had the constitution of a dock worker and would feel no effect. To add to her misery, she could hear Bela talking in the yard – the usual stream of self-important rubbish and claims of how the household would fall apart without her work; how she has to keep the mistress calm in the face of John Dee's impossible behaviour; how she was the only person Katherine trusted; how she had to organise the other servants; how difficult it all was. Then she claimed to have been a friend of Lord Pembroke. *Fie. his cur-dog was a more pleasant soul than you.* Margaretta vowed to put the vixen in her place – one day, when the time was right.

After her morning rub-down with coarse linens, Margaretta made her way to the laboratory. Dee was already at his desk, though his eyes were as red as hers. 'You are late.'

'It is before six in the morning. The sun is not even out of bed.' She sat heavily. 'Mother Dee opened a flagon.'

'And from the look of you, you opened your mouth to drink it down.'

She ignored the glaring and tidied her desk. 'What is the plan for today?'

'We go to the Alms-houses in Bethnal Green to check the death of that Huguenot woman. Then to Cecil. I have sent a note to say Walsingham should attend. I want to know the connection to Mabelain. I have told them I – we will be at The Strand by middle of day.'

'Good. That gives me time to see Clarissa. I will meet you at the north end of London Bridge at ten of the clock.'

Dee raised his head. 'You saw the book? Did you borrow it?'

'It is in Latin. Lady Mildred found another and told me to go to Clarissa. So, I…' *Oh, damn my fuddled head. I have let the truth slip and your face hardens in fury. Time to go.* She turned on her heel and went to the door ignoring his roar and insistence that she was a 'damned fool and slip-tongue.'

The apothecary store was just as it was the first day she walked in. Shelf upon shelf of glass bottles, jars and pots, each neatly labelled with the contents. All manner of flowers, herbs and barks of trees. On the very top shelf, out of reach from a foolish thief were the mushrooms, henbane and belladonna. These would need the ladder, kept well hidden behind the counter. The only difference was that Simon was in the shop instead of Clarissa.

'Miss Margaretta, 'tis a great pleasure to see you. Mother will be pleased.' He came from behind the wooden counter, the limp from the foot, broken as a child, now barely noticeable. He had grown into a fine young man – tall, reddish hair, blue eyes that shone bright and still the freckles that had given him the nickname of Spot when Margaretta had found him in the gutter. Who would have thought that the hungry imp begging an apple or a fist of bread would grow to be one of the most respected apothecaries in London? He took her hand. 'Come to the back. Mother is working on a remedy for the sweating sickness.'

'I heard there is no cure.'

He shrugged. 'She thinks the remedy is reducing the terrible heat in the body which drives out the soul.'

Clarissa was bent over a small weighing scales, and an

array of glass jars. The sun was shining through the window, making the glass cast rainbows across the room. But for all the colour, she dazzled brighter. Her amber eyes lit up as she walked over to embrace her friend. 'It is a good day when you walk through the door, my dear. But so early? You must have left Mortlake in the dark.' She looked into Margaretta's eyes. 'Have you been imbibing Katherine's malmsey wine? You are as red-eyed as a bulldog.' She winked at Simon. 'A tea of mint, marshmallow and much honey.' He grinned and left them.

Margaretta sat heavily. 'Mother Dee's wine. But I am here on other business. It is my sister's household again.'

Clarissa raised an eyebrow. 'Another dose?'

'It is her husband this time. I have never seen such a sight. Even with all my hatred of him, I was moved to pity.'

Clarissa took up a pen and started writing as Margaretta listed the symptoms, tears wetting her cheeks.

Simon came in with the tea and his face fell. 'Oh, Margaretta. What ails you?' He put his hand on her shoulder.

My, you have learned the kindness shown to you by this woman. I recall the day she took your little hand and offered to be your mother. I think God looked down that day and decided to make the world a little better. You certainly made my world better. When you left together, my mother was kind to me for the first time in years.

Clarissa handed him her note. 'This is Margaretta's brother-in-law, Angus.'

He took it to the light of the window and read quietly before shaking his head and speaking quietly. 'The latter stages of the French Pox. Advancing quickly.'

'What can I do?'

'Nothing,' said Clarissa. 'He is doomed, Margaretta. All you can do it try to get your sister to take control of his business before she finds herself in the gutter in which her husband so often wakes up.'

Margaretta rose, wiped her eyes and pulled on her shawl.

'I will go to her now. One more thing. Do you have a salve for a leg ulcer? I cannot say for whom I seek it. And my master will take all the glory. But I will ensure he pays you.'

Clarissa smiled and put her head on one side to tease. 'I will make it up over the coming days. I assume it is a silk-stockinged leg.'

'It is. A more noble leg you will not find.'

Susan was wide eyed, holding Maria's hand when Margaretta walked in. In the corner, Jack was rocking, his face to the wall.

'Send the children out, Susan. We need to talk.'

A nod to the maid and in a minute, they were alone. Susan's indignation flared. 'You should not come here without giving me notice.'

'Why? So that you can cover the wreckage of your life? So that you can pretend you are not scared witless? So, you can pretend to be the grand woman you always thought yourself to be and forget that as children we ran together – barefooted in fields?'

Susan turned away. 'Go away.'

'No Susan. For all your bile and bitter words, you are my sister, and those poor children are my kin. Dada would turn in his grave if he could see you now. Your husband is dying of the French Pox and I must help.'

Silence.

'Where are the papers for Angus's business? He would have had them when old Mr McFadden died a few years ago.'

A shrug.

'Might they be in the house?'

Silence.

'Stop this foolery, Susan. There is no time for disdain.' Margaretta grabbed her sister's shoulder and yanked her around to see a face crumpled in desperation, tears flowing down her cheeks. For a second, they stared at each other. Then she gathered her sister into her arms as she wailed out her misery.

Half an hour later, Margaretta was leaving through the front door, telling the maid to leave Susan a while for she was tired. In reality, her face was so swollen from crying that they feared frightening the children. The maid gave a knowing nod. Susan had agreed to search the house for any papers. Margaretta mounted her horse and looked at the darkening sky. *Oh Dada, where are you now? I need your strength. Mam's too. How the hell do I manage a wine business... with Susan. I hear something. A name. Huw. No. Impossible. Or is it?*

Chapter Seventeen

'Where the hell have you been? I've been waiting an hour.' Dee was hunched in his saddle, scowling, cloak buttoned against the rain, his cap askew. His horse picked up the tension through her reins, pulled and whinnied.

'Saving my family.'

'Pah. Your sister is a lost cause. And we do not have time for meddling. It is days and we are no closer to finding the killer.' He wheeled round his horse and ignored Margaretta's call that she needed food. She beckoned to a street urchin trying to sell a basket of shrivelled apples, bought one, and set off after her master. They made their way through the damp streets, rain hardening and the east wind making a bitter cut between the close built houses. She was soaked to the skin and shivering when they arrived at Bethnal Green.

The streets teemed with people. Merchants carrying bolts of cloth, children running between legs with spools of cotton and baskets of food, women sitting in windows for light, heads bent to cloth and the glint of a needle as they stitched hems and embroidered edgings. Others, their hands a blur as they moved and clacked lace-making bobbins. From inside houses came the clump, clump of looms.

Dee passed a penny to a small boy for directions to the alms-houses and they were led through narrow streets and alleys, damp with mulch. Merchant houses had signs swinging above the doors, each with a name rather than the symbols and pictures found in the great market of Eastcheap.

The child pointed to a set of tiny houses, built in a row, the centre house barred and nailed shut with wooden slats. He grinned in hope of another penny, but Dee was already dismounting and striding towards the houses. Margaretta gave the child her apple.

Inside the door of the first house an elderly man, evidently blind, was sorting through a basket of remnants with gnarled fingers, putting them into different baskets. He raised his head on hearing Dee's footsteps and looked to the sky with dulled eyes. 'Good day, friend. Who is with us?'

'Greetings, sir. I am on business relating to the death of Lucille. I think she lived here.'

The smile vanished. 'We do not speak of it.'

'Why? I hear she was old. It was expected.'

The man shook his head. 'I will say no more of the Devil's business.'

Fear. It was subsiding, but the doctor has reignited it. Oh my God, you think of a... 'Mae e'n meddwl am ddiafol.' He is thinking of a devil. She nodded at the middle house.

No amount of pulling would prise off the slats. Dee hailed a young man and demanded a hammer and bar. He looked, frowned, shook his head, and disappeared down a dark alley.

Fear is everywhere. Strangers usually bring stares. We are making people look away and scurry on.

Dee marched to the first house with a sign, rapped on the door and demanded to speak to the merchant. Margaretta could hear voices and then Dee shouting. 'I care not what you will not speak of, sir. Send one of your weavers to get the warden of the alms-houses – on the orders of Sir Cecil.'

It was a long fifteen minutes of waiting in a deluge of grey rain before a portly man walked warily up the path carrying an iron bar and hammer. He made no greeting.

You have been dreading this visit.

Dee stepped forward holding up an arm to keep the rain from his eyes. 'Are you the warden? I want this house opened up. I am investigating the death of an old woman called Lucille.'

'We want no trouble, sir. We live a godly life and abide by the law.'

'Then you should have no concern about opening the house. If Lucille died of old age, why all this secrecy?'

The man hesitated. 'There is nothing to see in the house.' Despite the bitter cold and rain, he was sweating.

Untrue. Your gut is turning. You are thinking of the floor. 'Mae e'n dweud celwydd.' He is lying.

Dee made a small nod and pointed to the door. 'Let me in or you will be explaining yourself to Sir Cecil and the Earl of Leicester.'

Reluctantly, the man stepped forward, prised off the wood and pushed open the door. From inside came the acrid stench of dried vomit and excrement. Dee reeled back and then stepped inside, snapping at Margaretta to follow. The warden refused to enter.

The interior was simple but orderly. Just a bed, made up neatly, a table and two chairs. Over the small range, a pot, still filled with pottage, now green with mould. The floor was no more than damp, tamped earth with a thin covering of rushes. But across the floor were patches where the woman had emptied her stomach. In the corner a privy pot, full like that of Pierre Perotin. The walls were lime-washed with three pristine and one stained red.

'We need to look at the floor,' whispered Margaretta. 'I felt it.'

Dee nodded and stood still as he looked around. 'The reeds by the fallen chair are disturbed.' He called back to the warden, 'Where did you find her body?'

'By the table, she had fallen from her chair. She was cold.

She must have died on the Tuesday evening or in the night.' He stepped further back, refusing to even look into the house.

'Was she visited that night?'

'The women had given her food at four in the afternoon. She was happy as usual. They ate with her and left. It was a night like this, sir. We were all keeping dry in our houses. We found her in the morning.'

Horror. I hear a man's scream. You are trying to think of anything but that. I must get your thoughts. She whispered in Welsh, 'He must think of the body.'

Dee nodded. 'Had she been sick or ailing before that?'

'No.'

'She had evidently been very sick in her last hours. I want the details of everything you saw.'

Outside the man made a little mew and began to stutter. 'She was lying there. Cold. There was nothing to be done except pray and cover her body to hide… to hide her sickness. I kept the women out and called one other weaver to help me.'

No. You screamed. Her face. 'Beth oedd ar ei hwyneb?' What was on her face?

'The face of a corpse tells us much. Describe it.'

The man began to weep, holding the doorframe as if he might fall to his knees. Dee went to the door as Margaretta whispered to, 'be kind and get more.' He put a hand on the man's heaving shoulder. 'Come, good man. We want to help.'

The man started gulping air and forcing out his words. 'Good sir, our people cannot take more persecution. We seek only peace and the ability to work.'

'Tell me what you saw.' Dee was stern and behind his back gestured for Margaretta to come outside. Quietly, she joined them.

'The Devil had carved his mark upon her forehead and – *mon Dieu* – sewn her.' The man shuddered.

Dee opened his bag and pulled out a wax tablet and stylus. 'Draw the mark on this – as best you can.'

With a trembling hand, the man scored a triangle pointing

left into the wax. 'That is exactly what I saw. God help me, I cannot get it out of my mind.'

'Very good. Now, you say she was sewn. Was it above her heart?'

A shake of his head and hands went over his eyes. 'No. Her eye had been taken and neatly sewn shut. But we could see...' He shuddered and began to weep again.

'Go on.'

'There was something put in place of her eye. We cut the stiches. The man retched and put his hand out to the wall. 'The Devil left a message in her eye. A piece of cloth.'

'Was it embroidered with a pentacle, centred with a B?'

The man slowly nodded. 'Yes. How did you know?'

Dee ignored the question and asked, 'Where is the cloth now?'

'We wrapped it in the winding cloth to hide what had happened. Then we called for Goodman Mabelain, who went to All Hallows to ask for a Christian burial that day. I had to press him hard, for he said Lucille should go to the morgue like everyone else and have her death registered.'

'Why did you not call the authorities and report this murder?'

The man gulped. 'Fear of being accused of doing wrong. Please believe me. I was trying to protect our people. I only...'

Dee wagged his hand to stop the man's babbling and narrowed his eyes. 'Did Mabelain know how she died?'

'Indeed, no. Only I and the weaver who helped me wrap her know. Though Blind Basile heard us cry out. We vowed silence to protect our people from fear. We have told people Lucille died of her long years. She was so yellow, we said she had filled with bile.'

'But why call for Mabelain, and not Vicar Tyrwhit?'

'Josef has gained much respect in the church, sir. For a foreigner that is rare, even with a good man like our vicar. He works in the church as a clothe mender, helping the Sacristan repair all the church linens, tapestries and banners.' The man made a small laugh. 'Yet when he arrived, he could barely thread a needle. He has learned his skills, and they think much of him. They would hear a plea from him better than the rest of us Huguenots.'

Dee nodded and pointed back into the house. 'The wall is stained. Was there something written on it?'

The man whimpered, 'In her blood. *D'abord la terreur, puis la mort.*'

'Something must have been seen or heard. Did her neighbours speak of a visitor?'

'No, sir. It was a dark cold night and people were beside their fires. Blind Basile claims he heard the sound of a blacksmith hitting metal, but the darkness of his eyes makes his ears sensitive to all manner of strange sounds, he also says he hears angels. He has been told to say nothing.'

Oh, no. My master will be noting that in his mind and the old man will be pestered at some point.

Dee glanced to Margaretta with a silent command to feel. 'Tell me anything else strange about this death.'

You are too frightened to say. You think of ground. A cross. It is near the cross. Margaretta stepped back inside and looked around. There on the far wall, above a small trunk was an ornate cross hanging on the wall. It was exactly the same cross as painted on Pierre Perotin's trunk. She walked to it and looked down. Scrapes on the floor showed the trunk had been dragged. She pulled it away from the wall and cried out.

Dee ran in and came to her side. Imprinted into the floor were the shapes of two huge cloven hooves.

Chapter Eighteen

Servants at Cecil's house took the horses for stabling and peeled Dee's cloak from his shoulders before he dripped all over the tiled floor of the fine entrance hall. Margaretta took off her own and handed it to a servant who took it with some resentment.

Why do the servants of the rich assume a disdain for their own kind? It is as if they think that scorn will elevate their station. But servants they remain, and base born they will always be until the day they go through the veil.

'Heavens, John. You will catch your death.' Mildred Cecil was coming out of the kitchens, wafts of baking and spice following her. She turned to a servant. 'Bread and hot wine for our guests. Blankets too and build up the fire in Lord William's office.' She took Margaretta's arm. 'Come see me before you leave, my dear.'

Cecil looked over a pair of spectacles, his forehead strained with staring at the documents in the light of a candle. He jabbed a finger towards the window. 'These dark days of March are no good for the eyes. I have your note. Walsingham has business this afternoon but will join us soon.'

'That gives me... us... time to give you the bad news.'

Cecil dropped his pen making a dark blot on his parchment. 'Go on.'

'Another Huguenot. A woman this time. Lived alone. Killed last week. Similar desecration of the body. Same message on the wall. Same double flux and yellow skin. She had been fed by neighbours who are well, so she was not poisoned in her home. Likewise, we have found that Perotin's bread was not tainted.'

Cecil groaned and pinched the bridge of his nose. 'Two Huguenots in two weeks. Tell me all.'

'More worrying – two Huguenots from the same church. When they found her, she too had been carved – on the forehead this time with another symbol.' He turned to Margaretta. 'Show the wax tablet.'

Cecil took it and leaned back in his chair. 'Similar to that found on Pierre Perotin. This must be part of a code. We will hand it to Walsingham. What else?'

John Dee poured himself a glass of wine from Cecil's decanter, taking no heed of the other man's raised brow. 'The old woman's eye was taken and the same coded cloth pushed into the socket. The same neat stiches used to sew her eye closed. We found the imprints of cloven hooves in the ground under her cross. Baphomet came in the night, unseen. No frightened beggar that time.'

There was silence while Cecil wrote notes. Dee watched him, his eyes narrowing like an archer focussing on his victim. When Cecil looked up, he released his quiver. 'It seems, William, that their connection to All Hallows is not the only one. We spoke to a clothe mender called Josef Mabelain. Ugly fellow with a twisted limp… and he knows you and Walsingham.'

Cecil jerked his chin up. 'How the hell did you make that connection?'

Dee swallowed but held his gaze. 'Intuition.'

Cecil rapped his fingers on the desk. 'Do not lie to me,

John. Have you been scrying with those wretched cards again?'

'No—'

'I said do not lie.' Cecil was pointing a finger at Dee's face.

And yet again you have put your foot in the mire and gotten it stuck, Doctor. I must rescue once more and for no thanks. 'It is true, Sir Cecil. Doctor Dee mentioned your name and the mender winced – then again at the name Walsingham. That was the clue.' *And God forgive me for lying. The man only winced at the name Lucille.*

Cecil peered at her through the gloom of the office, the flickering candle making shadows on his face. 'Impressive loyalty, Margaretta. Sometimes I think you would be more useful in my household than cleaning a house in Mortlake.'

'No,' snapped Dee. 'Margaretta is no more than a scribe – no use to you.'

You are dreadful. I keep pennies in your pocket with endless horoscopes. I keep your house organised. I log and keep the books of your library – even though that means handling stolen goods. I help your pupils, calm your wife, placate your mother and tolerate your bad choice of kitchen servants. Then I sense the feelings and words that are never spoken and feed them to you to present as intuition, brilliance, cleverness and deep knowledge of the human soul. The only things to stir your soul are your damned books... and Katherine. You do love Katherine.

Cecil was staring at her and raised a knowing brow.

Dee's ire was rising. 'And that is not the only connection you have hidden, William. Blanche has shown me letters from Mary Queen of Scots, Catherine de Medici, that rogue Mothe-Fénélon – all using the same words to demand Queen Mary's release and assurance of succession. And who the hell is Thomas Martinfield and his horoscopes predicting poisoning?'

Cecil glowered. 'Blanche should not have done so.'

Dee's temper was rising. 'Fie. Seems my kinswoman is keener to assist than you.'

Cecil's usual level voice rose to meet the fury of the other man. 'Calm yourself, John. I could not raise the terrible vista of a European plot on the basis of one body. Relations are delicate enough without accusing the French of sending a Templar assassin... unless we have proof.'

Dee raised his hands in incredulity. 'Dear God, William. Last year the Northern Lords tried to rip Elizabeth from her throne and replace her with Mary of the Scots. The long fingers of the French were stirring that plot. When a man is killed within a stone's throw of our Queen, we need to consider every terrible vista, delicate or not.'

'Yes, John, but...'

'No,' shouted Dee. 'If a cold wind of threat is blowing from the continent, we need to run before it.' He pointed to Cecil's feet. 'Your gout may slow your step, William, but you cannot allow it to hinder your mind.'

Oh no. I think you have gone too far this time, my master. Cecil has gone white with fury.

Cecil's voice dropped to a low, cold hiss. 'You may be famous for lecturing on Euclid, John, but do not lecture me on protecting our Queen. It is my life's work and duty. A second body changes everything and when Walsingham arrives, we will, all three, set out every connection. Until then I suggest you calm your mind and tell me about your progress with the Philosopher's Stone... and what investment is required.'

Oh, you clever man, Sir Cecil. You know my master is obsessed with finding the source of all alchemy and has been pounding your door for money. Like a hunting dog who has reached water, he is off the scent of Baphomet and onto his hunt for recognition.

To Margaretta's relief Lady Mildred entered the room and beckoned to her. Outside she took her arm. 'I heard shouting and thought you might want to escape. Did you go to Clarissa?'

'I did, but there is no hope. I have told my sister to find the papers of ownership for the business before she is on the streets with her children.'

Mildred nodded. 'When you have them, make sure you get you an appointment with Will Fleetwood. He will set your sister straight.'

Oh, God. My master's arch rival. A man he hates for his closeness to Lord Cecil. Lady Cecil is smiling at me. She knows.

'And John Dee can either not know – or know and keep his counsel. Now, let us get you warm with some spiced wine in the upper library.'

Chapter Nineteen

Half of an hour later, Margaretta was called down to Sir Cecil's office where Walsingham had just arrived. He was a melancholy looking man. A pale face framed with dark hair and a neatly cut beard, and a crease between the brows giving a look of perpetual concern. He perused the gathering with deep grey eyes, making no smile, only a slight downturn of his mouth when he looked at Margaretta. His clothes were dark, sombre, the only nod to lightness being a small white ruff collar. Everything about him was black.

So, that is why our Majesty calls you her Moor.

Dee shook a finger at Margaretta. 'Get pen and paper. We must have good notes.' He then turned to the younger man. 'Master Walsingham, I deduced that you have connection to All Hallows Church – through Josef Mabelain.'

Walsingham's impassive face quickly changed to startled. 'Did he speak of this?'

Dee took in a deep breath and assumed his pompous voice. 'No. Not at all. But I am trained in watching the human face, picking up those little flinches and ticks when a man knows something hidden. He did not betray you, but his eyes did.'

You are unbelievable.

Walsingham shifted in his seat and glanced at Cecil who gave a small nod. 'Very well. Josef Mabelain is an informant in the network stretching to France.'

'Informant? Network?'

Cecil leaned forward and growled, 'Do not play the innocent, 007. We have an assassin to catch and there is no time for pretence.'

You look at me, Sir Cecil. Worry in your eyes. You also have let slip my master's code name. You forget, I was there when Lord Pembroke told him to use it all those years ago in a dark, dank cell in the Tower. You forget, I see his letters. But as ever, I look down, give nothing away.

A peeved Dee snipped back, 'Then pray redress my innocence of this man.'

Cecil took a deep draft of wine. 'When Mary Queen of Scots landed in Scotland nine years ago and began her mad pursuit of our throne, which she had quartered into her own coat of arms, we needed eyes in France and on her Guise family, as they would see her as the path to taking control of England.'

My God the intrigues of the rich and ambitious are a treacherous midden.

Cecil continued. 'Soon after, Huguenots started arriving here, fleeing the persecution and massacres meted out by Mary's Guise family. Josef Mabelain was one of those poor wretches. He came to my attention when he sent a note reporting a merchant smuggling Catholic relics. We never found the merchant, but Mabelain had proven a reliable source of information. I had some sympathy for him with his twisted foot, and he was kind to…'

He was kind to Robbie. Your twisted little boy. Look at the sadness in your eyes as you look away to the window.

Cecil gathered himself. '…he is a skilled physik. He has made salves for Robbie's back aches and can make medicines for a weak stomach. He sails to France every three months to sell his woven cloth and returns with snippets of news. When Mary fled from Scotland to England two years ago, and started her claims on Elizabeth's throne, I decided to use him as a trusted informant. We needed those eyes in France… and on the Guise. Mabelain's number is 013.'

'And why is he in All Hallows? It is not Huguenot.'

'The Threadneedle Church was becoming overcrowded. He suggested the move to All Hallows as the founders of the church, Saint Earconwald and his sister Saint Ethelburga, had a mythical reputation for healing a deformed nun. So, being crippled, he could arrive in All Hallows claiming he had a calling to join.'

Dee frowned. 'Maybe easy, but why did you need a spy in All Hallows?'

Walsingham took up the story. 'It is the very church the first Catholic martyr, Bishop Fisher, was taken after execution. Then it was the resting place of Thomas More, executed by Henry for refusing to put him above the Pope. It is said they even keep the clothing of the Patrone statue removed in 1559.'

'Patrone statue?'

Cecil cut in. 'A life-size wooden carving of a man, dressed in real clothes – part monk, part warrior.'

Dee narrowed his eyes. 'Like a Templar.'

Cecil jerked. 'Yes. Like a Templar. And in another strange coincidence, All Hallows was the place where a group of Templars were imprisoned and put on trial for heresy back in the 1300s.'

'So, it is obvious that Catholics might be drawn to the church,' sneered Walsingham. 'The Vicar, Richard Tyrwhit, is a good Protestant, but also an innocent. We needed spying eyes. By becoming the clothe mender to the Church, Mabelain can sit in the vestry sewing quietly and hearing much. Their former mender – one William Armorer – had died in 1560, so Vicar Tyrwhit welcomed Mabelain with open arms.'

Dee nodded. 'Clever. But what is your personal connection to him?'

Cecil answered for Walsingham. 'As you know, Francis here also came fully into our circle in 1568 after advising me of the Guise family and their plotting around Mary Queen of

Scots. He speaks French and has good knowledge of Europe, having moved there to live out the terrible Catholic reign of Mary Tudor. So, I made him the spy-handler for Mabelain.'

'A sensible connection,' mused Dee.

Ah, Master Walsingham. You relax. Now you will feel safe and tell my master all. You fool. He will play you for his own knowledge and gain.

'And was the dead man – Perotin – a spy too?'

Walsingham shook his head. 'Not at all. Just a simple man who happened to worship in All Hallows. There is no connection.'

Sir Cecil sighed. 'I'm afraid there just might be a connection. John brings news of a woman killed last week. Same pattern, same church.'

Walsingham blanched.

Dee stared up at the ceiling, his voice dropping to the drone he adopted when thinking deeply. 'Not quite the same pattern. The bodies are left where they will be found. But the second more public than the first – with a beggar woman insisting he looked towards her. Baphomet is getting bolder.'

Walsingham shuddered. 'They say the Devil's confidence grows when evil wins. The marks are the sign of the Devil. How do we fight a spirit?'

Dee tutted. 'It is no spirit. It is a man who wants us to think that. The symbols on the body and mark of Baphomet sewn into the bodies are giving a message in a language we do not yet know. The manner of desecration and death is designed to instil fear. And looking at your faces, it is working. But if it were a devil, why would two God-fearing Huguenots give entry to their houses? No. The killer is known to them. Our killer is hiding in plain sight.'

The other men are looking at you with a mix of horror and admiration. You know it. See how you puff your chest and that tiny smile on your face.

Dee stood and went to the window to look at the rain coming down in icy sheets. 'Two symbols are not enough for any message, especially if they are a cypher. Baphomet knows that. There will be more bodies.'

The room seemed to drop further in temperature and Cecil groaned again. 'But who is behind this?'

Dee turned and clicked his fingers to Margaretta, demanding a large piece of paper and a pen. As she handed it over, she whispered, *'Gwylia'r dyn tywyll.'* Watch the dark man. He placed it on Cecil's desk, weighting the corners with candlesticks, then drawing a circle in the centre in which he wrote E. Then three more circles above, below and to the right in which he wrote north, south and east. 'We need to look at all possible threats. What links do we have? Who envies Elizabeth and her throne?'

Walsingham pulled his chair closer to the desk and tapped on the circle saying north. 'The seat of the Northern Rebellion and a viper's nest of Catholics.'

Cecil shook his head. 'But it is stamped out. Elizabeth's loyal men, my first born, Tommy, being one, are there now meting out terrible justice. There is not a crossroads north of Leeds that is not decorated with a gibbet of rotting Catholics.'

Dee snorted. 'They are hanging the sheep for bleating. The shepherds who herded them into Durham Cathedral to rip up the Bible, worship a Catholic Mass and call for the fall of Elizabeth, are still at large on the Continent. We will come back to them.'

What are you doing? I saw a small smile on your face. The logical next question is about the Lords, but you are delaying. What is your game, master?

Walsingham shook his head. 'But still residing in the North is the woman they would have used to replace Elizabeth. The Scottish whore, Mary Queen of the Scots – working her charm on her captors. The Earl of Shrewsbury is a kind man, fond of women. Mary is a flirt and will flutter her evil eyes at him. We have sent the Earl of Huntingdon to ensure the Scottish siren has not bewitched those who keep her. The *putain*.'

Cecil snapped at Walsingham to curb his tongue in front

of Margaretta. The younger man glowered and shot a look of contempt towards her. *Oh, Master Walsingham, I think you have little care for women. I smile and your frown deepens.*

'Has Mary Queen of Scots made a direct threat to Elizabeth's life?' asked Dee.

Walsingham shook his head. 'She connives and loves to communicate in cypher. We have broken all the codes and all her foolish attempts to smuggle letters. But she has never suggested murder.'

Dee slid his finger to the circle saying south. 'And here we have the Duke of Norfolk in the Tower – the man the rebels sought to marry to Mary Queen of Scots and make our King. In the next cell is the Bishop of Ross her great promoter. What do we know?'

'Norfolk insists he has no ill-will towards the Queen but is hard guarded,' answered Cecil. 'All letters are opened and copied before they enter or are taken out of the Tower. Visitors are searched. All presents are checked for hidden messages. As for the Bishop? He has had no visitors and communicates only with the Church.'

'And who are these visitors bringing letters and gifts to the Duke?'

'Usually his secretary, Billy Barker. Also, Mothe-Fénélon, the French Ambassador before he departed for France last month. De Speys, the meddling Spanish ambassador, has visited once. But everything on their person is checked,' answered Walsingham.

Dee nodded. 'And what are the gifts?'

'Nothing but fripperies from Mary Queen of Scots who still dreams he will be her husband because he sends her jewels. She sends small embroidered linens depicting animals or a cross. Sometimes just a pattern. The type of gift only the simple mind of a women would see as valuable.' Walsingham shot another dark look towards Margaretta.

Doctor Dee has just glanced my way. It is a sign that we will investigate these gifts. But you are looking uncomfortable,

Master Walsingham. That name Ridolfi again. You are hiding something. I cough. The doctor hears me. That little nod.

Dee poured more wine and held the flagon out to Cecil, seemingly oblivious to the look of indignation at being offered his own liquor. 'Who else goes to the Tower?'

Walsingham shrugged, 'No one suspicious.'

'I asked "who", sir... not their standing in your eyes,' barked Dee.

'Ridolfi.'

'Who is Ridolfi?'

The younger man looked peeved. 'Ridolfi is a banker. We think De Speys was hoping to use him to finance the Northern Rebellion. He has been interrogated and turned to our cause.'

You are tense Mr Walsingham. I hear raised voices. I feel dark nights. Long talks and tiredness. Hope. Satisfaction. But worry. Your head says to be sure but your heart is not. The doctor needs to push further. Margaretta pretended to cough again and through it whispered, *'Gwthia fe'*. Push him.

Dee smiled. 'Turned? Are you quite confident?'

'Yes. Senor Ridolfi now works for us,' was the reply.

I am not so sure. I will tell my master later.

Cecil cleared his throat to get attention and tapped on the circle saying, 'East. Let us look here, sirs. We have to consider Europe, notably the French.'

Dee returned to the desk. 'The Guise – Mary's blood family – with their determination to root out the Huguenots. Then there is Catherine de Medici, Mary's former mother-in-law, who is tired of trying to marry her son, Charles King of France, to Elizabeth and now calls for the release of Mary. I hear she has a nasty habit of poisoning her enemies.'

Cecil nodded. 'Perfumed apples are her choice of deadly gifts.'

'So those French players do combine an interest in Mary's destiny, a hatred of Huguenots, and a tendency to dispatch with poison.'

Cecil's fingers went to the bridge of his nose. 'Catherine

de Medici has been in dispute with the Guise for some time. But now we have information from our ambassador in France, Henry Norris, that she has welcomed the Cardinal of Lorraine, head of the House of Guise, back to Court. There appears to be a new entente cordiale between them.'

A cardinal and a queen. The Hierophant and the Queen of Pentacles. My master has just jumped. He has made the connection too.

Dee looked at Cecil. 'Is there a famous knight associated with either family?'

'Yes. The Duc d'Anjou, younger brother of the King of France, despite his penchant for boys and jewels, is a fearsome soldier and leads the charge against the Huguenots in the religious wars of France. He is held up as the saviour of Catholicism.' Cecil sighed. 'God help us if this is a Catholic threat coming from France.'

'Would they send an assassin?' asked Dee.

Walsingham gulped. 'I have a weekly report of all foreigners arriving in London, but no word of a Catholic assassin. But, as I always say, there is less danger in fearing too much than too little, and our informant, Captain Francois, has been bringing intelligence for months telling us to beware of poison and threats to the Queen's life. She has been told to check all her linens for harmful potions.'

'And who gives him this intelligence? Is it this Thomas Fieldhouse?' demanded Dee.

Ah. You have seen the opportunity. You have waited for this opening. I see the wolfish look on your face. You are digging. But your anger is rising again.

Cecil looked away. 'I hoped you had forgotten that, John. It matters not who he is.'

'I disagree. His letter, held by Blanche, suggested he was using divination and prophesy of horoscopes. In the wrong hands such tools are dangerous... or misleading. Who is he?'

There was a long silence. Eventually Cecil answered. 'It is John Prestall, using a false name. He now sends information on the Northern Lords who fled to the Low Countries. He calls me Lord Conway. He seems to be able to foretell what the future brings.'

Dee jumped up and yelled, 'Prestall? You use that fake and foolish fiend to guide your thinking. For the love of God, William. He is the worst of all scapegraces and a traitor. He was in league with the Northern Lords – who were in turn helped by the French royals – and now you believe his claim to spy on them. Are you turned a fool?'

My, my master, how your confidence has grown. A few years ago, you were begging this Lord for money and now you shout and call him a fool. But these days you are the Queen's philosopher. She calls on you for advice and guidance and has even visited your laboratory in Mortlake. Oh, I remember that day. I thought Mistress Katherine would burst through her farthingale with excited pride. But this display is as much for Walsingham as Cecil. You want to put him in his place.

Cecil stood. 'Do not berate me in my own home.'

There was another agonising silence in which Walsingham looked between the two. At last, Cecil gestured to Dee to sit and lowered his voice to the tone of a calming father. 'We cannot afford to be at war in this room, John. Protecting our Queen is more important than our rivalries. If we can break this terror then all recognition will flow to you.'

Dee glared for a few seconds, then looked back at the circles. 'So, Elizabeth has a chain of Catholic threat around her and a Papal Bull has given them the right – no the duty – to kill her. We do not know if the players are connected in one great plot to get her throne or if they work alone. But there is only one way to break a chain. You find the weakest link and work from there. Who would break?'

'Norfolk,' snarled Cecil. 'He is also a poltroon fool who bends to the whispering of others.'

Dee stood and nodded to Margaretta to gather his papers. 'I will need a letter for the Tower guards tomorrow.' He paused, eyes narrowing. 'I could visit Lannoy the alchemist to check his progress.'

'No,' snapped Cecil. 'Having promised all the gold in Christendom, he is held there to do his alchemising and prove his word. I want you to focus on Baphomet and add to what we know.'

Dee muttered his irritation and moved to the door, turning with a grim smile. 'Gentlemen. For all your spying, watching, decoding, and foolish use of madmen like Prestall... you know nothing. Maybe Baphomet knows that Mabelain is your man and his Huguenot compatriots are chosen as a deadly message to you that your spy is seen – but you are blind. As I said, I think Baphomet is hiding in plain sight.'

Both Cecil and Walsingham paled, and silence fell as John Dee closed the door with a smile.

Chapter Twenty

The journey back to Mortlake had been exhausting. Dee, as ever, had moved between delight in having pulled together the connections and then fury at the credence given to John Prestall, his sworn enemy. She had to sit and listen to the diatribe until he mollified himself by thinking how he would question Norfolk and make him leak. He was further calmed when she told him that Walsingham was nervous about Ridolfi.

Having settled him in his room and begged Katherine to go and better his mood, Margaretta had changed her damp clothes and warmed a beaker of wine to pull the chill from her bones. Then she heard the clattering of hooves in the courtyard of Mortlake house and in seconds she was racing out, as every Friday, to greet her guests.

Each one was hugged and the chatter started, first with her brother, Huw, who held tight the hand of Grace, his wife these five years. Margaretta spoke in Welsh, knowing that Grace, being the loving woman she was, had insisted on learning her husband's language. 'Well Huw, how goes the world of big business?'

He smiled, looking slightly to her side, for the strain of looking in another's eyes was still too hard – excepting Grace. 'It goes well, sister. All is pink and yellow.'

Ah, you speak of the gifts you hid for all those years – the ability to see a person's soul in the colours around them and the goodness or evil of a situation in the colour of the air. You are a special man, my little brother.

Huw pointed at the older man. 'Siôn has news.'

Siôn Jenkins, the tall man at her brother's side who eight years ago had risen from destitution to become their friend and business partner, grinned and put an arm around his blushing wife. 'God has graced us again. Delyth is expecting our fourth.'

Delyth looked up, patted her husband's chest with a sweet smile. 'Pray it is as strong as the first three.'

Margaretta took her hand. 'Well, with you as parents, the child starts life blessed.'

Who would have thought we would be here today. Eight years ago, while the doctor and I were pulled away to investigate the case of The Cygnet Prince, Siôn Jenkins was plucked from the gutter and raised from beggar to hero – protecting Huw and rescuing Master Constable's business from certain ruin. God was looking down on us the day we found you, Siôn Jenkins, and then God blessed you with Delyth.

She moved the conversation to business. 'How goes the cloth trade?'

Siôn pulled a bag of coin from his saddle bag. 'I was a lucky man the day, Mistress Constable sold me her husband's business for a weekly percentage.' He shook the bag. 'A good week for her.'

Margaretta clapped her hands. 'Then you will be most welcome in her kitchen. And I have another proposition for you.'

Suddenly, Bela's shrill voice from the door. 'Why are you all talking like the monkeys in the Tower? Jibber jabber, jibber jabber.'

'*Cath ddu*. Black cat,' whispered Huw, only to get a tug on his sleeve from Grace, followed by a pat to show she was protecting and not cross.

Bela's eyes narrowed. 'I will tell Mistress Katherine of

your roguish talking. She will not like it. You know how she likes me more than…'

'That is because Katherine has not a dollop of wit.' The voice was loud, angry. They all turned to see Mother Dee standing in her doorway, a shaky finger pointed at Bela. 'Get back in your rathole, vermin.'

As Bela scampered away, fury was replaced with smiles and greetings, Mother Dee doing her best in the Welsh she had learned from Doctor Dee's father. As ever, she insisted they met in her kitchen. Margaretta gave a knowing look to Siôn as they both knew this was not kindness – she wanted to know what Katherine was earning.

After the usual fresh bread and cheese bought by Grace from Leadenhall market swilled down with small beer and much chatter about business, life, and gossip, Siôn crossed the yard to present Katherine with the bulging pouch. They could hear the squealed delight as she smacked him on the arm and declared that he was, 'the best man her old husband ever found.'

Siôn returned, making play of rubbing the arm, squeezed his wife's shoulder, and sat by Margaretta. 'You said you had a proposition.'

She looked to Mother Dee. 'Can you hold our family business private, Mother?'

'Pah,' spat the old woman, 'with a son like mine and his father before him, I have had to hold more secrets than Whitehall.' She tipped the flagon to fill her beaker and sat back to listen.

Margaretta looked around the table. 'Angus is living out his last days, riven by his sins.'

Grace whispered, 'For all their mean spirit, I am sad to hear this. What about the children?'

'Damaged. But we have much to manage before we steady them.'

Huw frowned. 'Margaretta grey. Worried.' He began to sway in agitation and Grace put out a calming hand. 'Angus black?'

'Yes, Huw, in every way. He is in the last stages of the French Pox and will die badly. Our sister, Susan, is sunk to living in a mouldering house, with little money and two children who hide in corners.'

'Jack same colour as me,' muttered Huw.

'Yes. But he does not have Grace's colour to make good his world.'

Huw nodded, looked at his wife and took her hand. 'Grace all violet. Kind, good, friend.'

'So true, my brother. But Susan is grey. Angus has left the business in the hands of the lanky lad and he must be stealing, for Susan has nothing.' Margaretta took Huw's hand. 'I need you to take over the business.' She turned her eyes to Siôn. 'Will you help?'

Siôn nodded immediately, but Huw jumped up, his chair clattering back 'No, no, no. Not go back. Bad place, black place, cruel place.' Grace rose to calm him, but he shrugged her off. 'No, no, no.'

Margaretta took his arm. 'Huw. I know it holds bad memories, but we have to care for our sister. I cannot run the business. Susan is too much a goose-head to know a barrel of wine from a barrel of vinegar. That leaves you.' She held fast as he tried to pull away. 'It is now seven years that you have managed the Constable business with Siôn. You have proven your great ability with counting and money.'

'No, no, no.'

Oh, little brother. I must be unkind. 'Well, Mam and Dada must be looking down in sorrow now, Huw.'

Grace marched to her husband's side, pulling Margaretta's hands away. 'You have said enough, Mistress Margaretta. I will calm my husband from here.' With no further word, she took Huw's hand and pulled him through the door into the yard. Slowly she walked him up and down, talking softly. At last Huw fell silent, nodding at his wife's words. Margaretta came away from the window, put her face in her hands and tried to stem the tears. 'What have I done?'

Siôn spoke quietly. 'Huw has grown strong with the care of Grace. He manages well in business because of his abilities, but the world is a hard place for a man like him.'

Delyth took his hand. 'Then be ready to help, husband.'

It was half of an hour before Grace and Huw came back into the kitchen. Grace spoke. 'My husband will help your sister, Margaretta, for that is our family duty. But the Vintry boys must know that he is master. Also, it must be agreed that I will help in the business with him every day. Your sister must accept that her former maid, and the brother she so abused, now provide for her and her children.' She looked to Siôn, 'And we ask your regular advice, sir.'

Siôn stood and held out his hand to Huw. 'It will be done, my friend.'

Huw straightened and spoke, with only a hint of a tremor in his voice. 'Must establish myself first. Or boys see me as weak. Will attack.' He shot out a hand for Grace.

'I will tell them,' said Margaretta.

'No,' snapped Huw. 'I must be a man. Like Dada.'

Oh, brawd bach. Oh, Little brother. My heart bursts with pride for you. But I wonder what the hell I have done. What if they throw barrels at you again?

Huw frowned at her. 'Stop being grey about me, sister. I need you pink.'

Grace was looking at her husband with pride. 'Together we can be yellow, husband.' She turned to Margaretta. 'Do we have a deal, mistress?'

My, my little Grace. When we met you were the sweet little maid who chortled at my tales of Susan on the farm. But marriage to a man who finds the world hard has grown you into a strong woman. I thank the Lord he sent you into our lives.

'We have one last hurdle. We must tell Susan. If you can manage her fury, Huw, you can take on any villain in The Vintry. We will go on Monday. You have two days to prepare.'

Chapter Twenty-One

The Tower yard was stinking. Traders jostled their way through the mulch of mud, detritus and rotting rubbish. A steady rain hazed the air making the scene one of damp misery. Walsingham was hunched outside the guard's office, hat tugged down over his head and cloak clutched tight around him. He looked up, grim-faced, when Dee and Margaretta pulled their horses to a halt.

Inside, the guard complained about the water running off their oiled cloaks, but it made him hasten to read the letter handed over by Walsingham. 'You'll find him in the Bloody Tower. His secretary, the fancy boy, Billy Barker, is with him, writing letters. I hope you've brought good food. Might stop him whining to us about his fare.'

Lucky that I thought to bring a bottle of wine, bread and cheese for you two men are looking between the guard and each other in worry. 'We have, sir.' She pulled the cloth bag from under her cloak.

Dee looked at Walsingham, a self-satisfied smile on his face. 'The first lesson in interrogation, Master Walsingham. Make a friend of your target.'

You old scut.

* * *

Norfolk was immediately on his feet when the heavy oak door squealed opened on a rusty hinge. The room was well appointed with a desk, four good upholstered chairs, and a separate table for eating. In the corner a shelf of books and a coffer laden with good plate and a flagon of wine. A dish held a few winter-wrinkled apples.

The duke was a tall man in his early thirties, though the strain around his heavy-lidded, dark eyes made him look older. A long pale face made more pronounced by his elongated nose and prominent, bearded chin shone pale in the thin light from the cell window. For all his height, he was a puny figure. He said nothing, but stared at Walsingham, his mouth opening though no sound.

I know little of this Master Walsingham, but whatever his reputation it has withered this noble to a frightened babe.

Sitting at the desk was a small, thin man, attired in bright clothes, all silk and stripes of yellow, red and blue. The large ruff beneath a small head and the padding on his shoulders reminded Margaretta of a dairymaid's yoke. He stood, pursing his lips, annoyed to be interrupted. The puff of his trousers, also striped, were even wider than his shoulders. Margaretta put her head down to cover her mirth.

'My Duke of Norfolk,' spoke Dee, stepping forward. 'We come to ask if you might assist us. It is a matter of security for our Queen.' Walsingham said nothing, but slowly, deliberately took off his cloak, placed it over the chair and sat, never taking his eyes off the prisoner. He leaned back, folded his arms, and raised one brow. Norfolk shuddered and mumbled he was, 'at their service.' He then turned to the striped man and said he may wait outside. The response was a tut and a strut to the door, slamming it behind him.

Ooh, resentment. You have a need for importance, little Billy Barker.

Dee saw the impact of Walsingham's silence and followed, going quiet while he ceremoniously removed the dripping oilskin, placed it on a hook, gestured to Margaretta to prepare the paper and ink, then sat on the other chair, opposite Walsingham, leaving Norfolk between them. 'Where shall we begin?'

Norfolk looked between the two, and stuttered, 'I will begin with my allegiance to our Majesty. I thought only to support our Queen by being a strong husband to the Queen of the Scots, bring her to heel, to moderate – nay – prevent her foolery of mind. It was Elizabeth's own idea back in 1564 to suggest me as a suitor. I am a loyal Englishman – badly used by ill-intended men.' The voice was weak, light, slightly woman-like with elongated vowels that gave the slick of disdain so often heard in those born to a belief in their blue blood.

Dear Lord, I doubt you could bring a puppy to heel. I do not have to sense your feelings, sir, I can smell the sweat of fear dripping beneath those fine clothes. It beads on your brow, even though this place is as cold as a cellar. But also, fury. The words 'base-born' go through your mind. You resent being questioned by men you think far beneath you. But fear commands you.

Dee smiled. 'Much has happened since 1564, sir. Not least, last year's Northern Rebellion seeking to put the Scottish Queen on our throne along with a husband – you.'

Norfolk gulped and his eyes flicked towards Walsingham who just continued the steady stare. 'I had no part in that, Doctor Dee. Indeed, I wrote to the lords from Kenninghall, begging them not to continue their madness. I have done nothing to earn this indignity of being the most prominent noble in the land yet tethered like a common dog.'

'Interesting that you knew exactly who should receive your letter and where to send it,' cut in Walsingham.

There was a desperate silence before Norfolk pulled up his head to look down at Walsingham and spluttered, 'It was well known who they were and where they were heading. You probably knew better than I, sir, with your network of watching eyes.'

Walsingham just stared.

Panic is rising in you Norfolk – at your own foolery. You look at these two men as lowly, yet they frighten you. You are covering something. You think of a diamond. 'Gofynna am y diemwnt.' Ask about the diamond.

Dee ignored the other two men frowning at Margaretta. 'Tell us about the diamond, sir.'

Norfolk gasped and his hand went to his chest. Then he almost shouted. 'Who is behind your visit here? Is it that disloyal viper, Leicester? Or the low-born whisperer, Cecil?' He looked between Walsingham and Dee, eyes wide in alarm.

'Just tell us of the diamond, sir,' purred Dee.

More alarm. But it is not just Norfolk. It is you Master Walsingham. You jumped a little when my master asked the question – thinking only you knew of the gem.

'It was only a gift between nobles. When I presided over the enquiry into the death of Lord Darnley last year…'

'I think you mean the enquiry into whether Queen Mary had her hand in the blowing up of her regretted husband in Kirk o' Field. And whether she is aiding Lord Bothwell, who she then married in indecent haste – the same Bothwell who she now leaves to rot in his Danish jail so that she might marry you, sir,' spat Walsingham.

'And she was found innocent,' answered Norfolk, his voice going higher with anxiety. 'She complained of all her jewels being taken by Elizabeth – even her treasured Medici pearls. I simply wanted her to have a bauble of some beauty now that she is a royal guest in our country.'

Walsingham tilted forward slowly and spoke low and cold. 'The casket letters prove she has blood on her hands, though your enquiry reached no verdict. Now she is imprisoned for plotting to overthrow our Queen. Hardly good marriage material and yet you gave a diamond. Is that not a noble's betrothal gift?' He paused. 'And if merely an innocent token, why does our lady wear it close to her heart below her clothes? As she told you in a secret letter only three months ago.'

Norfolk raised a hand to point at Walsingham but snatched it down as soon as he realised the extreme of his trembling. 'It was a charity.'

Walsingham tutted. 'It was a promise.'

I hear the name Ridolfi again. From you, Walsingham. He is informing you about Norfolk. I will tell my master later. In the meantime, I can only pen this game of cat and mouse. Ah, you sit back and start the staring again. Clever.

Dee opened his bag, pulled out the paper with the symbol etched on the body of Pierre Perotin, placed it on the table and tapped. 'What is this?'

Norfolk bent to see it in the dim light. 'Just a shape. Why ask?'

'Because it was carved into the body of a murdered Huguenot – a palace guard protecting our Queen.' Dee then pulled out the wax tablet. 'And this was carved into the forehead of a murdered Huguenot woman. Any ideas?'

Norfolk paled and stood up. 'I know nothing of these shapes nor of butchery.'

A half-truth. You winced and your brow furrowed when you looked at the shapes. And a vague glimmer of memory. I sense colours. A picture. The name Ridolfi again. Also, Billy. But you look straight into my masters' eyes, and I feel your genuine confusion. Dee turns to me pretending to check if I am writing diligently. I write B large on my paper.

'When did you call on Baphomet to assist your leaping ambition?' Dee raised an eyebrow and stared at the trembling Duke.

Norfolk opened and closed his mouth like a fish in the throes of death. 'What?'

'You heard me.'

'That is the name of a demon.'

'A Catholic demon,' snarled Walsingham.

'No. Not I. I would have no part in such Godlessness.' Norfolk's voice rose to a strangled scream.

Truth. The shock is pulsing from you, Not fear. Horror and despair. You may be a bad one, but you are not a disciple of Baphomet. I cough again. My master turns. A small shake of my head and he knows there is nothing more to be drawn from this Duke. He looks to Walsingham with a small nod to take over.

The younger man stood and walked to the window, speaking over his shoulder. 'What news from the French Court – the lair of the Medici's and the Guise faction – who were behind the rebellion that would have had you king?'

Norfolk looked perplexed. 'Why ask me?'

'Come, come, sir. Mary Queen of Scots is a Guise. The family plan to put her on the English throne and expand their popish lands. We already have information about plots to poison Elizabeth. Catherine de Medici is former mother-in-law to your wanted bride and supports her release. The old serpent will be watching you... writing to you.'

Norfolk gulped and his breathing quickened further. 'Untrue. I have no truck with the French Catholics. Was I not the soldier who expelled their forces from Scotland ten years ago?'

Walsingham turned his eyes glittering. 'That was before you set eyes on the Scottish whore and your own path to the throne, sir.'

'No, no, no. I am a Protestant and loyal to the Queen.'

'You are born to the greatest Catholic family in England,' sneered Walsingham.

'For God's sake, I was the organiser of her coronation.' He pointed at Dee. 'On the date he defined as most auspicious. The idea of marrying Mary was a folly, foisted on me by others. Men like Leicester.' He snatched up the paper with the symbol. 'I know nothing of plots, nothing of killings, nothing of strange carvings.' He sat heavily and stared at the floor, shaking.

He is thinking of Mary. Colours again. A picture. A gift. Billy. Dee was now standing behind Margaretta, looking over her shoulder. She quickly wrote the words in Welsh on her paper.

Dee gestured to Walsingham and stepped forward to stand by the shaking Duke. 'Sir, if you send pretty tokens to Queen Mary, what pretty gifts do you get in return?'

Norfolk stiffened and balled his hands. 'She is kept in penury. What the hell could she send me other than a few kind words… and… nothing else?'

'What about her sewing?' snarled Walsingham. 'Are those nothing?'

Sweat was dripping down Norfolk's neck. 'Just embroidery… n… n… nothing more.'

The panic is rising. I get a stronger image. A picture. Colours. But I do not understand. Margaretta made a slight shake of her head.

Dee held the silence a little longer and then said in a low voice, 'We will leave you to ponder, sir. Maybe the shapes will come back to mind… and the memory will save your skin.'

Without a word, Walsingham walked back to his cloak, plucked it from the chair and walked out. Dee nodded to Margaretta to pack their papers and leave in silence too.

As they closed the door Norfolk whispered, 'God help me.'

Half of an hour later, Dee and Walsingham were shutting the door on the cell of the Bishop of Ross, wiping the spittle off their clothes. They had pulled the holy man from prayer to confront him with his links to France, his support for Mary, and his knowledge of the strange shapes carved on dead Huguenots. Every challenge was met with a look into their eyes, a snarled rebuttal and derision of Elizabeth. It had taken only a few responses before Margaretta shook her head to Dee indicating that the spit-slicked lips of this angry man spoke true. He was not involved.

Chapter Twenty-Two

Walsingham had left the Tower with a terse agreement to meet at Sir Cecil's within the hour. As soon as he was gone, Dee had asked to see Lannoy the alchemist, only to be told his passport letter stated he was not allowed to see the Dutchman in his prison laboratory. Indignation boiled as he and Margaretta pressed their horses into muddy streets, navigating around carts, animals and merchants. Then, 'Tell me every sense and thought. But ride close and use no names.'

'The Duke is a fool who still aspires to greatness. He tells the truth that he was used, but he was a willing fool. He thinks little of Cecil, Walsingham… and of you too.'

'Why?'

'To him you are all base-born and have no right to tug his hem let alone interrogate his motives.'

Dee twisted in his saddle, furious. 'But I am the Queen's philosopher. I am more learned than he could ever think of being and…'

'… you were born to a merchant not a Duke.'

Dee growled, geed his horse past a slow-walking donkey and snapped at Margaretta to continue.

'He has seen those symbols before and was full of alarm. But his memory is muddled. I saw colours. A picture. A gift. I could not understand.'

'What else?'

'Little Billy in his stripes resented being told to leave.'

Dee shrugged. 'He is only a secretary… though he looked like a fucking marchpane cake.'

'Yes, but as soon as the Duke thought of the gifts, he thought of Billy too, and that name Ridolfi again. There is some kind of link.'

Dee frowned. 'The turned spy. I think this is a mangled web. What about the Scottish bishop?'

'Full of hate. Angry. But he saw nothing in the shapes.'

Cecil was waiting in his office with Walsingham. Cecil limped to the side of the room and poured four glasses of wine.

Dee leaned forward. 'You are limping. Gout again? You need to go to the physik woman.' He turned to Margaretta. 'Go and see Clarissa and have her make up a remedy.'

'Yes, yes, John,' Cecil tapped on the desk. 'My feet can wait for Mabelain's tincture. News of Norfolk and the Bishop of Ross cannot. Young Walsingham here says they are still plotting to put Mary on the throne, and that they are up to their lugs in this murder.'

Dee turned to look at Walsingham. 'Is it not amazing how two men in one interrogation can hear two different stories?' He raised a hand to stop Walsingham cutting in and turned to Margaretta for her notes. 'The Bishop of Ross has no involvement at all. He is vehemently angry but showed absolutely no reaction to the shapes. As for Norfolk? My analysis is that he still aspires to great office as a birthright. But he does not have the wit or the spine to take forward a plot.'

Cecil nodded and looked at Walsingham. 'This is true. When his foolish plan to marry Mary was uncovered – or more like blabbed by Leicester – Norfolk ran home to Kenninghall, pleaded sickness, had to be ordered to Court and squealed like a child when he was arrested on route and taken to the Tower.'

'But he sent her a diamond. He is setting up his betrothal

and now makes his move on the palace, starting with the guards,' insisted Walsingham, his voice peevish.

'A pretty bauble does not make a murder plot,' insisted Dee. 'And when I presented the symbols, he showed only a vague recognition – as if they reminded him of something. Speaking of murder and Baphomet created genuine alarm. No man can falsify true fear. No. Norfolk is not behind this killing – but he has seen something that reminds him of those shapes.'

'Hah. So, he recognised them,' sneered Walsingham.

Dee sighed. 'If you are going to be a spymaster, Walsingham, you need to learn to read your fellow men. Those little winces, a frown, a flicker of an eye, a reddening cheek. All the language of the mind coming into the face. The difference between a man caught and a man shocked. The difference between guilt and unease. Without that, you only have crude accusation.'

You are outrageous. You cannot even read your own face. Without me you would be as blind as Walsingham. Damn you.

Walsingham jabbed a finger. 'There is only one way to decide between our theories. The rack.'

Cecil spluttered on his wine. 'Gad, sir. You cannot rack a Duke of the realm.'

'I will not,' blustered Walsingham. 'I will rack a traitor. That is all he is – a common traitor.'

My, you are an angry man riddled with resentment. I felt some of it earlier, but here, when you see your path being barred, it bubbles up like molten iron.

Walsingham began to pace. 'We will rack him, gain the confession and then the scaffold.'

Cecil pinched the bridge of his nose. 'Without real evidence? He is the highest noble in the land, even considered for kingship when Elizabeth was struck down with smallpox in 1562 – and it is many a year since our Queen has agreed to an execution.'

'She is too weak stomached. We need to send a message to those who would tear her from the throne.'

You are thinking of Elizabeth. She dislikes you. This is what Blanche meant when she warned you of needing better manners. But now you are taking things off track. 'Excuse me, sirs. But surely a weak man breaking on the rack and telling you what you want – not truth – will only assist Baphomet.'

The three turned, Walsingham reddening in fury. 'And why does a scribe – a woman scribe at that – think she has the wit to have a voice?'

'Enough, Walsingham,' snapped Cecil. 'Mildred tells me this woman has greater wit than most and her words are wise.'

How proud I feel that your wife speaks well of me, for she has the wit and wisdom of a hundred men. We are both wishing she was here now to give this little pup a dressing down.

Walsingham sat, heavily, glaring at Margaretta. She glared straight back. Dee shot her a warning glance and closed the conversation. 'Norfolk has been a puppet in the past and may well be linked to the shapes but not directly. He takes us no further in finding the killer.'

Cecil slumped back in his chair. 'We must make progress. Blanche has written that Court is in terror and Elizabeth has fallen into one of her bouts of vomiting again. Fear is overwhelming her.'

Dee perked up. 'I will concoct a physik for her. Mallow, camomile, and…'

Cecil raised a hand. 'You need to spend every waking – and sleeping – hour on the pursuit of this demon, John.'

'But I can be trusted to—'

'No, John. Focus your skills on Baphomet. Josef Mabelain is in the circle of trust – and skilled with remedies. I have already charged him with creating a soothing tonic for her.' He looked to Walsingham. 'It is urgent now. Chase him on progress and provide a passport of entry to the palace. I will write to Blanche and ensure he is given priority.'

Dee packed his bag with sharp and angry motions. The atmosphere was brittle.

'What do we do, John?' asked Cecil in a tone meant to ameliorate.

'Wait for more evidence,' snapped Dee.

There was little waiting time. Bellot arrived at the door and bowed to Sir Cecil. 'A messenger for you, my Lord. From the city morgue.' The atmosphere went to ice.

The messenger was no older than seventeen, dressed in a dark tunic and breeches. He cowed as he entered the treasure-laden realm of Cecil and jumped back from one of the roman statues as if it might move. Another jump as Bellot pulled off his cap and pushed him to Cecil's desk with a command to speak up and speak clear.

'The officer of the morgue sent me, sir. He said a body was delivered this morning with evidence of a strange death. He did not say what he saw, but said he knew from street gossip that you were to be informed. He begs your instruction.'

Cecil gave nothing away in his face. 'Your officer is wise to inform me. And you would be wise to say nothing of this to any living soul.'

The boy nodded. 'Shall I take a message back, sir?'

'No. You will take Doctor Dee back with you.'

Chapter Twenty-Three

The officer of the morgue was a small man, bald as a coot and slightly hunched from years of bending over a desk making notes in his ledger. The writing was even, straight, testifying to a man of great pride in neatness. Every movement was precise, small and definite. When the boy led them into his office, he placed his pen on the desk, moved it slightly to be in exactly the right place, blotted his ledger and placed the blotter just behind the pen. Then he sat up, peered at Dee through eyes in need of spectacles and pursed his lips.

Dee handed over a note from Cecil. 'A note of authority, sir. Please show me the body you report.'

With the noted checked, stamped and carefully placed on the ledger for copying later, the officer rose, told the lad to leave and pointed to the door. 'I have him on ice in a side room. Not a pretty sight I am afraid.'

Oh, God. To a man who witnesses the evils of death every day, that means it is terrible. The doctor is giving me a warning look. For the love of Christ, when will he accept that I cannot abide dead bodies?

The officer unlocked the door and the stench was immediate. Rotting flesh and the putrid smell of flux. Margaretta reeled back clasping hand to mouth as she retched. Dee pinched his nose and stepped in barking at her to follow and be ready to scribe.

The body was yellow just like the others, skin stretched over the skull of a man whose eyes were open and the mouth gaping as if giving a last, silent scream. But what made Margaretta cry out was the holes in his face and neck, ragged and uneven. 'Rats,' muttered Dee, leaning towards the cadaver. 'Must have been lying dead some days.'

'The body collectors say he died Tuesday night,' agreed the morgue officer.

That is the same night as Pierre Perotin.

The officer shook his head. 'It is strange the rats have not taken more. As though they bit the body and then left it. Usually, I have bodies with the whole face and hands eaten away by the damned creatures. But whoever killed this man did more damage than a rat. Look under the covers.' He shrugged an apology as Margaretta whimpered.

Dee pulled back the linen and even he cried out. Just as on the other bodies, there was a symbol carved into the chest. Different again from the others. But worse was the stomach. The flesh had been cut away leaving the guts exposed. Grey, purple, swollen and sending out a stink beyond description. Dee turned away, pale and asked for water-soaked linens to cover their mouths, and a knife with which to probe.

Minutes later he was bending over the body dictating to Margaretta. 'Carved into the chest is a diamond shape but the base elongated. Draw this as before, exact in shape and size. The flesh of this man's stomach has been cleanly cut – so with a very sharp knife or even shears. I think our message will be in here.' He carefully took up the knife and lifted the intestine, bending to peer underneath. Then a satisfied nod as he spied a small oil-cloth pouch and pulled it out. It had been sewn shut with seven perfect stitches which, when slit, revealed another perfectly embroidered pentacle centred with a B. 'Baphomet again,' whispered Dee and then turned to the officer. 'Where was this man found?'

'In his Spitalfields workshop. Neighbours broke in after

a simpleton kept whimpering about the Devil running from the house.'

The same story. Alone. A Tuesday night. Only one witness. But the other side of the city.

'What did you find other than the body?' demanded Dee.

The man nodded towards Margaretta. 'Maybe better we move this lady away from this sight. I have my report in the office.'

'We will follow in one minute.'

Oh no. Please. I know what you are going to do.

The door closed and Dee turned to Margaretta. 'Look on the body and feel. What happened? No shirking girl. Your job is to feel, mine is to analyse. That is why Cecil calls us back. Now do your work.'

Margaretta forced herself to look into the dead man's eyes. Slowly, dull at first, then rising in waves, the feelings came through. 'Surprise. A new person. No face. Who walks here? Quiet. I feel interest. The door opens. A figure. Coated and cloaked. Hooves. I look up. Oh, help me… no, no, no. A claw. Horns. Stay away. No, no, no…'

'Come back.' John Dee was holding her shoulders then took her face in his hands. 'Calm, girl. It is only a vision. It is all done. Breathe.'

The door opened and the officer ran in. 'What is happening here? Why the screaming?' He looked at Margaretta and then glowered at John Dee. 'Why did you bring a woman to witness such evil? Come madam, let me give you some wine to calm your fears.' He took her hand and led her out, weeping.

In his office, Margaretta wiped her face with a clean linen and sipped the wine while the officer read out his notes. 'The body was discovered this morning at the man's workplace in Spitalfields, but estimated time of death was Tuesday night. That is when the simpleton started shouting about the Devil. Seems the neighbours thought the man had gone away a few days. It was a normal thing for him.'

That is what I was seeing. I was seeing through the eyes of the simpleton. He was terrified.

The officer checked his note and continued. 'The man was called Lucien Moreaux, a Huguenot weaver. He lived alone since the death of his wife some months ago. There are no children. Inside the workshop, my body carriers found evidence of a bad flux and the body – just as you have seen it. A few dead rats. But the worst for them was writing on the wall… in blood.'

'Did they say what it said?'

The officer shook his head. 'The body carriers cannot read or write. But they pick up rumours. I have had the house locked.' He opened his drawer and took out a key.

Dee nodded, took the key and stood. 'You have done right, sir. I ask you to keep this very secret.'

The officer raised his brows. 'Too late, Doctor Dee. The neighbours discovered the body and were gathered around the house when my men arrived. The news is spreading in every street in Spitalfields – and with it the growing fear. People say the raving of the simpleton is true – that the Devil came to take the soul of Lucien Moreaux.'

Chapter Twenty-Four

Dee pushed open the door of the weaver's workshop as Margaretta tethered the horses. People gathered into a small crowd and stared, silent but for a few whispered words that this was the Queen's conjuror and so it was certain the Devil was abroad. At the back of the group a young girl began to cry and was harshly hushed by an old woman.

There is deep fear here so strong it makes my own heart pound. Some of you think that the evils from which you have run have followed you here. The younger ones sense the fear of the elders and it terrifies them.

Margaretta followed through the door and shuddered at the stench. Just as before, a pail of shit and vomit. On the floor, blood which must have flowed from the weaver's wounds. Still on the floor his own shears, black with blood. Dee pointed to the back wall. A Huguenot cross had been pulled down and thrown to the ground, breaking it in half. Daubed in dry, black blood were the words, *D'abord la terreur, puis la mort.*

'Cut open with his own shears. But the blood was not congealed. He was probably still warm.' Dee walked around slowly, staring at the floor, then stopped. 'Look. We were meant to find this.'

She walked over, stepping over the stain on the floor.

Under the loom was a square piece of white cloth. On it were two perfect prints of cloven hooves in blood.

'We need to find the simpleton.'

The boy was cowering on a chair, his mother patting his shoulder and whispering comfort from a toothless mouth. He looked up at Dee, eyes wide, mouth slack and a stream of drool flowing down his chin. When Dee walked towards him, the boy hunched over and put his hands over his head making little mewing sounds. A brindle dog pressed against his leg and whined.

'Do not be afraid, my boy. I mean you no harm. Just tell me what you saw.'

A shake of the head, fingers scrunching into matted hair as the boy rocked to and fro. Dee looked to Margaretta, before turning back to the boy. 'Then speak with my assistant. She has a brother afeared of strangers. She understands you.'

Margaretta waited for her master to leave before speaking to the mother. 'Does your son fear people looking at him? That is true of my brother.'

'Yeth. He ith not bad. Moonsthruck.'

'His name?'

'Milo.'

'And when did his fear start, Mistress?'

'Tuesday night, just after dark '

Margaretta sat next to the boy, looking at the floor with him, and lowered her voice to a purr, exactly as she did with Huw when he was a little boy and upset. 'Milo, your dog is trying to comfort you. What is his name?'

The boy reached for the animal, pulled it close, and buried his face in the fur of its neck. 'Puck. My friend.'

'He is a good dog. Kind eyes and a tail that wags. You hold him tight and he will make you brave as you speak with me.'

Milo nodded but kept his face buried in the fur.

'I think you and Puck saw something that frightened you a few nights ago.'

The rocking slowed and the boy made a grunting noise, still pulling at his hair with one hand and clutching the dog with the other. Then he whispered, 'Devil.'

'Ah. You were brave to even look. Where did you see this devil?

'Ran from Lucien's house. Chink, chink, chink. Stopped. Looked at me. Eyes. Bad, bad, bad.'

Chink, chink, chink. The same sound reported by Alice.

'Did this devil speak?'

Rapid nodding of the head. 'Stopped, looked at us. Said "Bath". Milo afeared. Puck growled.'

'Just Bath?'

'Puck barking. Milo not hear rest.'

'Did you see the face of the devil?'

'No, no, no. Black.'

'So, tell me how you knew it was a devil?'

Milo began to rock and mew again, reaching out for his mother's hand. 'Horns, a claw, silver hooves. Taller than a horse. Chink, chink, chink.' *I feel your confusion. You saw two people.* 'Was there more than one devil, Milo?'

'No, no, no. Man went in. Chink, chink. Devil came out. Chink, chink. Stopped looked, laughed, spoke, ran.' Drool dripped to the floor and his mother wiped his chin, cooing comfort.

'What did the first man look like?'

Shaking of the head. 'Covered in black coat. Carried bag. No face.'

'So, a man visited Lucien and the devil walked out?'

'Yes, yes.'

'You said the devil was tall. Was the first man tall?'

Milo shook his head. 'Like other men. Chink.'

'Did Lucien let him in?'

Milo shook his head. 'Man walked in. Then devil...'

'So, a man arrives, is let in and the devil emerges and laughs at you. Then says "Bath".'

The boy began to rock frantically and cry. 'Milo shouted. No one listened. Milo frightened. Puck frightened.'

Margaretta patted his arm. 'You are a brave boy, Milo. My master works for Sir Cecil and will speak well of your courage.' She looked up at the mother. 'Where did Lucien worship?'

'All Hallowths.'

I was afeared you would say that.

Outside, Dee was sheltering in a doorway, trying to avoid the rain which had started to tumble down again. 'Well?'

'Exactly as before. Lucien worships at All Hallows. He was alone and let in a man wearing a black coat and cloak. A tall devil emerged. The boy heard the word "Bath" before the dog started barking and drowned out the rest of the word.'

'Baphomet,' snarled Dee. 'Anything else?'

'The boy keeps saying "chink, chink, chink". Alice described the same sound. Blind Basile claimed he heard the sound of a blacksmith hitting metal. But not just Baphomet. They are hearing it when the man arrives too.'

Dee's eyes widened. 'They are hearing metal on stone. Good work, Margaretta.'

'But we have a problem, master. How can Baphomet be in both ends of the city at the same time? Only a spirit can do that.'

Dee went silent and narrowed his eyes. Margaretta waited, knowing better than to break his train of thought. Then, 'Follow me and do not mount your horse. We walk south.'

Thirty minutes later, they arrived at the banks of the Thames. Margaretta looked around and pointed west. 'This is close to All Hallows, master. We met at those steps.'

'Indeed, we did. And just over there is Belin's Gate, full of wherries stored overnight.' He stared out over the water. 'Nearly dusk and the tide is running out. Six days ago, it would be turning to flood the river. By dark, the water would be running fast towards Westminster.'

'Doctor, we have been walking through busy streets from Spitalfields. How does a tall, clawed, horned devil with iron cloven hooves walk that mile unseen?' Margaretta shuddered. 'I am not sure you are right about Baphomet being a man, Doctor. Maybe it really is a devil walking our streets.'

Dee shook his head. 'No. Hiding in plain sight. A mystery for us to unpick. But for now, we go to All Hallows and break the bad news to Vicar Tyrwhit.'

Chapter Twenty-Five

'Vicar Tyrwhit? I will speak with you.' John Dee's voice echoed in the wooden rafters high above.

The vicar shambled out of the vestry, rubbing his eyes. 'Why the shouting Doctor? This is a house of God, not the Southwark bear pit.'

Dee ignored the rebuke. 'Another of your flock is dead. A man called Lucien Moreaux.'

Tyrwhit paled, grabbed the back of a pew and sat heavily. 'Dear God. What is happening?'

'A good question. Three Huguenots from this church. One last week, two this week. Each one has died of a terrible flux days after being in this church. Someone, who knows they live alone, arrives and carves them with symbols and hides an embroidered message in their body. In the case of Lucien – in his guts.'

Father Tyrwhit gave a little cry and bent over to put his face in his hands.

'Do they eat anything other than the holy bread in service?'

Tyrwhit looked up, horrified. 'You suggest they are poisoned in a house of God? That is blasphemy.'

Oh Lord, we do not want a churchman shouting religious law-breaking. We need his help not his fury. 'The doctor means no accusation of evil from your church, sir. But the Devil does not recognise goodness.' *I will make a hopeful smile to soften you.* 'We need your help to protect these good people… and your goodly church.'

Tyrwhit slumped again. 'Seemingly, you have more sense and sensibility than your master, mistress. The Huguenots of the congregation are a close-knit group, sharing a history of evading murder and threat. One of our congregation, Admiral Wynter, who is also a merchant, gives them space in his warehouse to gather and speak their own language.'

'Where is this warehouse?' demanded Dee.

'Just a short walk up Seething Lane, where the old chapel of Lady Mary stood – until the reformists tore it down.'

'Why does this Admiral Wynter give them the warehouse?'

The priest gave a small smile. 'They supply the goods he trades from his ships. Of course he wants to keep his suppliers happy. But more than that, he is a good man, so when Josef requested the use, he agreed.'

'Do they eat in this gathering?' snapped Dee.

'I think they bring food to share. But I am never there as I have no knowledge of their tongue.'

Dee growled his frustration and sat in a pew.

Margaretta spoke up. 'Vicar Tyrwhitt, does anyone in your congregation wear metal soled shoes? Maybe a blacksmith or farrier?'

Tyrwhit rubbed a furrowed brow. 'Not on a Sunday. But Josef will know. He will be in his workshop in St John's Yard today. It is getting late in the afternoon, but you should find him there.'

Dee stood and marched up the aisle, then suddenly turned back. 'I hear you have the clothing of the old Patrone statue here. Has anyone in your congregation shown interest in it?'

The vicar shook his head. 'Few of us even know of them. They are in the trunk in the vestry.'

'May I see them?'

With a nod, Vicar Tyrwhit walked them to the vestry and unlocked a small oak chest gathering dust in the corner. Gently he pulled out the carefully folded garments. Just as

Cecil had described they looked like the habit of a monk but overlayed with a tabard of white with a red cross and short cloak of a warrior. At the bottom of the trunk was a wooden sword. 'These have not seen the light of day for a few years now. I think the last time they were taken out was when Josef mended a hole in the sleeve made by the carpenter who took the statue down in 1559.' He smiled and pointed to the stitching. 'His first work would not make a beggar's rag.'

Dee grunted. 'Like a Templar Knight. Keep that chest well closed, Vicar. Our killer is invoking a Templar curse and we do not want them getting their hands on this.' Without another word, he strode out of the vestry and up the aisle, leaving Margaretta to the pleasantries and thanks. She ran after him, leaving Tyrwhit to refold the Patrone clothing, praying as he did.

Chapter Twenty-Six

St John's was a tumble of colour and wood. Folded tents, timber stages in pieces, carved animals and even wooden cut outs of mountains and trees. The buildings around the yard were ill-kept with stone missing. Noise was everywhere. The shuttle-clap of looms from workshops, shouting from taverns, women sitting on stools and gossiping in French, hands a blur as they moved lace bobbins faster than the eye could follow. Men carrying large baskets shouted greetings into workshops and stores, then friendly insults at each other. Margaretta looked around as she tethered their horses. 'What is this place?'

'The remnants of St John's Priory, built by The Knights Hospitaller, who made it into a hospital for the sick and needy. A place of goodness, deconsecrated and destroyed.'

'Why?'

'Because the knight-monks were staunch Catholics. A break-off from the Knights Templar, but just as zealous, they were first healers and then warriors for their faith. Their mission in life was to preserve the Catholic faith and rid the world of what they perceived as heresy. That was a problem for old King Henry when he wanted to rid himself of Katherine of Aragon and wed our Queen's mother, Anne Boleyn. So, the Knights Hospitaller of St John were cast asunder in his great dissolution of the monasteries. Now this place is a holding yard for all the tents, stages and props for her majesties' revels. Old Henry rid himself of nay-sayers, but he also rid London of the best healers his city had ever known. The fool.'

'Doctor, it is treason to insult the monarch. Your growing closeness to our Queen makes you bold. But maybe the fool if you press your luck too far.'

Dee shrugged. 'He's long dead. And I only speak what others think. When a man rids the world of knowledge in order to feed his lust… he is only a fool.' He batted his hands to indicate he wanted no more discussion. 'We need to find Mabelain. The other weavers will know him. Go ask.'

A weaver told Margaretta that Josef's dwelling was a small workshop with a blue door along Clerkenwell Street. But this being a Saturday would see him in the old Church, mending costumes or ripped tents. He pointed to the side of a dilapidated building, where more than twenty brightly coloured tents were propped up against the wall.

Dee and Margaretta walked to the once grand entrance, now ragged walls with stones lying around. 'Blown up by John Dudley, our Earl of Leicester's father, to make his great house on the Strand, back in 1550. Another fool,' said Dee.

Inside was evidently a revels storeroom. Racks of costumes, shoes and wigs making it a blur of colour. With it came the musty smell of old clothes, long unworn. Dee shouted into the void for Josef. Silence. 'We will go to his workshop.'

Hammering brought no answer. Despite Margaretta's protestations of rudeness, Dee turned the handle and entered. It was silent. A loom filled most of the front room, leaving space only for a seat and a shelf where the reels of silk and wool were stored. At the back, a door led through to the living area. A table, chair, wooden trunk decorated with the same Huguenot cross. On the table lay a cup, a pewter plate, a spoon and a loaf of bread. In the middle, a grate with coals still warm, straddled with a tripod from which a cooking cauldron dangled. On the back wall, long pieces of cloth hung from wooden poles to keep them free of creases. On a hook on the door was a leather coat. 'So where is he?' growled Dee.

Margaretta looked around. *Something tells me there is more to see.* She moved around and peeped behind the long cloths. 'Another door, Doctor.'

Again, Dee pushed through without knocking and stopped still. 'Dear God. Is he an alchemist?'

Looking over his shoulder, Margaretta could see a bench with a pestle and mortar containing a light brown powder. Above it a shelf full of glass conical flasks. The fusty smell of damp floated to their noses. 'Well, he doesn't have all the equipment that fills your office. But he certainly makes a stink like you.'

Dee huffed, backed out and pulled the door. 'Where the hell is he? Do you feel anything?'

Margaretta stopped, closed her eyes and breathed deep. 'I feel closed in. Dark. Damp.'

'The crypt,' shouted Dee walking out, ignoring Margaretta's insistence that working in a crypt made no sense. He marched back up Albemarle Street through the church door and turned to the side. There was a carved wooden door with an iron handle. 'Go ask that weaver for a candle.'

Minutes later they were stepping down into the realm of the dead over stone steps. The crypt was dark with a meagre light coming through a window at the far end and slit windows high on the wall which were evidently at the level of the ground outside. Margaretta noticed that the first window on the right was bricked in. 'Doctor, why is one window blocked?'

He turned to look. 'That was more likely a place for a candle or even a relic but they made it look like the window to retain the pattern. The Templars and Hospitallers liked balance and order.'

Margaret shrugged and followed. The smell was strong.

Dust, damp. Dead wood. Holding the candle high, Dee shouted for Mabelain. Silence.

At the far end of the central aisle, two archways led to further spaces either side. To the left a small area with steps leading up to a small door that opened onto an empty chamber. To the right, they stepped through into a wider space but half the length of the main aisle. At the end was a table covered with a linen cloth below a small window. On it were three red, snuffed candles. One had been burned low. Next to them various pieces of fabric cut into squares and a bowl with skeins of silk, wool and cotton. On top of these a small cushion, pricked all over with pins and needles of various sizes. To the side, two pairs of tailor's shears, one small, one large. Margaretta's eyes went to the wall behind the table and down to a hole. She bent to see what it was and reeled back from the smell of rotting wood. 'What is this? It stinks like a dead mouse.'

Dee came to her side. 'An old drain. The priests used to put unused holy water through these. They did not want needy people getting their hands on something which gave them hope. That would stop the dependency. Damn Catholics.'

Margaretta raised her brow. 'Some words from a man who went into the house of Bishop Bonner as an accused conjurer and emerged only three months later a fully ordained Catholic priest.'

'That was survival, woman. And years ago.'

'But you also came out using the number 007 – used by Sir Cecil and our Queen.' Margaretta raised her hand in enquiry. 'Are you one of Cecil's ring of secret spies?'

'Stop questioning, Margaretta,' was the snapped reply.

Damn you. Still, you keep me down. 'I am your assistant. I should know…'

Dee turned, eyes bright and raised a finger to within an inch of her nose. 'Apprentice. Now do your work… apprenticing.'

I hate you. I do everything for you, and yet you treat me like a nobody when it suits you. I feel the tears. But I will not give you satisfaction by showing my hurt.

There was a long silence while Dee was looking around,

already forgetting the conversation. 'Well, this is obviously his mending place. Nothing strange. What do you feel?'

'I feel fear, Doctor. I sense death.'

Dee held up the candle making his face look like a hideous mask. 'Of course you do, woman. You're in a damned crypt. Once full of rotting bodies. What else do you expect to feel?' He turned and stamped out, grumbling that Mabelain should be at his work and not causing delay.

Margaretta looked back at the table. *Why do those candles bother me?* As Dee disappeared into the central aisle, she was plunged into pitch black and reached out to the table to steady herself. Under her thumb she felt the ridges of something carved into the front of the table. Slowly she traced it. *It feels like a star.* 'Doctor, come back.'

'Why are you dallying, woman?' The candle came towards her. 'What is it?'

'There is something carved under this cloth.' She pulled it up and they both stared. The table was not made of wood, but a strange stone. Four legs supported a thick table-top. Into the front had been carved a star within a star. Dee peered at it. 'Well, well. Looks like old Henry's men missed this.'

'What is it?'

'The cross of the Knights Templar and the Knights Hospitaller. This must be an old altar. Once used to pray for their fanatical faith and cruel crusades… only to be used as a sewing table for the mending of frippery and fun. Hah.'

As they emerged into the fading light outside, Josef Mabelain appeared from the side of the church where the tents were propped against the wall. He limped and scraped towards them, rubbing his hands down the sides of his legs to clean them. His face was creased with worry. 'I hear you seek me, Doctor Dee.'

'I have been shouting for you,' snapped the other man. 'We've been to your home and your workshop in vain.'

Mabelain pointed behind him. 'I have been working the physik garden.'

Dee gestured to the church. 'We will speak in your workshop. Away from flapping ears.'

Alarm. Why does the thought of going into the crypt worry you, Frenchman? Or are you alarmed that the doctor is seeking you and wishes to speak in secret. Whatever it is, you keep clenching your hands and twitching your eyes in worry. I feel threat. And you smell as fusty as your workplace.

In the rot-reeking undercroft, Dee placed his candle on the table and sat on the wooden stool the weaver used for his work. Shadows flickered over the white walls and in the arches of the ceiling. 'It seems we are of the same circle of trust, Master Mabelain. Has Walsingham spoken to you?'

The Frenchman's shoulders relaxed. 'Of you, yes. Of the woman, no.'

Dee smiled. 'I think Master Walsingham is a little disapproving. But Sir Cecil includes Margaretta in all our meetings as a note taker. You can trust her too.'

Mabelain nodded to Margaretta. His wall eye seemed all the more twisted in the candlelight. 'Very well, Doctor. I hope you come to tell me how I can assist your investigation.'

'I have bad news. I have found that Old Lucille was murdered and now another – Lucien Moreaux.'

Mabelain gave a little wail and reached out to the wall as if he were about to crumple. 'Dear God, help us. When?'

'Seems it was the same night as Pierre Perotin. That makes three bodies, all carved with a symbol; all with a strange message sewn into the body. My analysis is that these killings are by a maddened Catholic assassin who is invoking the very people who are seen as the guardians of the faith – the Templars and Hospitallers.' Dee swept his hand around. 'The very people who built this church.'

Mabelain nodded and pointed at the table. 'Indeed, they did. If you raise that cover cloth, you will find the Templar Star. I think it might be an altar missed in King Henry's dissolution.'

He smiled. 'As a Huguenot, I should smash it to pieces in fury at our suffering at the hands of Catholics. But there is some strange justice in using it to mend frippery and foolery – the very things the Templars hated – so I just keep it covered so that I do not have to look upon it.'

Dee made a small laugh. 'My words exactly.'

You are calming Master Mabelain, and relax when you realise that the doctor thinks like you.

Mabelain frowned. 'Why do you say the killer invokes those wretched knights?'

'Every death has the same pattern. A person living alone dies on a Tuesday night of a double flux we think is poison; they are carved with a symbol; and they have a linen sewn into them. That linen is embroidered with a pentacle centred with a B.'

Mabelain held out his hands in question.

'It is the sign of Baphomet. A Pagan goat-headed deity that the Templars were accused of worshiping. When they were wiped out for their supposed sins, the last Templar uttered a curse. That curse is written in blood on the wall of every victim.'

Mabelain made a mewing sound. Margaretta gestured to Dee to give up the stool for the man to sit, but she was ignored. He took some deep breaths and looked up at Dee. 'What is the curse?'

'First terror, then death. Written in French – the mother tongue of the victims. This killer is bent on creating terror in your people – and through them, your protector – the Queen. Have there been any threats in the past few weeks?'

The Frenchman shook his head slowly. 'We are always threatened, sir. The English do not like a foreign face... until they want our fine silk, starched lace and silverware.' He shuddered. 'Our people whisper of a devil seeking us.'

Dee nodded. 'A beggar woman claimed she saw a devil emerging from Pierre Perotin's house. Then a simple boy called Milo insists a man entered the dwelling of Lucien

Moreaux and a tall devil emerged, looked at him and said "Bath", which we think is really Baphomet. But it is possible he had heard rumours. Does the lad have fancies of the mind?'

Mabelain shrugged. 'I know little of him. His mother keeps the boy close. Usually, he chatters only about his dog.'

Margaretta stepped forward. 'The boy heard metal on stone. Does anyone in All Hallows wear metal soled shoes?'

Mabelain frowned and then glared at her. 'Are you suggesting, Madam, that a Huguenot is slaughtering his fellow… ?' His voice was brimming with fury.

My God, you turn like a wildcat.

Dee cut across him. 'No need to snarl at Margaretta. The assassin knows your people, knows they live alone, knows how to poison them, knows when they will die. As I have said to Cecil and Walsingham, they are hiding in plain sight. I am afraid, Monsieur Mabelain, it might well be a member of All Hallows. Which is why I will be at your church tomorrow.'

Mabelain nodded and turned to Margaretta. 'Forgive my reaction, mistress.'

You say the words, but your anger remains. No. It is alarm. Deep alarm. Little wonder.

'Father Tyrwhit says you all gather at a captain's warehouse in Seething Lane to eat after service on Sunday. Tell me about that,' demanded Dee.

Sudden fear. You feel caught.

Mabelain shifted on his twisted foot and winced. 'We gather to share news of our people. Many people are here in Clerkenwell, but others are in Spitalfields and further afield in Bethnal Green. We share a past of sadness, even horror. It is good to gather but we speak no wrong.'

You think of horror. Oh, God. I hear screaming. The clash of swords, Children screaming. You think of pure hate. People dying. Terror. I must sit.

Dee turned to her and peered through the low light. 'Are you sick?'

She made a small nod towards Mabelain. 'I remembered

the stories of what the poor Huguenot people faced in France. It makes me feel ill.' *My master knows I am leading him. That small smile he makes when I give him information.*

Dee made a small nod and turned back to the Frenchman. 'And what horror made you flee, sir?'

Screaming. A child shouting that her arm is gone. A mother begging to put the children outside. Men running, unarmed. Swords going through them like knives though butter. 'Oh, God.'

'I was at Wassy,' was the bitter reply.

Dee raised his brow. 'The massacre eight years ago? I understand. Now let us speak more of the meeting in Seething Lane. Do you eat?'

The man seemed to snap his head back towards Dee. 'Yes. Huguenot food. Pottage, honey cakes and good bread. What of it?'

'As I said, it seems each victim was first afflicted with a terrible flux.'

Mabelain waved his hands in agitation. 'We share as is our custom. If there were a Huguenot poisoning the food, we would all be dead.'

'Unless the person serving taints only the food of the victims.'

The small man snorted. 'You do not know our ways, sir. We bring food in baskets – I could take cake from the centre, the edge or the top. We all take pottage from the same cauldron. Your thinking is foolery.'

Dee bristled. 'So how do you explain that two days after Sunday service, a person becomes sick – always a single person – and then dies, only to be desecrated?'

Mabelain put his hands over his face. Again, the sleeves slipped to reveal the scabs on his lower arms. 'The pamphlets speak true. The Devil is abroad. Tell me what I can do. What you can do.'

'I am working as fast as I can, Goodman Mabelain. Now

let us get out of this place. I do not understand how you work in the dark and the dank of it.'

Yet you make our home stink like a pig-yard in your mad pursuit of conjured gold. But there is another question. 'Master Mabelain, where does this hole drain? It seems the smell down here comes from there.'

The Frenchman turned sharply and made a twisted smile. 'Just to the earth, mistress. But it is like sitting next to a dead rat when I work.'

Margaretta followed the men. As she reached the steps to go up out of the crypt, she looked sideways at the bricked-up window. She calculated it was above the drain out of the side crypt. But there was no time to ponder. Dee was already gone. When Margaretta reached the top of the steps and blinked in the light, he was walking past the tents leaned against the wall in the direction from where Mabelain had appeared. 'I will see the garden. I am something of a physik myself, you know.'

You liar. You are jealous of his making a salve for the Queen. You just want his recipe.

Mabelain scraped after him, insisting that the garden was really nothing to see. Dee ignored him and they walked to the back of the church, through a stone arch into a well laid out garden, each bed set with various herbs, all drooping low and straggling across the paths as if just awaiting the sun of spring that would awaken them from the winter sleep. In the centre a yew tree, its dark branches hanging low to the ground.

Dee stared around and then down at the paths. He paused, his brow making little furrows as he considered the vista. 'What do you use in your salve?'

Mabelain was silent a minute. 'It is a personal recipe. Just lavender, mallow, some marigold when in blossom. I mix by eye, not measure.'

Dee was irritated. 'Science needs precision. It might work better if you were more consistent in your mixing. In your home, I found pestle, mortar, glass bottles with various mixtures. Do you practice alchemy, sir?'

A sudden surge of worry.

'No, no,' stuttered the other man. Then he began to nod rapidly. 'That is my experiments for salves. And dyes for my cloth.'

Relief. It cannot be you, Doctor. You are the one person who can hide everything from my strange abilities. So, it must be the Frenchman. Little wonder. But the doctor warms now that he realises that you are not a competitor in the pursuit of gold. You see it too, Frenchman. Your shoulders sink in relief.

Mabelain leaned towards Dee. 'I have been asked to create a salve for Her Majesty and a tincture for her stomach but there are so few herbs growing in March. I will share the recipe with you, Doctor Dee. But more pressing is the threat to my people. Tell me what I can do – anything you ask.'

Dee nodded and leaned forward conspiratorially. 'Keep your eyes and ears open. Anything that makes you wonder should be reported directly to me. Either at my house in Mortlake, or through Sir Cecil or Walsingham. Every message must be signed 013. Then I know it is a true message from you.' He made an exaggerated wink. 'I will see you in All Hallows Church on the morrow.'

Mabelain feels relief. Even delight. He is taking your hand to shake it and seal your agreement. This man feels a surge of good feeling.

Dee turned to Margaretta. 'Come. First Westminster and then we go to the Strand.'

Chapter Twenty-Seven

Alice Burton was asleep when the palace guard unlocked her cell and roused her with a call unusually gentle. Seeing the visitors, she jumped up stammering her apologies and gave a small smile to the guard, who left the door open. Dee went to sit at a table and chair that had not been there before.

Margaretta looked around. 'This cell is certainly sweeter than it was a few days ago, Alice.'

The woman nodded. 'This is the first roof I have had over my head in years, mistress. I asked the guards for a pail of water and some rags to clean it. I was always a house-proud woman. Then they brought me that chair and table – and food to eat on it.'

'And you are dressed more warmly too.'

'A lady called Blanche did send me this dress, a shawl and shoes. I never knew a prison could be so kind. Even the guards speak nicely to me.'

'Because you are here for safety, Alice. Not punishment,' said John Dee softly. 'And we have questions for you.'

Alice pinked as anxiety returned and she began to stammer. 'Ask anything, sir. If I can help you find that devil, I will speak until my tongue splits.'

'I am afraid we must ask you to take your memory back to that night.'

She shuddered but nodded. 'I will recall all I can, though it do make my heart thump.'

Margaretta took her hand and led her to sit on the bed. 'Alice when you told me of the killer, you said "chink, chink". What did you hear?'

Alice started slowly. 'Yes. He sounded like a horse on the cobbles. The way their shoes chink in the stone. That is what made me look up when the man arrived at the door. I heard him before I saw him.'

Margaretta glanced at Dee. 'So, both the visitor and the devil creature made the sound?'

Tears fell as Alice gulped down her fear and gripped Margaretta's hand tighter. 'Like they were shod. And the devil were as tall as a horse too.'

'What time did the visitor arrive?'

'It were some hours after dark had fallen. I would say near nine of the clock for I had heard a bell inside the palace wall sound eight chimes long before he arrived.'

Dee leaned forward his voice low and kind. 'I know the memories afear you, madam, but you must be brave for Her Majesty's sake. You said the devil looked towards you and spoke a word beginning with B.'

Alice began to shake. 'Yes, but I did not understand it.'

'Did he say, "Baphomet"?'

Alice jumped and let out a little cry. 'Yes. He looked right at me and said that. God help me. Am I cursed?'

'No, mistress. You are blessed to be assisting us as we are protecting the Queen.'

For the first time Alice made a watery smile.

Having asked the guards to give Alice a beaker of warmed wine to calm her, Dee and Margaretta mounted their horses and turned towards the Strand. Dee called over his shoulder, 'It is good of Cousin Blanche to be so kind to her, but Alice should have further reward for her courage.'

'I already have an idea, Doctor.'

Chapter Twenty-Eight

Burcott looked tense when he opened the door of Sir Cecil's so-called cottage on the Strand. 'Good you are here, Doctor. The Earl of Leicester and Mistress ap Harri are here, asking about your progress.'

'Ah, Robert,' chirped Dee. 'And Blanche is my cousin, you know.'

Burcott made a small bow. 'Yes, Doctor. You have told me many times.'

Oblivious to the dig, Dee strode through the central hall to the staircase that would take him up to Cecil's office. Margaretta nodded to Burcott with a knowing smile and for the first time ever, he made a small smile back.

Inside the office, Leicester was sat bolt upright in a chair, his magnificent brocade glistening in the candlelight. He was staring ahead, face dark with discontent, as he passed a piece of paper hand to hand. In the far corner, Blanche and Cecil were deep in conversation bending over a book.

Leicester jumped to his feet. 'Have you found this evil spirit, Doctor? Court is in deeper fear.' He held out the paper. 'Look at this.'

Dee nodded to Blanche and Cecil, took the paper and tutted. 'Damned pamphleteers.'

It was a single side of printed paper, at the top a scrawled image of a devil's face. Under it the script ranted about England being in the last few days before Armageddon caused by the Serpent Queen and her heretical men. It went on to insist that the Queen's casting aside of the council and nobility and filling her palace with obscure men, heretics, false preachers and ministers of impiety had brought to England the wrath of the True Faith and made this a Devil Land where Satan roams free.' Dee frowned and looked to Cecil. 'Where is that Bull?'

Cecil limped over to his desk, unlocked the drawer and pulled out the rolled parchment. Dee came to his side and laid the pamphlet next to it. He tapped on the words serpent, obscure men, heretics, false preachers and ministers of impiety. 'Whoever wrote this pamphlet knows about the Papal Bull.'

Cecil groaned and sat heavily. 'We wanted to supress all knowledge as long as possible.'

'Who delivered the Bull? Could they spy it?'

Cecil shook his head slowly. 'Sent by special envoy with multiple seals and a clever letter-lock. If it had been opened, we would know.'

Dee tutted. 'Does anyone else have a key to the desk? What about your secretary?'

Cecil bristled. 'No, John. The only people who know about it are in this room.'

An uncomfortable silence fell.

Blanche picked up the pamphlet in the tips of her fingers as if it were smeared in filth. 'It is likely those gossiping ambassadors, De Speys and Mothe-Fénélon. Whoever it is, the word is out and Elizabeth is hearing all manner of terrors from her ladies. One of them was wittering this morning that the fool, John Prescott, has warned of death by poisoning, yet that letter has never left my locked box. But the terror spreads.' She ignored John Dee huffing at the mention of Prescott and looked sharply at Leicester. 'Terrors which add to her pain.' Then she turned to Dee. 'She has not slept in three nights for weeping. The dark of the night is a cruel place for such a mind of imagination. Then in the morning she is fearful of dressing in case her garments are poisoned. She will not eat.'

And you are up all night with her Blanche. I see the dark circles under your eyes. Like a woman with a newborn babe, your face has that hard, wan look that only sleep can soften. Yet I feel your motherly love. I remember Mam being like that when she looked at my brother Huw. Love and concern and fear all mixed into a terrible ball of worry. You look at me and make a weak smile. You know I am feeling you.

They all looked to Dee. He reached for Leicester's goblet of wine, drank it dry, and then beckoned to Margaretta to hand him his bag. 'Well, I do not come with good news. The morgue holds a third body with exactly the same pattern of death. It appears he died the same night as Pierre Perotin.' He glanced at Blanche. 'Do not tell Elizabeth, but this one had his belly cut open by his own shears. The same messages were found – a symbol carved into the chest, the embroidered pentacle containing B pressed into the exposed guts.'

Dudley went pale and put a hand over his mouth.

Dee continued. 'We went straight to the killing place. A simpleton gave the same story as the beggar woman. A man entered the home with no force. We now know this visitor has metal soled shoes as witnesses hear the chink on the cobbles. Then Baphomet emerges, taller, with horns and silver hooves. In the case of the last two victims, he looked at the witnesses and said the word Baphomet.' He winced a few times as his mind put together clues. 'So, a pattern becomes more clear. The first victim was a shock – no one saw the devil. The second murder was flaunted by laughing and stopping to stare at a terrified boy as he said, "Baphomet". The third murder was made public by leaving the body in the alley and ensuring the beggar woman had seen him sew. This devil is getting more courageous… or more determined to frighten us.'

'But how can he be in two places on the same night?' demanded Cecil.

'Already investigated, William,' replied Dee smugly. 'The

Spitalfields murder was just after dark. The killing of Pierre Perotin was around nine at night.'

'But they are five miles apart.'

Dee nodded. 'But any adult can walk from Spitalfields to the river in thirty minutes. The tide was making strong last Tuesday. A stolen wherry would have you in Westminster by eight. Easy.' He smiled as Cecil gave an impressed nod.

'What else do we know?' snapped Leicester.

'That every victim is Huguenot, they live alone, and worship in All Hallows. After their service, they meet in a warehouse in Seething Lane owned by Admiral William Wynter, who trades their goods.'

Cecil raised his eyes and rolled his lips together as if supressing any look of surprise.

Your eyes look side to side, Sir Cecil. Your mind is torn between secrecy and concern about the threat.

Margaretta pretended to take something out of the bag by her master. As she leaned close to his arm, she whispered, '*Gofynna am y morwr.*' Ask about the seaman.

Dee did not flinch. Just that tiny nod. 'I must investigate the Admiral. If any crime is committed in the warehouse, he is under suspicion.'

Cecil took in a sharp breath. 'No suspicion follows him. He is a man to be cherished.'

Dee sat back, eyes narrowing. 'Why so defensive, William?'

Leicester was looking between the two men as silence stretched. 'Gad, Cecil. Enough of your secrets.'

Cecil turned slowly to Leicester and glared. 'In these days of naughtiness, sir, secrets are necessary.' He looked to Dee. 'Admiral William Wynter is a skilled commander, the surveyor and rigger for the navy, and, four years ago, made Master of Navy Ordinance. He acts as a merchant for added income, giving him connections in every port from here to Africa.'

'So, he is another spy in your secret circle,' barked Dee.

'And does he know that Mabelain is one of your hidden watchers?'

Cecil nodded. 'Wynter takes Mabelain to France with his goods. They rendezvous at The Pelican Inn at Wapping.'

'Is that dark drinking hole not a bed of pirates?' snapped Leicester.

Cecil glowered. 'That dark drinking hole, as you call it, sir, is a place where Wynter can collect Mabelain out of sight of the London Docks. It is also a good source of seaman's loose talk. It serves them well.'

'Mabelain and Wynter work as a pair?' asked Dee, his voice rising in indignation. 'And you did not think to inform me... as one of your trusted circle?'

'I saw no need to... connect you.'

Leicester feigned laughter as he pointed at one of the Emperor statues. 'Julius Cesar who declared, "divide and rule". Gad, Sir Cecil, you are taking your Latin learnings to heart.'

Cecil ignored him and kept eye contact with Dee. 'Mabelain and Wynter bring rich news from Europe. Wynter covers the seamen, Mabelain the merchants and dock purveyors as well as a string of tavern keepers. How do you think we know so much about the Guise, Catherine de Medici and even the rantings of John Prescott? Yes John, they delivered that letter that so angered you. They pick up everything that is hidden from our ambassador, Henry Norris, in Paris.'

Dee was silent a second and then growled. 'It does not help to use curtains of mistrust, William. This is no time for guarding your power. We need to preserve the power of the throne... of Elizabeth.'

'Well said,' snarled Leicester. Behind him Blanche made a small nod, her face pinched with worry.

The brittle tension was broken by the door opening. Walsingham walked in, eyes darting between the people in the room as if scoping friend from foe. He made a slight frown when he looked at Blanche who nodded and looked him straight in the eye until she won the battle of who would look away first.

Oh, Mistress Parry. This man has annoyed your beloved Elizabeth and you are going to insist on some manners.

Walsingham nodded to the men, ignored Margaretta and sat on a chair near Cecil's desk.

Cecil turned to him. 'Have you made progress on the cypher?'

The younger man shook his head. 'With only two symbols? My code breaker needs at least eight.'

Dee picked up the drawing of the symbol carved on Lucien Moreaux. 'Well, this makes three.'

Walsingham snatched it from his hands and studied it, his head shaking slowly. 'This is the strangest code I have ever seen. The symbols are so similar.'

Dee took out the other two drawings and put them on Cecil's desk, taking the third from Walsingham and putting them all in a row. 'I agree they are similar. But we cannot wait for another five bodies.'

'I cannot work with so little,' said Walsingham, almost shouting.

Dee stood and started to pace. 'Then let us look at what we have. Baphomet leaves a calling card – the pentacle up-ended and centred with B. The shapes are spelling something out. Either a message or a name.' He returned to the symbols and put them in the order of the killings, snatched up Cecil's pen and wrote E under the first, L under the second and I under the third. 'This is our worst nightmare. For if I am right, not only is Elizabeth in mortal danger but another six Huguenot souls will face a terrible end.'

'Is Tuesday night significant? Is it special or sacred to a Huguenot?' asked Blanche.

Dee smiled. 'You think well, cousin.' He ignored the sharp look of rebuke at claiming kinship and resumed his pacing.

'A killer always has a pattern. We have desecrations, the calling cards, the shapes. But we also have a pattern of time. Huguenots of one church gather to eat after Sunday service in the warehouse of a merchant who buys their wares. Exactly two days later, one of them who lives alone falls to a terrible flux. A man arrives at their door and enters unchallenged. That tells me the visitor knows the person inside will be dead or dying alone and is known to them... and they know the time of death.' He looked to Margaretta. 'The victims live in different parts of the city – so the only common link in the pattern is gathering for food on Sunday. We need to know a poison, easily given to one, that kills in two days.'

Margaretta nodded. 'Clarissa.'

'The herb-woman of Southwark?' asked Cecil frowning. 'I am not sure we should tell anyone else of our fears. Southwark is a hotbed of evil gossip.'

Walsingham nodded. 'Mabelain has knowledge of physik. Ask him.'

Cecil nodded. 'He is working on a tonic for Elizabeth's sickness. He must know what poisons. Go see him this evening, Walsingham.'

Walsingham sat up straight, his eyes brightening.

Oh, spy man, you have suddenly smiled. Hope. You think of Elizabeth's harsh words. Those green eyes, glaring at you. But if your man can crack the mystery, then you can be a hero.

Walsingham stood. 'I will indeed and will collect the salve he is working on and deliver it to the palace.'

Dee bridled. 'But I am going to All Hallows in the morning, I can speak to him and collect the salve. I should—'

Cecil raised his hand. 'It will assist Walsingham in earning the trust you already have. Now be generous.'

Dee peevishly gestured to Margaretta to pack his bag. 'Tomorrow I will attend All Hallows to observe. We will gather here in the evening.' He marched to the door, stopping only to make a bow to Blanche.

She patted his arm. 'We may not see eye to eye, John. But

we both love the same soul. Do your work and salve her mind. It will be felt deeper than her leg.'

Dee flushed with gratitude, nodded and walked to the door, calling over his shoulder for Margaretta to follow. With the door closed, he turned, eyes bright with anger. 'Do you remember I once said forgiveness is easier reached than permission?'

'Yes – you say it often, Doctor.'

'So, go to Southwark. Ask about poison. Get a salve and also a tincture for sickness caused by fear.'

Margaretta winked. 'I ordered the salve a few days ago, master.'

Then one of those rare moments. He patted her cheek and smiled. 'We are a good team, Margaretta.'

Chapter Twenty-Nine

Margaretta opened her eyes on a dark and dreary Sunday morning and pulled the covers up to shut out the day, but there was little point. Katherine Constable was already clanking around the kitchen, hauling down the pails and cauldrons to start boiling water. Sunday was wash-day – not the shirts and linens of the week – but her husband. Ever since John Dee had advised the Queen to reduce the miasmas around her body with clean and perfumed water every week, he had decided to follow suit – and Sunday, being a holy day was the bathing day of choice.

She shivered in the damp dark of the morning and rubbed herself hard with rough linen before pulling on a loose smock which was going to get soaked anyway, then made her way to the kitchen. Katherine turned around. 'I have the fire going. Will you bring in the water? The barrel was filled just a day ago.'

'Where is Bela? She is the lower maid.'

'She is unwell. Couldn't even get out of bed when I knocked. I told her to rest.'

'Really? Interesting how she is always sick on a Sunday. Either she is shirking, or her soul is fearful of the holy day.' Margaretta stamped out, ignoring Katherine's plea to be gentle. She kicked open Bela's door. 'Get your backside off that pallet, slugabed.'

There was a shout and Bela sat upright, pulling the covers over her naked breasts. 'Get out. I'm sick.'

No woman lies naked in bed in the cold of March.

'More like frightened of the heat of hard work. This is the second Sunday you have...' she stopped and stared at the bed. 'Well, whatever illness you have it seems to have grown your backside to the width of two people.'

Bela was silent, just shaking her head.

'Who is in there with you?'

'No one.'

'Liar.' Margaretta marched over and smacked the rounded cover, ducking to avoid the other girl's hand as she tried to push her away. There was a grunt. 'Show yourself.'

Slowly, reluctantly, fearfully, the mussed head of Thomas Digges emerged from the covers. 'I... I... I can explain.'

'Good Sabbath morning, Mr Digges. Did Bela's Ptolemaic system need a little attention?'

The man burbled as Bela hissed, 'Don't you say anything. Do you hear? You'll be sorry. I'll tell the Mistress...'

'... that you're a slattern? Go ahead. But first move your lazy bones to the basins. The doctor will bathe in half of an hour.' She grinned sarcastically. 'He says a clean body makes for a clean mind. You evidently need a bath, Bela.' She left, slamming the door on the other girl's stream of indignation.

What is it with me? Does every man who claims to like me, lie?

Back in the kitchen Katherine was red-faced and puffing as she heaved the water pots onto a table. 'John will be here in his bare legs soon and his water is not ready. She looked up. You will need to fill the pans.'

'Bela is coming. She can fill them.'

Katherine swiped sweat from her forehead. 'I hope you have not tumbled her out of bed.'

Margaretta smiled. 'No, Mistress. Any tumbling was

already done.' She walked away leaving Katherine, open mouthed and very confused. Thankfully, John Dee arrived in the doorway, and Katherine was instantly fussing around him, getting a blanket to warm his knees until the water was ready. Margaretta pulled her cloak from the door and told Dee she would go immediately to Southwark and get a wherry across to meet him at Custome House Steps, close to All Hallows. Outside she pulled up her hood against the rain and smiled to see Master Digges running across the yard to his rooms, like a piglet racing from a fire.

Well, you have given me my excuse, Master Digges. A good thing too. For I think marriage to you would see me in The Bedlam.

Clarissa was at the counter when Margaretta walked in. Her amber eyes lit up and arms outstretched to hug her friend. 'A holy day is made lighter by your company, my dear. But why so early again and before Church? Have you come for the salve for a precious leg? I have it here ready for you.' She opened a drawer and pulled out a package.

'I came for different wisdom today.'

'Your sister? Are there symptoms?' She pulled up a chair to the fire and took down a bottle from a shelf with a wink. 'Dandelion – good for worry.'

Margaretta shrugged off her damp cloak and sat heavily. 'Not my sister this time, Clarissa. Though, no doubt, I will be back about her. This time I need to ask about poison – but I cannot tell you why.'

Clarissa raised a single eyebrow. 'You do not trust your old friend?'

'Oh, I do. But there is much secrecy because of the threat to Court.'

Clarissa nodded. 'Give me the symptoms.'

'Flux of belly and bowel. Then a sudden death. The bodies are always yellow. The first victim was a big man and had been finished off with a slit to his throat. But the other symptoms were exactly the same.'

'Do the victims live or work together?'

'No. They all live alone. Each one has eaten in one place after service on a Sunday and all three have died on a Tuesday night.'

A sudden surge of panic. Fear. You think of a man. Husband. Screaming. Vomiting. A yellow face freezing into death. Oh, God. I feel sick. But now relief, Joy. 'Why are you shaking, Clarissa?'

The other woman rose, walked to the counter and poured another glass of dandelion wine, downed it and poured another. 'Dark memories.' She bent her head, closing her eyes.

Margaretta stood and walked over to take her hand. 'I hear the word husband. But you said your husband and son died of the sweating sickness.'

Another gulp of wine and Clarissa shook her head. 'That was my second man. The good husband. The one I mourn every day.' Tears started to pool in her large eyes and she gripped Margaretta's hand as she forced a smile. 'Let us not speak of the first.'

There is a deep secret here. You fear me knowing. But I feel your pain too. A deep pain that lingers within. You are my dear friend and deserve my trust. 'He seems not worth our breath. But what can cause people to die on one night in the week if it is not witchcraft?'

Clarissa raised her brow again. 'Or a devil roaming the streets? You are too late – the news has been chattered around here for days. But it is not a devil. It is a Destroying Angel – a small, white, and deadly mushroom. You eat it, enjoy your food, feel well. Then two or two and half days later a violent flux and sudden death.'

'But people pick mushrooms every day. Why do we not hear more of this kind of death?'

'Because it grows not in a field but in the dark, damp

rotting wood of a forest. Usually an oak forest. You would need to seek it out.'

'But there is no oak forest near London. We are building so much, the wood must be brought from the North.'

Clarissa nodded. 'Your killer is growing it.'

Minutes later Margaretta, the salve made safe in her bag, tied her horse at the back of Clarissa's for safe-keeping and was stepping through the filth of a Southwark after a Saturday night of revelling before the Sabbath. The stench was rising with the temperature of the day. Drunken men were stirring in gutters, one vomited and dropped his head into the mess. Cats prowled and somewhere, down an alley, a doxy yelled that she wanted five pennies for the soiled straw mattress. Children ran barefoot, staring at the ground, eyes keened to find a dropped penny or something they could eat.

She reached the steps to the river Thames and stepped down the weed covered stone. A wherry man was lying in the bottom of his boat, snoring. A kick on the prow of the vessel opened his eyes. 'Will you row me across to Custome House Steps?' She pointed straight across the river.

He tutted. 'Hardly worth my waking. Why can't you walk the bridge?'

'I cannot walk below the piked heads. I hate the way they stare.'

He cackled a laugh. 'The only heads are worn to the look of a turnip. Good Queen Bess kills few on Tower Hill. Very well, but I will charge a fare and a half.'

Margaretta crossed her arms across her chest. 'You will not. I am friends with Sam the wherry lord and manager of the building yard where you bought your boat. Cheat me and he will chase you off the water.'

There was a long silence and the man's face clouded. 'The poor bastard. They say he is still screaming.'

Margaretta grabbed the wall trying to stop the world from shaking. 'Is he hurt?'

'Not him. Little Lottie and the two boys.' The man shook his head and seemed to sniff back tears. 'Laughing at breakfast, dead at dinner. The Sweat took all three in a day.'

Margaretta heard a long animal wail as she bent over and covered her face. Then she realised it was her own voice.

Chapter Thirty

John Dee walked quickly towards Margaretta. She was sitting on the wall at the top of Custome House Steps where the wherry man had led her and spoken soft words of comfort before turning away, refusing any fare. She looked up, white faced and red-eyed, trying to speak, but only choking sobs came out.

'What has happened?'

'Lottie and the boys. Dead.'

Dee patted her shoulder. 'I am sorry. May they rest in peace.' He pointed up the Watergate in the direction of All Hallows. 'Service will start in a few minutes. Come. We need to get a good pew.' He turned to lead the way.

Damn you. I feel my grief turn to rage. 'Did you hear what I said?' *I did not know I could shout that loud.* 'My best friend and her children are cold dead. And you want me to find a good pew to feed your ambition?'

Dee turned, face hardening with fury, and raised a finger to her face. 'I am sorry that your friend has died. But Elizabeth is in danger. My reputation is in danger. You can be the grieving friend later. Right now, madam, you are my apprentice in saving our realm from evil. Come at once.' He turned and marched away.

I hate you. I hate you. I hate you.

They walked into the church with only a look to Vicar Tyrwhit who made a nervous nod to Dee, then a concerned glance at Margaretta's red-eyed misery. They pushed into a pew towards the back and Dee looked around to ensure they could see everyone.

Satisfied, he asked, 'What says the herb woman?'

Margaretta refused to look at him and kept her voice low and cold. 'She thinks it is a mushroom called Destroying Angel. All the symptoms fit. You eat, feel well, fall with flux two or two and a half days later and die yellow.'

Dee's eyes widened. 'I was right. The poisoning is on a Sunday. So, Baphomet will make his move today.'

The service was long and solemn. Vicar Tyrwhit preached about protecting thy neighbour as a brother. If they knew anyone walking through this life alone, they should reach out their hand and offer the comfort of a shared fire, broken bread and the warmth of friendship.

Oh, you are such a good man. This whole congregation knows that they have evil among them. The Huguenots, obvious by their dress, are all tense. See the way they glance at each other as your words ring out. Fear is filling your church.

At last, the vicar descended from the pulpit, went to the communion table and blessed the bread and wine. The congregation started to rise, the first being the front pew where clothes were rich. After five pews had walked forward to take the bread and wine, the first of the Huguenots rose. Dee leaned sideways and whispered. 'Watch for those who do not walk forward with a wife or husband. Count them. And take care not to miss anyone.'

I hate you. You want me to count as my heart breaks. I think you feel my thoughts – even though I can never feel you. You wince each time I think how much I hate you.

When the last person had returned to their seat, Dee leaned again. 'How many?'

'Seven adults, including Mabelain. The boy Milo appears to have no father for he was only with his mother, so I counted her.'

He sighed. 'That's a lot of victims.'

As the congregation filed out, Dee hung back to the very end and then moved forward to greet the vicar who was standing with Josef Mabelain. 'A good service, father, and wise words.'

Tyrwhit looked pale. 'I fear for my flock. What do I do?'

Dee put a hand on his shoulder. 'Say nothing, keep your eyes open and tell us anything that worries you.' He turned to Mabelain. 'Has Walsingham seen you?'

The man nodded. 'I told him I will enquire, but I know only of healing herbs.'

Dee made a self-satisfied smile. 'I thought as much and so have used my own knowledge. Baphomet is giving out poison in your gathering at the warehouse – a mushroom.'

Mabelain supressed a little cry and his hand went to his mouth. 'No. It cannot possibly be one of our people.'

Dee nodded. 'I am afraid it is very possible.'

Panic and confusion. Your head is a blur. You feel threat.

The small man shifted awkwardly on his twisted foot. 'How so? We all eat from one pot.'

Dee nodded. 'Let us go to your gathering and pay special attention to the Huguenot's who live alone. See who speaks to them, sit close or hands them food.'

Mabelain shook his head. 'If we just watch, then another might die. No, I cannot agree to that. I will serve the food. We will see who seeks to help me. That must be enough.'

Dee walked into the warehouse, followed by Margaretta, still trying to hold in her distress. Men were arranging chairs and stools. In the far corner, Milo and his mother were taking the cloth off a basket of bread while a younger maid was lighting the brazier for the pottage cauldron.

You are wondering why we are in your midst. Words are

whispered in French. I understand nothing but I feel your worry. This is the great Doctor Dee. Some of you fear him. Others nod but do not smile.

Dee turned to Mabelain. 'Is everyone here?'

The Frenchman looked around. 'Yes... nearly. We have a new member, a silversmith, but he does not come every week. He was not in Church. Maybe not in London.'

Dee glanced up at the suspicious faces. 'Tell them I come as a friend.'

The man limped over and raised his hands to get attention as he was a head shorter than any other adult there. He pointed back at Dee and spoke in a low voice. The words *amis* was used several times and the huddle nodded. Milo reached out for his mother's hand.

The meeting progressed. First talking, then a woman sang a mournful song as everyone stared at the ground. Mabelain explained, 'She sings in memory of those slain by the Guise. The slaughtered martyrs.'

Oh God, I see the images again. The severed arm; the screaming child; the wailing woman. The noise. The smell of blood. I feel...

Dee reached out and held her shoulder as he murmured to the Frenchman. 'Margaretta is a sensitive woman. Tales of Wassy upset her. I will take her to get some air. You watch those who live alone. Note who sits by them.' As the other man nodded, he took Margaretta's arm and led her to the door.

Outside she gulped air and leaned against the wall.

Dee stood in front of her, his face close. 'What are you feeling? Do you feel hatred? Fear? Revenge? Evil? Who is it coming from?'

'The slaughter at Wassy. It is as if I were in the midst of it. Josef's memory is strong – and terrible.'

'You need to block that and feel the others. Our devil might be in there. Now concentrate, woman.'

Margaretta closed her eyes and took a deep, shuddering breath. 'Do you have beating heart in that cold breast of yours

– or just a swinging stone? My friend and her children lie dead just half a mile down the river. Sam is screaming his grief – and you want me to concentrate on other people's feelings. Really?'

Dee's eyes narrowed. 'I have already said, I am sorry you are saddened. But we cannot allow sentiment to block our investigation.'

'Well, I am sorry Doctor. But I cannot block my sentiment.'

'Do not shout at me, woman.'

'It is the only way you hear me. I am going to my friends.' She shoved him away and strode down the street, ignoring his furious demands to return and do her duty. She still had his anger ringing in her ears when she reached the river and hailed a wherry.

Chapter Thirty-One

'Why? Why *my* wife? Why *my* boys? Has God not taken enough from me? He took my first family and now the next? Why?' Sam bent over and howled like an injured dog. Behind him Goodwife Tovey pressed a linen to her eyes. Next to her, Tillie, her adopted daughter, sobbed. The only person not crying was Master Tovey, who just sat still in the corner, staring at the fire, face twisted in grief.

Margaretta took Sam by the shoulders and put her head to his. 'I am so sorry, Sam. The world is a lesser place without her... and your little ones.'

He reached out, put his hands around her waist and screamed out his pain.

An hour later, Sam was seated at the table, Goodwife Tovey coaxing him to take a beaker of wine and bread. Margaretta sat next to him, still holding his hand.

The sadness of this place is almost too much to bear. I can feel Sam's distress pulsing through my hand. Goodwife Tovey keeps fussing around, finding anything to do, patting her husband each time she passes. My word, you are a different woman to the harsh and bitter snip-tongue who ordered me around in the house of Sir Cecil fifteen years ago. Love found you in the shape of Master Tovey and the good woman you are was released. Lottie moved from being the silly maid you snapped at, to being a daughter. Sam, when they married, became your son. But best of all was Tillie – the wailing orphan who stole your heart and made you the mother you had always dreamed of being. I see the love between you. Tillie is a young woman now. All grown up. But you are still her mammie. Not the mammie who birthed her – but the mother who gave her a life of hope.

The conversation was muted, factual, simmering with sadness. Lottie had kissed her husband goodbye at dawn, told Goodwife she felt unwell at nine, started sweating at ten and gasped her last breath at midday. She did not know her younger boy fell sick at eleven – then the eldest within the hour. Sam had been out on the river as usual, working as a wherry manager for the morning before returning to run the boat-building yard for the afternoon. A young apprentice had been sent out to find him. But it was too late. He ran through the door to see his wife dead and cold next to his boys. The morgue men took them away. No coffin. No service. Just the hope of a prayer in the church on Sunday – for Lottie, two children and every other soul in the area who had been snatched away by the Sweat.

There were long silences. Tillie cried again and Goodwife held her close. Master Tovey read from his Bible and Sam glared at the table before saying he had no time for God's word and rose to leave. Goodwife took her husband's hand and told him not to be offended. Sam was only angry. He would return to the Lord. The old man grunted, nodded, and swiped a tear from his eye declaring that Lottie was as good to him as any daughter. Then he reached out to Tillie and hugged her close.

Goodwife turned to Margaretta. 'Go with Sam. He will be on the riverbank. If anyone can comfort him, it is you.'

Sam was staring and rocking. Margaretta sat by him on the damp grass. After a few minutes he spoke. 'What will I do, Missy Margaretta? What is left for me?'

'You move through time, Sam. You keep living, keep working, keep trying, keep breathing, keep putting one foot in front of the other – and keep praying for them every day. In time, you will remember them with a smile instead of a rage of tears. In time, you will look around and see the world again instead of the dark cloud of grief.'

Sam reached out and took her hand. 'I have you to thank, Missy. You opened my eyes to her goodness.'

And I broke my own heart in the doing of it. I pushed you to Lottie thinking I was going to carry my mother and brother for ever. When you learned to love Lottie, I realised how much I loved you. The feel of your hand in mine. But this gesture is not feeling for me – as I feel for you. You think only of her. 'I knew you were meant for each other.'

Sam made a weak smile and nodded. 'And I thought you were the one. But you were right, Missy. Lottie was my girl.'

Oh, this hurts. I still feel the loss of you. 'She was your girl from the day she saw you on those river steps and jumped in your wherry calling it a ship.'

Sam gave a laugh, cracked with a sob. 'Do you remember how she used to squeak? Like a mouse who had found a truckle of cheese. I will miss that every day I have left on this earth.' He squeezed Margaretta's hand harder. 'Don't stay away, Missy. I need a friend. Someone who recalls my Lottie.'

'I will always be here for you, Sam.' *And God forgive me for even thinking of those old feelings. My friend is dead. Damn my bad mind.* 'You are getting cold, Sam. Let us get you back for warm wine.'

Another strangled laugh with a sob. 'Lottie and I used to sit here and make our plans.' Tears fell. 'We never noticed the cold. Her soul would warm an icicle.'

Oh, this hurts. 'Her soul is all around you Sam. It is in the earth, the water, the air and the fire.'

Sam nodded. 'I hope so, Missy. For I cannot face life without her.'

Pain, pain, pain.

Chapter Thirty-Two

It was after four of the clock when Margaretta wheeled her horse into the yard at Mortlake and clambered down onto the mounting stone, blinking to steady her eyes. Clarissa had given her three goblets of strong wine and a hug of kind words when she arrived back to collect her horse. The ride along the southern bank of the Thames had been long, cold, wet and, with every step of her stead, her pain had grown. She looked around. All was quiet. But then a scrape of a door and her heart sank. There was Bela, head cocked on one side, mouth in a sly smile. 'The Doctor is angry. Told the mistress you are no good to him with weepy eyes and a muddled mind.'

She took a deep breath ready to respond. But a door opened behind her and out stepped Mother Dee, her gnarled finger pointing. 'Button your mouth, Lemon-head. And run back to your rathole.'

She did not wait for an answer but turned to Margaretta and held out her arms. 'Come, girl. Johnny told me your woes. You need a mother for a while.' And Margaretta cried again.

When light started to fade, Margaretta crossed the yard to John Dee's laboratory. He was bent over his desk, looking at the cards, scribbling notes, and did not hear her enter. She stood by the table. 'I am sorry, Doctor.'

He lifted a hand, pointed to the stool at his side. 'Sit.'

She placed the packaged salve on the table to which he gave a short glance and grunted, then turned back to his writing.

A few agonising minutes later he raised his head. 'Worry made me harsh. I am sorry.'

Am I really hearing this?

Dee cleared his throat. 'Mother heard me talking to Katherine and spoke her mind. Apparently, I am the worst of my father.'

I cannot feel you, though I see your regret. 'Bela said you are very angry.'

'Mother calls her a lemon-headed rat.'

'Your mother is wise.'

Dee chuckled and patted her hand. 'Just remember that grief takes time to heal. Make sure you are not burned by a widower's fire.'

I feel threat. Not from you but your words. 'What do you mean?'

'Just keep that advice fixed in your mind.' Dee tapped on the cards. 'I asked the cards to tell me what and who to look for. Look at what I pulled.'

There were five cards in front of Dee. Margaretta turned them so that she could see the images and shuddered. 'My God, the first card is terrible. A man lying dead, ten swords driven into his back. Beyond is a black and stormy sky.' She looked up. 'I counted seven single Huguenots stepping up to take the bread and wine. Three are already dead. Surely, this does not tell us all those people will die?'

Dee nodded slowly. 'Maybe not all. If I am right and Baphomet's shapes spell out Elizabeth then another six will die. We need to alert Vicar Tyrwhit.'

'But this card has ten swords.'

Dee looked grim. 'The name Elizabeth has nine letters. Nine dead Huguenots for the terror before death. The tenth sword is for Elizabeth herself. Puis, la mort.'

Margaretta stared as she took in the threat and then turned to the other cards. 'The Tower. We have already seen this. It foretells disaster and threat to those in power. Also, the Five of Pentacles. Two poor people outside a beautiful church window in the cold. One on crutches.' She looked more closely. 'Could this be Josef Mabelain? He is crippled with that twisted foot.'

Dee contemplated. 'Good thinking Margaretta. Catholic churches are known for their glorious windows and their priests expel the Huguenots.'

'And Josef Mabelain recalls Wassy, where people were murdered and ejected.' She picked up the fourth card. 'The Devil. The card of warning and disaster. The pentacle above the Evil One is upside down, just like Baphomet's calling card.'

Dee sighed. 'The cards are darkening – warning us that disaster is coming fast. But we do not know from where or whom.'

'But we do know a powerful woman is involved. We saw her in our first scrying. The Queen of Pentacles. Could Baphomet be a woman?'

Dee raised his eyebrows. 'Interesting thought, but the women who threaten Elizabeth would not bloody their own hands. Mary Queen of Scots, Queen Catherine de Medici, or even the wives of the Northern Lords who see their people swing on gibbets. They would not risk their own necks. Nor would they be strong enough to carry a man up an alley.'

'What about Lady Douglas Sheffield?'

Dee frowned. 'The woman who asked me to do her horoscope?'

'Yes. She is in a dalliance with the Earl of Leicester. Blanche is trying to stop it. But that woman is passionate for him.'

Dee slammed his hand on the desk 'Why was I not told?'

'I thought it just a flirtation.'

Dee leaned forward, his face inches from hers. 'No secrets.

I detest secrets.' He rose and gathered up the cards. 'Get your cloak and have the horses saddled. We ride to Cecil.'

'So late? What about robbers?'

A wry smile. 'We will howl that I am a conjuror. Sometimes it is useful.' He picked up the salve. 'And I will be the one to conjure away Elizabeth's pain and be loved for it.'

You are unbelievable.

Chapter Thirty-Three

Cecil was dozing at his desk, candles burning low, when Burcott admitted them to his office. He looked up, groggy, then took a deep breath and straightened his back. 'It is late, John.'

Dee ignored the rebuke and peered at the book on Cecil's desk. 'I was reading Cicero for inspiration on how to lead men through threat.' He snatched it into his lap. 'No. You cannot borrow it.'

Ah, you have also lost a few precious tomes to my magpie master. I have no doubt I catalogued them and set them on the shelves of his great library.

Dee sniffed his indignation and turned back to Burcott. 'I am sure William would wish us provided with warm wine as we have tramped our horses through the dark and the cold and across the river to furnish his curiosity.'

Cecil nodded and ordered, 'And then fetch Master Walsingham from the library... where he is reading with my absolute trust.' Dee ignored the barb and sat by the fire, resting his chin on his fingertips, in a display of contemplation. When Walsingham entered, he began his presentation. 'The threat is growing. Today we learned that there are seven more single Huguenots at All Hallows, which means further deaths... though I hopefully averted that by having Mabelain – your spy – hand out the food. I have deduced that there are ten deaths planned, Elizabeth being the tenth victim. A powerful female is involved in the plot.'

'How do you know all this detail and the number of deaths?' snapped Cecil.

'I just know.'

Cecil limped across his office and pulled a chair towards Dee. 'What have you used this time? Cards? Crystals? The madness of talking with Angels? I want proof, not conjuring.'

Dee sniffed again. 'Yet you are happy for me to use the cards to give advice to betroth your daughter to Philip Sidney and not that feral imp, the Earl of Oxford.'

Cecil glowered. 'Affairs of the heart and money are very different to affairs of our Queen's safety, John. Now, give me your thinking.'

Dee stood and started to pace. 'Catholics want Elizabeth thrown from her throne for her religion. Huguenots are living proof of Elizabeth's protection of Protestantism. Slaughtering them creates the terror before death. The fact that they belong to a church known for Catholic and Templar martyrs, deepens the message. So, who is the powerful woman?' He raised a hand to stop Cecil interrupting to ask again how he knew. 'Norfolk thinks of Mary Queen of Scots – but you insist she is well-guarded.' He raised an eyebrow and made a crooked smile at Cecil. 'I do hope you are right, William.'

Cecil groaned and rubbed between his brows. 'Lord Huntingdon has clamped down her freedoms and has everything checked. Apparently, she just sits and sews every day with Lady Bess, talking of fripperies such as satins, silks, hair dressing and… well women's matters. But we have no evidence of further plotting.'

Walsingham snarled, 'Fie. The Scottish whore is a schemer using any weakness in those around her. Lady Bess Shrewsbury is as ambitious as her charge and her weakling husband…'

Cecil slammed his hand on the desk. 'Enough. You cannot speak so roughly of those above you in station.'

Walsingham glowered. 'The Scottish whore…'

'And do not use such language or harshness of words about women in front of a gentle-minded woman,' snapped Dee pointing at Margaretta. 'I say again, this lady does not deserve your rough tongue, sir.'

And even after fifteen years you surprise me. I like you again. I just give a small nod of appreciation.

After a few tense seconds, Cecil commanded Walsingham to, 'Tell John the news you received today.'

'Prestall is claiming a definite plot to poison the Queen by black magic, and it comes from France.'

Dee started to mutter about hocus-pocus meddlers, but Cecil silenced him. 'You may dislike Prestall, John. But we cannot ignore a threat so alike to what is happening here.'

Dee huffed and started wincing in thought. 'Last year, that gutless ape was promoting Mary Queen of Scots and the Northern Rebellion. Now he changes alliance in the blink of a rat's eye. Does he say who makes the threat?'

'No,' said Walsingham.

Cecil cut in. 'There are only two possibilities. The Guise faction – the blood family of Mary Queen of Scots; or her marriage family – the royal household – led by Catherine de Medici.' He paused. 'And Catherine de Medici poisons.'

'Certainly, a powerful woman,' muttered Dee. 'But she negotiates to match her son to Elizabeth. What about the Guise – the blood family? Any suspicion there? Any powerful women?'

Cecil shook his head. 'We know they promote Mary of the Scots to be our Queen, that they are Catholic fanatics, that they kill Huguenots, but—'

'We have no intelligence about them using poison and their women are not powerful,' finished Walsingham.

Dee poured more wine and began to pace and jab his finger in the air. 'Norfolk gets messages from Mary in cypher.' He turned and pointed at Walsingham. 'My gut tells me that Norfolk is linked to your spy, Ridolfi, who is linked to France.

Yet you insist you have turned him back to English loyalty. I ask again – are you sure?'

You scut. I felt that link and you use it again for your own glory.

Walsingham jumped up in fury, making his chair clatter over. 'I am not the handler of a traitor. And I will not be insulted by—'

'Stop,' shouted Cecil. 'We do not have time for arguments, nor can we question Catherine de Medici. But we can find out if this the next evil scheme of Mary Queen of Scots? That is the next step in your investigation, John. You will go north.'

Dee jumped and started shaking his head. 'No. I am needed here in case there are more killings.' He pointed at Walsingham. 'Send your spymaster. He speaks French like Mary.'

'You are my spy, 007. Now prepare to travel to Tutbury and use your advantage. Uncover the mind, the thoughts and feelings of Mary Queen of Scots.' He pointed at Margaretta without looking at her.

Oh, God. He knows my secret.

Back at Mortlake, Dee slammed the door of his office, stamped across the room, sat heavily behind his desk, and roared, 'Ten days. That is what it will take. It is one hundred and twenty miles to Tutbury. Damn Cecil.'

In the corner, Thomas Digges watched wide-eyed, then blushed and bent his head when Margaretta looked in his direction. 'Good evening, Mr Digges.'

He nodded, still head bent and mumbled a greeting as he started to gather his books and papers, stuffing them into his bag as fast as he could.

Oh, sir, I can feel the heat of embarrassment coming off you. But I am afraid I must play this if I am to get the better of Lemon-head. 'You look tired, sir. Maybe your bed is less than restful.'

The man gave a muffled yelp and made for the door. Predictably, Dee noticed nothing. Margaretta turned to him. 'Cecil suggested he knew our secret... my secret. Have you told him.'

'No,' scowled Dee. 'Who have you told?'

'Do you take me for a damn fool, Doctor? The witchcraft bill has been in place seven years now, every day of them a worry in case someone notices. Would I expose myself to accusation of sorcery?'

Dee's eyes narrowed. 'Who has guessed?'

'Blanche ap Harri.'

Dee raised his brows. 'Then speak with her... and tell her your special gifts tell you I deserve more recognition. In the meantime, I will send the salve made by Clarissa for Elizabeth's leg. That will soften her. You do the rest.'

Damn you. Here I stand scared of being accused of sorcery and being sent to the ducking chair, and you try to find a path to Blanche's favour. 'I will see her when we get back. I must see my sister before we leave tomorrow.'

'We are not leaving tomorrow. We leave Wednesday. I want to know if there is another body.'

But Sir Cecil said...'

'To hell with Sir Cecil. This is my investigation.'

Margaretta left the office allowing Dee time to plan their journey north. Outside, Bela was standing in the shadows and stepped out. Margaretta lifted her candle and smiled. 'Ah. Our little dishwater doxy.'

Bela lifted her hand as if to strike and then pulled it back, but the hand was still in a fist. 'I will tell Mistress Katherine that it was you.'

'Then you are a fool as well as a strumpet.'

Bela's face twisted in fury, but her eyes showed alarm. She turned and stamped down the corridor as Margaretta watched. *I will have you in the gutter yet.*

Chapter Thirty-Four

As the sun rose the following day, Margaretta, Huw, Grace and Siôn Jenkins were standing outside Susan's house. She patted her brother's arm. 'This will be your greatest test. If you can fend off Susan's forked tongue, you can batter those Vintry boys into silence.' Grace took his arm and squeezed her strength into him. Huw stared straight ahead, saying nothing.

Susan was sitting in front of a miserable fire, giving more smoke than warmth. Jack and Maria, sat together on a wooden bench at the far side of the room. Jack began to rock. Maria stared. Susan looked up, eyes heavy and red-rimmed. 'A delegation at this hour? I suppose you come to gloat.'

'No, Susan. We come to rescue.' Margaretta sat before her sister. 'I suggest you close your mouth, curtail your tongue and concentrate on what our brother has to say.'

She turned to Huw who was staring ahead, his shoulders as tight as knotted wood. At his side was Grace, and behind him stood Siôn. Huw took a deep breath. 'I will manage The Vintry for you, sister. You, Jack and Maria will have income to keep you in food and comfort. Your husband will be given as much aid as any physik can provide. But from now, I am master. Grace will work with me. Jack will learn the trade.'

Susan stood, her face white with anger. 'No. I will not

have our family business ruined by a half-wit. Angus would never...'

Margaretta stood, but she was not fast enough to speak before Huw stepped forward and spoke, his voice strong and loud. 'Silence sister. You have no choice. Your husband is mouldering out his last days, his mind rotted by wine, his body by immoral living. You are no longer the sister who can flaunt and jaunt her way through life. You can no longer taunt and jibe at me. I am no half-wit, but you have not the full-wit to see that you need me.' He reached for Grace's hand. 'And my wife too.'

My God. Even I am speechless. Grace looks up at you, her eyes glassy with tears of pride. You and she have practiced this speech repeatedly until your voice stayed strong. Behind you Siôn is trying to control a proud smile.

Susan let out a wail of fury. 'You cannot speak to me like that.' She looked to Grace. 'And you are just a servant. How dare you...'

Grace lifted her head. 'No, Mistress. I stopped being a servant the day I walked out of your door. I am a wife and partner to my husband. And right now, I, and Huw, are your salvation.' She looked around at the bare room, all the fineries she once dusted now sold for food. 'Your star is falling, Mistress McFadden. I suggest you get the papers of your business and let us stop you falling as far as the gutter – your children with you.'

Susan turned on Margaretta. 'This is your doing. You are living out your curse. You are a witch. You—'

'That is enough, sister,' shouted Huw. 'If it were not for Margaretta's pleading, I would not be saving you. If our dada and mam raised a witch, it is you. Now bring me the papers of ownership.'

'I will not.' Susan turned her back and folded her arms.

This is exactly what you did as a child when given orders to work. I want to step in, but Siôn is staring at me in warning. I must not undermine you, little brother.

'Then you must save the business and manage the Vintry boys yourself,' snarled Huw. 'It is your choice, sister. Take a helping hand or get your own hands dirty.'

The atmosphere went brittle. Jack rocked and pulled at his hair. Maria's attempt to stop him resulting in a wail of alarm.

Huw looked to Margaretta. 'We will go. Susan has made her foolish choice.' He turned and walked to the door.

Before he turned the handle, Susan broke. 'What about my children?'

'As I said, Jack will come to work with me. I understand him. So does Grace. Maria will stay here with you, but she will have a tutor. My niece is not to live a life of dependency like you.'

Susan was shaking. 'And what of me?'

'You will nurse your husband until God releases him from this realm. You will be provided for once we stop the Vintry boys stealing from you. This house will be repaired.'

Maria ran across and took her mother by the shoulders. 'Uncle Huw is right. What will become of us if you refuse?'

Susan crumpled. Maria forlornly patted her shoulder as Jack rocked harder and grunted his distress. Margaretta kneeled, and once more held her sister as she sobbed. Grace moved to Jack and calmed him as she used to do.

Half of an hour later, Huw walked out of the front door holding the papers of McFadden's wine merchants of The Vintry, London. He shook the hand of Siôn Jenkins and they agreed to go to the business the next day. Then Huw would see the lawyer, Will Fleetwood.

'You do not need me, Huw,' smiled Siôn.

'But I would like you there, friend. We are good business partners. I think we can build the best vintners in London. I want you in the business.' He put his hand out to his wife. 'And so does Grace. We agreed last night.'

And the deal was done.

Chapter Thirty-Five

It was only late morning when Margaretta reached the Tovey boatyard. The air was rich with the ring of hammers on nails and saws through wood. A few men looked up and one shouted to his master that a visitor was at the gate.

Master Tovey walked over, his wooden leg making the familiar lurch of his gait. In an instant, Margaretta was transported back to the day a wide-eyed, young Lottie had declared that a man who walks click-step, click-step had arrived at the door and made Goodwife Barker smile. Within hours a sad and bitter woman had been laughing like a tinkling bell. *Oh, you good man, you have brought so much love into other's lives – Goodwife, Tillie who you took to your own, Lottie, Sam and their children. Pain rips at your heart. Life is surely cruel to the good.*

'My I am surely glad to see you Margaretta,' he greeted in his deep Bristolian accent. 'Sam has declared every day that he needs your kind company.'

'I will do what I can to soothe him, Master Tovey. But I think you are all bereft, as am I.'

The big man's eyes welled with tears. ''Tis true, Missy. Lottie and her boys might well have been my own flesh and blood. No one can ever replace her.'

Pain, pain.

Master Tovey looked abashed. 'Forgive me, Margaretta. I forget she was your dear friend. Sadness is writ all over your face.'

Inside the house, Goodwife Tovey and Tilly were kneading dough. Tilly ran to the stairs to shout up to Sam, while the older woman brushed her hands on an apron and hugged Margaretta, whispering into her ear. 'He has not left his bed in days. See if you can get him to walk for it is good for a troubled mind.' There was a thump above of someone getting up and then footsteps on the wooden stairs.

Sam was dishevelled, pale of face and eyes heavy with dark circles. He made a weak smile. 'It is kind of you to come a visiting, Missy.' Tears fell down his cheeks.

'Let us walk and talk, Sam. Bring a good coat for the March wind is surely biting cold.'

'Not as cold as my heart, Missy. I think it is iced over.'

Outside, Sam made straight for the river, saying they should walk where he had been happiest. For over two hours they trod the river path, Margaretta listening, Sam slowly talking out all his memories. Little slivers of his life with Lottie that added up to a picture of total love. At last, he stopped, turned and looked into her eyes. 'I am sorry, Missy. I speak only of my loss. I forget you lost your one great love too. The man Christopher Careye. Lottie never did tell me the full tale, but she was sore worried for you.'

Margaretta nodded. 'Yes, Christopher was dear to me, but he was never really mine, Sam. I thought he would be – but fate took that away before his life was ended.' *Oh, if I could tell you truth. Yes, I loved Christopher; yes, I thought he was to be my man; yes, I thought I was to be his. But he was not you. They say a first love never dies; you just learn to live without it. My hands twitch to reach out and comfort you.*

Sam gently wiped the tear from her cheek. A small smile and then two strong arms pulled her close as he buried his face in her hair and whispered, 'Don't stay away, Missy. We understand one another, you and I. Two broken hearts can help each other with friendship. Let us be kind friends as we remember the ones we have both lost.'

Pain, pain.

Chapter Thirty-Six

Wednesday morning dawned cold, grey and wet again. Margaretta packed her bags and went to the kitchens to give orders to Bela. 'While I am away, you will be in charge of cleaning, washing of clothes, keeping people fed and the rats out of the flour sacks.'

'I do that anyway.'

'Only because I kick your door every morning.' Margaretta turned to leave. 'And remember you are in Mortlake, not the stews of Southwark.'

Bela's ire was halted by knocking at the door. It was Josef Mabelain. Margaretta greeted him and tried to block his view of Bela who stared at him in horror. 'Is there news, Master Mabelain?' He shook his head. *I feel relief from you. And triumph.* 'Please follow me to the doctor's office.'

He limped over the threshold and followed Margaretta along the passage, his foot scraping along the stone floor. He shuffled in and made a small bow to Dee. 'I have had reports from Bethnal Green, Spitalfields and Clerkenwell. All our fellow Huguenot's are alive this blessed morning.'

Dee pointed to the chair in front of his desk. 'Please sit, sir. This is good news indeed. Our strategy of you serving the food has worked. Who usually gives out the pottage?'

Mabelain shifted in his seat and shook his head. 'No one

person, Doctor. But we are respectful of age and so the young will serve the older members of our group.'

Dee turned to Margaretta. 'Get our notes. I think I recall there were four younger people there.'

Mabelain nodded. 'Indeed, but I cannot believe they would do harm. Three are women and, as you know, the boy Milo is a simpleton.'

You are thinking of a man. I see no face though. You feel nervous.

Margaretta picked up some of Dee's papers and placed them on the desk before him, whispering, '*Gofynna am y dyn. Arian.*' Ask about a man. Silver.

Mabelain looked between them, suspicious. 'What tongue does your servant speak?'

Dee wagged a hand. 'She comes from the Welsh hills and sometimes forgets herself. Because I am descended from Welsh Royalty and even Arthur himself, I understand her muttering.'

Damn you. I speak the language of Heaven. And if you descend from Arthur, then Bela is the Queen of Sheba.

'What about the man you mentioned. A silversmith I think,' asked Dee.

'Young Devereaux? He is recently arrived in London. Maybe four weeks. He seems a devout and goodly man.'

'What else do you know of him?'

Mabelain shrugged. 'Little. He is a silversmith, recently out of apprenticeship. That is why he was able to gain his papers and come to England.'

'And why did he not attend church or your meeting on Sunday?'

Mabelain shrugged, raised his hands in a silent expression of not knowing.

Dee frowned. 'Strange. His face. Anything strange about it. Does he have two eyes?'

Mabelain was quiet a second. Then a shrug. 'He always keeps his hat on. Even in Church.'

I sense your rising discomfort, even fear, and nod to my master.

'He has attended the warehouse meeting?'

'Of course. He is welcomed into our community.' The Frenchman's eyes were wide. '*Mon Dieu*. You do not think…'

'What do you know of his connections in France?'

'He worked as an apprentice in Paris. His master served the French Court. Devereaux told us he could no longer abide adorning the people who would see us slayed.'

Dee frowned. 'Connected to the French Court and worked for Catholics. Are you quite sure he is a Huguenot?'

Mabelain gulped. 'He showed us his Méreaux coin – the sign we always use to identify ourselves to others of our faith.' He took a silver coin from his pocket and placed it before Dee. It was small with an image of Jesus standing among trees, a staff in one hand, a trumpet in another and sheep at his feet.

Dee turned it over to show the image of a sun and a tablet with writing on the other side. 'Hells' teeth, man. If he is a silversmith, he can make a hundred Méreaux coins. Find him. Watch him. Ask if he has any connection with an herbalist. And, for the love of God, do not let him serve the pottage. Whatever you find, you pass to Walsingham. I leave for Tutbury today but will go to Cecil and have this man's background investigated.'

Margaretta cut in, 'Is the silversmith tall?'

Mabelain shook his head but Dee wagged his hands. 'A mere detail. Any man can be made to look tall.'

Damn you. It is one of the most striking features of this devilish killer. I glare, but you are already basking in your own satisfaction.

Mabelain clasped his hands together in prayer. 'Let us pray, Monsieur Dee, that you have identified the evil one – and I am honoured to assist you.'

Relief. You feel gladdened. Not surprising, because my master just might have found our killer.

Margaretta took Mabelain to the door. He put his head

down as he walked past Bela to cross the yard. *You poor man, I feel your shame when she stares at you, her lip curling in disgust. Little do you know that her soul is as twisted as your foot.*

There was a shout from Dee's office and she ran back to find him pacing, smacking his hands together. 'Our first breakthrough. What did you feel of Mabelain?'

'Relief when you honed in on the silversmith.'

'Good. It all fits. The time of his arrival, he served food, Catholic connections and he works metal. What did Milo say of Baphomet?'

'Silver horns and silver hooves. Black face.'

'Yes. By sheer wit and deduction, I have identified the killer. He could have brought the mushrooms from France.'

'But Mabelain shook his head when I asked if he was tall. Both Milo and Alice said that Baphomet is taller than a man.'

Dee sat down at his desk, drumming fingers on the wood. 'Shoe pattens can add inches to a person's height. Mix that with horns and fear and anyone would appear bigger, taller. As I have always said, Baphomet is flesh and blood and hiding in plain sight.

But, Doctor…'

'No, Margaretta. My wit has won through and I am on a path to glory. All we do now is find the connection to Mary Queen of Scots and give Cecil the evidence he needs to have her dealt with. Now get ready.'

'We are going to get evidence to kill a queen?'

Dee looked indignant. 'We are going to save a real queen. Our Queen. Elizabeth. Now, as I said, get ready.

Dee bade farewell to his mother and a tearful Katherine, who insisted on kissing each cheek twice for every day he would be away. Margaretta mounted her horse and glowered at Bela, then called farewell to Mother Dee who was glowering at Katherine.

Two hours later, having crossed the Thames on the horse ferry and ridden to Cecil's house to report on progress and the need to investigate Devereaux, they made their way to the great North Road and began their long journey to Mary Queen of Scots.

Part Two

Tutbury Castle, Staffordshire

Chapter Thirty-Seven

At last, Tutbury Castle loomed out of the mist. It had been a hard ride of forty miles a day, changing horses at every inn they had stayed in along the way. However, it was four days in which John Dee had been able to tutor his apprentice in the long and sorry saga of Mary Queen of Scots. Here they would find her miserable and her goalers too, as Elizabeth was keen for her cousin to be well guarded but not so keen to pay for it. Hence, she had chosen the Earl of Shrewsbury and his wife Bess of Hardwick as they were rich beyond riches – for now.

It was high on a mound rising out of the flat, boggy, bleak and barren land. The horses made slow progress up the hill, slipping on the greasy stones of a rough path. The packhorse carrying Dee's box of books had to be pulled hard by the reins. A miserable guard held up his hand to stop them at the gate and gave not a care for Dee's fury that he was not recognised and admitted with a fanfare. He shrugged. 'This is a prison, sir,' he said.

Inside, the vista was no more welcoming – just a cluster of old buildings within a high wall, towers on each corner. To the left, a long two-storey building, with a few chimneys belching smoke and the promise of a little warmth. To the right, a smaller building, obviously a dwelling, one window lit. At the far end, decrepit outbuildings, a stable and stores.

High walls were no protection against a bitter wind. But even the icy blasts and the woodsmoke could not take away the stench of open privy pits.

A few stable boys ran out over muddy, rough ground, pulling oilcloths over their shoulders against the rain. As they took the horses to the far stables, a servant emerged from the long building. 'Greetings, Doctor Dee. My Earl of Shrewsbury expects you. Food, drink and a warm fire awaits.' He looked to Margaretta. 'I will have a maid take your servant to…'

'My assistant, not servant,' snapped Dee, ignoring the man's confusion. 'Take us to our hosts. I want to get to work quickly.'

Inside, the smell of damp and mould was overpowering, and limed walls were patchy with black. Dee held a linen to his nose and coughed as they were led along a corridor and up a spiral stairway into a dark panelled room, the windows covered with heavy cloths. Candles gave light and at least a fire burned in the grate. Before they even sat, a door opened in the far corner and three people entered. The first man smiled and walked over to Dee, his hand offered in greeting. 'Good Doctor Dee. Welcome.' He turned to Margaretta and frowned but gave a small bow. 'Mistress.' He was a kindly looking man, pale skinned and a long face with eyes that spoke of worry. The hand he held out was gnarled and red.

Fretting seeps from under your skin. You are a man riven with worry – as if the world is upon your shoulders.

The woman was next forward, greeting Dee with warmth and asking about the journey, listening with a look of concerned sympathy as he listed the trials and evils of riding through March rains and easterly winds. She nodded to a servant who poured him a large glass of wine from a flagon warming by the fire. Lady Bess Shrewsbury bid him sit and get the damp from his bones, apologising for the coldness of the place. Apparently, it was only ever meant as a hunting lodge for the summer and they had been given little time to make it ready for winter living. She looked around with uncontained derision at her own house, then changed the subject, asking Dee if he has seen her son of late, for he had been taken into the house of the Earl of Leicester. She purred her delight that he had gained such a place and won the favour of Robert Dudley.

So, this is the famous Bess. Blanche has told me of you – wealthier than Elizabeth due to clever marriages. Our Queen loves her one day and rages against her another. Maybe they are a little alike. Haughty, determined, arrogant and strong, yet a gentle mother to her brood. When you speak of your son, I feel triumph.

All through the greetings, the second man stood back, evidently irritated at being excluded. Eventually, he could restrain himself no more and interrupted. 'Doctor Dee. We have not been introduced. I am Lord Huntingdon. Here to ensure our prisoner is properly guarded.' The voice was high, imperious, arrogant.

The atmosphere iced as the Shrewsbury's turned to glare at him.

Dee nodded. 'I was told you would be here, sir.' He gave a half smile and turned back to the Shrewsbury's. 'Have you been appraised of our mission?'

Earl Shrewsbury nodded then rubbed at the gnarled hand, rocking a little as if overcome with more worry. 'Cecil sent word of some dark deeds in London and that you wish to ensure that our guest…' He shot a look at Huntingdon who was raising one eyebrow. '… I mean our prisoner, has had no opportunity to involve herself in such matters. I assure you Doctor Dee, we have been diligent. I refute any suggestion of our being lax or lazy in our protection of our Queen or realm.'

Ah, so clever Cecil has told you we are here to prove her innocence. Yet we are really here to prove her complicity. But your belief will lower your guard. And my master, as clever as Cecil, has noted this. Look at that sly smile.

Earl Shrewsbury pushed a hand through his hair as he listed everything they had done to ensure Mary Queen of Scots was impotent in her scheming. All the time, Lady Bess glared at Huntingdon.

It was of little use. When the Earl stopped to take a deep breath and wipe the sweat from his brow, Huntingdon stood. 'Now that I am here to instil some discipline, the prisoner is less staunch in her demands. I have taken away half her household, her horses and all access to the outside world. Her letters are read and even her clothing inspected before she rises to dress. We have also curtailed her habit of taking long horse rides and the opportunity to meet villains.' He shot a sharp look at Shrewsbury. 'Her pretty words and fluttering will have no truck with me.'

The other man glowered. 'Stem your naughty words, sir. My good wife and I are grey... and poor... from the efforts we make. We cannot forget that Mary of the Scots is an anointed Queen. You may like to treat her as if she is a slattern in a bridewell, but it is us who have to manage the grievous outpouring after your limitations on her life.'

Huntingdon shrugged. 'Imprisonment is a limitation on life, sir. It is your job to keep the lady within her limits. There is little merit in being a goaler who is incapable of saying nay to a fawning prisoner.'

'Who our Queen says should be treated as a guest,' barked Shrewsbury looking to his wife who was sitting, her mouth in a straight line of suppressed fury. Huntingdon shrugged.

Bitterness, also hurt. This Earl and his wife believe they are doing their duty and are affronted that they might be seen to be lacking in loyalty. Underneath the lady's anger is another feeling. Ambition.

Dee stood and raised his hand to stop the sniping. 'Gentlemen, please. I have not come here to set one against another. I have no doubt – nor does Sir Cecil – that you are both determined to keep Elizabeth safe. However, with three killed horribly in London I need to ensure Queen Mary is clean of all knowledge. A mere formality.'

My, how well you lie.

Lady Bess, having given another withering look towards Huntingdon, turned smiling to John Dee. 'Good doctor, before I take you to meet Queen Mary, give us news of Elizabeth's health. The dark months of winter suit her not, but I am sure she has sought your good advice.'

Oh, you clever woman. I can see my master's chest puff in pride. You are a diplomat, but also, a schemer, and want him on your side against Huntingdon. I cannot blame you. He emits malice – seeking glory by belittling others. A small man.

'She is troubled with a little wound on her leg. But I have sent a physik, made up to my own recipe. She will soon be dancing again.'

Damn you and your lies. I did that... and it is Clarissa's intelligence not yours. Does your need for glory have no morals?

To the relief of all, servants arrived with plates of bread, meat, cheeses and a hot pie. Mugs of warm ale and spiced wine sent steam into the air bringing some relief from the smell of damp. Huntingdon excused himself and flicked a finger towards a servant with a sharp barked command to bring a plate of good meat and a jug of wine to his room. When the door closed, Shrewsbury slumped. 'I swear on my life, that man and Queen Mary will be the death of me. My hair turns grey and my head aches every day with fretting.'

Lady Bess patted his arm. 'Hush, my dear. When Doctor Dee finds that Mary is well guarded, he will report back to Elizabeth – and Sir Cecil – that we have no need of his presence. After all, Doctor Dee is the Queen's philosopher and most trusted advisor.' She turned with a beguiling smile and Dee puffed up further.

So that's your game, lady.

As they ate, all talk was of Mary – a demanding guest constantly trying to increase her household by insisting that there were special tasks to be done. Bitter tears had flowed when Huntingdon forced his limitations. She was served by a few trusted ladies in waiting, the main being one Mary Seton, kept close for her skills in dressing the Queen, creating wigs, and making an art of her hair. Another favoured friend, Lady Livingston, was much affected by the damp and so rarely in attendance. Mary spent hours doing needlework at which she was most skilled. The greatest trial for the Shrewsbury's was her hatred of Tutbury – a feeling shared – and every day they were met with weeping and wailing, claims of illness and warnings of dire disease.

Dee winced. 'I hope she keeps dry eyes when I speak with her.'

The Earl laughed harshly. 'You will be disappointed, Doctor. She reserves all her waters for men.'

'Maybe she is laid low by the death of her brother. It is only weeks—'

'Pah. She hated him. She first smiled and then pretended to grieve in order to be given more wine in which to bathe.'

As Dee went to ask another question, a weary-looking servant opened the door and announced in a flat voice, 'Queen Mary demands your company, Lady Bess. The pain has returned and she suspects poison.'

Bess groaned. 'The pain she causes in my head cannot be less than the one in her side.' She looked to John Dee. 'This is as good a time as any to meet our guest, Doctor. You can witness for yourself the demon we host.'

Chapter Thirty-Eight

The room was a fug of heat as a huge fire crackled in the grate, though a poor chimney rendered the air hazy and thick. Nestled in high-backed settles were two women, heads bent to the linens in their hands and needles glinting as they worked. Every wall was hung with tapestries and the floors covered in more. In the far corner a grand carved chair was topped with a canopy cloth of state. Silver ware and ornate boxes covered every table.

Both women stood. One was a head taller than the other and grandly attired in deep red brocade, her red hair ornately fashioned under a frilled lace coif. She was fair skinned with a face that could be both plain and beautiful. Dark eyes appraised the entrants. So this was Mary, Queen of the Scots.

'I have new company?' The voice was light and pretty – a mix of Scots and French.

'This is Doctor John Dee, philosopher to Her Majesty. I told you of his visit,' answered Lady Bess.

Mary looked him up and down, then broke into a warm smile. 'I am so happy to meet a man favoured by my cousin. What message does she send with you?' Her hand floated towards her neck.

Ah, you have not anticipated that, have you master? You have been so consumed with grumbling about the rain, the roads, the riding and raucous taverns that you never gave a thought to how you would explain your visit to this twisty woman.

Dee made a short bow to the woman. 'No message, my lady. I come only to enquire about your living arrangements and health.'

And that is your first mistake. Did you not hear Lady Bess groan behind you? And look at the Scottish Queen's face – a flash of fury, now indignation.

'Cousin Elizabeth knows of my misery here so you are to take me to a place more befitting a queen. Yes?'

'No, my lady. Just to talk with you.' Dee shifted on his feet and gave a little shrug of resignation.

Mary slumped dramatically back into the settle, and clasped her brow. 'Dear God, Doctor, have you opened your eyes since you walked through the gate into this hell on earth? It is but a barn upon a hill and all around is desolate and barren.' She gripped her left side. 'I am sick – poisoned by the evil cold of the air, the damp that grows green on everything. An ague lives inside my belly and my legs stiffen. I beg go to the spa at Buxton as it is owned by the good Earl. But no. All healing is refused.' She sat up straight and pointed at the walls. 'Did they tell you that anything left against a wall in this place is black in a week? My hangings are damp with evil water. My furniture goes mouldy. When my bed linens are changed each day, there is no sweet smell – only the stale stench of misery.'

Dee looked aghast. 'I am sorry, my lady, but…'

'Have you been outside? Have you smelled the privies? Even the pigs are offended by the mud and the stink.' She turned to the other woman, a small woman also red haired, about thirty years of age with a severe face not helped by the black dress and black coif. 'Mary, open the windows and let our visitors face the ordure of this animal pen.'

Dee saw his chance to change the direction of conversation. 'Ah, another fair woman called Mary. What a coincidence.'

Queen Mary turned, her dark eyes blazing. 'The only one left. When I went to France I had four Marys – all high born and loyal to their Queen. Now? I have only Mary Seton. One by one, my ladies are snatched from my household.'

Lady Bess stepped forward. 'That is not quite true, Mary. Three of your ladies married. Only Mary Seton remains unmatched.'

In the shadows, Mary Seton winced.

You poor sad woman. Your face tells of a hard life – given over to a woman who behaves like a wanting child. You have had no chance of love, of marriage, of hope. I feel I know you.

Mary Queen of Scots ignored the correction and stood to pull Dee towards the window which Mary Seton was opening. 'Stand here, Doctor. Do you smell the evil?'

A terrible waft of human waste filled the room and Dee put a hand to his nose. 'Not pleasant, my lady. Keep the window closed against bad humours.'

Lady Bess groaned again.

Queen Mary made her way back to the fire, leaving the hapless Mary Seton to close the window, though she had to tug the damp-warped frame with all her might, grunting with effort. She was ignored. Margaretta went over to assist and was rewarded with a wan smile.

You are nervous, lady. What do you know? You think of sewing.

Queen Mary suddenly clutched her side again with a loud groan. 'The pain is back. The ill humours are killing me. Is that my cousin's plan?'

'No Madam. Your cousin only has good will towards you. But evil forces have used your name in ill deeds previously. Last year—'

Oh, Doctor. You have said too much. Weariness has dampened your wit. Now this wailing queen sees you as a threat. The Lady Bess groans again.

Mary jumped up, 'So the truth at last Doctor Dee – you come to see if I plot against my cousin. I am accused of such evil every day. Yet I am bound and tied. Pray, how does a prisoner, watched in every minute, sow the seeds of evil?'

Her hand went to her neck again. 'I am accused of sending secret messages, of writing schemes and laying plans for escape. But all is a lie. Everything I touch is snatched away for inspection.' She began to weep loudly.

Margaretta walked to her master's side. '*Paid â siarad. Tyrd yn ôl yfory.*' Do not talk. Come back tomorrow.

Mary Seton had edged back to the settle bench, sitting in silence next to her mistress, eyes to the floor. Mary of the Scots ignored her, preferring to focus those dark, weepy eyes on Dee.

'So, ask any questions, Doctor. I have nothing to hide.' The voice was now high-pitched like an angry child.

Oh, you are lying madam. See how your eyes flick side to side and I hear the name Norfolk. But another man too. And why do you keep touching your neck?

Dee bowed. 'Madam, sleep beckons. I beg forgiveness – to rest and resume our discussion tomorrow.'

Mary sniffed and declared, 'If I must suffer another night so mis-understood, so must it be. Yet another night of misery as I lie thinking only good thoughts of my cousin and yet abandoned by her. I will pray for her as I do every night.'

Next to her, Mary Seton winced.

You are uncomfortable lady. You know she lies. You know it all.

Mary frowned then put her head on one side like a coquette. 'My chefs will soon bring the evening meal. No less than thirty-two plates on silver platters. You must stay to partake.' She made a childlike giggle. 'I eat so well I must take to my bed to rest by two of the clock every day. Just for an hour.'

'I thank you, my lady, but my body demands I lie down and recover.' Dee started for the door.

'We have venison and duck… in spices.'

'Maybe tomorrow.'

As Dee and Margaretta closed the door, they heard Mary Queen of Scots, wail at Lady Bess. 'I thought you had brought help. No. Just more torture.'

Chapter Thirty-Nine

Dee and Margaretta were led across the muddy yard by a servant explaining these were the Shrewsbury's living quarters, and he had made up rooms on the upper floor for John Dee. His assistant would be given a bed in the kitchens. Dee started to object until Margaretta nudged him and whispered, '*Na. Dw i'n gallu clywed mwy yn y gegin.*' No, I can hear more in the kitchen.

Inside, Dee was told that his trunks and chests of books had been taken to his rooms and a fire set for his comfort. Warm wine would be brought at once. He puffed in self-importance and loftily told Margaretta to get settled in her servant's quarters and then come up to take some notes.

She smiled, bobbed a curtsey, and poked out her tongue when he turned to the stairs.

The kitchen was warm at least. A busy crowd of women was plucking geese, and another, younger woman was peeling onions, wiping at her eyes and sniffing. They fell quiet as Margaretta approached and one stood, smacking her hands on a round stomach creating a cloud of feathers. 'Good day, mistress. You must be the servant of the man they call Doctor Dee. Winnie will get you some warm ale.' She nodded at the younger girl, who jumped to fill a beaker from a jug near the fire.

She was a pretty girl of about seventeen, as plump as a

babe and yet shapely. A round face, pink cheeked and fair skinned, was well balanced with light blue eyes and a rosebud mouth. Fair, frizzy hair was pulled tight under a coif. As she handed over the beer, her eyes widened. 'They say the doctor can read the stars and the heavens. That he comes to see if the Lady Mary is destined to be our Queen – that he will—'

'That's enough, girl,' snapped the older woman. 'You focus on your pottage and not the business of our betters.'

Winnie squeaked and returned to the cauldron.

My God, you remind me of Lottie when we first met. Young, wide eyed, not a jot of diplomacy. Just saying what she thought and what she heard. It makes me think of Sam and wonder how he fares. But you will be useful to me, Winnie. I sense loneliness and sadness. You need a friend.

After drinking her ale and making friendly talk with the women, Margaretta left to see John Dee. When she knocked on the door, he had the cards ready, and crystals were spread across the desk.

'Why have you brought these when you know Cecil's spies are in this house? Do you want the word to go back that you were conjuring instead of interrogating?' She looked to the door and around the room. 'Have you checked for peepholes?'

Dee grunted. 'There is no one around. Now stop fussing girl and sit. We need to scry. But first, what did you pick up?'

'The woman, Mary Seton, is nervous. She thinks of sewing. As for Queen Mary – she has Norfolk on her mind. And maybe another. But she keeps touching her neck every time she speaks of messages. But I am not sure what it means. Not yet.'

Another grunt. 'Good. We will look at her pretty embroidery tomorrow. Now, you shuffle the cards as you think of the questions I give you. First the Shrewsburys – are they loyal or do they know more than they say?'

Margaretta sat and shuffled the cards, her eyes closed as she thought on the Earl and his wife. One card fell and Dee bent quickly to snatch it up. 'A message. Keep going.'

His apprentice stopped, spread the cards in an arc and put her hand above it, slowly moving left to right. Her hands dropped and she gave the card to Dee. Seconds later she dropped on another card. 'That's all I feel.'

He turned the cards in the order. 'This one dropped. The Seven of Swords. A sign of deception. A man stealing swords, his face full of foolish satisfaction. But because as he looks behind, he does not see ahead.'

Margaretta nodded. 'There is deception everywhere. The gaolers work against each other and Queen Mary wails that she is the victim of unkindness while she is up to something. We just do not know what.'

'Not yet,' smiled Dee. 'That is your task for tomorrow.'

Margaretta picked up the second card. 'Nine of Wands. A man tired and wounded with a white bandage to his head. His face full of concerns, worries, feelings of betrayal. This is the Earl of Shrewsbury.'

'Every inch of our Earl and everything we see in him. The poor man was delighted to be trusted by Elizabeth and took to his role as Mary's guardian with gusto. Now he is exhausted, watched by Huntingdon, fearful of being called a betrayer and—' Dee tapped on the image of the man. 'Fast moving towards the poverty depicted by this man's clothing. Shrewsbury is not a strong man. You heard him say that this was making his hair turn grey and he complains of headaches. He is bent and limps with the gout.'

'But he is loyal. He keeps toiling.'

'Indeed. Now look at his wife, Bess.' Dee passed the card to Margaretta. It was a woman in a white dress, seated, blindfolded, her arms crossed holding two swords.

Margaretta frowned. 'You taught me that this is a card of indecision, of hiding one's face until the chosen path is clear. The moon above the woman shows she is staying in the dark.' She looked up at Dee. 'If this is the Lady Bess, then she is playing a dangerous game. She is waiting to see if Mary of the Scots wins over Elizabeth and takes the throne.'

'Exactly,' murmured Dee. 'That describes our Lady Bess. Always tactical – moving from widow to wife, and each husband richer than the last. She has angered Elizabeth on more than one occasion by showing her power at Court.'

'So this is why she is so friendly with Mary, sitting for hours over needlework and gossip.'

Dee chuckled. 'And it also explains why she is so delighted that her son has been favoured by Robert Dudley, Earl of Leicester. She has a perfect line of information between Court and this God-forsaken hole.'

Margaretta picked up the card. 'But this is a woman playing her position… not scheming.'

'Well said, Margaretta. So, our focus is Mary. Shuffle again and ask what we look for.'

Margaretta sighed and did as he asked. She shuffled. Shuffled again. Then again and spread the cards, holding her hand aloft. 'I am tired Doctor. They will not speak.'

'They must – or we are stuck in this hellhole for days.' Dee stretched across the desk, picked up the white crystal from his collection and put it in the centre of the arc of cards. 'Sit and stare at the stone. As you do, repeat over and over, "Uriel I beg your help. Uriel, I beg your help". He is the Angel of wisdom and alchemy. He will help us.'

Margaretta jumped up. 'No. You know what calling angels does. My belly is already aching from all the riding. I'm not going to spend an evening hunched over a bucket.'

Dee scowled. 'You are an apprentice and you do as you are bid.'

'It is sixteen years and still you treat me as a chattel. I deserve… to be respected as your assistant.'

'Silence, Margaretta.' Dee was red in the face with fury, his eyes dark. He pointed at the crystal. 'Do it.'

I hate you. I will leave and then see how you fare.

Margaretta sat without looking at Dee and stared at the crystal. After a few seconds she began to murmur the incantation. Soon the vibration started deep in her gut, then the tension. She balled her fists, gulping down bile between the pleas. Then a strange hum started as it did, sweat beaded on her forehead. The candle spluttered. Dee stood before her, urging her on. She began to shake. 'I cannot. I will be sick.'

'Keep praying. Keep looking.'

The hum increased until Margaretta lurched forward, sweeping the cards to the floor with a wail. She put her head on the desk and wept, her hand over her mouth and breathing hard to stop her stomach from heaving into her lap. Dee was on his knees. 'Every card face down except one. Uriel has shown us.' He pulled himself up and placed the cards on the desk next to Margaretta. 'Look at this.'

Slowly she raised her face to look at the cards and frowned. 'Pentacles again.'

'Indeed,' said Dee. 'The Five of Pentacles is the card signifying gifts. And this is a gift from a wealthy person. See the red cloak? It usually denotes a person of power and means.' He patted her hand. 'You have done well my dear. I am proud of you. Now take some wine to settle that stomach and then go to the kitchens and see what you can hear.'

You are like a cat. One minute cruelly torturing a mouse, the next soft and purring as a sweet kitten.

Chapter Forty

The kitchen was hot and airless. Steam rose from many pots and the spit was turning joints of meat over the fire, a sweat-soaked boy at the handle wiping his brow and glugging small beer. The young maid, Winnie, trotted over. 'Hello, Miss. My, you is looking pale. That long journey maybe. You will need to drink well if you stay in here such is the heat. The Queen of the Scots is upset and her chefs have been told to make all her favourite dishes.' She pointed to the fire. 'Poor little Justin has to keep five spits rolling.'

'I thought she had her own kitchen.'

'Quite right, Miss. But with thirty-two dishes to make for each meal, she keeps the kitchens of Earl and Lady Bess busy too.' She looked suddenly alarmed. 'And I's behind making the little loaves.'

Margaretta patted her shoulder. 'I am good with bread. My mam taught me. Between us we will have a hundred loaves baking in no time.' *And you are a talker, Winnie. Just the woman I need.*

'But you's a guest and—'

'An assistant. Not a great lady. So let me assist you. And you can tell me all about the Scottish Queen and this castle as we work.'

The girl grinned, took Margaretta's hand, and led her to a table holding five bowls full of risen dough. As they began the kneading and cutting and shaping, Winnie stood close to Margaretta, her voice low. 'I's not allowed to speak of her really. The chef says there are spies here, sent up from London.' She suddenly stopped and turned to look at Margaretta, eyes wide. 'Like you.'

Margaretta laughed. 'Do I look like a spy? No, Winnie. My master is a great scholar and advisor. He would never stoop so low as to be a spy. He thinks them lower than rats.' *And God forgive my lying tongue. But I feel your loneliness child – and a useful yearning to talk.*

Winnie let out a long breath and her shoulders relaxed. 'Thank the Lord. I am too scared to talk to anyone in case I am pulled in front of Lady Bess and scolded.'

'She seems a very strong woman.'

'Strong, proud and speaks her mind. She has to be with the Earl laid so low. Poor man. All he does is pace the floor, pull his hair and hold his hurting head. And since that Lord Hogshead arrived, he has been all the worse. Oh, the arguments.'

'Hogshead? Do you mean Huntingdon?'

Winnie giggled. 'We call him that for all the wine he drinks. The Earl has had to send to Uttoxeter for more barrels. We like him not. He came in here the day he arrived, strutting like a little bantam, looking at all of us and asking who we worked for and what money was put in our pocket. Three days later, half of Queen Mary's kitchen people were gone and we all had to work to help make her daily platters – never less than two dozen with each meal. More when she is upset – and that is nearly every day.' She sighed. 'Then the servants went and the grooms. Then the ladies who sat with the Queen. Then the shouting really started.'

'Who shouts?'

'Oh, Hogshead shouts at the Earl, who shouts at Lady Bess, who shouts back. Then Queen Mary shouts and wails at all of them.'

Margaretta chuckled encouragement as she smacked

another fist of dough into the shape of a loaf and put it on the baking tray. But Winnie was looking away, her face sad.

You think of a boy. Freckle-faced. Tall. 'Did you make friends in Mary's household? A sweetheart?'

Winnie jumped and looked around. 'You must not tell. We were secret. I did not lift my skirts or anything bad.'

'Of course you didn't, Winnie. I only know because your face fell to sadness. Tell me.'

'He were a groomsman. Donald was his name. Tall, strong as his horses, and a face full of freckles and cheer. And he were good at his job. The Scottish Queen would only have him to groom her horse.' She sighed. 'But he were sent on his way. Hogshead did not even give 'im his last wages.'

'Back to Scotland?'

The young woman shook her head and sighed. 'To London seeking work. He said he would get enough money and send for me. But that could take a year so I will be stuck in this stink-hole 'til then.'

Maybe not. I feel the start of a plan, deep in my gut. I will ponder on you, little Winnie. But now I must change the subject. 'Let us not think sad thoughts. Tell me more of the house. Does Queen Mary wail a lot?'

Winnie giggled. 'We call her the weathervane, for each time she turns her weather changes – sunny, stormy, raining tears, racing like the wind to complain to the Earl and make him groan. With Hogshead she is ice, with Lady Bess as warm as spring time. And they know all about scandals at Court.'

Oh, you sweet girl. You are spilling all I need to confirm the cards. 'I hear they like to sew together.'

'Hours every day – for Hogshead said that Queen Mary was not allowed to go riding. My, that caused a storm. But Lady Bess buys her bright sewing silks and linen. The Frenchman too.'

'Frenchman?'

Winnie shrugged. 'I know not who he is, but he speaks French and is called a moth.'

Ah, so the French ambassador, Mothe-Fénélon, has been here. And he assists her sewing. 'I hear she is a very clever needlewoman.'

'Better even than Lady Bess – tapestries finer than any in a palace or than those brought from Chatsworth to line the walls here.' Winnie leaned in conspiratorially. 'They say that every linen Queen Mary embroiders has a story and a message. She sewed our Queen as a ginger cat and herself the mouse.' Then Winnie frowned.

You are recalling something strange. Something you see.

'Have you watched the Queen doing her sewing?'

Winnie nodded and smiled. 'I carry up the trays of sweetmeats or biscuits. She never looks at me, but I see her.'

'Well, she is probably looking at her needlework.' *And you are recalling something that puzzled you. I felt it when you said Mary never looks at you.*

Winnie nodded. 'The needle and her necklace.'

Margaretta turned with a quizzical look. *I pray silence works.*

'Maybe it hurts her neck, for it is surely sharp with edges. She puts it on the table before her when she sews. She must like it because she looks at it all the time.'

'Is it a grand necklace?'

'No. Plain gold and made of many shapes.'

And my gut has just jumped. Mary put her hand to her neck when she spoke of messages. We have to see that necklace. 'I think we have every loaf done, Winnie. Let us take them to the baker.'

'And then we will eat together,' chirped the young girl. 'For it is good to have a friend for a few days.'

And even better to have a sweet friend who leaks like a holed bucket.

Chapter Forty-One

Next morning, Margaretta was torn from her dreams by chefs screaming for boys to get pots and kindling for the roasting fires. She closed her eyes and tried to hold the image of Sam, but it faded as sleep ebbed away. She pushed away the damp-reeking blanket and shivered in the cold and black of her room, the cramp of four days on a horse gripping the back of her legs. She stamped her feet, said her prayers, and pulled on her clothes, not even bothering to rub down with coarse linen. Cleanliness could come later when she found a room with a fire.

She emerged into a circus of cooking. In the corner a young lad was plunging heated pokers into jugs of spiced ale. He grinned and handed one to Margaretta when she said she would deliver it herself to her master. As she left, she put two of Winnie's loaves into the crook of her elbow.

Dee was already up and making notes, hunched under his cloak by a fire. He glanced up and pointed to the desk. 'There are two beakers waiting, though you might want to check them for mould.' He reached out a grateful hand for the loaf and ripped it apart to eat. 'My God, the cold in this place makes a man's stomach groan.'

Margaretta filled the beakers and pulled a stool over to

the fire. 'I spoke to a maid called Winnie. Sweet natured and talks like a jaybird.'

Dee's eyes lit up. 'Anything useful?'

'There are many storms around Mary – only Lady Bess stays on good terms with her by buying linen and silks for embroidery. They gossip about Court.'

Dee raised a brow. 'The Two of Swords.'

Margaretta nodded. 'Apparently Queen Mary's embroidery is full of stories and messages. Indeed, she has sewn our Queen as a ginger cat and her the mouse. When she sews, she places a necklace on the table next to her. My gut clenched.'

'In a good way or a frightened way?'

'In a way that told me we need to see that necklace. Also, the French ambassador, Mothe-Fénélon, has been here and brought her sewing materials.'

Dee made a satisfied sigh.

The conversation was broken by a sharp knock as the door opened without wait for invitation to enter. It was Lord Huntingdon. He was the most mournful looking of men. No more than mid-thirties – but a long face, long nose and eyes which seemed pulled down at the outer edges could have him taken for seventy. The puritan black of his clothing and felt hat only made the pallor of his skin more apparent, and the wispy beard fade into his ruff. 'I have not been presented with your passport, Doctor Dee. Nor that of your servant.' He said the word servant with a leer.

Dee stood, eyes glittering with anger. 'I have a passport, sir. Though it is hardly necessary when I come on the Queen's business.'

The other man bridled. 'I represent the Queen here.'

'I understand you have power of passport checkage North of Leicester City… if not south of it,' responded Dee through gritted teeth, turning to Margaretta. 'Please give our documents to Lord Huntingdon.'

The papers read, checked, refolded with slow deliberation and deposited in a leather bag hanging from Huntingdon's belt, he lifted those dull eyes. 'What is the exact nature of your business here, Doctor?'

'To establish that Queen Mary can have no connection to the killings in London; to discern what is beneath the words. Call it gut-feel.'

Pah. I do it all and you take the damn credit and claim your brilliance. Fifteen years and you still deny me.

Huntingdon sniffed and looked even more dismissive. 'I check all letters. I have servants who listen to her conversations. I have her clothing, her food, even her perfumes watched. There is no secreting while I am here.'

'The expected toils of a gaoler – aided by Cecil's spies. But checking everything that is seen, leaves much to be missed.'

Huntingdon's pallor was pinking in indignation. 'Missed?'

'What she does not say, what she does not write, what she does not show. That is where real evidence lies.' Dee's face fixed in a grim glare.

A slow, sly smile spread across Huntingdon's face. 'Which is why they call you the conjuror, sir.'

Dee snorted his fury. 'I am the Queen's philosopher, Huntingdon. That old slander is only used by those not close to Court.'

Huntingdon's voice faltered. 'I meant no slander, Doctor Dee.'

'Good. Then please inform Mary of the Scots that I will see her this morning.' He waited until Huntingdon was turning to leave. 'And make sure she is sewing.'

The door slammed and Dee sat. 'Damn him and his puffed-up importance.'

Margaretta put on her soothing voice. 'He is like a small pup trying to scare a bulldog. They think a lot of yapping works until they get their ears nipped.'

Dee smiled, nodded and tension ebbed away.

The room was warm with a fire blazing and candles burning on every surface. But still the stale smell of damp. Mary raised her head and smiled sweetly when Dee entered, then a frown when Margaretta came in. She put down her needlework on a small table. Just as Winnie had said, there was a gold necklace laid out in a line. 'You seem to have your maid at your heels every minute of the day, Doctor.'

'Margaretta is not a maid. She takes notes.'

Mary shook her head. 'A woman secretary? The strange ways of this land will never stop amusing me. Come sit with me, good doctor. You can tell me of Court.'

Dee gestured to Margaretta to sit in line of sight to Mary, then went to sit next to her. 'You look very elegant this morning, Your Majesty.'

Mary smiled and patted at her hair. 'One of Miss Seton's creations. She makes the best wigs. And God knows I need them to keep my head warm in this dreadful place.' A coquettish tilt of her head. 'I hear my cousin also wears wigs – but because the hair has fallen from her head.'

'She wears them for fashion, my lady. I have not heard that she has lost her hair. But as no man enters her bedroom chamber, I would not know.'

Mary gave a little tinkling laugh. 'Ah yes, her horse master has found another red head to chase around a bed. I hear Lady Douglas Sheffield is quite the future wife, sending letters and trinkets. How sweet to be lovebirds at their age.'

So, you are getting gossip from Court. This must be from Bess's son. He would have sight into Leicester's antics. This woman's spite falls out of her mouth like rotten apples from a tree.

Dee made an unreadable smile. 'I would not depend on the gossip of a seventeen-year-old boy – lads are want to use their imagination.'

Well done, Doctor. See how she stiffens as she realises you have recognised her indiscretion. She was thinking you were under her spell.

Mary made a little huff. 'I assure you, Doctor, I am well informed. I just regret it is by everyone other than my cousin. I only want to be on sisterly terms with her and be recognised for who I am and who I will be.'

'And what will you be, my lady?'

Mary stood to ensure she was looking down her nose at Dee and pointed to the canopied throne at the back of the room. 'Your Queen when Elizabeth dies, the line will move from Tudor to Stewart, through my grandmother, King Henry's sister.'

Dee turned slowly, paused and then warned, 'I am aware of your lineage and claims, my lady. But I must caution that speaking of our Queen's death is treason.'

Mary bit back. 'It did not stop you predicting the death of my cousin, Queen Mary. Bess has told me of your imprisonment and that they call you The Arch Conjuror.'

Dee pressed his lips together to hold in a tirade. He walked to her throne and pointed to the gold-embroidered motto across the velvet Cloth of Estate. '"*En ma fin gît mon commencement.*" My end is my beginning. Strange words. What do they mean?'

Mary walked to his side and took his arm. 'Gifted by my mother-in-law – Catherine de Medici. I think it refers to the endless spirit of the Stewarts. We rise from flames.' She turned with a sweet smile.

Ah, you think again that my master is falling for your tinkling charms. Look at how you flutter those lashes.

Dee nodded. 'Ah. Like the salamander, so loved by your other mother-in-law, Margaret Douglas. I understand it is the spirit animal of her family.'

Mary walked back to the fire. 'Maybe. I rarely hear from her these days.'

That is because you stand accused of having a hand in the blowing up of her son in Kirk o' Fields last year – found naked and strangled amid the ruins of an explosion – minutes after you suddenly remembered you were invited to a wedding the other side of the city. But there is not even an inkling of sadness coming from you. The only time your heart beats fast is when you think of yourself.

Dee turned to follow Mary, nodding at Margaretta that he was about to start his real questions. He pointed to the linen she had placed on the table. 'Lady Bess tells me you are a better needlewoman than anyone she knows. May I see?'

Mary nodded and said nothing but watched him like a hawk.

Dee moved the linen into the light of a candle. 'Exceptional. Come and see, Margaretta.'

Margaretta, put down her paper and joined them. The linen was certainly exquisite. Silk stitched in rich colours of red, blue, purple, gold and white, depicted a man with a lion bowing before him and another lying at his feet. Mary was part way through a border made of triangles, diamonds and pentagons. Margaretta shuddered. *Like the shapes carved into the bodies.*

Dee made a tiny nod. He had seen it too. 'I understand you make these as gifts.'

'A queen must show generosity and love. Being imprisoned, the only gift I can give is my heart through these meagre sewings.'

'I think this is Daniel in the den of lions. Who is your Daniel, My lady?'

Mary turned away with a small flick of her hand. 'I have yet to decide who has this.'

Norfolk. I hear the name clearly. I will look at my master and mouth the name. But I also get the sense of a young man's face.

Dee made an imperceptible nod. 'It makes me think of the Duke of Norfolk. He certainly feels he is in a lion's den.'

Mary gave a little cry. 'I did not think of dear Norfolk. Of course, you are right.'

Liar. You are making it for him. Winnie said messages. I am drawn back to the border. Not a single pattern, but many

shapes. Necklace. You look at a necklace. I will take a risk.
'That is a beautiful necklace, Your Majesty. So unusual.'

Mary looked irritated at being addressed by a secretary and snatched up the golden trinket to fasten it around her neck. 'A gift from my family in France. Just a little trinket to put a little prettiness on my clothes.' She turned to Dee. 'I hear my cousin wears my pearls – handed to her by my brother.' She raised a hand to her eyes and sank dramatically into her chair. 'My poor dead brother. I pray for his soul every day.' She began to weep.

Dee shifted in discomfort and looked to Margaretta, who shook her head. *This is all display. You have not warm feelings at all for your brother. But my master does not know what to do with you.* 'Maybe some wine, Your Majesty.'

Mary took the goblet and sniffed her pretended distress. Margaretta stood close with the decanter in a pretence of waiting to fill it again. *That necklace. A heavy chain and hanging all around it are strange shapes. Triangles, pentagons, diamond shapes, shapes like the letters V and X. Some have a pearl hanging inside as if they make a dot within the shape. But there is no repeated pattern. Necklaces always have a repeated pattern. This is not a necklace.* 'Oh, my God…'

Mary started and looked at her. Dee scowled.

'Apologies, Your Majesty. Days on a horse has cramped my legs. A sudden pain.'

Mary sighed. 'Well, you are lucky you are allowed on a horse. I am trapped inside this prison while my horses strain at their harnesses in need of riding. In this place a secretary has a better life than a queen?'

Is everything only about you? Oh, look at Mary Seton. She saw me looking at the necklace. She is nervous. Her eyes flick to the linen. She is wondering if I have noticed. I have, mistress. I have. I see the connections.

Chapter Forty-Two

'Are you sure? Quite sure?' John Dee was pacing in his room, smacking one hand against another.

Margaretta was pulling the drawings of the carvings on the bodies out of his bag and placing them on the desk. Look. These shapes are made of triangles and diamonds. The border around Mary's embroidery is triangles, diamonds and pentagons. Her necklace is made of triangles, diamonds and pentagons and other shapes too.'

'Baphomet's cypher.'

'Yes. And how do we break it without her knowing?'

Dee stared into the fire. 'We use weaknesses. What is her failing?'

'She thinks only of herself, paying no attention to the thoughts or feelings of others. Do you not see the misery of Mary Seton, her loyal lady-in-waiting? But she has one weakness greater than anything else.'

'Go on.'

'She thinks herself intelligent.'

Dee smiled and took a long quaff of wine. 'And like all those who think they are above others in being better of wit and knowing, she believes little people like us cannot see through her. She is blinded by her own sense of magnificence.'

'She also thinks you are blinded by her charm and beauty. That is why she moves from coquette to weeping woman. It has always worked for her. Is she not on her third husband and now manipulating a goaler who cannot say no to her?'

Dee nodded. 'What is our next move?'

Margaretta winked. 'We play the fools and win her foolish faith. We pretend to scheme for her. Then we get the linen and the shapes on that necklace.'

Dee's face wrinkled in confusion.

Margaretta grinned. 'Only a woman's guile can win. You will have to rely on me – your lowly apprentice.'

'Mistress Seton – may I speak with you?' Margaretta ran across the muddy yard, hopping over the deeper patches of water.

The other woman stood, holding her hood down against the wind; her stance was stiff and face hard.

'I wish your advice, Mistress Seton. May I speak plainly, woman to woman?'

Just a non-committal shrug of her shoulders under the heavy cloak.

You are suspicious. I need you to think me naive.

'My master has upset Queen Mary more than once. It worries him as it will not gain him favour with Queen Elizabeth,' Margaretta looked over her shoulder as if worried she might be heard. 'And that favour is most precious to him.'

Mary Seton pulled her chin back to her neck and raised her brows. 'And what do you expect? He has not come to help her, has he?'

You do not trust. But nor have you walked away. Your toes turn to me so you want to speak further. 'He does not think ill of her, Mistress Seton. But helping her is not in his gift. He can only report back truth.' I smile to try and soften you. 'He is a man not well versed in female emotion. He is married only recently, and his wife would swear he could walk on water. So, he gets little education at home.' *A vague smile. This is working.* 'She praises his brilliance just for coming home to eat her pottage.'

Mary Seton took a deep breath and gave a slight nod, her eyes dull.

'I see your sadness when your mistress weeps. How do I guide my master to keep her smiling?'

You are relaxing. Thinking of using my eagerness.

'I think it impossible while we are overseen by Lord Huntingdon. The man is a cruel gaoler. He makes life as miserable as it can be.'

Margaretta looked over her shoulder in a play of checking for listeners, then whispered, 'A maid told me they call him Lord Hogshead for the amount of wine he throws down his muzzle. It is a wonder he can see Queen Mary let alone spy on her.'

This was the breakthrough. Mary Seton giggled, putting her head down in case she was seen, then fell serious again. 'Believe me, Mistress, there are spies a plenty to inform Lord Huntingdon… Hogshead. Everything is checked – letters, laundry, candles, every casket of food delivered. Constant suspicion. Mary may not even have guests unless they have a passport, so they are either spies or have nothing to tell her.'

'Cruel. She must feel abandoned by Queen Elizabeth.'

Mary Seton fell silent. Margaretta waited as she plotted. Then she looked up, eyes narrowing as she went in for the test. 'We are told your master has the ear of the English Queen. That he is her conjuror.'

Oh, you are warming. You think I am a willing fool. Good.

Margaretta made play of a sharp intake of breath. 'Better to call him the Queen's philosopher if you want to avoid a wailing that will drown out any distress of Queen Mary.' A smile and Mary Seton whispered conspiratorially. 'Maybe he could relay my Queen's good intention to Queen Elizabeth. Maybe he could make a nativity to show she means only good.'

Margaretta put her head on one side as if considering the

idea. 'I will surely ask him, mistress. But I beg you to tell no one. I am already looked upon with suspicion by Hogshead for being a woman who reads and writes instead of prettying her face and hair like your queen.' *And now time to get closer.* 'I said to the doctor, what you can do with Queen Mary's hair is as wondrous as anything we have seen on our Queen.'

Mary Seton's eyes lit up. 'You have seen Elizabeth's wigs?'

'Indeed – they are as high and grand as the marchpane cakes upon her table. All set with jewels and pearls. And pretty plaits in all directions.'

'Can you explain them to me?'

I will wait a few seconds, looking thoughtful as if my mind is churning. Now a frown and a smile. 'I can draw them for you, Mistress Seton.'

'Do that. My poor Queen is so fearful of losing her appearance. Already I have had to take out the waist of her gowns since Hogshead stopped her from riding. Her face and hair are so important to her. It is her only daily joy.'

Margaretta gave a warm smile. 'If I can help you lighten the darkness of her days, I will be pleased to help, Mistress Seton. Where will I find you?'

'Come to the last door from the S end of Queen Mary's quarters. That is her pantry. Find the servant, Elsie, and tell her to come for me.'

'I will, Mistress. This evening when light has fallen.'

I am in her trust. And I feel almost guilty at how easy it was.

Chapter Forty-Three

'Well? What have you found? Can you get the necklace?' Dee had been watching Margaretta's conversation from the window of his room.

'I need you to describe Her Majesty's wigs.'

'What? I send you to get secreted information and a cypher and you witter in the wind about fucking wigs. What the hell…?'

Margaretta slammed the door and raised her hand to silence him. 'Stop it. I told you it needed a woman's guile… something that eludes you no matter how many books you read. I have found a way to make her trust me.'

'By talking about wigs? For hell and—'

'Stop your cussing, master. I deserve it not. I have been standing in that bitter wind making a woman warm to me. This evening, I will visit her to give her drawings of our Queen's wigs and let her feel she is getting special information for Mary of the Scots – who is very concerned about winning the battle of beauty with our Queen.' She walked over to the bag and pulled out three wax tablets and a stylus, ignoring Dee who was pouring himself wine and muttering about women being strange creatures. She sat by the fire and ordered him to describe the wigs.

'For the love of God, woman. I go to talk philosophy with Elizabeth not the shape of her damned hair.'

'Just describe what you see when she wears her wigs.'
'Curls. Jewels. Pearls.'
'Give me the shapes and where the plaits go.'
'What the hell is a plait?'

Margaretta groaned and there began the slow and painful drawing of three hairpieces, each one created by eking clumsy descriptions out of Dee. It took over an hour, but she finally had three designs. She downed a glass of Gascon wine to celebrate surviving frustration and her master's ill-temper, and said she was going to the kitchens. She left, leaving Dee muttering about the mad humours of women.

Winnie was at the kneading board again. Margaretta rolled up her sleeves to be rewarded with a grin and a barrage of chatter about the day; how Hogshead had shouted at the Earl of Shrewsbury in front of a groom, and how Lady Bess had turned on him like a tiger protecting her cub. Now the Earl was abed with a headache again. Then she asked Margaretta what Holborn was like.

'A parish outside the London Wall and to the west. It is close to where the lawyers work, so some good houses. Why?'

'It is where my Donald said his aunt did live. Are there maiding jobs around there?'

'I am sure there are. But should you not wait until your young man calls you down?'

Winnie turned, bright eyed. 'I is just dreaming, miss. For the dreams are the only thing to keep me warm in this place.'

Winnie's mouth pinched in misery. 'I is worried that one of those London girls will lift her skirts and rope Donald into marriage.'

Margaretta leaned in. 'If he has a good heart and that heart is yours, he will wait for you, Winnie.'

The young girl looked puzzled. 'Why do you look sad when you say that, miss?'

'Oh, nothing.' *I lie. It was the thought that no one has ever waited for me. But no time for regret.* 'But I do know one very sad woman here, Winnie.'

'Who?' she asked.

'That poor Miss Seton, a drudge to her Queen's tears. What can I take her to cheer up Queen Mary?' *I feel bad at lying to you Winnie.*

Winnie was wide eyed. 'You will not get anything past Hogshead. He counts everything.' She looked towards a pantry in the far corner. 'There are sugared plums in there but he says she is only to have four a day.'

'Get me a linen cloth and walk away so you cannot see me.'

'But—'

'Hush. If you are going to London, you will have to get crafty.'

Winnie scooted across the kitchen to get a linen, pressed it into Margaretta's hand unseen and then ran over to the other maids to help cut vegetables. She did not even look round. *I like you, Winnie. Maybe I can repay you.*

As soon as dark fell, Margaretta was leaving the kitchen with eight sugared plums under her apron. She collected her wax tablets and made for Mary's pantry.

Margaretta asked for Elsie, who ran for Mary Seton. Minutes later the woman arrived in the heat of the kitchen and beamed when the linen was pulled back to reveal the red jewels of sugar. 'My lady will be so pleased. Hogshead has refused to give her cook the recipe so we cannot make them for her.' She took Margaretta's hand. 'We will go to the dressing room and you can show me your drawings.'

They walked down a dark corridor to a room with a strong smell of damp, but also the tang of rosemary, thyme and lavender in bowls placed all around the room. There were huge chests against every wall, the polished wood gleaming in the candlelight. The centre of the room had a small table with a carved dark wood box resting on it, the key in the lock. In the far corner were five round balls of wood on stands, everyone holding a red wig – each one a different mix of curls, plaits, braids and ribbons. 'Here they are,' said Mary. 'My daily duty is to rework the one used the day before to ensure there is a different appearance every time. It is a toil, but one I cherish.'

Margaretta pulled out the wax tablets. Mary Seton looked surprised and snapped. 'I was expecting drawings on parchment. I cannot use these.'

Oh, God. I need to twist this to make her feel safe.

'My master is short of parchment, my lady. If we ask Hogshead for paper, we risk questions. More than that, if anyone found you or I with drawings of Queen Elizabeth's hair we would face the wrath of your lady's gaolers. I can explain these drawings to you and then scrape away the evidence.' She grinned. 'So, we help each other and keep your mistress safe from accusation.'

Mary Seton patted Margaretta's hand. 'True. Hogshead cannot read scraped wax. Now tell me all.'

The women spent a good while poring over the wax tablets, Miss Seton asking detailed questions about the narrowness of the braids and the height of the wigs above the head. Most answers were a guess or taken from a vague memory, but she was too enthralled to notice Margaretta wincing with each lie. Then she moved to the jewels. 'What colours are they?'

'Every colour of the rainbow. Pushed like sugared fruits into a marchpane cake. But every wig has many pearls.'

Mary Seton sat upright with a sharp sniff. 'I bet she has pearls – my lady's pearls.'

I think those are the pearls as big as mistletoe berries Elizabeth uses to adorn her plainer dresses. I will stay silent and look puzzled. It worked.

'My Queen's half-brother took her jewels to London and used them as a cheap bargaining gift so that he could snatch the throne of Scotland. Queen Elizabeth bought them for a pittance and gave no care for their meaning to my Lady.'

'What was that meaning?'

'They were a gift from Catherine de Medici. A reminder of the French Court where once she had been adored. King Henry of France idolised her, putting her above even his own sons on the dining table. He treated her like a doll and never let the word "no" defile her ears.' Miss Seton looked down quickly and swiped a tear from her eye. 'She was raised to be France's most glittering queen but only a year after the crowning, fate infected the ears of a young boy king and, as he faded, so did her future. Widowed at only eighteen, her life withered into tragic persecution.'

'Surely, she was not persecuted in France.'

'Hah,' was the sharp response. 'Queen Catherine de Medici made it apparent that she was surplus to requirements in the Courts of France. She froze her out, married off her ladies – except me – and reduced her household. Just like Hogshead does today on behalf of your queen.' The voice was now low and bitter. 'Why do all my Lady's kin turn against her?'

Because she has a bad habit of plotting, making very poor decisions, getting too close to Italian servants and... maybe... killing husbands. Oh, and then there is the little issue of claiming our throne and quartering the arms of England into her own. 'I see that you hurt for your mistress.'

Mary Seton nodded and sniffed back her tears.

Now for the test. Where will you look? 'But Queen Catherine de Medici seems to have renewed her kindness. She sent her that beautiful golden necklace of many shapes.'

Mary Seton glanced towards the box in the centre of the room. 'No, it was Mary's Guise uncle, the Cardinal of Lorraine, who sent that necklace. Catherine de Medici stands with him to demand my lady's release, but she sends no gifts.' Mary's eyes went back to the box.

A cardinal. The Hierophant. The gift from a rich man in the cards last night. And that necklace is in the carved box. 'I am so sorry for your sadness, Mistress Seton.'

The tension was broken by a squawking cry from

somewhere down the corridor outside. Miss Seton jumped up. 'I have left her too long. She is upset.'

Margaretta picked up the linen full of sugared plums. 'Take these to her.'

Miss Seton's footsteps faded as she ran the length of the corridor. Margaretta moved quickly to the box and lifted the lid. At the bottom was a purple silk bag. She undid the cords. 'There you are.'

But then the sound of a door opening and footsteps returning. Margaretta pushed the necklace back in the bag, tied the cords, and dropped it exactly as she found it. The lid clicked as she shut it. Then the rush to the stool to pick up her wax tablet as the door opened. She looked up with a smile, steadying her breath. 'Is Queen Mary calmed, Mistress Seton? I have been working my memory. I think I can point out where the pearls are placed in the wigs.'

Mary Seton smiled her delight.

And God forgive me. For I think you are a good woman, and I am going to use your trust against you.

Chapter Forty-Four

'Why the hell did you not take it and hide it in your skirts? Damn it girl. That was your chance.'

Margaretta groaned. 'For one that is called the most learned man in Europe, you are often a goose-head, Doctor.'

Dee stiffened, eyes hardening with anger. 'I am no goose-head.'

'Then a gander-head – mixing madness with manhood. A deadly combination.'

The finger rose. 'You overstep yourself, madam. You are my apprentice not my better.'

Margaretta raised her eyebrows and put her head on one side. 'But I certainly *know* better. We must not raise alarm or even suspicion. Knowledge is power. For one, I have found out that the necklace was sent by the Cardinal of Lorraine, not Catherine de Medici, though they stand together demanding Mary's release.'

Dee fell silent. 'Her uncle?'

'And what was the very first card you drew?'

'The Hierophant. My God, maybe this is a Guise plot. Maybe the silversmith, Devereaux, made it. I will write to Cecil and have it messengered tomorrow.' Dee took a deep quaff of wine and picked up a pen. 'And what mad idea do you have for getting that necklace without Queen Mary or her sad servant knowing?'

Margaretta grinned. 'Friendship, Doctor. At which few men are clever.' She picked up her wax tablets and made for the door, leaving Dee staring after her, shaking his head.

Winnie's face lit up when Margaretta entered the kitchen, now quiet while the staff ate their food in the side room before beginning the labours for the evening meal. Chatter and laughter drifted from the gaggle of cook, washers, bakers, spit boys and then the lowly pot washers. 'It is surely good to see you, Mistress.'

'Why are you not eating with the others, Winnie?'

The girl shrugged. 'One of the baker boys keeps grabbing at me and saying he will take me walking and the cooks will do nothing to stop him. So, I take my bread and cheese and eat it here.'

'Are you afeared of him?'

Winnie sniggered. 'No. He's so big around his belly that I can outrun him on a road of ice. I just feel I should keep away and stay honest to my Donald.'

Then I need to make you useful... and give me reason to argue for you.

'As it is just you and me, will you help me make up my writing tablets? I want to try a new method. Is there any oil of almond on the kitchen?'

The young girl grinned. 'A new thing to learn. Better than bread, bread, pots, pots. Maybe I can be a tablet maker in London.' She disappeared into a pantry and emerged with a lidded jar. Guided by Margaretta she put two pans in the fire ashes and broke the wax out of the wooden tablets putting half in each. To one pot was added spoons of almond oil.

'Now slowly pour the almond wax into the wooden tablet frames. We will put them outside the door to harden.'

Winnie frowned. 'But the oil will keep them soft, mistress.'

'Yes, making a good bed for the hard wax. Now where will we get some oil cloth and some sheers?'

A puzzled Winnie ran to fetch cloth from the stables and watched as Margaretta cut three rectangles. The tablet frames were brought in and the oil cloths placed inside, then the rest of the wax poured to create perfect writing boards.

'You have just made tablets fit to serve a queen, Winnie.' Margaretta winked, then put her finger to her lips in a signal to say nothing.

Chapter Forty-Five

The morning was dark and damp. Margaretta put her feet on a wet floor with a groan and rubbed her legs to try and reduce the lingering stiffness. No good. She dressed, picked up her bag of writing materials and wrenched open the damp-warped door.

At least the kitchen was warm. She sat to eat with Winnie who was keeping a wary eye on the kitchen boys. Margaretta patted her arm as reassurance. The reward was a bright smile. *Oh, you poor lonely soul. You are desperate for a friend in this grim place. And forgive me but I will use your need.*

The food eaten, Margaretta pulled Winnie to the door where she whispered, 'Do you know how they make those sugared plums?'

The girl nodded.

'I think you could make the Queen of the Scots look very kindly upon you if you were to tell how they are created. The poor women is so very miserable here and she was good to Donald, was she not?'

Winnie's eyes opened wide and she gulped before shaking her head and stuttering, 'Hogshead shouted that we are not to tell her cook about their making.'

Margaretta held her by the shoulders and looked into

her eyes. 'If you help me, Winnie, I think I can get you to Holborn.'

'How?'

'Never mind. You will need to trust me.' *God forgive me – I do not know.*

Winnie bit her lip and frowned as she wrestled with her thoughts. 'How do I do it?'

'You come to the door of the Queen's kitchen at fifteen minutes to three of the clock this afternoon and ask for a maid called Elsie. Tell her to bring you to me.' Margaretta reached into her bag and pulled out a wax writing tablet to put in Winnie's hands. 'If anyone asks what you are doing, you say I left this behind by mistake.'

Winnie nodded, wide eyed, and watched Margaretta disappear through the gloom of a wet March dawn.

It was mid-morning when John Dee went to visit Mary Queen of Scots for his third interview. It was agreed that he would be fawning with sympathy and then engineer her away from Mary Seton. At that point, Margaretta would make her move.

The fire had yet to build up, so Queen Mary was on the settle, a blanket over her knees, linen and needle in hand. Next to her was the faithful Mistress Seton and opposite was Lady Bess. As Dee stepped in, an uncomfortable silence hit the room and furtive glances questioned whether he had heard their gossip.

You were talking about him being naive about women. Good. That means Mary Seton is repeating all I say.

Dee bowed, seated himself and asked about their health. Mary's hand went to her side and she let out a groan before moving into a long speech about how the evil humours of Tutbury would bring her to an early grave. Then the acid barb, 'Which will please my cousin, Elizabeth, for I will no longer be the thorn upon her Tudor Rose.'

My God. This is like listening to Mam whenever I asked

her to stir the pottage. But I cannot think of those dark days now. They are gone and so is she. I just pray she is happy in heaven, Cadi the cat on her lap, listening to my father and laughing as she used to do when I was a child.

'Mistress Morgan. Did you hear me?' The sharpness of Bess's voice ripped Margaretta from her memories. 'I bid you sit.' Bess was looking at her as if she were a feckless child and pointed to a chair in the far corner.

Dee was already assuring Queen Mary that he was quite convinced Elizabeth meant only good for her. But he was rebuffed with, 'Fie. I am called guest but I am retained in a pigsty. If this is English Royal hospitality then I can only pray that a queen of England marries the Duc d'Anjou such that you can learn some taste.' She smirked and stabbed at the linen to make another stitch. Opposite her, Lady Bess closed her eyes and sighed.

Strange. You said 'a queen' not 'the Queen'. A slip of your tongue in a second language? No. There was a smirk on your face. And how would you know about the ideas to present the Duc to Elizabeth. I cough to get my master's attention. A little nod. He has heard it too.

'I think you mean the King of France, my lady. It is he who has been presented as a suitor for Queen Elizabeth.' Dee cocked his head as if perplexed.

Mary shrugged and did not look at him. 'I made a mistake. King Charles used to be Duc d'Anjou before he took the throne and it passed to his brother, Henri. Just a little mistake.'

You lie. A woman so obsessed with being queen would not muddle a king and a duke.

Dee glanced at Margaretta then changed the subject, asking about her embroidery and if her depiction of Daniel was completed. She nodded and her hand went to her chest.

Not to your throat this time. You do not think of your necklace but something else. A diamond. You are thinking of the diamond sent to you by Norfolk. That embroidery is meant for him. We have to get it. I need my master's attention. A cough. He turns. Good. 'Ewch i ôl y lliain.' Get the linen.

Bess stared at Margaretta. 'What did she say?'

Mary was also staring. 'Her tongue sounds a little like my mother tongue.'

Dee wagged a dismissive hand. 'Sometimes she forgets herself and speaks the old tongue.' He shook his finger at Margaretta. 'Mind your manners, girl. No rough tongue in here.'

Damn you. That's God's language – or so you always say.

Dee turned back to Queen Mary, his voice lowered to a cajoling purr. 'She simply asked to see the linen. Last night she said it was the most beautiful embroidery ever seen and begged to see it finished. Even at Court we never see such skill.'

It worked and Mary nudged Mary Seton. 'Get the linen so that Doctor Dee can tell my cousin that, if she were a little kinder, I could sew her a true message instead of having to write – only to have all my letters ripped open and read before they reach her eyes.'

Mary Seton rose, her face etched with weariness, pulling a shawl closer as she moved away from the fire. As she passed, Margaretta whispered without looking at her. 'A word later if you please, mistress. Something to make your Queen smile.' Lady Bess shot a look over towards them with a frown but then returned her gaze to Mary of the Scots, who had taken Dee's hand and was looking into his eyes like a doe deer.

'Dear Doctor, you must understand the privations and hardships I endure. I threw myself on the mercy of my cousin with a loving heart. But I found the soldiers were not to protect me but to imprison me. I arrived in the clothes I wore and my head shorn – like a waif on the streets and the miserable rags sent from London were not fit for a servant.' She dabbed at a forced tear.

I recall talk of that in London. Even Sir Cecil was embarrassed.

Queen Mary continued. 'At least in Carlisle, I could look out of a window in the warden's tower – though it was cruelly barred – and see my beloved Scotland in the distance. Even that small mercy was stolen away when they took me south to Bolton with walls so high I have never seen the like.'

Dee was trying to pull his hand away, but Queen Mary was now clinging to it with both hands and her voice rising in pitch to that of a miserable child. 'Then they wrenched me out into the freezing cold and made me travel by horse to this godforsaken hole – the weather so terrible that my lady-in-waiting, Mary Livingston, became too sick to ride and I was afflicted with a frozen neck for weeks. It was cruel. Within a month of being here I was facing death.' She made a dramatic fall back into a cushion.

Lady Bess sat forward and snapped. 'Your Majesty, do not forget that your cousin was kind and had us take you to our houses in Derbyshire for your recovery. You liked both Wingfield and Chatsworth.'

Queen Mary glared. 'They were more appropriate for a Queen, but then you brought that terrible man. I was treated like a foul traitor and my life threatened. I lived in fear every day. Then he forced me back to this hole of hell.'

Bess sighed. 'Lord Huntingdon was sent to help us guard you, Your Majesty. Not to kill you.'

Queen Mary put her hand to her side and the voice went up a pitch. 'I have had this pain since he arrived and have faced death on many nights.' She turned glittering, angry eyes on Bess. 'He has taken away all my household and reduced us to living likes rats in a gutter. We are half-starved and have no good water, and we freeze in the damp and cold. Wind comes through every window to chill us to the bone. I live like a beggar.'

This was too much for Lady Bess who was on her feet, her ruddy complexion rising to red. 'Hardly a beggar, Madam. You have your own servants, groomsmen, a stable of horses in the town. You have your own baker, apothecary, chef, launderer and seamstress. You are bought linen and fine coloured silks to amuse your love of sewing. And you can hardly say you are starved when we are buying enough food to prepare at least sixteen dishes at every meal for your whole household, and they drink two tuns of Gascon wine every month.' She raised her hands in despair. 'You even use the wine on your face.'

Mary shrugged. 'I need something to retain my beauty.' She turned a shoulder to the fuming Bess and looked at John Dee. 'I hear my cousin bathes in perfumed water and had potions mixed for her face.' Then a sly smile. 'Though I think she is much scarred by her pox in 1562.'

Dee frowned. 'We are thankful to God that her illness left no mark on her fair face, madam.'

Ah. So even you are getting riled, Doctor. I do not have to feel our thoughts to see the set of your jaw against this spite.

Mary shrugged and gripped his hand harder. 'Did they tell you of Coventry? They put me in an attic. A room so small I could not turn and a door so low that it was unfit for anyone higher than a child.' She looked pointedly at Bess then back to Dee. 'It was an insult to all except those of low height and manners.'

A barb at your host. Lady Bess is a good head shorter than you, but that small stature holds a mighty temper and passion. She is so red I think her head might blow like a cannon.

'That was because the Northern Earls were rising against our Queen, Your Majesty. It was for your safety,' said Dee in a placatory voice.

Queen Mary shook her head. 'I had no part in that.'

I look to Mary Seton. She is frozen next to me, holding the linen, just staring at this emerging maelstrom. Look at your eyes. Dull, sad, devoid of hope. I think you have given up on yourself, Mary Seton. You pray for sanctuary. Strange I see you in a nun's habit. You feel my gaze and turn to look at me. I smile and get a wan, pleading response. 'Let us meet just after two of the clock when others sleep.' *I get a tiny nod. And the trap is set. I feel almost guilty.*

Queen Mary was oblivious to the looks of weariness around her and continued her bemoaning of her lot in life. 'Doctor, if you want proof of how they plot against me, then look only to the casket of lies they used to slander me – and in a false court where I could not even defend myself.'

You speak of the casket letters and the investigation at York and Westminster. A damning mix of love letters, marriage contracts and sonnets which set out your conspiracy to have your second husband, Lord Darnley, murdered and marry his killer, the far from pleasant Lord Bothwell. My, my, you have a poor choice in men. It makes me think of Sam's goodness.

Dee cleared his throat in discomfort. 'But I think the good Duke of Norfolk has allayed the worst rumour of your character, my lady.'

'Ah, my poor Norfolk. For all his kindness he moulders in a desperate prison – The Tower.' Her hand went to her breast again.

You are touching the diamond he has sent you. For he wishes to marry you does he not? But a movement to the side of me. Mary Seton clutches the embroidery further. Yes. It is meant for Norfolk. For while he may be a puny man, he is warmer than a cold bed in Tutbury.

Queen Mary had slumped back again, one hand clutching Dee, the other over her face for dramatic effect. Opposite her, Lady Bess was breathing deeply to quell her fury. Margaretta touched the arm of Mary Seton and nodded towards the linen and then John Dee. The other woman saw the chance to change the atmosphere and stepped quickly across the room, putting the embroidered cloth on John Dee's lap and proclaiming loudly, 'Do you see what beauty my lady makes?'

Dee made his bid for escape, and proclaimed he needed better light to see the full glory of the work. Dragging his hand from Mary's clutches, he walked to the window to hold the linen up.

You are checking that she has completed it and that the border of many shapes is finished. He held the embroidery towards Margaretta. 'Come see this work of wonderment.'

Margaretta smiled and joined him. 'I think Daniel would be most loving to the person who depicted him so gloriously.' For a second, Queen Mary stopped her weeping and looked up. Then she buried her face in her hands and started again. Lady Bess poured herself a large glass of Gascon wine, gulped it and poured another.

There was palpable relief when a servant arrived to bring up the dishes for the next meal. Queen Mary sat up, asked what had been prepared and demanded extra wine to ease her pain. She turned an alluring smile on Dee. 'Good doctor, you will stay and eat with me. I am determined to know what omens are in the stars.'

He sagged and looked to Lady Bess who smiled and agreed it was a very fine idea, before she bolted to the door saying she would eat with her husband.

Margaretta lifted her bag and made to follow her, whispering, 'Just after two of the clock,' to Mary Seton as she passed.

Chapter Forty-Six

Margaretta kept glancing through the window of John Dee's office waiting for him to emerge from the building opposite while she etched a series of gowns she recalled seeing on Queen Elizabeth.

As predicted, at exactly a quarter of an hour to two of the clock, he appeared. looking as if he had been into battle. Hunched against the wind, he ran across the yard and up the stairs to kick open the door and stormed in shouting a tirade of foul language before he saw Margaretta in the shadows and muffled his cussing. She poured him a glass of wine and held in her mirth as he raved. He quaffed two glasses and sat with a sigh. 'She demanded I did her horoscope to determine when she would take the English throne. The woman is crazed.'

'She was raised to be adored, master. Mary Seton has told me how she was the angel of the French Court, adored by King Henry of France and made to believe that she was superior to all around her, including his own wife, Catherine de Medici. Little wonder she is confused when people do not love her and bow to every request she makes.'

'But she is a fallen queen, accused of murdering her husband, marrying her accomplice and now of plotting against Elizabeth and raising a rebellion.'

'Because those who are told they are always right and

perfect never see themselves through the eyes of others, master. Now to our mission. Did you see that linen? The border is complete and made of all the shapes in the necklace. It must be her cypher.'

'Yes. But how do we get it?'

'Friendship is a powerful tool in the face of loneliness. Now leave me to work my own guile.'

Dee just frowned his confusion as Margaretta picked up her bank of wax tablets now covered in drawings of gowns.

Margaretta first went to the kitchen to find Winnie at the pot sink. 'Have you remembered? Just fifteen minutes before three of the clock.'

Winnie nodded and looked around. 'Am I doing wrong?'

'No, Winnie. You are doing our Queen's business and will be rewarded.'

Just after two of the clock, Margaretta knocked on the door of Queen Mary's pantry. As before, the maid, Elsie, ran along the back corridor and soon Mary Seton appeared out of the gloom. She gave a wan smile. 'Do you have something for me, Miss Morgan?'

'I do. May we sit as yesterday?' Margaretta winked and tipped her head in the direction of the dressing room. When inside, Margaretta walked across the room to the far table, checking that the key was in the jewellery box.

And here begins the cruel lie.

She made a point of looking around the room before whispering, 'Can we be heard?' A shake of Mary's head. 'So where is your Queen?'

'Sleeping. Telling your master her story has tired and upset her.'

'It upset my master too. He is terrified of distressed women and fearful that her sadness will be made worse by his visit.

He has told me to give information which means little but that may cheer her, but I must ask for your confidence.'

Mary Seton's eyes lit up. 'I promise I will say nothing.'

'You said you had worked to create some wardrobe for the Queen. But you are so far north, it is hard to know what fashions are arriving in England.' She smiled. 'But with the magic of my wax tablets, we can give you the very latest styles in the English Court.'

The other woman put her hands to her mouth with a gasp of delight and came to sit. Together they pored over the wax tablets, Margaretta explaining the colours, the cloth, and the jewels, Mary Seton listening intently, asking questions and checking details.

At exactly fifteen minutes to three, Elsie knocked on the door and said a kitchen servant had arrived to speak to Margaretta. Behind her was Winnie who announced, 'You did leave this outside, mistress. Must be from last night when you was mending them.'

Margaretta thanked her heartily and then announced. 'I think you can assist us, Winnie. Can you spare a few minutes?' Without waiting for 'yes', the girl's hand was taken and she was pulled into the dressing room to face Mary Seton, who looked less than amused to have a poorly dressed servant among the finery. Margaretta pushed Winnie forward. 'This is the girl who found the sugared plums for Queen Mary.'

A smile from Mistress Seton and a nod of the head. It is working. 'Mistress Seton is to be trusted, Winnie. Tell her how your cook makes the sugared plums.'

Responding to Winnie's squeak of fear, Mary Seton spoke gently, 'I swear never to reveal your kindness in making my lady happy. Those plums are the one sweet treat that brightens her day.'

I think that is not true, but the plan is working. 'Go ahead, Winnie. Just say what you have seen.'

The process of soaking in wine, boiling in honey and soaking again described in detail, Margaretta patted Winnie's back. 'You are truly kind. Now wait in the corridor and I will walk you back in a few minutes in case anyone asks where you were. You let me do the talking.' Winnie nodded and stepped out without another word.

The room silent again, Mary Seton narrowed her eyes. 'Why do you do this for us? Why take such risks?'

'For I despise injustice of men, Mistress Seton. I see your queen in this poky, damp place and what has she ever done but trust men? The men of Scotland imprisoned her; her half-brother took her place and her pearls; men have held her here, and men have raised a rebellion using her name. She has been cruelly treated by two husbands and now, my master's men insist she is interviewed for treachery when all she can do is sew a picture of Daniel in the lion's den.' A long sigh. 'It seems the only man who has shown her any kindness is my Duke of Norfolk.'

'You speak truth, Margaretta. It is cruel indeed.'

And you use my first name, like a friend. This is working.

Mary Seton shook her head. 'She is mistrusted in everything she does.'

And you know she is not to be trusted. I feel your lies. That is why you will not look at me. But your mind is ticking. You are wondering how else you can use me for you think me naive. Good. 'I noticed how she smiles when my master speaks of Norfolk. She must know his fondness for her.'

The other woman nodded. 'But she cannot write without her letters being copied and sent to that damned man, Cecil.'

With a gentle hand on Mary's arm, Margaretta whispered. 'But no one can copy her embroidery. Why can she not send a gift of sewn linen? Maybe a message that she understands he is in a lion's den – and that Daniel prevailed by keeping his faith.' A pause. 'If only someone trusted could press it in his hand.'

Mary Seton took in a long slow breath. Then a nervous enquiry. 'Could your master take this one? The French ambassador, Monsieur Moth-Fénélon usually does it and brings her sewing silks too. But he is away in his own country.'

Oh, you poor fool. You have just confirmed that other linens have gone. Those are the bright pictures I sensed in Norfolk's cell. I will pretend to think. 'Yes. And as Cecil's man, who would ever question? You are clever, Miss Seton – and loyal.'

Mary sat back. 'I will ask him.'

Oh, hell. 'And how can you do that without someone hearing? My master cannot be alone with either you or your queen. It is a risk.'

'Then how?'

Margaretta pointed to the ceiling. 'Is anyone up there now while your queen sleeps?'

A shake of Mary's head. 'Only the servant who watches her door.'

'Then run, Miss Seton. Get the linen and I will give it to my master on our return journey. Then he can never leak knowledge of it while he is here. It will be our women's secret – for we are so much better at silence than men.'

Mary pondered for an agonising moment then rose, opened the door and looked along the corridor – empty except for Winnie sat on a bench, humming. She whispered, 'I will be but a minute,' and was gone.

As soon as the footsteps reached the top of the stairs Margaretta darted to the door, hissing, 'Winnie, come here quickly.'

The girl arrived and was told to watch the stairs. 'As soon as you hear Miss Seton, cough loudly and go back to your bench.'

Margaretta laid her frames by the jewellery box and pulled out the top layers of wax and the oil cloth. A turn of the key and she plucked out the velvet wrap and pulled out the necklace.

Winne looked in and gasped, 'What is you doing?' She was silenced with a glower.

Margaretta measured the first third of the necklace, pressed it into one of the soft beds of wax. She made a single mark with her nail at the top, then covered it with oil cloth and the hard tablet. The middle third was pressed into the next, labelled with two indents and the impressions were completed on the third soft tablet with three indents.

Winnie coughed and Margaretta looked up, terrified. Too late. No time to get the necklace back. With a nod, Winnie scurried towards the stairs where Mary was descending and stood in her path. 'Scuse me miss, I is terrible frightened I will be punished. You will not tell cook what I did tell you… please, mistress. I am so afeared.'

In the room, Margaretta quickly wrapped the necklace and put it back in the jewellery box, turning the key with a prayer that Winnie's pleading would cover the click of the lock. Then a race across the room, dropping the tablets in the bag and sitting exactly as before.

Mary walked through the door, saying a kind word of assurance to Winnie then showed the linen. 'I have it.'

And I have you well fooled, Miss Seton. I feel guilty. But I make a conspiratorial smile and raise a finger to my lips in a sign that we will never speak of it again. You poor innocent fool.

Chapter Forty-Seven

John Dee's eyes gleamed like an eagle spying a rabbit as he traced the shapes sewn into the border of Mary's tapestry of Daniel.

'And this is not the first, Doctor. Others have been delivered by the French ambassador. That is why I sensed bright pictures. But I think the Duke does not know the code.'

Dee nodded and turned his attention to the imprints of the necklace. 'We need a decoder who is fluent in French. Mary is now able to speak in English – thanks to the kind tutelage of the Earl and Lady Bess. But her writing is poor. We saw that in the letters held by Blanche.'

He smiled and declared her, 'Better than any other student I have ever tutored. Even Thomas Digges. I think those copper curls are a sign that you have the cunning of a fox, girl. I am proud of you. Now – some good wine to take the chill out of your clever bones.'

It is these moments that you make my heart soar with pride.

She replaced the oil cloth and then the hard wax on top of the soft bed with the shapes of the necklace and stacked the frames. 'I suppose Master Walsingham is our best bet.'

Dee nodded as he poured her wine. 'Indeed, he is a speaker of French and a lover of cyphers. He will crack this message in a day. Now that we have what we need, we can prepare to leave this godforsaken place. The wind is south and so it will be dry tomorrow. We leave at dawn. I will inform the Earl.'

'We need to take Winnie.'

Dee's face crumpled in confusion. 'Who the hell is Winnie?'

'A kitchen girl who has helped me – innocently.'

Dee's good mood shifted to irritation. 'Damn it, Margaretta. I cannot walk out of here taking half the staff with me for no good reason. And I am certainly not going to drag a witless kitchen-wench over one hundred miles because you happen to like her.'

Margaretta slammed down her wine making slops over the table. 'When you found me, I was only a witless laundry girl, yet I have just delivered to you the code which might break open this mystery and the killer within it. Winnie – who is far from witless – gave me everything I needed to gain the trust of Mary Seton and then saved me from discovery while I imprinted the necklace. Without witless Winnie, you and I would be uncovered as spies – 007.'

Dee growled, 'Do not use my code name. It is secret.'

'And thanks to Winnie it remains so.' *I can see your face move to stubborn. How many times have I witnessed that set of the mouth and narrowing of the eyes which means you will argue the sky is pink rather than admit you are wrong.* 'It only takes one word from Mary Seton to her queen and then it will all tumble out in one of her passions of weeping. I can hear it now.' She assumed the accent of Mary Queen of Scots and raised her hands to her face in a display of anguish, 'See how my lady-in-waiting is reduced to using a lowly secretary and a common kitchen maid to help me get a simple gift to the only person in their cruel land to show me a petit gentilesse.'

Dee chuckled at the acting and then returned to serious. 'And how do you suggest I magic away this maiden?'

'The Earl bemoans his growing costs. Simply offer to take Winnie off his ledgers.'

Dee huffed. 'And how do I explain I want Winnie and not

a more useful or expensive servant? You have not thought this through.'

'You simply request a servant who can manage a horse and assist me in organising as we travel. You leave the rest to me.'

A moment of thinking then another frown. 'And what the hell do I do with her when we get back to Mortlake?'

'You leave that to me, too.'

That evening, they sat down to eat with the Earl and Lady Bess. Dee announced that he was fully satisfied that Mary of the Scots was so well guarded that she could have no part in the London evil. Margaretta noted how well he lied. The Earl was relieved but returned to his anxieties, voicing the costs of housing Mary's household, complaining that the forty-eight shillings a week sent from Court – if in fact they arrived – was not even covering the cost of her food let alone the two barrels of wine they consumed. Opposite, Bess tried to soothe him. Huntingdon watched with a look of superiority and repeated all his successes in curbing Queen Mary's servants. His comments only riled the Earl further as each point was like a stab at his competence.

Dee looked to Margaretta and interjected. 'Maybe I could assist with a reduction to your costs. I would appreciate a servant – one who is strong, able to ride a horse and able to manage victuals. It would be one less mouth to feed.'

Bess shook her head. 'I do not think we can reduce Mary's household further. We have daily wailing that she is bereft of help.'

Margaretta leaned forward. 'There is a kitchen girl of yours called Winnie who is strong and knows food.'

Bess waved a dismissive hand. 'No, we will give you a stable-lad.'

Damn this. Lady Bess is as stubborn as my master and will not appreciate being addressed by the likes of me. 'If I might say, my lady. Winnie has intention to go to London anyway to follow a friend, and, going by the size of her, she eats like a horse. We would be saving you a few months of feeding.'

Bess went to snap at Margaretta, but the Earl cocked his head. 'How much does she eat?'

'More than my master and I put together, sir. I have never seen the like.' *And forgive me my lies.*

Bess went to refuse again, but the Earl looked to Dee. 'Take the greedy wretch.' Then the conversation moved to Mary of the Scots, and Dee set about learning all the gifts and visitors she had received in the past months. The only person who brought gifts now and who took her letters away was the French Ambassador, La Mothe-Fénélon. The Earl nearly spat his name. But any letters had been copied and analysed before being handed to the wily ambassador.

Dee nodded. 'Does he take gifts from Queen Mary to others?'

Bess answered. 'He takes little embroideries. But he is also generous in bringing her linen, silks, coloured threads and gold twine to keep her amused.'

'And thank God he does,' grumbled the Earl. 'For I cannot be keeping her in silks and fripperies.'

'And does he bring news and gifts from France?'

The Earl nodded. 'News, yes. Letters, no. We have to keep our ears open but Bess has a good ear for French. The only gift was a golden necklace saying it spelled out her Uncle's love for her. She was delighted by it, though it must be uncomfortable for she always puts it on the table. Strange thing it is, too.'

Dee glanced at Margaretta who gave nothing away, but the links were being confirmed. Margaretta stayed silent and mused on her master's look of worry. *Because now there is a very good chance that this strange affair goes all the way to the French Court.*

Later than evening, Margaretta found Winnie huddled in a corner, head down. When she approached, the younger girl glowered. 'I don't know what you are doing Miss, but you have brought me into mischief. It is wrong.'

Margaretta crouched in front of her. 'I am sorry, Winnie. But there is a reward for your silence. Can you ride a horse?'

The other girl huffed. 'We do not have your pretty London streets up here. We learn to ride before we walk – that way children do not drown in puddles and ruts.'

'And how would you like to ride to those pretty streets and take a maid's job just across the River Thames from Holborn, Winnie?'

Open mouthed silence followed by a loud squeak, and Winnie was racing to her bedding place to stuff all her worldly goods into a sack.

The dawn was grey but dry. Formal goodbyes were made to the hosts, with the Earl whispering a plea to ask Cecil to recall Huntingdon. Horses were reigned up for Dee and Margaretta and a mule for their new maid who was pink with cheer as she waved farewell to her kitchen friends and reminded another young woman to be sure and tell her mother where she had gone. Margaretta pulled her cloak close to cover the bulge of a tapestry hidden in her dress.

By the following evening, they had reached Atherston in Warwickshire and took food and beds in a small inn on Watling Street, where the landlord was known for changing horses for travellers. Cold and saddle sore, they made for an early bed as Dee insisted on another dawn start to make the best of the meagre daylight.

But at five of the clock in the morning, hammering at the door woke them all. A red-eyed, angry potman pulled up the bar and roared at the horseman for waking the dead before daylight. Then he stepped aside when the messenger announced he was on the Queen's business and seeking the travellers from Tutbury.

Minutes later, Dee and Margaretta were out of their beds

looking at the bedraggled messenger, covered in mud and stinking of horses and sweat. 'I am sorry to wake you Doctor Dee, but I come from Sir Cecil. You are to make haste to London. We must leave immediately.' He shifted on his feet.

'How the hell did you know where to find me?' growled Dee, rubbing sleep-heavy eyes.

'You would have to use the old Watling Street road between London and Tutbury. I have stopped at every inn, then a market trader putting up his stall said he had seen you arrive here last night. Thank God, for I have ridden two full days with no rest.'

Dee gave a loud sigh and then looked concerned. 'And why has Sir Cecil sent you riding through night and day to find me?'

'Sir Cecil says, "Three more souls".'

Chapter Forty-Eight

Winnie was left at the outskirts of the Hyde deer park and the messenger given money to take her to the Lambeth Crossing and onto Mortlake by road. Margaretta pushed a letter of introduction addressed to Katherine into her hand and told her to ensure she made herself as useful as possible until she and the doctor arrived home. An impatient Doctor Dee was already turning his horse west towards the city walls and The Strand.

The horses trotted into Cecil's yard, a thunder-faced John Dee, having been refused time to go and see his wife first, dismounted and stamped to the front door. Margaretta followed, clutching the bag of papers and carefully wrapped wax tablets. Bellot opened the door and raised an eyebrow as Dee stormed past him without taking off his cloak, heading straight to Cecil's office, banging open the door and coming to a sudden stop.

Oh, Lord. Something has shaken you. Your back is stiffening even further and the shoulders rise, like a cat seeing another on its territory. I peep over your shoulder. Ah. Your sworn competitor. Mr Will Fleetwood.

'Come in, John. We are glad you are here.' William Cecil rose from his desk and beckoned. He called to Bellot and asked for a carriage to be sent to collect Walsingham.

Will Fleetwood also rose and made a small courteous bow. 'Doctor Dee, I am pleased to meet you again.'

Dee ignored him and looked only at Cecil. 'I have not even seen my wife.'

'Ah, yes. Mistress Constable, who I understand is now your good wife,' said Fleetwood. He looked to Margaretta, winked and bowed again. 'Mistress Morgan. Delighted to be of service again. Your brother has been to see me, and all is now in order.'

Dee turned to his apprentice, eyes wild and face furious. 'What?'

Oh, Lord. I will not hear the end of this. 'Master Fleetwood, who was so kind to Mistress Katherine eight years ago, has helped Huw again with some legal papers.' *Let's hope the reminder that your wife had to be rescued from a contract in which she sold my brother for a barrel of malmsey wine will stop your ire. I smile sweetly and try not to look at the lawyer who is pinking as he tries to mask his amusement.*

Dee gave a low growl, sat on the seat in front of Cecil and reached for the wine and then Cecil's half-empty glass. 'The messenger said three more souls. Tell me.'

'All three must have died in one night and put in a wherry tied under the landing pier of Sheen Palace which, as you know, has been given as residence to our most political guest, Odet de Coligny, the Huguenot Bishop of Chatillon, who fled here begging Elizabeth's protection. Leaving the bodies so close is a strong message of threat from Baphomet.' Cecil turned to Fleetwood. 'We called in Will as a trusted lawyer and kept the bodies away from the morgue. Little good it did. They were found by a wherryman.'

Dee huffed. 'You might as well tell the town criers. Is it the same pattern of death?'

'Yes.' Cecil nodded to Will Fleetwood to continue.

'All three victims were Huguenot, and…'

'From All Hallows?'

'Yes, and they…'

'Did they eat together on Sunday? Did they suffer flux?'

'Yes, but...'

'The bodies carved?'

'Yes, and...'

'Is Mabelain informed? What says he?'

Cecil banged the desk. 'Stop this snapping, John. Mabelain was sent to France the Friday after you left for Tutbury and so was not in London on the Sunday these poor souls started their road to death. Now, listen to Will.'

Will Fleetwood leaned forward to look directly into Dee's eyes and lowered his voice to a calm friendliness. 'Doctor Dee, be assured, I mean only good will and, like you, have the safety of our Queen foremost in all I do. I have conducted a thorough investigation – thinking what you would ask at every step and twist. Now, allow me to fully appraise your great mind of the details.'

Oh, clever. Methinks you are more intelligent about people's hearts than is the doctor, Will Fleetwood. A nod to his brilliance and he is settling back with his wine – well, Sir Cecil's wine.

Cecil nodded to Fleetwood and the lawyer continued. 'Yes, all three were Huguenots from All Hallows, living alone. Each victim had bread left as a gift on Sunday evening- after dark. We know because all three boasted to their neighbours the following day, for it was good bread. Nothing was heard – certainly not the chink, chink associated with the previous deaths. At least not on Sunday.'

Dee sat forward. 'So, are you telling me Baphomet was not seen this time?'

Fleetwood raised his hand. 'In good time, Doctor, let me tell you as events unfolded so that your great mind can see the patterns.'

And as predicted, my master sits back with a satisfied smile and clicks his fingers to me to keep note taking. Scut.

Fleetwood pulled letters from his case and put them in front of Dee. It was written in French. 'The bread was not the only thing in the bags. Each person had received this note, telling them to be at their killing place on Tuesday morning and to await information. These victims did not die in their homes; they were lured to empty warehouses or shacks near the river. Every lane is a working place, and so the streets at night are deserted.'

Dee snatched up one letter and read it. 'This says they will learn "the real instigator of Wassy, the dirty dower". That revenge can now begin. Did the victims have any connection to that massacre?'

'No,' answered Cecil. 'We had to bring in that poor Vicar Tyrwhit from All Hallows to identify them and where they lived. I have never seen a man so bereft. Apparently, every one of them had arrived in London in the past five years – not one of them from Wassy.'

Yet, when I have been the company of that congregation, there is strong memory of Wassy. I have felt the horror. The Doctor recalls this. He makes a slight glance in my direction.

Cecil continued. 'However, Huguenots name Wassy as the start of the great war of persecution. Within two months, there were further massacres of Huguenots in the towns of Sans, Castelnaudary and Bar-sur-Seine. And it went on. Persecuted Protestants were soon boarding ships and begging refuge in our cities.'

Dee looked back at the letter. 'The writer of this letter calls Wassy, "the dirty Dower". What does that mean?'

'Another connection, John. The town of Wassy was part of the Dower of Mary Queen of Scots – given in trust to her by her Guise family when she was married to the French Dauphin in 1558.'

Dee blew out slowly, looking to Fleetwood. 'This is a new twist. But what about the bodies? Were they carved?'

'I will come to the bodies and what was seen in just a moment. First let me report what I found in the killing places and what was seen in the surrounds. Inside every building was the evidence of violent flux, and on the walls was written the same terrible message in blood.' Fleetwood reached for his notes.

'*D'abord la terreur, puis la mort*,' muttered Cecil, pinching the bridge of his nose.

Dee refilled his glass. 'Marks of a cloven hoof?'

'In every place. And also in Anker Lane where the devil was sighted and heard.' Fleetwood looked to his notes. 'It was nearly ten of the clock when the warden of the Vintner Hall and Almshouses at the top of the lane was awoken by a knock at the door. The poor man answered and found himself face-to-face with a huge creature, taller than a man, cloaked, and with silver horns. It pointed with a silver claw, whispered "Baphomet" and ran away on metal hooves. He reported the same chink, chink and, in the morning, huge cloven hoof marks were still in the mud leading to the river.'

'So, he becomes even more bold,' snarled Dee. 'Did the man see his face?'

Fleetwood shook his head. 'He insists the face was covered in a leather mask.'

'Did no one make chase?'

'The warden is old. People living in the alley were roused by his screams, but when they ran to the riverbank, there was nothing to be seen except the usual few wherries out at night. Though one of them, no doubt, held the bodies.' Fleetwood reacted to Dee's frown and pulled out a map. On it were three crosses in ink. 'These are the locations of the three murders. Each lane leads to the river and we found marks showing something was dragged. But only the third had hoof marks. The tide was making on Tuesday night. So, if the first murder was here in Wirehale Lane and the body placed in the wherry, the tide would easily take it to Bretaske Lane, where the second victim could be killed and loaded. That leaves Anker Lane as the last killing and loading place and the tide would be running fast to take the wherry down to Sheen Palace where it was tied up and left for discovery.'

Cecil cut in. 'Baphomet could easily get away. On these

cloudy nights of March, there is little moonlight to illuminate a killer escaping along the riverbank. Let Will tell you about the bodies.'

Fleetwood nodded towards Margaretta. 'This is not for a woman to hear. The details are terrible.'

'Pah. She is Welsh... and well used to talk of blood and guts.'

Damn you. I shake at the sight of death and the hearing of the wounds is often more terrible than seeing them as I have imagination to add to the horror. But I look to Will Fleetwood with a nod to continue. More for his sake, for he looks aghast at exposing me to such terrors. I like you, Will Fleetwood.

'Very well. Each one was terribly desecrated. I have drawn the wounds. As before, each had a linen sewn into the body. One in the mouth, one had his ear sliced off and the linen inserted, the women was cut near her private parts. Each linen was the same.' He pulled out a pouch and spread three bloody linens on the desk in front of Dee, each one exactly as before, a pentacle, centred with a B.

Dee looked at each one. 'What symbols were on the bodies?' he demanded.

Quickly the lawyer took out three papers. 'These are exact in shape and size.' The first was a diamond on its side with a dot in the narrower end, the second like the letter V and the third a V on its side.

'Walsingham will be here soon,' interjected Cecil. 'He has already had these and so I hope he has cracked the cypher.'

Dee raised his head. 'I have already found the cypher.' He clicked his fingers to Margaretta. 'Give me the wax tablets and the drawings of the first three symbols.'

Margaretta grimaced at his arrogant tone and pulled the tablets and papers out of the evidence bag. She placed them in order in front of Dee and pulled up the hard wax to reveal the imprints below.

Dee picked up the drawings and quickly looked between them and the necklace imprints, his brows wincing as he thought. Then he frowned and groaned. 'Our worst fears. Baphomet is spelling out Elizabeth.'

Cecil gave a yell and jumped up to come round to Dee's side of the desk. 'Explain.'

'This is the imprint of a necklace owned by Mary Queen of Scots in which she studies when embroidering her gifts. It is so basic that the shapes along the necklace are the alphabet. He counted along five shapes. 'This is E.' He tapped on the symbol found on old Lucille. It was the same. Then he picked up the symbol found on Lucien Moreaux before counting along twelve shapes. 'This is L and they are the same. The symbol on Pierre Perotin is I.' He continued until ELIZAB was spelled out. 'The next victim, if we do not stop Baphomet, will be the same as on Old Lucille. It will be an E.'

Cecil returned to his seat.

'Has Walsingham found the silversmith – Devereaux?'

Cecil shook his head. 'No silversmith of that name is in the city. Walsingham is creating a list of all new arrivals in the last three months – but many are scattered far and wide.'

'You are assuming Baphomet is new to our city, Sir Cecil, yet he seems to know our lanes, alleys and warehouses well – and where he will find those who live alone,' cut in Will Fleetwood.

All four stared in silence, only broken when the door opened and the dark face of Walsingham looked in and clouded further as he picked up the fear in the room.

Chapter Forty-Nine

The three men listened intently to Dee's report on Tutbury – of Mary being a demanding guest; her flirtatious behaviour and her foolery at thinking no man can see further than her pretty face and speech; that her goalers were honest, but that Lady Bess was keeping her rackets braced for the long game. Cecil smiled when he learned that leaks in Leicester's house enabled Bess's young son to carry gossip to his mother. They grunted in admiration as Dee revealed how he had suspected the necklace, and ordered Margaretta to carry out his cunning plan of befriending the naive lady in waiting, Mary Seton, and steal impressions of the necklace; how he had also fooled Mary into handing over one of her embroidered linens with a cypher border and how he had, due to the kindness of his heart, rescued a poor servant who had been an innocent helper. Only Cecil noted Margaretta glowering behind him and winked.

Walsingham picked up the wax tablets. 'We were close to cracking the code, but this will speed up our work. May I have the linen?'

Dee clicked his fingers at Margaretta, took the present and handed it to Walsingham. 'I suspect it is in French. I could do it myself, but I have ridden well over eighteen hours today and wish to see my wife. By early tomorrow, you need to have this in the care of the Tower guard for collection, and I will deliver it to Norfolk. Then your job is to follow it. There are no embroideries in Norfolk's cell, but Mary let slip this was not the first. We need to know where they are going and who it is meant for.' He ignored Walsingham's resentful glare.

Dee stood to leave, but Cecil raised a hand. 'Not yet, John. We have news too – further developments have our eyes on France. Walsingham will explain.'

Dee sat as Walsingham opened his bag and pulled out letters. 'Doctor Dee, when you drew the chain of threat, you drew a circle to the East representing France. Well, it seems we are right to throw suspicion that way. Early in this investigation, we sent word to Norris, our ambassador in Paris. His letter of response arrived the day you departed for Tutbury. It was in cypher, and this is the translation.'

He handed the letter to Dee, who read silently and suddenly looked up. 'Is he quite sure?'

Cecil nodded. 'Norris is thorough.'

Dee looked to Walsingham. 'Catherine de Medici dabbles in the occult and uses pentacles?'

'She has always used methods of divining the future, especially that of her sons. Michel de Nostradamus was her key advisor and soothsayer.' Walsingham raised a hand to quieten Dee's muttering that Nostradamus was a mad fool who used poor practice and wizardry not mathematics and true methods. 'The old man used to divine their future through various means. He once inspected the moles on her son to predict his reign. But he has also coached Catherine in spells. When her husband, King Henry, died, she was determined to rid the palace of his lover, Diane de Poitiers. Lady Diane was dispatched to a magnificent palace in Chaumont. She found rings of candles, strange symbols and pentacles etched into the floors and the walls. Such was her fear she fled that palace and never returned.'

Dee leaned over and picked up one of the linens embroidered with a pentacle. 'Do you think Catherine de Medici is behind these murders? Is she so angered with Elizabeth for dallying over King Charles that she would resort to terror and murder?'

Cecil shrugged. 'We do not know. It might be a way of frightening Elizabeth into seeking the protection of a Catholic husband.'

'But Elizabeth has long-resisted Charles of France.'

Cecil nodded. 'And we know from Blanche ap Harri that Mothe-Fénélon, the French ambassador, has hinted at changing negotiations to marriage with Catherine's third son, Henri, Duc d'Anjou. Norris confirms this change of strategy.'

Blanche referred to that son as a dreadful man-child with the morals and dress of a Southwark doxy. This will not go well. Elizabeth likes her men to be manly.

Dee looked back to the letter. 'Norris refers to the Cardinal of Lorraine, Mary's uncle, as meddling. Another link. It is he who gave Mary her cypher necklace.'

Walsingham nodded. 'The Cardinal has been out of favour for some time but his recent rapprochement with Catherine de Medici coincides with her demanding Mary's release and hinting at d'Anjou marrying our Queen. Recently, the Cardinal has made moves to become close to d'Anjou and has asked him to become the protector of the Catholic Church – a huge honour and mission.'

Cecil cut in. 'We seem to have a triangle – Mary is connected to the Cardinal of Lorraine, who is recently connected to Catherine de Medici, and they are both connected to the Duc d'Anjou. Norfolk is the blind fool in the middle. But did they send Baphomet?'

Dee narrowed his eyes and raised a finger to silence anyone who might stop his train of thought. After a long minute, the eyes widened. 'Of course. If Baphomet's murders frighten Elizabeth into a hasty match with the protector of the Catholic faith, then England's future is set for return to the Holy Roman Empire. Mary would be released to await the throne, putting England under the total rule of the French royals. Clever.'

'And deadly,' snarled Cecil. 'If Elizabeth is frighted – no

terrified – into this scheme, we of the new faith will all be fleeing to the Low Countries.'

Margaretta leaned forward and tapped on Dee's arm. 'Queen Mary said it would be good for *a* queen of England to be married to the Duc d'Anjou in order to learn some taste.'

Dee turned with a frown. 'I was just about to say that.'

No, you were not. You had forgotten. Lord Cecil looks at me with a knowing smile.

Dee pointed at the embroidery in Walsingham's bag. 'I predict Mary of the Scots is feeding them information through her cyphered linens. But we have one glimmer of hope.'

'And pray what is that?' snapped Walsingham, his voice sharp with cynicism.

Dee turned a hard glare on the younger man. 'If Baphomet is trying to frighten Elizabeth into marriage, then he is not trying to kill her – yet. We have a little time to find him and expose the people behind this plot. You say Mabelain is in France. We must use him. Norris too.'

'We have already set this in motion, John,' broke in Cecil. 'Mabelain has been sent to Joinville – the seat of the Cardinal of Lorraine. He will pick up any information about the churchman's politicking. But, as he rightly said, he will not be permitted within the Court of Catherine de Medici. She has a horror of deformity and only beauty is allowed in her presence. Even her troupe of dwarves are handsome and perfectly dressed.'

Dee raised his brows. 'So, Norris will need to investigate the Court of Catherine de Medici and see if she has sent someone with her evil pentacles.'

'No John. An ambassador cannot spy and present false friendship. That will be your challenge.'

Dee stood, face reddening. 'No. I have suffered Tutbury and brought you the cypher to unlock any correspondence between Mary and her French relatives. I must stay here and attend to the killings.'

Cecil pointed to Fleetwood. 'You must agree, Will has

conducted his part of the investigation with good speed and skill. No, John. We need you in France. You have the perfect foil.'

'What?'

'Nostradamus died five years ago, and Catherine de Medici misses his strange advice. The plan is that Elizabeth will send you on a diplomatic mission to attend the French Queen and her children to cast their horoscopes and divine their future.' Cecil smiled. 'You depart in three days.'

'No!'

Cecil picked up a pen. 'I will write your passport now, to be signed by Elizabeth tomorrow. You have three days to sort your affairs. Tomorrow, you see Norfolk and also Elizabeth for she will only believe word of Mary Queen of Scots from you. Also, I am sorry to say I have had word that your dear wife has received bad news.'

'What?'

Cecil looked up, his face suddenly softened. 'The Sweat is a cruel killer, John. I hear she has lost her only sister. Now go comfort your wife and then prepare to go and save your Queen.' He rang a bell and Bellot arrived to take away the passport for signing by Elizabeth.

Chapter Fifty

The ride to the Lambeth crossing was filled with Dee's fury until he pulled up his horse so suddenly that Margaretta nearly rode into him. 'Cosimo Ruggieri.'

'Who? Have you lost your mind, master?'

'Just remembered. I heard word that he resides in the household of Catherine de Medici. I'm sure Tycho mentioned it in his letter to Digges. Full of contempt, of course, but I'm sure he said it.'

'Who is Cosimo, Rug... Rug...'

'Ruggieri. Replacement for Nostradamus. An Italian. Started with horoscopes but moved onto the higher order of knowledge. He is also an alchemist, fully funded by French coin. Useful. A good contact. Come girl, we must make haste.' He rode away into the dusk.

You are unbelievable. We are running home to your weeping wife, and you are already getting excited about our next journey. No thought for others. No thought for Katherine. None for me. I am wanting to see Sam and see if he fares better. Do you think of that? No. Just your damn stinking experiments.

The stable boy ran out to take the horses as the door to the main house opened. It was Winnie, hair pulled back and her dress covered in a flour-spattered apron. 'It is good to see you, Doctor Dee. Mistress Katherine is in the main dwelling room. I have made her a posset for comfort.' She stood aside for Dee to stride through. As he opened the door, they heard a wail from his wife and his voice dropped to soothing as he wrapped his arms around her.

'He seems to be a such a good man, despite what Mistress Bela says of him,' whispered Winnie at Margaretta's shoulder. 'She says his wife will not manage without her friendship, though she is tired already with the burden of comforting such a difficult woman. And the loss of the sister is even harder for Bela. So sad to lose a dear friend so suddenly.'

Margaretta turned, eyes wide. 'Mistress Bela? Loss of a friend? Worse for her?'

Winnie nodded and sighed. 'Why, yes. She has been weeping in the office. Says she cannot even help such is her grief and duty to stay with Mistress Katherine. Then she must protect us from the witch who lives in the yonder cottage across the yard. So, I have just muddled along myself.' She patted the apron making a small plume of flour.

Margaretta bent down to be eye-to-eye with the maid. 'Winnie, you have much to learn. Lesson number one is that some witches have lemon hair. Now where is she?'

Winnie pointed down the corridor and said that she was in the office comforting Mr Digges. Margaretta put a finger to her ear in a sign to listen well and tiptoed to the office door. The bang as she hit it back on its hinges was quiet compared to the scream from Bela and the yelp from Thomas Digges. Winnie squeaked and slapped her hands over her eyes to block out the sight of the woman she called Mistress Bela lying on a desk, skirts hiked high and legs in the air. Between them was a bare-legged Thomas, breeches round his ankles, face white with horror. 'We… we… were just trying to…' He jumped back, making Bela tumble from the desk as he tried to cover his manhood with his hands.

'Trying to find the Philosopher's Stone? I doubt you will find it there, Mr Digges.'

Bela scrambled to her feet and started to argue but was silenced with, 'Hold your tongue, Lemon-head and get back to the kitchens where you belong – for now.' Margaretta, jumped aside as she stamped past, face red with fury, and deliberately shoving little Winnie. The door was closed on a gibbering student Digges. 'Now Winnie, I will take you to meet the doctor's mother – who is no witch.'

Mother Dee was seated at her fire, beaker in hand. 'Ah, you are back. Is my John with you?'

'He is, Mother Dee, but he has gone to comfort Katherine.'

The old woman shrugged. 'I did try to be kind. Sent her a flagon of wine with warm spices to help her sleep. I found it placed back on my doorstep this afternoon not even opened. That told me she wants nothing of my help.'

Winnie made a little squeak and stepped from behind Margaretta. 'That were me, missus. Mistress Bela said it were tainted and I should take it from the kitchen and leave it back at your door.' She gulped. 'I is truly sorry if I has caused upset. I—'

Mother Dee bridled. 'Mistress Bela? Did you call that lemon-headed rat 'Mistress'?'

Margaretta raised her hand. 'Enough, Mother Dee. This is Winnie – brought here from Tutbury. Like all innocents who do not lie, she does not expect dishonesty in others.' She turned to a wide-eyed Winnie. 'Bela is a low maid with even lower morals. She is not companion to Mistress Dee, nor has she ever even met the dead sister. And the good woman you look upon now, is the very kind mother of Doctor Dee – not a witch.'

This brought a chortle from Mother Dee who declared it was good to have sense back in the house and insisted they pulled up a chair and have a glass of good wine – Winnie too, so that they could give her a lesson in managing lemon-headed rats.

Chapter Fifty-One

The following day started early. Margaretta groaned as she tried to stretch the stiffness of three days solid riding out of her limbs. But she warmed as she imagined walking into Sam's yard. *Will he call me friend again – say he needs me to stay close? I loved Lottie. But I never stopped loving Sam. Now I can be his friend.*

Then a knock at her door. It was Winnie. 'What can I do, Miss Margaretta? Lemon-head will not let me in the kitchen. Says she is the one to tell me what to do and I have no work here.'

'Ah. This will be her next tactic. To make you look useless and herself the saviour of the household. Come with me.'

Winnie trotted along at her side. 'Are there really such awful people, Miss?'

'Yes, Winnie. Lucky for us there are few in the world. But some are born with a strange belief that the world revolves around them. They will cheat, lie, claim greatness, claim innocence and make themselves the centre of all situations – whether that is happiness or grief. They must be the most important.'

'They must be surely bad souls, Miss.'

'Yes, Winnie. You can always spot them – they say falsehoods about anyone who is their better. And that is most people. Now go and get that flagon of spiced wine we brought back from Mother Dee.'

Katherine was sitting in a cold sitting room, a blanket around her shoulders. She looked up, red-eyed, as Margaretta knelt before her and took her hands. 'Oh, Mistress. I wish I could take away your pain. But you are surrounded by people who will care for you.'

Katherine shrugged. 'I had forgotten the sorrow of loss. I am sorry Margaretta. You lost a friend to the Sweat only weeks ago, but I said nothing kind. You see, Bela said you were not bothered.' She bent her head as tears fell.

'Now, Mistress. Do not fret. Let us agree to speak to each other and not through a kitchen maid.'

'But she has been such a comfort.'

'I am sure, Mistress. But we can speak of Bela later. I want you to meet Winnie. She has come all the way from Tutbury after assisting the doctor and she brings you a flagon of good, spiced wine from Mother Dee who sends it as a kindness as it will help you sleep.'

Katherine frowned. 'Mother Dee sent that? Bela said she had turned away when told of my dear sister.'

'She would have turned away to go and get the spiced wine to send with kind words. Sometimes half a story tells us exactly the opposite of truth.' Margaretta looked to the new maid. 'Winnie, please pour a glass of Mother Dee's wine for Mistress Katherine and stay a while to tell her of your experience serving in an Earl's kitchen and how you helped cook for a queen.'

As Margaretta closed the door, she smiled to see Katherine sitting straighter, supping wine, and nodding with enthusiasm as she now had an earl's servant in her household – and one that kneaded bread for Queen Mary at that.

* * *

Dee was already in his office, bent over his desk, writing furiously. He sensed Margaretta entering and pointed to the stool before him without looking up. 'I am just finishing a horoscope for Elizabeth. It shows tumult well into the year. A sudden upsurge of negativity in August. God help us if Baphomet is still not trapped by then. We need to agree our day's work.'

Margaretta walked over and nodded to Thomas Digges who was staring at his desk, pen poised, hand shaking, writing nothing – only dripping blots of black ink onto his paper. 'Good morning, Mr Digges. Has that Philosopher's Stone tumbled around your desk this day?'

Dee looked up. 'What nonsense are you speaking to Digges, Margaretta?'

She smiled sweetly. 'Just enquiring, Doctor. Seems the search requires experimenting with some very base materials.'

Dee shook his head and muttered that the ride from Tutbury must have made a muddle of her head. He turned to Digges and ordered him to leave as he needed privacy and to, 'Ask that yellow-headed maid to bring bread and ale as you pass the kitchen. She is to leave it outside the door.' He did not notice Digges' panicked groan.

The office empty, Dee pulled the casket out of his desk. 'We need to ask about the French Court. What we can expect.' He took out the cards, passed them over the flame of a candle and shuffled them before spreading them in an arc across the desk, face down. 'Use your abilities. Ask the cards what we look for.'

Margaretta held both hands over the cards and moved them side to side. Nothing. She tried again. *No tingle. Oh God. Surely my gift is not fading. Not now.*

Dee frowned. 'Something is blocking your feelings. Maybe your own feelings. He raised a finger towards her. 'You are planning to go to the boatbuilders yard before we go to France. I have warned you, girl. Beware.'

Damn this. Why can you sense me and yet I can never

access your thoughts. You are the only one who blocks me, yet I am laid bare. 'I think I am just tired, Doctor.'

'Rubbish.' He handed her the crystal on a silken string. 'Use this. It will add the energy your thinking is dampening.'

Margaretta took the crystal and asked the question again as she moved it along the arc of cards and then yelped in sudden pain. She dropped the crystal and pulled her hand back. 'It was like fire.'

Dee turned the cards and just stared. Margaretta shuddered. Then they jumped as a sudden loud rattle at the window broke the silence. The turned to see a magpie clattering it's beak against the glass and flapping. It made its cruel, hacking call and flew away. They turned back to the card. 'The Devil,' whispered Dee. 'The worst of the cards. A goat creature, horned and a reversed pentacle as a crown. We are walking towards evil.'

Chapter Fifty-Two

Westminster Palace was heavily guarded. Dee grumbled at having to wait in the receiving office while his passport was sought and checked. People came and went in a strange silence with frightened eyes. Margaretta shivered as the feelings came. *Fear is everywhere. Fear that evil is coming unseen. Fear that the one foundation in your lives – the Queen – might be struck down by a devil creature. Whispers, rumours, tales invade your souls.*

At last, the guard returned and beckoned. 'Follow me, please. You will be first met by Mistress ap Harri.' As they walked, they passed a huddle of women, staring and whispering behind hands. Among them was Lady Douglas Sheffield who went to speak but was hushed by another.

Blanche was pale and dark shadows hung below her eyes. 'What progress have you made? Elizabeth is riven with fear. We cannot stop her stomach purging. Every time she is sick, we think Baphomet has entered the palace.'

Dee assumed his gentle tone. 'We are advancing our investigation. I have uncovered a cypher used by Mary Queen of Scots and we have found possible links to the courts of France.'

'Cyphers, ambitious queens, French rogues – all well and good. But how close are you to uncovering this devil who roams our lanes? We cannot lock down Court any further without turning away food supplies.'

Dee was silent and twitched his discomfort. 'We sail to Calais in two days and I will not rest until Elizabeth and her loyal subjects are safe.'

'Oh, fie your grand words. I get the same from Cecil, Leicester and Walsingham. Every one of you with the same look of sickened fear in your eyes.' Blanche stood, banging the desk with her fists. 'When will you uncover Baphomet?'

Dee gulped. 'We are working as fast as time allows, Cous... Mistress Blanche. I will create a soothing physik for Elizabeth's stomach.'

Blanche batted away his words with agitated hands. 'Cecil has already sent something created by his herbalist. But some damned fool has lost the package. We will find it and begin her treatment. We cannot risk anything else coming in unchecked.'

Dee jerked at the insult. 'I understand the Queen wishes to see me.'

Blanche nodded. 'She is locked away in her bed chamber. Only I, Leicester and Cecil are admitted unless by special request. I even have to watch the cleaning maids while she cowers in her bed. Every night she is prowling her room, waiting, waiting for the sound of iron feet in the corridor.' She sat again heavily. 'For the love of God, John. Give her a little peace.'

Elizabeth was sitting on a cushion, knees pulled up to her chest and a blanket around her shoulders. Her copper hair was loose. No wigs, pearls, or jewels this time. Just a thin, pale woman, pulling the covers close but still shivering. There was a faint tang in the air. Someone had recently been sick.

For all your grandeur, you are just as frightened as the beggar woman called Alice in your cells.

Elizabeth rose and stepped unsteadily towards Dee, her

hands reaching out for his. 'Tell me you have caught the devil.'

Dee took her hand and led her back to the fire. 'Sit and rest, good lady. We are making progress, and you are safe in these walls.'

Elizabeth gripped him tighter. 'But what do the stars say? Do they say a queen will fall and another rise? Do they see the death of dynasty?'

'They do not. I took the liberty of looking at your horoscope last night. It shows a period of unrest in which Mars meddles with the other stars. But no death. As for the death of a queen and the rising of another. No. Your friend, Bess of Shrewsbury, and her husband guard Queen Mary well and my investigation has uncovered her last means of communicating in secret.'

Elizabeth straightened. 'She still secrets her letters.'

'Not letters, my lady. Linens. Pretty embroidered linens. But we have the method and her cypher. It gives us eyes on those who would support her against you.'

'Norfolk. Does he plot?'

'I think he is a witless conduit, my lady. But the trap is set for those he foolishly feeds the messages. We will know more later today.'

'A witless fool is still dangerous, Doctor.'

'But witless and watched is your safety.'

For the first time, Elizabeth made a wan smile. 'What now in the search for the devil, Doctor?'

'France to flush out any foreign schemes. But first The Tower.'

Elizabeth nodded and seemed to sink. 'God speed success, good doctor – before I lose my life or my wits.'

Dee patted her hands. 'Cleave to Mistress Blanche, my lady. She is like a tiger protecting her cub and there is no greater wild-cat than a Welsh wild-cat.'

Elizabeth nodded and held out her hand to Blanche. 'How

true, Doctor. I am blessed.' She did not see the tears gathering in the older woman's eyes.

As Dee and Margaretta reached the door, Elizabeth called out. 'Meistres Morgan. *Dw i eisiau siarad gyda ti.*' Mistress Morgan. I would speak with you.

Dear God. She wants me. I look at the doctor who is surprised but nods. My stomach churns. She looks at me with those dark eyes. I do not know whether to look her in the eyes or not. '*Eich Mawrhydi?*' Your Majesty?

Elizabeth leaned forward and whispered, '*Brenhines yr Alban. Beth oeddet ti'n ei deimlo?*' The Queen of Scotland. What did you feel?

Margaretta answered in Welsh, 'Ambition, arrogance and foolery. Never trust her.'

'*Dych chi wedi weld a merch, Douglas. Beth amdana hi?*' You have seen the woman, Douglas. What of her?

'Ambition and desire – a dangerous combination. Beware.'

A blush of pain and a nod. 'You go to France. *Y bachgen Medici. Teimla fe.* The Medici boy. Feel him.'

'*Wna i.*' I will.

You are reaching out and touching my hand. A small smile. I feel you. A terrible mixture of fear, regret, anger and pride. But most of all, loneliness. Surrounded by hundreds and feeling so alone. You turn and put your head on Blanche's shoulder. I curtsy and leave to let you cry.

Chapter Fifty-Three

The Tower guard wrote their names in a ledger, then nodded towards a dark corner where a young man was sitting on a bench. 'I was told to point you to him.' He looked like a market lad, simply dressed in brown serge.

Dee approached, he rose and whispered in an educated voice. 'I am sent by Master Walsingham, sir. I am to say, "follow the linen" as proof of my service.'

Dee nodded and spoke low. 'We will leave within the half hour. Watch for anyone leaving the cell of the Duke of Norfolk. Follow and see where they go and who they meet. It will likely be a man called Barker. Fear not, he will be hard to lose in a crowd.'

The man nodded, made a twitch of a smile at the side of his mouth and sat, staring ahead. Dee returned to the guard. 'A package has been delivered for me, by Walsingham or his secretary.'

'Already taken to the cell, sir.'

'By who?'

'Master Walsingham himself. He arrived some quarter of the hour before you.' The guard tapped on the visitor book to show the name recorded and a package of a linen.

Dee exploded. 'That meddling fool. Why did you let him in? Why did you not make him wait for me... us.'

The guard stood back abashed. 'I did not know, sir. Master Walsingham did say nothing of it.'

Dee barked his frustration, grabbed Margaretta's arm and tugged her through the door towards the Bloody Tower. 'We have to hope we are not too late. The fucking fool. He is ruining the plan. If he has handed it over without you there, we cannot sense.'

Oh, dear, oh, dear. You are already irritated that Elizabeth spoke to me. You are even more irritated that I insisted she only asked for a woman's opinion on the Queen of Scots. You don't believe me, and I have had the fork of your tongue all the ride here. But this has sent you into a fireball of fury.

Dee banged open the door and stood glaring. Norfolk looked up, frightened eyes widening with more concern. Walsingham, who was sitting back to the door, turned slowly and made a small bow of the head. 'Good morrow, Doctor.' As he moved, the bright colours of the embroidered linen placed on the table before Norfolk came into view. Then a movement in the corner and someone clearing their throat. Dee turned angry eyes towards Billy Barker who pursed his lips and glared back, before sniffing and returning to his writing. Today he was adorned in yellow and blue with a ruff so wide he had to pull it down to see his own writing. Then another sniff, when Margaretta slipped from behind her master to take a seat by the door and open her bag to take out her pen and paper.

There is alarm in here. The fire makes it hot and the room stinks of sweat. It is the bitter smell of fear not the sweet sweat of hard work.

'I see you have handed the Duke his gift, Master Walsingham. The gift *I* brought him from Queen Mary.' Dee's voice was like a simmering kettle just about to scream its boiling point.

'There was no time to waste. The Duke was most grateful.' The cold, dull tone made Norfolk gulp.

Dee clattered another chair across the room to sit by the

desk, taking care to sit such that Margaretta had full line of sight. 'And what do you think of your pretty gift, sir?'

Norfolk shrugged. 'It is most kind and exquisitely made. Queen Mary has a gentle hand with silk.'

'Shame she is not so gentle with her scheming,' snarled Walsingham and Norfolk dabbed his brow. 'Before you arrived, Doctor Dee, the Duke was just about to tell me about his news from the French Courts – of his dealings with Catherine de Medici and the Cardinal of Lorraine.'

Oh no. My master's back has gone as rigid as a ram-rod. You are ruining his plan, Master Walsingham. Even I can see that spilling your suspicions at this point is a foolish move. Billy Barker has turned with a look of confusion. There has been no contact from France.

Norfolk began to splutter that he had no such dealings, but Dee cut across, pointing at the embroidery. 'Daniel in the lion's den is an interesting tale is it not? A great man maligned by jealous princes is cast into the den of lions but is saved by his goodness. When he is released, all those who had malintent towards him are cast in themselves along with their children and devoured by the beasts. What message is Mary sending you?'

Well done, master. Not perfect, but I can see his reaction and sense his thoughts. He looks at the linen, brows making little furrows. Sweat is beading further. But that is because the linen is causing him fear. Suddenly he is wondering what it holds. He does not know... and I do not think this man has the wit to think it through. He shrugs. The doctor glances back to me and a little shake of my head tells him to change tack.

'And such a fine border,' continued Dee, his voice going oily.

Norfolk's gaze went to the surround of Daniel and his lion and the brows knitted again. 'Yes, but what of it? This is much like the oth... other tapestries I have seen in great houses.' He turned his head away knowing he was not quick enough.

Walsingham opened his mouth to speak but Dee stepped

in. 'Yes, the others. Where are they? Mary told me this was not the first she had sent through the French Ambassador – Monsieur Mothe-Fénélon. A regular visitor I hear.'

Norfolk began to breathe rapidly. 'I do not recall others.'

'Oh, come, sir. How can you forget such kind and exquisite gifts from a gentle hand?'

There was an agonising silence until Billy Barker spoke, his voice like an indignant woman. 'My lord has gifts from ladies who fear for his comfort. All of them delicate, like the feelings of those ladies. They cannot be kept in this place of damp and death – it would only sully the sensibilities of the sweet senders. Anything of heartfelt thought is taken away to be graciously stored until my Lord is granted justice.'

My word, Billy Barker. You not only look like a mummer on a stage, but you speak like one. The other men stare at you. But you are quite unruffled. Just purse your lips, sniff, pull down your ruff and pick up your pen. The doctor looks back to Norfolk. He taps the border and comments on the strange pattern, so irregular. The Duke peers at it. Shrugs. He really does not know, though he is worried. He is thinking the name Ridolfi – again. Dee has his ear to me. 'Digon. Dilyna'r llian.' Enough. Follow the linen.

There was a terse farewell, leaving Norfolk slumped in his chair trembling. His interrogators descended the stone stairs but Dee's foot was not off the bottom step before his temper cracked. 'Why the hell did you not wait for me, Walsingham?'

The other man jerked to a halt and turned angrily. 'We are short of time, Doctor. You leave in two days. I needed to…'

'Needed to what? All you have achieved, sir, is to prevent us seeing the first reaction to the linen. The reaction which would tell us all. It was the impetuousness of a fool, man.'

Walsingham frowned his confusion. 'What do you mean "prevented us"? I hope you do not elevate your scribe to any position. I am the investigator here. Not a simple woman with a pen and only the wit to write what she hears.'

Damn you, Master Walsingham. Your high-handed

dismissal of women makes me like you not. And I sense you like me not either.

Dee began to shout. 'Do not deflect onto your opinion of my scribe, sir. Your thoughts on her are immaterial. But your foolery in overleaping my investigation – yes, *my* investigation – is both material and maddening.'

Walsingham's swarthy skin went deep red. 'You overstep your manners, Doctor Dee.'

'And you are too young to see how you overstep your abilities, sir. Stick to your cyphers and leave the intelligencing to those with experience of using intelligence.' Dee started to walk away. 'I will meet you at Cecil's in an hour for report on the message in the border – and where that linen is taken.' He did not turn back. Margaretta gathered up her bag and ran after him, through the guards' office, through Baynard's Tower, over the walkway traversing the stinking moat, through St Martin's Tower, and onto the gate. He did not stop stamping until he reached the end of Tower Street where he slipped into a shadowy alley, gesturing to Margaretta to step in close. 'We wait here. If Billy Barker moves, he can only move this way. I wonder where he will go.'

'Norfolk thought of the name Ridolfi again.'

'Did he indeed. The turned spy – or was he?'

It was only a wait of twenty minutes before a flash of blue and yellow under a black, billowing cloak was seen moving up the road towards them. Close behind was the man from the guard's office. Dee huffed, pulled back into the shadows and whispered, 'Well at least Walsingham's man is doing his job. But Barker's hands are empty. The guards would have checked his jacket. Where is the linen?'

Margaretta peeked out and supressed a laugh. 'His breeches are better filled than before.'

Dee looked out and then at his apprentice. 'Really?' Then the first smile of the week. 'For his sake, let us hope those lions don't bite.' He waited for Billy to be well out of sight and stepped out. 'Come Margaretta. We go to All Hallows. Fleetwood has left a gap in his questioning.'

And you are delighted.

Richard Tyrwhit was ashen white. 'Dear God, Doctor. What evil abounds in this city? How many more of my congregation will fall to this demon? I pray night and day, but weekly he takes another few. Like a fox in a hen-house he gets greedier with each visit.'

This time Dee was gentle in his speaking. 'I understand your distress, vicar. We need more details from you. Each person had a note saying they would learn the killer of Wassy, yet they had no connection.'

Tyrwhit looked puzzled. 'That is true.'

'Who else in your congregation is of that place?'

'Only one. Josef Mabelain. After the massacre, he picked up a few tools of his trade and fled. I am afraid he is away on one of his trading visits to France so he cannot speak with you. Gone since last Friday. Thank God – for he lives alone too.'

'Does he speak of the town?'

'Rarely, Doctor. Though all Huguenots think of Wassy as the start of their misery. It rises fury in all of them. Little wonder the note brought them from their homes.'

Chapter Fifty-Four

Walsingham did not look up when Dee and Margaretta entered Sir Cecil's office. Leicester was there, pacing, smacking his hand against his thigh, stopping only for a second to greet the doctor and then continue. With every pace, a golden sword rattled at his side. 'We need progress. Elizabeth is making herself ill with grief; Court is in panic, and the streets are humming with rumours that the Devil stalks our streets because Elizabeth has angered God.'

'You speak of the pamphlets,' Cecil replied. 'The trouble with such papers is that they rely on a snippet of truth. We cannot deny that the last few years have not been good for her standing with the people.'

'What do you mean?' snarled Leicester.

Cecil pulled a sheaf of pamphlets from his desk. 'These are what drive the anger towards Elizabeth. First, the spiteful imprisonment of the Grey sisters for the sin of marrying for love. One dead, the other locked away – their popular husbands broken. The people do not like women of the blood being so treated.'

I think Elizabeth has as many facets as the jewels she uses to adorn herself. Loving, angry, joyful, fearful, an imperious mistress, a frightened child, a kindly friend, a spiteful cousin, a confident Queen and a cowering wreck. And the only one who really sees her is a Welsh woman who rocked her cradle.

'They were threats to the Crown,' snarled Leicester.

'No. They were young, beautiful, in love, and chose to be happy with honest men.' Cecil paused while the point landed. 'Now the imprisonment of her cousin, Mary, angers the Catholics. He picked up the last pamphlet and flung it across the desk to the Earl. 'And then there is this.' It was a crude drawing of Elizabeth riding a horse with her skirts above her thighs, the horse's head was Leicester's.

Leicester picked up the pamphlet and ripped it to shreds, throwing the detritus on the floor. 'Why are you not finding the printers who churn out this evil?'

'Because we are busy trying to find a killer. If you want to be useful, my Earl of Leicester, then marry Douglas Sheffield, for love, and encourage Elizabeth to marry for her country. And leave this investigation to those who seek to protect her for no personal gain.'

Leicester opened his mouth as if he were going to scream. Then went silent, marched to the door and left, leaving the room in tense silence. Dee raised his eyebrows. 'Well, William. Your confidence has grown since events of last year.'

Cecil smiled. 'Conspiracy is a risky game, John. Last year, Leicester was part of a plot to marry Norfolk to Mary and send me to the Tower. This year his colleagues are scattered to the wind as traitors and I have the ear of the Queen – again. But enough of his strutting. We need to discuss Norfolk. Tell us all, Walsingham.'

The younger man was still scowling and refusing to look at John Dee. He pulled a parchment from his bag and placed it on the desk. 'This is the translation of the border. Each side had a single sentence.'

Cecil reached for it and read out loud. 'A duke and queen are kindly matched. I pledge my troth to destiny. We are God guided. Let the future begin.'

Dee leaned forward to take it. 'Seems she is still promoting marriage to the Duke of Norfolk – Daniel in the embroidery

– and sanctioning a plot. It makes sense.' If she is wedded to a Duke, and her former brother-in-law is King, Elizabeth will have to release her.'

Walsingham shrugged and responded sullenly. 'As I have said before, we need to extract confession from Norfolk.'

Dee shook his head. 'It was apparent this morning that he does not understand this border message. No, this is meant for someone else.'

'You cannot know that,' snarled Walsingham.

Dee's tone turned to ice. 'I say again, let experience lead the way. Now where did Billy Barker take the linen?'

Walsingham shrugged. 'He went to Norfolk's house, but we think he knew he was followed. My man said the guard whispered to him as he was searched for letters. Then Barker turned and smiled at his follower as he entered Norfolk's house.'

'Incompetence,' spat Dee.

'Enough,' barked Cecil. 'We will watch and wait. If Barker goes anywhere other than The Tower, we will follow. For now, John, you need this – your passport for travel and request for entry to the Court of Medici signed by Elizabeth. You will board The Northern Star at St Katherine's Dock the day after tomorrow at eight in the morning. We have prediction of good weather and so should arrive in France the following day. Norris will await you, take you to Court and translate.'

Dee looked at the documents. 'These only have my name.'

Oh. No.

Cecil smiled as he pulled out another sheaf and handed them to Margaretta. 'Mistress Morgan has not escaped our notice. She will travel as your secretary. Or is it partner in detection?'

Chapter Fifty-Five

They arrived back at Mortlake late afternoon, where Dee announced that he would spend the evening with his wife. It had been arranged that an official barge would collect them at turn of tide the day after tomorrow and so they had only a day to prepare.

Margaretta took a breath. 'I need to visit with my family and friends, Doctor. I will organise the house in the morning and then travel to them.'

Dee looked stern. 'Family I understand. Then you come home.'

Damn you. I will not. 'Yes, Doctor.' *And I hope you do not know my fingers are crossed behind my back to undo the lie.*

Winnie trotted out of the house. 'How has been your day, Miss? I have made bread, cleaned the kitchen and prepared the vegetables for evening pottage. Can I get you some ale?'

Margaretta put her arm around Winnie's shoulders and walked with her. 'It is good to have you here, Winnie. You are the antidote to Lemon-head.'

The girl stifled a laugh. 'She has spent the day trying to become my friend. Told me how she has to calm Mistress Katherine; how she keeps their marriage together; how you know nothing of running a house.' Suddenly she halted. 'Maybe I should keep quiet, Miss.'

Margaretta chuckled. 'Just listen and agree, Winnie.

While I am away in France, pretend to be stupid and believe everything she says. If she gets vicious, go to Mother Dee.'

Winnie nodded. 'I went to the riverbank today, Miss. When I look across do I see Holborn?'

'Not from here, Winnie. Oh, do not look sad. Your job for the next few weeks is to prove yourself an excellent housemaid. That way I can get you a position. When I get back, we will seek your Donald. Now get me that ale.'

Winnie squeaked and scampered into the house.

Chapter Fifty-Six

The Vintry was already a hive of activity when Margaretta urged her horse through the gate of McFadden's Wine Merchants. With the sun just up, Huw was out in the yard organising the stacking of barrels being unloaded from an Italian ship. Margaretta watched for a while.

Look at you. Dada and Mam would be bursting with pride. You look at no one, but you count as fast as the wind and, with one look around the yard, decide where you want the barrels stored. You give orders loud and strong. The men nod and run. No arguing. No sly comments.

Grace came out of the wooden shed that served as an office and spotted Margaretta, her face showing delight. 'Welcome, sister. A good day to visit. Huw thought that with all the rumours of France and Spain trying to take our lands we might make a virtue of Italian wine.'

Margaretta jumped down. 'This makes my heart sing, Grace. Let us speak inside.'

Over spiced ale for warmth and a slice of good bread, Grace chattered about their progress. The first week had been hard with the friends of the lanky lad showing their defiance. Huw had given them their papers, but the threats to burn his yard had been ended by a 'friendly visit' from Siôn and a few wherry men happy to show their muscles for a few beakers of good Gascon. Within the hour, Huw had the loyalty of the remaining men when he announced that he had studied the books and found they had been cheated. Every man was given three shillings and asked for his commitment to making McFaddens the best Wine Merchant in London. There had been good cheer ever since and no slacking.

'And what do you do, Grace?'

'I make food, clean barrels, and also wash the pots and measures. It is hard work, sister. I would like to learn to help with the books and the entertaining of customers. I think we could make a wine tasting room where people can try our goods before they buy. But there is much cleaning to be done. I have told Huw that as soon as we are turning a good profit, I should be getting a bottle boy. Delyth agrees with me.'

'As do I. And I have the very person – a hard-working woman who has met hard times. Her name is Alice. We would be taking her from the gutter…'

Grace smiled. 'I think Siôn would approve of that and Huw listens to him.'

'Well, I go to France tomorrow. So, you get that brother of mine turning a profit by the time I return.'

And the deal was done.

Huw came through the door and smiled without looking. 'It is surely good to see you, Margaretta. All is yellow here.'

'So I see. Dada and Mam would be so very proud. But how is our sister, Susan, behaving?'

He began stepping until Grace walked over and took his hand. 'Keeps shouting that she should have all the takings. I send money every week and bought physik for Angus. She wanted money for a new dress and a French hood. Shouted when I said "no".'

Margaretta groaned. 'Will she ever change? Saved from certain poverty and she can only think of her looks. I am heading east and passing the house. I will call in.'

'Beware, Margaretta. She keeps saying you have hexed Angus. There is talk everywhere of a devil roaming and killing. You do not want her shouting such things of you.'

I cannot tell you the truth of Baphomet. But your words strike ice into my heart. The sister I have saved – many times – could be the very one who brings me down. 'Do not fear, Huw. I will quieten her.'

The usual maid opened the door. 'Your sister is busy, Mistress. The master has had a bad night.'

Margaretta shrugged and stepped through the door. 'No matter. I must see her. Is she attending Master Angus now?'

The maid made a worried nod and scuttled away.

The room was stinking from an unwashed body, rotting flesh, and foul breath. Margaretta almost cried out when she saw Angus. The purple boils were larger and pus filled. One had closed his left eye. He began to rave and shake his head side to side when he saw her, as if she were an angel of death come for him. Susan, who was slumped in a chair by his bed, jerked out of her sleep and stared through the gloom at the figure in the door. 'Who is it?'

'Your sister.'

Susan jumped up. 'I suppose you have come to gloat. My husband cursed, and our business stolen.'

'I have just come from our brother who is fulfilling his promise. As for curses. Your husband is living his own curse.'

I came here to shout at you. But you look like a cat who has been left out in the rain. Spitting and snarling, yet bedraggled and sad. I will try kindness. 'Let us not argue, sister. Huw said he had ordered a physik. Is it helping?'

Susan slumped back on the chair and slowly turned her head to Angus. 'Quietens him for a while. Makes him sleep. I sit here and remember the man I met when I came to London. So handsome. So fine. So…'

You were going to say rich, but you have the sense to stop your tongue. 'Huw will take good care of you. Your children too. He is Dada's son.'

Susan said nothing but stared at her husband.

'Susan, I am going away for a few weeks. Maybe we can try to be more sisterly when I return.'

Just silent staring.

'I must away. I will look in on the children before I go.' Margaretta turned and left the room. As she reached the bottom of the stairs, she heard the door of Angus's room open and her sister's face appeared over the banister. 'Tell Huw I will need a new gown, sleeves and a hooded cloak for the funeral. Shoes too.'

Dear God. For a second up there I thought you had a heart. No. You are quite dreadful.

Chapter Fifty-Seven

The boatyard was the usual thrum of activity and thick with the smell of newly sawn wood. Men, their shirts damp with sweat and hair made blonde with sawdust, shouted their conversation above the din and laughed at jokes. In the far corner, Sam was shaking hands with a well-dressed man. It looked like the end of a good deal. As he turned to walk the man to the yard entrance, he saw Margaretta and waved. A quick farewell to his client and he ran over. 'It is good to see you, Margaretta.' He reached out for her hand. 'Come. Let us speak away from this noise.'

You still look so sad. That dimness of your eyes. No smile. It is as if your soul is sapped away. 'You are back to work, Sam. That is good. I think Lottie would like that.'

He gulped and quickly looked away. 'I had no choice. Master Tovey has taken Goodwife and Tilly away for a few days to see his brother. Told me I had to shake myself out of bed and run the yard.'

What a very wise man. 'Maybe that was a gift from heaven, Sam. Work will keep your mind busy.'

Sam looked up at the sky. 'I think my Lottie sent him a message from above, for I have never heard him want to see his brother before.' He seemed to shake himself. 'Come to the house. I have a fire burning and can make you some warm wine.'

They settled in front of the fire, legs warmed by the flames and their stomachs with wine. Sam talked about Lottie and his boys, how he woke every morning thinking all was well and then the black cloud of misery would descend. He shed tears about the years and future he would never see. Margaretta listened, comforted and patted his hand. She passed him linens to blow his nose and put her hand on his shoulder when he started to weep. Hours passed and beaker after beaker of wine was poured. Suddenly she realised that the room was vague and her head a fug. She looked down and realised that Sam was holding her hand. He was slower in speech and less clear.

I feel the warmth of you. Warmer than the fire. The feel of your hand squeezing mine. The sound of your voice. You are speaking of the business of the future of your dreams for the yard. I wish I could take this moment and put it in a bottle, like those little ships that never sail.

'You're squeezing my hand like you will never let go, Missy.' He was looking at her, smiling.

'Sorry, Sam. I think the wine makes me unsteady. I must away. It is a long ride to Mortlake.'

He was silent a second. 'I was hoping it meant more, Missy. Sitting here with you makes me realise how much I miss the touch of a woman. It is not natural for a man to be without it. We have always had good feeling for each other have we not?'

I am confused. You are smiling at me, though with sad eyes. You touch my cheek. I want you to kiss me. No. This is wrong. I mustn't.

'Yes. Since the day you picked me up at St Dunstans.'

'And made you angry by asking why your master had given you away. You wouldn't talk and then you slipped on the weed and I had to catch you round the waist – like this.'

Is this happening? Those strong arms wrap around me. I feel the warmth of your breath and the smell of the wine. Closer. I should push you away. But I want your touch. Your lips on mine. Gentle. Hungry, Probing. It feels as if we have done this for years. You hold my face in your hands, look into my eyes, yours full of tears. I feel dizzy – and not from wine.

Sam kissed her forehead. 'Don't think me bad, Missy. Lottie would not want me lonely – nor her dear friend.'

Margaretta smiled, put her head on his shoulder and told him she must away to France for some weeks.

'I'm not going anywhere, Missy. Just hurry back.'

Another kiss and she had to go. As Margaretta geed her horse through the gate, she wept tears of joy – and guilt.

As dusk settled, Margaretta trotted her horse into the Mortlake house yard. Out of the shadows jumped Thomas Digges. 'Miss Morgan, I have been waiting for you.'

'For what reason Master Digges?'

Even in the gloom his blushing was obvious. 'I... I... hope my small indiscretion has not ruined my chances.'

Margaretta dismounted, her face bright and she smiled as she patted his shoulder. 'Oh Mr Digges, it is not your indiscretions that have ruined your chances, but a gift from heaven itself.' She walked away, leaving him staring at her back.

Part Three

France

Chapter Fifty-Eight

Despite a good sea and a fair wind, it took two days to reach Calais. Margaretta had suffered through the usual phases of sea sickness. First feeling ill, next, thinking she might die, by the end of the day wanting to die. But all through her retching, delirium and begging Dee to take her home, she kept thinking of Sam with a strange mix of warmth and guilt. Then she would open her eyes and find John Dee, looking down, eyes worried, voice gentle. He lifted her head to give her water, wiped her mouth, smoothed her hair from a sweating brow. Then the blessed sound of a sailor shouting, 'port-ho'.

She walked unsteadily down the gangplank, ignoring the muttering of sailors that she was bad luck on a ship and so deserved all her maladies. Dee walked ahead, directly to a well-dressed man on the quayside next to an impressive carriage. 'Henry Norris?'

The man smiled, shook hands and looked behind Dee with a look of disdainful horror. She knew she looked a wretch. She could smell herself. 'Your wife, Doctor Dee?'

'Good God, no. My secretary. Retched with every wave and we can expect more of it if we put her inside the carriage.' He pointed up to the driver. 'She'll have to sit by him. But is there somewhere she can clean herself up?'

You old rogue. Talking about me as if I were a dog whose gone rolling in horse muck. Sam would never do that.

After a tavern woman was paid a few francs to provide hot water, linens and some dried lavender, Margaretta emerged smelling sweet in a clean dress. She had washed her mouth with salt water, rubbed her teeth with a course cloth and had filled her stomach with bread. This time, Henry Norris was polite. 'Mistress Morgan. Forgive me for not realising that the poor woman staggering from the ship was the very woman Sir Cecil has written to say is essential to the work of John Dee.'

Dee bridled. 'Essential? Fie. Margaretta is simply a servant who can write.' He handed her the bag. 'Ambassador Norris has given information we must write down. Load your pen.'

Norris raised a brow as he offered Margaretta a seat at the table, and the story was repeated, his voice low to avoid eavesdropping. 'In the past few days, I have investigated any links to the information sent by Sir Cecil – that the killer is masked, uses poison and has metal shoes. There is a link to the Guise family. The Cardinal of Lorraine's apothecary wears a leather mask and is known as "*le cheval médecin*" – the physik horse – because he walks on metal feet and makes the sound of a stallion on stone.'

Margaretta looked to John Dee. 'Every sighting of Baphomet has said his feet chink, chink on stone and witnesses have described a leather mask. This is a very close co-incidence.'

Dee nodded. 'Where will we find him?'

'Joinville, the seat of the Guise,' answered Norris. 'I understand Cecil has sent a spy there. Though, as I was not informed, I have not given him the information.' He made a sigh of exasperation. 'Cecil needs to understand that sometimes trust is stronger than suspicion.'

'Can you get a messenger to Joinville? Someone trusted who can instruct Mabelain to investigate the apothecary and see if he is there or if he has travelled to England?' demanded Dee.

Norris nodded. 'My secretary. Marcus. He will leave today.'

Outside, Norris handed Margaretta an oiled cloak and helped her to her seat by the driver which had been furnished with a cushion.

Well, let's hope my master will pick up a few of your good manners, sir.

Three days later they entered the gates of Paris. The streets were crowded like London, but the buildings closer together, and in the centre, grander, larger, all white with black timbers. As they crossed a bridge over a river thick with detritus and scum, the driver turned to the right and made the sign of the cross. Margaretta pointed at the steeple, so tall that it seemed to touch the sky, and tugged his sleeve. 'Notre Dame,' he replied. Another bridge and they turned north, then the opulent Palace de Louvre came into sight. Guards, perfectly dressed as if going to a royal occasion, ran forward to greet the guests and carry bags. She clambered down and waited to be told where to go.

I sense discomfort. Embarrassment. It is you Master Norris. You keep looking at me and that ruddy complexion of yours is brightening with every look. You whisper something to my master and he looks me up and down and whispers something back. Do I still smell? They are looking at my dress.

Dee stepped over. 'Now do not take badly, Margaretta, but Ambassador Norris says you need a little – well, dressing. This court expects beauty in everything. His wife, Lady Margery, will assist.'

'This is a clean smock.'

'We need you to look like a woman of breeding. You will go with the Ambassador now and come back dressed so you do not embarrass me. Margery is of Welsh nobility. You will like her.'

Damn you. My clothes are plain because you do not pay

me. You would see me naked if it saved you money to buy another damn book... 'Very well.'

'Do not sulk, girl.' He turned away and followed the servants who carried his bags and box of books.

Two hours later, Margaretta stepped down from Norris' carriage, laced into a bodice and gown, with kirtle and sleeves so heavy it felt as if she were wearing the sheep whose wool had made the cloth. The small ruff scratched her neck, and the pins securing her hood tugged at her hair. The servant who had accompanied her, handed her passport to the palace guard and explained that she would be taken to her rooms to wait for Dee. He bowed low and stepped back into the carriage.

My – what a bit of brocade and lace does for a woman. First looked at like a mangy dog – now I deserve respect and sweet words. Well, I will gladly live this charade for a week. When I go back, I will be back in my brown smock. Though I might save for a blue dress to step out with Sam. No. I must try not to think of him, for I think my heart will burst out of this damn corset with joy – and worry.

The room was a large as the courtyard at Mortlake. Windows looked out onto a large garden, perfectly manicured. Beyond the green, a huge building swarming with men carrying bricks, plaster, tools – a whole new palace being built. Margaretta stared around. She was used to a wood-walled room with a single bed, straw mattress and a wooden box for her clothes. Here there were fresh rushes on the floor, walls of stained oak, a bed big enough for four people with rich coverlets. She pressed it. Not the crunch of dry straw but something soft and silent. There was a dressing table with a brush, perfumed oils for her hair and a mirror to see her face. On another table was a crystal decanter full of dark liquor and small glass next to a dish of sugared fruits. She just stood and looked around. Then the wicked thought. *I must tell Susan of this.*

There was a knock at the door and a small woman, brightly

dressed, her hair in a silk coif entered. 'Madame Morgan?' The accent was heavy but the language clear. 'My name is Marianne – your assistant for your stay as I speak your language.' She made a smile that did not reach her eyes and bowed her head.

Resentment. A woman of intelligence desiring respect but told to look after a servant. You feel affronted. 'Thank you, Marianne. But as an assistant myself, I do not warrant the same. However, I would be most grateful if you would educate me in how to conduct myself in this grand court.'

The other woman narrowed her eyes, cocked her head on one side. This time the smile reached her eyes. '*Mais oui*. My pleasure.' She wrinkled her nose. 'Who gave you that dress?'

'Lady Margery, the English ambassador's wife.'

Marianne made a small puffing sound and shrugged. 'This court likes beauty, madame. Take off that dreadful ruff. So very English.'

'Willingly. I am Welsh. But, why do you smile so widely?'

'Breizhad on i.' I am Breton. 'We can speak.'

Your tongue is so different but so alike mine. 'Siaradwch yn gyflym.' Speak slowly. *Your face lights up. I think I have a friend. Good for my heart and good for our investigation.*

In seconds, Marianne was fussing around Margaretta, undoing the front of her dress, folding the material back to create a lower neckline and pulling off the hood, dressing her hair into falling curls. She stepped in front of the looking glass and gasped. The other woman laughed. 'Maybe you have a sweetheart? Would he like this?'

Oh, to hear those words and think of Sam. 'I would say... he might be... well, surprised.'

Marianne grinned. 'I think he would like. Your eyes brighten when you think of him.' Then she disappeared and returned with a necklace of bright blue glass and a matching brooch that was pinned to the front of the dress, centred to draw attention to the low neckline. '*Gwelloc'h.*' Better. She handed Margaretta a large pomander. 'You will need this.'

It was time to go out into the Court of Catherine de Medici.

Chapter Fifty-Nine

It was like walking out into to a mummers fair. People paraded the corridors, constantly glancing around to see who gazed at them. Women glided along, eyes peering over fluttering fans to check for admiring glances. Many of the men were dressed in pure white from their silk tights to their velvet doublets, all threaded with gold sparkling in the candlelight. Others were gaudily clad in every colour of the rainbow.

Dear God, it is like walking in a crowd of Billy Barkers. These men wear more jewels than our Queen and swing their hips better than a Southbank bawd.

Marianne nudged her and whispered in Breton, 'Eyes ahead. You are gawping like a child in a shop of sugar.'

'But I have never seen the like – or smelled so much perfume.'

The other woman made a small laugh and whispered even lower. 'Oh, this is the parading corridor where the lowly but ambitious strut daily, hoping to be seen. You will notice they are all beautiful. Only money gives you allowance to be ugly in the Court of Medici.'

Eventually, Margaretta was steered towards a door guarded by a well liveried guard who nodded to Marianne to continue. She nudged Margaretta. 'Use your pomander.' The huge, gilded door was swung open to reveal a long walkway of marble walls, hung with rich tapestries and paintings in golden frames, pestles topped with porcelain vases and crystal. A crowd of people milling around or walking, all dressed in rich silks, sparkling with jewels. Margaretta gasped – not at the sight but at the heat and terrible stench of sweat and heavy scents. Her companion chuckled.

As they made their way through the crowd, women smirked and lifted their fans to hide the comments between them, eyes narrowing in contemptuous laughter.

Oh, you think I do not feel your spite. You look at me as if I am a little drudge and yet, with my dress opened so low, I feel like a doxy. I have not felt one kind thought since I walked through that door. Your minds are as vile as the stench you make.

There was the sound of a trumpet followed by clamour as people shuffled to the side to make a walkway. The far door opened and through it came a parade of beautiful women, every one of them with a neckline so low that Margaretta turned away. Marianne whispered, 'The squadron,' then winked in a sign to say nothing. As they paraded through, heads high, noses in the air, a smile of triumph on every face, the whispering courtiers stared, and the men made flourishing bows. As the last of the parade disappeared through another door, the babble of noise erupted.

Gossip and spite. That's all I can feel. Suddenly, I am of no interest.

They had reached the end of the corridor and were admitted to the next chamber before Marianne bent her head to Margaretta. 'The squadron is Queen Catherine's posse of woman with special power. They whisper sweet words, lift their skirts, bring men to their knees and play them like puppets. The power of the putain touches every dark corner of this court.' She laughed. 'Come, I think you have seen enough for one day. I take you to your Doctor. He is in the library.'

Oh, no. A library. You have no idea how foolish that was. And you thought I was the child in a shop of sugar.

Dee was immersed in a large volume, head bent and scribbling furiously. Margaretta went to his side. 'Doctor?'

'Nicolaus Copernicus. His greatest work. Published just a day before he died,' muttered Dee, still writing. 'If I work non-stop, maybe I can copy the whole text. Take it back to Digges.'

'What is it?'

'His treatise. *De Revolitionibus Orbium Coelestium.* The revolution of planets. Wonderful. This will change the science of the stars.'

'But Doctor, we need to…'

'Hush, woman.'

A pox on you.

It was over an hour before a servant entered and cleared his throat to get attention. 'Doctor Dee. Her Majesty Queen Catherine will see you now. Your Ambassador, Norris, is waiting in her salon to translate for you.'

Dee raised his head, scowling, then sighed and started gathering his copy papers, handing them to Margaretta to sort and put in his bag. He looked at her for the first time and froze. 'What the hell… you look like a harlot.'

She blushed crimson. 'This is more fashionable. Will help me… blend in.'

'Pah. I'm not sure I want you blending. Come. And cover your chest. I can almost see your belly.'

Maybe I will not dress like this for Sam. I want him to be proud of me. A respectable wife.

The salon was opened with a flourish by two liveried guards. Dee stepped through first and bowed to the dowager Queen Catherine. She was like a tar-barrel. Dressed in ink-black silk, a black headdress and a small veil over her forehead; the only nod to decoration were her jewelled silk shoes with thin narrow heels. Her face was pale, fleshy, with heavy jowls over a chin with many folds. Steady, hard eyes were puffy above a broad nose. The only sign of earlier prettiness were her full lips. She coldly appraised the doctor as he approached, then turned to Norris who stood and told Dee he was, 'most welcome by Catherine, the Queen Mother of France.'

Margaretta glanced around at the walls, painted with vivid frescos of birds, and other animals all placed in forests and fields. Plaster cornicing glistened with gold leaf. Crystal lights hung from the ceiling, their glass twinkling in the hundreds of candles within them. A fireplace the height of a man burned a fire that would keep an army warm. There was a loud squawk and Margaretta turned to see a huge green parrot on a golden pedestal. It opened its wings and screeched, '*Merde, merde, merde*,' making the plump dowager chortle and clap her hands. As she moved there was a whiff of perfume, strong and lemony.

Dee bowed low and declared he brought, 'the good wishes of Queen Elizabeth of England and the hope that he might give her insights into the stars.' When this was translated by Norris, she made a tiny shrug and stated that there were more pressing questions on her mind.

Then Dee's attempt to offer her a horoscope was killed like a bird flying into glass. Catherine wagged her hand and demanded to know, 'why has the English Queen has been so reluctant to grasp the honour of betrothal to Europe's most eligible King? If you are her philosopher, you must be able to illuminate me on her reluctance.'

Dee gulped and Norris looked as if he had sat on a wasp. He tried to answer for Dee, but was silenced with a sharp, 'Shush.'

My, this woman is as dark as her dress. She is riddled with anger, anxiety and indignation. Yet when she speaks of her son, there is a flash of joy. I think she is a serpent who happens to love her snakelets. When she says the name Elizabeth, she feels fury mixed with hurt.

Dee took a deep breath. 'Queen Elizabeth wants the best for her beloved country and also for your great land. I think she is concerned at the difference in age.'

Norris cleared his throat in a very evident warning to say no more.

Catherine shrugged. 'But not too old for a gallop with her stable-boy. Well, she has left her decision too late. We are negotiating with Austria... for the hand of a much younger Elisabeth. When there is a new Dauphin of France, your Queen can be godmother as reminder of the child she never had.'

You wicked, spiteful old woman. I must have reacted, for you are peering past my master to look at me. Eyes down, Look away. Pray. Norris is looking alarmed. He knew nothing of this new negotiation.

Queen Catherine glared at Dee. 'Why are you really here, sir? Do you expect me to believe my cousin in England has sent you all this way to calcule a horoscope when she knows I have my own foreteller of the future.'

Dee looked to Norris who was stiff with tension.

Seeing their discomfort, the Queen made a vicious smile. 'Ah. Two men and not one tongue between them. Well, let me tell you why you are here, Doctor. You come to see if my reputation as the Serpent Queen is true and if I seek to poison Elizabeth of England. You are here to see if this strange man of a cut face and one eye is sent from me... maybe with a tainted apple.' Dee tried to allay further accusations and was silenced with a bark to, 'listen well and take back my message, sir. If Elizabeth of England wants to avoid the wrath of France, then she should stop supporting our Huguenot enemies. She should release Mary Queen of Scots and find herself a good husband – not a stable boy. The protection of France would be to her benefit and she would be advised to accept the protection of a man who rides a horse to the true Church and not one who rides a horse to the hounds.'

She turned to Norris, who was almost breathless having had to translate her ranting. 'Cecil is not the only one who can slit a letter and read it before it gets into the hands of your messengers.' She put her fingers into a V and tapped below her eyes. 'These serpent eyes are all seeing, sir.'

The silence in the room was like a layer of ice but Norris was now sweating profusely.

Catherine de Medici clicked her fingers and pointed to the side of the room where a high table groaned with food. Servants ran to fill two gold plates. She immediately started jabbing at the offered delicacies with an implement like a knife with spikes upon the end. With every mouthful, her cheeks ballooned and her lips smacked in gluttony. Her guests kept their eyes down and said nothing.

You eat like a woman starved, through the belly belies that, Madam Medici. You are a glutton.

Eventually, her fill taken, she jutted her chin to be wiped with a silk handkerchief, before a flick of her hand sent the servants scattering away. 'How do you vision the future, Doctor Dee? Do you own a magic mirror?'

Dee looked abashed. 'No, Your Majesty. I use the science of the stars.'

'And do the stars see my son wearing an English crown?'

Dee glanced at Norris who looked equally abashed. 'You have just stated that you are pursuing negotiations with Austria, Madam.'

She sneered. 'Unlike the Tudors, the Medici's are fertile, sir. I have two sons yet to be matched. Henri Duc d'Anjou and young Hercules.'

Dee made an ingratiating smile. 'I presume you are thinking of Henri, Your Majesty… though he is younger still than the King.'

Catherine's eyes narrowed in irritation and her tone lowered to threat. 'With a mind much advanced for his years, a warrior, and a man of faith… making him an excellent king for the salvation of your Devil's Land.'

Not from what Blanche ap Harri has said of him. And Ambassador Norris is paling fast.

Dee smiled again in an attempt to warm the atmosphere. 'I have no authority to negotiate a betrothal, Your Majesty.'

'But you can prepare one of your horoscopes. You can ask

if my son will be a king of England – and alleviate some of the offence you have created in coming under false pretences by answering that question.'

My master is lost for words and Norris is too fearful to speak. If we leave now, I can have no feeling about this queen's link to the murders. And we do not know if Henri is a willing player in this scheme. I am blocked. Always try paper.

Margaretta took a parchment and her pen out of her bag, dipped the quill into the ink horn and stepped to her master's side, whispering in Welsh, 'mention the killings and ask to see Henri.'

Queen Catherine barked at Dee. 'Your servant is ill-mannered, sir. She moves without bidding. And what is that tongue?'

Oh, my God.

Dee bowed. 'She is simply trained to bring my paper and pen when I require them. She speaks her own tongue as a sign of secrecy and respect – that she will never repeat a word of what she hears. Now, may I have the date and place of your son's birthing?' Norris nodded and quickly translated. Then sank in relief when the dowager gave a satisfied smile.

She flicked her fingers for the doors to be opened. 'In the morning my astrologer, Cosimo Ruggieri will give you the information you require and oversee your work. He may even educate you in the art of visioning.'

Dee hid his resentment well, bowed and started walking backwards to the door.

What is he doing? He needs to mention the—

Dee suddenly stopped and smiled again. 'Your Majesty, you mentioned earlier a man with a scar face and one eye boarding a ship. It is indeed true that we face terrible events in London. Do you want your son coming to a place that you call the Devil's Land?'

The response was imperious. 'He will sweep away the sins of your country, sir. Be assured of that. I know of the evils happening in your streets.' She turned with a knowing look to Norris. Then suddenly she softened and shook her head. 'Doctor Dee, tell Elizabeth that I mean her no harm. But a woman leading a court is very lonely without the protection of a man... I know it.'

And you are not lying. Below this black and brittle front is a woman of feeling... and fear. And maybe you are right. I feel safer simply thinking of Sam.

Dee bowed again. 'I always like to match the messages of the stars with the features of the face, Your Majesty. It gives a stronger prediction. May I present my horoscope to your son?'

Catherine de Medici nodded. 'The Duc d'Anjou is in Joinville where he has been in conference with the Cardinal of Lorraine about the Huguenot problem. He returns tomorrow.'

She turned away and clapped her hands for more food. As Dee, Norris and Margaretta backed out of the room, she was stuffing sweetmeats into her mouth.

Outside, Norris leant against a wall and mopped his brow. In a second it was slicked with sweat again. 'Dear God, I have long begged Cecil to return me to England. Now it is essential. If she does not trust, she kills.'

Dee spoke softly to ensure he was not overheard. 'But you knew she was contemplating matching the Duc d'Anjou to our Queen.'

Norris made a shuddering sigh. 'Yes, and I have told Cecil it would be the end of any refuge for Huguenots in England and bring years of misery to our Queen. I will not be party to any such discussion. She has just made it very clear she sees every word of my correspondence. My poison is probably already in an apple.' He started to walk away speaking over his shoulder. 'I will write my plea this very day.' And he disappeared into the crowd of courtiers.

Dee led Margaretta back to the library, which was empty but for one studious looking young man, but they spoke in Welsh for safety. 'What did you feel of her?'

'A storm of feelings. But not murder. When she said she meant no ill to Elizabeth, she spoke truth. She is not behind these killings.'

Dee frowned. 'If the threat is not here, then Cecil has sent us to the wrong court. Damn it.'

But Josef Mabelain is in Joinville and you have sent message to investigate the apothecary. He will be able…'

'No, Margaretta,' snapped Dee. 'Mabelain is no more than a lowly weaver and will have no entry to Court. He will never stand in the presence of anyone we identified as in the ring of threat around Elizabeth. That fool Cecil has played his game of divide and rule and created divide and fail.'

He snatched the bag from her. 'Now leave this with me and go and walk around Court. See, feel, spy. Bring me everything you can.'

'Why do you want the bag?'

He looked away. 'To hold my papers.'

'Or to magic away a book? Don't you dare play magpie here.'

'You overstep yourself, apprentice. Now, leave me to my work and thoughts and go and step around the Court of Medici.'

Chapter Sixty

Margaretta felt the presence of Cosimo Ruggieri before he entered the room. She was sitting with the doctor, telling him of her impressions of Court – the oily stink of perfumes, the lewd behaviour, the bawdiness of the squadron. Suddenly, her skin began to crawl and her eyes were drawn to the library door.

When the Queen's soothsayer entered, he stared at Dee for long seconds before nodding but never breaking eye contact. 'So, you are the famous Doctor Dee.' The voice was deep and heavily accented. 'Come to take my work from me.'

Dee stood and made a polite bow. 'I come only to share knowledge.'

A long silence and the other man stepped further into the room and the candlelight. He was short, round and fleshy like the Queen, but the folds of his jaw were covered in a long, thick beard. Bright, dark eyes kept their intense gaze on Dee like a raven viewing a bug. Though a head shorter than Dee, he appeared large, imposing, threatening. Suddenly, he shot an arm out to point at Margaretta without turning to look at her. 'You bring a spirit see-er.'

Margaretta jumped. *Oh, God. He frightens me. I cannot stop the tremble. I look to my master, but he is transfixed.*

Dee shook his head. 'Just my servant and scribe.'

'You lie.'

Another long silence, Dee glanced at Margaretta. 'Well, she does have a good sense of other people.'

Ruggieri made a dragging, slow chuckle, bulbous lips shifting as if forming his thoughts. The silence stretched. Then, 'My Queen says we are to work together to predict the marriage of her sons. You will do a horoscope, I think.'

Dee nodded. 'I can do that, sir. But the stars will only tell me if there will be a marriage – not the name of the bride.'

Ruggieri was silent again. 'Then my methods are superior.'

Dee bristled but held his tongue.

Another chuckle and the Italian pushed a paper across the desk. 'The information for your little calculations. Then you come to my office and we will do real magic. We will see the bride to be.' He stood, turned to Margaretta. 'She will see.'

He walked out, leaving Dee glaring at the shut door. 'Impudent snoutband.'

'He frightens me, Doctor.'

'But what did you feel of him?'

'Nothing. Just my own fear.'

'So, he can block you too. Sit. We will get this horoscope written and keep the Serpent Queen off our backs. We need to keep her thinking Elizabeth is a future bride.'

Chapter Sixty-One

Two hours later, Dee and Margaretta were led along the long corridors of Le Louvre holding the horoscope. Again, Margaretta was assaulted by feelings of pity, derision, spite. But her strange senses were not needed. As they passed, women lifted their fans and sniggered, one pointed at her dress and pretended to gag. Dee took her arm and whispered. '*Pen i fyny.*' Head up. 'You are the red dragon of Wales walking through sheep – and dragons eat sheep for breakfast.'

Sometimes I do like you. I wonder how you will react when I tell you am going to be a boat-builder's wife.

The nervous servant leading them knocked exactly seven times on the door. When a call came to enter, he ran away down the corridor. Dee stepped in first. The office was dark, fugged with candle smoke and a heavy scent of burning herbs. Ruggieri was seated at a desk in the far corner. In front of him a tray full of bloody mess. As Dee and Margaretta approached, the stink hit them.

Dee looked closer. 'Entrails?'

Oh God, I think I will be sick. The stench is terrible.

'You do not use this method? It has been used since the time of the Romans.'

'No, sir. I find calculation of destiny is better found in the stars rather than putrid guts.' Dee made a wry smile. 'Pray.

What has this hapless creature revealed to you? That Her Majesty will have a good meal tonight?'

Ruggieri glowered and held out a bloody hand. 'Your calculations?'

Dee held the papers tight. 'Henri Duc d'Anjou will marry in 1575.'

Ruggieri shrugged. 'But does your horoscope of Elizabeth show her marrying in 1575?'

Dee stiffened. 'In England we do not predict the life or the death of a monarch.'

The Italian lifted his hands in exasperation. 'What use is an astrologer who cannot predict?' He stood, walked across the room and unlocked another door, beckoning for his guests to follow.

The room was pitch black until a single candle was lighted. Immediately, Margaretta jumped back. On the floor had been drawn a huge pentacle. In its centre, a black mirror on a stand. Dee was transfixed. 'Of what is it made?'

'Magic stone. But it takes a seer to see its messages.' Ruggieri slammed the door shut and turned to Margaretta. 'Go to the mirror.'

'My master is the one who—'

'—depends on you to see.' He took her arm and pulled her roughly into the pentacle. 'Ask the question.'

No. No. No. I do not want to do this.

Margaretta pleaded, 'Please, Doctor. I do not want to look…'

'You must. We must do our duty,' he replied. Then in Welsh, 'Ask our questions not his.'

Shaking, Margaretta turned back to the mirror. 'Who is the bride of Duc d'Anjou?'

Behind her, Ruggieri began to chant. The words made no sense. They were not in French, Italian or English. After a few seconds a low humming started, and the room seemed to close in. Margaretta stepped back in panic but the Italian barked at her to look at the mirror. 'Do not turn away and anger the spirits.'

The humming grew louder. Margaretta began to feel her skin prickling, then the nausea started. She clasped her hand over her mouth and tried to control the shaking. 'Keep looking,' shouted Ruggieri.

Suddenly a light appeared in the middle of the mirror. The face of a woman flickered into view. 'Describe what you see,' was the command.

'Pale of face. Dark eyes. A mane of hair.'

'Is it your Queen?'

'I think so.' *A lie. That is not Elizabeth.*

Then a call from John Dee. '*Pwy yw'r llofrudd?*' Who is the killer?

Ruggieri bellowed at him that he could not use the mirror for his own questions. Margaretta kept looking as it went dark again and then suddenly the ghostly face of a woman, though the features blurred as if she were in the dark. Then a man, dressed in red, handsome, angry. The third image was a younger man, dark eyed, a face full of spite. Black again and Margaretta screamed as the third face came into view. It was masked, horned and a terrible smile below the face-cover. Another sound started above the humming; the sound of metal clanging on stone as the mirror began to shake. Ruggieri jumped forward, shoving her out of the way as it tumbled from the stand and shattered into shards.

Then the scream. 'Get out. Get out. Get out.'

In the library, Dee poured wine for a trembling Margaretta and patted her arm. 'You did well.'

'But Doctor. That face. It was terrible.'

'You were looking into the face of Baphomet. Our killer.'

When Dee had gently coaxed every detail from her, he walked to the window and stared out for several minutes. 'So, we have confirmation, a clue and calamity.

'Confirmation?'

'Who did you not see in that mirror?'

'Queen Catherine de Medici.'

'Indeed. Your senses told us true. A serpent she may be – but not in this evil plot.'

'The clue?'

'That Baphomet is linked to or working for two men and a hidden woman.'

'Calamity?'

'The bride you saw was not Elizabeth.'

'Surely that is a good thing if the reputation of Henri is true.'

'Yes – but if Queen Catherine finds out that Elizabeth is not destined for her son, then what little protection she gives is gone. She could switch allegiance to Mary of the Scots.'

'What do we do?'

'We lie with thin words.'

'Are we in danger?'

'Yes – and it will worsen. I feel it.'

Chapter Sixty-Two

The trumpets sounded the arrival of Henri Duc d'Anjou. Margaretta watched out of a window, Marianne at her side. The entourage seemed to go on and on. At the front was a white horse ridden by a man bedecked in bright jewelled clothes, surrounded by guards, each one riding with an unsheathed sword. Behind them a group of male riders with hats, plumed with huge feathers.

'The prince,' said Marianne. 'Now the madness begins.'

'I have heard he is – interesting.'

'Puh. He is dreadful. Come, you can see him for yourself.' She took Margaretta's arm and pulled her towards the steps that would take them down to the parading corridor. When they reached the lower floor, she steered them into an alcove and nodded towards the entrance.

Trumpets sounded again and the end doors swung open. Immediately, every person in the corridor bent into low bows and started to call their greetings. Margaretta was pulled down into a curtsy and could only peep through her eyelashes at the swarthy prince whose eyes darted like a bird seeking a worm.

Oh, God. The younger face in the mirror. But this person is no man. He wears a bodice – lower than any woman here and rows of pearls. His hands have rings on every finger and his clothes sparkle with diamonds. He looks around, drinking in this adoration. And is that berry stain on his lips? Yes.

Behind the Duc traipsed a string of young men, all wearing large hoop earrings and necklaces, looking smug at the fawning of the gathered courtiers. One smacked the head of a young man who evidently was not bowing low enough and laughed when he tumbled to the floor. Another grabbed a young woman and kissed her on the lips, crushing her breast with his hand, then pushing her away and walking on making a comment, evidently spiteful. She looked after him bereft, but no one comforted her.

When they had passed through, the bent backs were straightened and there was a cacophony of chatter again. Marianne took Margaretta's hand and pulled her over to the stairs. 'So, there you see the Duc d'Anjou in all his glory. The men are his mignons – a bunch of poodles who bark at his command. I think you and your master are set to meet him. Beware. Pretend you respect him. Anything less and he is vicious.'

Margaretta ran to Dee to tell him that one face in the magic mirror was now in the palace.

One hour later, Dee and Margaretta were outside the salon of the Duc. Norris came running up the corridor having been summoned to translate. Screeching laughter could be heard through the door. The servants pulled the door open and announced the guests. Dee stepped in first and froze.

Inside the salon, young men were scattered on various chairs, most now without their shirts. Seated on a chair elevated on a dais was the Duc, his legs dangling over one of the arms. Next to him, his mother, Catherine de Medici, looking adoringly at him and stroking his hand. In the middle of the room, and the cause of the raucous laughter was a troupe of eight dwarves, beautifully attired and dancing and tumbling for the entertainment of the men. The room was rank with the smell of sweat and wine.

Seeing Dee, the Duc d'Anjou clapped his hands and

silence fell. 'Ah. The doctor from merry England and our illustrious ambassador.' His English was perfect though heavily accented. He beckoned them forward. 'Maman says you have conjured my future.' A sly smile.

Someone has told you to use that word. For spite – to make my master uncomfortable – for he hates to be called a conjuror. It brings dark memories.

Dee and Norris bowed. Margaretta curtsied. When they rose, the Duc pointed at her. 'Your wife or your whore, Doctor?'

Damn you. But I will be the wife of a man one hundred times your better.

'My secretary, sir.' Was the response through gritted teeth. Next to Dee, Norris tensed further and explained in French that every philosopher in England was accompanied by a scribe.

The Duc made a disinterested shrug. 'So will I be a husband, Doctor?'

'Yes, sir.'

'And what will she look like?'

'Dark eyes and a mane of hair.'

'So not old. Not a *putain publique*.'

Another reply through gritted teeth. 'No.'

Catherine de Medici leaned to her son and patted his hand again. 'Henri, my child. You must think of France.'

The Duc turned to his mother with a sickly smile. 'Oh, I do, Maman. I think of our country, our faith, our mission for God. I think of a beautiful, young queen, who could produce an heir. Someone who speaks my language – not horse talk.'

Oh, my God. I hear the name Mary. You are thinking of Mary Queen of Scots. Now a man, older than you. A promise. A plot. Money offered. The Queen is looking confused. She does not know what you are thinking.

The Duc picked up his golden cup and took a long quaff of wine. When some dribbled down his chin, he jutted it for a servant to jump forward and wipe away the offending liquid.

'I am bored of this conversation. You may go. I will see you alone tomorrow, Doctor.' He clapped his hands to the dwarves who began to dance again.

In seconds, servants stepped forward and ushered Dee, Norris and Margaretta to the door. When the door slammed closed, Dee turned to Norris, furious. 'Did he really call our Queen a *putain publique*?'

'A common whore. Yes. That is the nature of the Duc. Pure venom.'

Margaretta tugged at her master's sleeve and whispered, '*Mae e'n meddwl am Mair o'r Alban.*' He is thinking of Mary of Scotland.

Dee froze then went quiet as if he were contemplating. 'That strange statement about a young queen, producing an heir, speaking his language. He was talking of Mary Queen of Scots.'

Norris paled. 'Surely not. How do you know?'

'I am skilled in observing men, ambassador. I tell you his scheme is to marry the Scottish Queen not Elizabeth. Maybe an obvious match. If Mary was so smitten with the Lord Darnley and his liking for having his bed warmed by male servants, why would she refuse a French popinjay who dresses like a woman and wears pearls?'

Norris groaned and hunched forward as if he had been hit. 'And he has just been at Joinville, the seat of the Guise family, visiting the Cardinal of Lorraine, Mary's uncle – and the man who has asked him to lead the Catholic faith. A more devious promoter of ambition you will not find.' He pushed his hands through his hair. 'Of course. If he can join Anjou to Mary and she remains imprisoned, then France would have to invade. It would be the Northern rebellion all over again – but with a French army at their backs.'

'But if Elizabeth were poisoned, he does not need to invade. There is no one else to put on the throne than Mary,' said Dee. 'Would the Cardinal stoop to such a plot?'

'He will not dirty his own hands, but he will stop at nothing to get what he wants. He may be a man of God, but he sees God's hand in his own power,' answered Norris, his agitation growing.

'We have to go to Joinville. I must see this Cardinal,' insisted Dee.

In truth, you want me to see if he is the older face in the mirror.

Norris shook his head. 'Impossible. They will ask our reason for going and we have no answer. And to lie to this family is to die.'

'Then we create a reason for them to send us,' muttered Dee as he walked away.

Chapter Sixty-Three

Margaretta was dragged from her sleep by Marianne shaking her. 'Get up, quickly. Your master has been summoned by Queen Catherine. She is angry. Pray and pray hard.'

'Why?'

'Ruggieri had audience with her this morning and says you broke the magic mirror. All Court is saying you will be flayed.'

'Flayed?'

'As the mad Italian does with sheep.'

God help me.

Dee was pacing outside his rooms, face drawn and fingers twitching. 'Let me do the talking. I need to see the Duc alone and make him think me an innocent ally. I might be able to talk us out of this.'

That does not give me peace. 'Yes, master.'

A servant arrived and silently led them through the palace. The chatter and sniping of yesterday had given way to raised eyebrows, looks of sympathy and shaking heads. Many just turned away.

This is what you see when a prisoner is dragged on a hurdle through London on his way to the gallows. I feel sick.

Mam, Dada, look down from Heaven and save me. Shaking overwhelms me. My mouth is dry. Please, please help me, God. Do not be so cruel to show me all I have wanted and then take my life before it is real. Please God, I want to get home to Sam.

The door opened. This time there were no tumbling dwarves, no parrot, no servants scurrying around with laden platters. Just Queen Catherine de Medici and the Duc d'Anjou. From the side of a room a severe, narrow-faced man stepped forward. 'I will translate. Your ambassador is not summoned.'

Dee bowed to the royals and then looked to the translator. 'Please tell Her Majesty and her fine son, the Duc, that I am delighted to have this opportunity to talk to them of a bright future.'

Queen Catherine almost spat her response. 'You have destroyed our method of seeing the future. Cosimo tells me you misused it and brought such evil to his office that the mirror shattered.' She pointed at Margaretta. 'She broke it. We are told you have brought a bad spirit from Elizabeth's Devil land.'

Oh, no, no, no. God, help me.

Dee stepped back to stand by his apprentice. 'Margaretta brings no evil, Your Majesty. Nor do I.'

The Duc piped up. 'And what religion do you follow, Dee? Are you a Huguenot heretic?'

'I am an ordained priest of the Catholic faith, sir. Tutored by England's most ardent leader of the faith – Bishop Bonner. He brought me into the centre of the faith in 1555 and we remained friends until he sadly died last September.'

Well, that is the truth – and the first time your so-called ordination has been used for any good. But this has silenced the spiteful Duc.

'Yet you serve a heretic queen. A putain publique who shelters the dregs who flee our pure-faith lands.'

Dee clenched his fists under his sleeves in an attempt to control his fury. 'I serve Queen Elizabeth, yes. My role is philosopher, astrologer and physician – not to look into her soul.'

The Duc leaned forward with a sneer. 'Does she have one?'

Oh, that has worried your mother. She wants Elizabeth as her daughter-in-law. This could ruin her plans to marry you off as King of England. This is our chance. But the doctor is stumped by his own fury. This may be my greatest risk.

Margaretta sank to her knees, bent her head and spoke in Welsh. 'Tell them the horoscope shows the duke marrying a queen. The mirror confirmed.'

Queen Catherine clapped her hands in anger. 'What does she garble – this bad spirit?'

Dee apologised for his apprentice's poor language and repeated her words. Both the Queen and the Duc sat back.

'The face of my bride. Tell me of her,' demanded the Duc.

Margaretta spoke again. 'Tell him she was beautiful, spoke French.'

Dee repeated.

Queen Catherine relaxed. 'Elizabeth speaks French.' Next to her, the Duc grimaced.

Margaretta lifted her head and looked directly at him. The first reaction was fury, but the tiny shake of her head changed his expression to curiosity. He turned to his mother. 'I wish to speak to the doctor and his spirit alone.' When she started to object, he screeched like a child and slammed his hands on the arms of his chair. No amount of petting would calm him. He just screamed louder.

My God. You are dreadful, but we can use this. As the fury continued, she whispered to Dee, 'Now become the innocent ally.'

Queen Catherine snapped at a servant who opened the door and she thundered out. In an instant, the Duc was calm again and his voice turned to oily. 'Who did you see in my future?'

Dee bowed. 'A beautiful queen, sir. But the mirror clouded. As if she were trapped. I do not wish to upset your mother, however, the face was very similar to Mary Queen of Scots.

But then another face – of a man who threatens the future. So evil was he that the mirror cracked.'

It worked. The Duc faltered. 'What do you mean?'

'My work indicates a threat to Elizabeth that would bring terrible revenge.'

The Duc frowned. 'Revenge?'

'In England, there is a belief that the beautiful Mary Queen of Scots – your brother's widow – is the root of all threat and counsellors call for her death. Elizabeth protects Mary and wants only for her to find a steady husband who will calm the waters.'

You lie like truth. But it is working. Suddenly this nasty little man is thinking of the masked man but with alarm.

The Duc sat back, forehead creasing as he contemplated. Then the lie. 'I know nothing of a masked man, but the Cardinal of Lorraine, Mary's uncle should hear this directly.' A small shrug. 'He can stop – I mean, help things.'

Dee bowed lower and made an ingratiating smile. 'I can leave today if Your Grace would give me and the ambassador a passport to travel.'

The Duc nodded and then turned away to signal that the interview was over. Dee stopped before he reached the door. 'May I beg one question, Your Grace? I hear your uncle has an apothecary. A cripple, I think. I always like to share knowledge. Where will I find him?'

Alarm. You juddered with it. The doctor has gone too far.

The Duc glowered. 'Michel Malpied. Why do you ask of him?' He raised a finger that shook. 'You speak to my uncle only. Any prying into our households will bring about the most severe of consequences.' *Devious confidence has moved to deep concern. I sense danger.*

Chapter Sixty-Four

'Do you know what danger you have put us in, Dee? For the love of God, you have deceived Henri into thinking his plot to marry Mary is possible, you have gone behind the back of his mother and now you have alerted them to our interest in the apothecary. Henri of Anjou will have a messenger on the road this very night and anyone asking about this man will be under suspicion. You had me send word to Cecil's spy to do that very thing. He is in peril – and my secretary is with him. That puts me in line of danger too.' Norris sank into a chair and began to shake, sweat poured down his brow and made rivulets down his cheeks.

Dee gulped and then wagged his hand in frustration. 'I used wit and intelligence to get us the result we needed – a passport to Joinville. Yes. I was the master of the room.'

Hell fire. You do not even say I was there. I fed you the wit and wisdom, and you created danger, but, as ever, I must sit here mute as you claim glory. And the terror pulsing from Norris alarms me.

Dee started packing papers into his bag but with difficulty.

Margaretta stepped forward. 'I will do that, Doctor.'

'Er, no. You carry my cloak.' He clutched the bag as if it contained jewels and started making for the door, calling to Norris, 'We will find Mabelain first and stop him investigating, then see the Cardinal. With clever questions I will know if his apothecary is implicated.' Ignoring Norris's objections, Dee put his head down and disappeared up the corridor.

As if we were not in enough trouble, I think you have stolen that book. Magpie!

In the carriage, Norris pulled out a map. 'Today we travel to the city of Sézanne. It will take the day and part of the night, but that will have us halfway.'

Dee took the map and turned it around, tapping on a town further east. 'Our journey takes us near Wassy, the place of the first great Huguenot massacre. I would like to see it.'

Norris looked aghast. 'You think visiting a Huguenot martyr site is a good idea, John? You are already walking on cracked ice.' He ignored Dee's huffing and ordered the driver to leave.

Two days later, in the late afternoon, they arrived at the gates of Joinville. Margaretta rejoiced that she could escape the persistent friendliness of the elderly driver who had spent the whole journey pointing at things, smacking her knee and then gazing at her with a toothless grin. Every touch had made her yearn to feel Sam's arms around her again. The town was small, and the cream coloured, red-roofed houses were dwarfed by the church that soared above them and a huge Chateau-fort. The driver pointed and said 'Maison le Cardinale,' then smacked her knee again. Norris called out of the carriage window to go straight to the church.

Inside the church was dim and fuggy with incense. A few people were kneeling, hands clasped in prayer. A black-robed priest walked around trimming the wicks of the thin candles burning before statues and relic caskets. Norris walked to one of the side chapels where a young man was seated before a statue of the Madonna. A few words were exchanged as the man shook his head.

Norris turned to Dee. 'Marcus has been searching for days – asking in every tavern, boarding house and Huguenot dwelling. He cannot find a man called Josef Mabelain and no one speaks of a visitor with a twisted foot and eye. However, there may be a reason. The Duc d'Anjou has been here a week.'

'Why is that relevant?'

'The Duc and his band of mignons like to make sport on their visits. They drink then rampage through the town harassing every man or woman they suspect of being Huguenot. The Huguenot's leave when the Duc is in town.'

'Where do they go?'

Norris turned to Marcus again and there was a short conversation. 'They just flee. Some into fields, others to nearby villages and towns to hide with friends. They are beginning to return now.'

Margaretta pulled Dee's sleeve. 'Josef would surely go to Wassy. His old home. There would be people who would remember him and give shelter.'

Dee gave a pointed look to Norris. 'I said I wanted to visit there. It was intuition.'

Rubbish. It was morbid curiosity.

Norris nodded. 'We can go tomorrow. It is but an hour's carriage drive. But this evening you meet the Cardinal and deliver your message and on your head be it, Dee. I will go and make arrangements – though I suspect they already know the reason for your visit. Anjou will have seen to it.'

Chapter Sixty-Five

'Not another foul-mouthed parrot,' groaned Dee as they walked through the corridors of the Chateau-fort, the creature shrieking from a room at the far end.

Norris shushed him. 'The Cardinal's parrot is precious to him and it would be sensible to be flattering about its colouring.'

Dee huffed and walked on.

The Cardinal was seated in a plush chair, upholstered with deep red velvet. He was attired in red and white silk, on his head a bishop's hat hiding a slightly receding hairline above a handsome face that gave no signal of his thoughts. There was just a slight nod in greeting.

Margaretta held in a gasp. *The first man's face in the black mirror. It is him.* She nudged her master's elbow and the little nod showed he understood.

Then another screech and they all looked at a huge parrot, feathers of all hues, bobbing his head as he perused the entrants.

Norris bowed deeply and introduced Dee, then Margaretta as his secretary. Another slight nod and the Cardinal pointed to the two chairs in front of him and then gestured that Margaretta should stand by the wall.

So, handsome man, you have little care for women. But this is helpful. I can just watch and feel and you will take no notice of me at all.

When the men were seated, the Cardinal spoke in perfect English. 'Doctor Dee. You are lucky to find me here. I travel to Paris tomorrow. But this is fortuitous. I understand you have recently visited my niece, Mary Queen of Scotland and England.' He gave an oily smile. 'Ah. I see you tense when I call her Queen of England. But surely you recognise her lineage.'

Norris cut in. 'Your Grace, I think we must recognise that—'

'—my niece is being denied her destiny and is detained in a cruel castle, Master Norris. Do not ask me to recognise anything other than the insult to the Guise family and France.'

Norris shrank back but Dee remained still. 'Your Grace, I spent some days with your beautiful niece. I assure you, her hosts, Earl and Lady Shrewsbury, are doing all they can to make her comfortable and are funding a full household to ensure she has the standing of a royal.'

The Cardinal turned cold grey eyes on the doctor. 'I hear she is made sick by the cold. Constant pain in her side caused by poisoned air.' He waved his hand around the room which glittered with gold leaf, paintings, tapestries, beautiful objects of silver and crystal. 'This is what she is accustomed to, sir. You have seen Le Louvre. To put her in a damp and mouldering hunting lodge is, as I say, an insult to her status – and my family. It is like clipping the wings of my bird.' As if it understood the parrot screeched.

Dee nodded. 'I am sure she will soon be given leave to move to Shaftsbury House. There she much enjoys the gardens and the large windows where she can do her embroidery. I will confer your concerns to Queen Elizabeth of England as soon as I return.'

His eyes narrowed when the doctor said embroidery. He is seeing something. He is thinking of something bright. Just like The Duke of Norfolk. I will cough. Yes. That little nod of the doctor's head.

'And does Elizabeth heed her philosopher?'

'She does, your Grace. She sees me as the diviner of wisdom as I can study the stars that guide us.'

The Cardinal gave a snort. 'Then I suggest you ensure the stars lead my niece to accession.'

Dee nodded, then turned to Margaretta, clicking his fingers as if summoning a dog. 'Bring my bag. I need my horoscope.'

Margaretta stepped forward with the bag and bent to put it on Dee's lap, whispering, '*Mae e wedi gweld llieiniau. Rhaid i mi eu gweld.*' He has seen linens. I must see them.

Dee opened the bag and pretended to rummage. 'I was astounded by Queen Mary's skill with a needle, your Grace. May I ask her to send one to you?'

Good thinking, Doctor. As if innocent.

The Cardinal made a slight shrug. 'There is no need, Doctor. My niece has a generous spirit and has already sent her gifts.'

'Ah, you have seen them.' Dee pointed to Margaretta. 'My secretary was so enamoured of Queen Mary's skills she has started to learn embroidery herself. As a kindness, may she see one of the linens? You see there was nothing complete to see at Tutbury, only a work in progress. I think it was Daniel and the lions.'

The Cardinal has tensed. Some alarm. But how can he refuse without appearing churlish?

The Frenchman took a few seconds to reply. 'Very well, but she goes alone. Such things are pleasing to a simple woman but of no interest to men.'

Damn you. But I bow my head and curtsy in grateful deference.

Dee pulled out his horoscope for the Duc d'Anjou. 'This was requested by Queen Catherine and then I was tasked with reporting to you by the Duc himself.'

'Yes. And the mirror showed a beautiful, French speaking woman.'

Dee faltered. 'You already know, your Grace?'

Another oily smile. 'You do not think we rely on the English to inform us of French destiny, Doctor.'

'But I am Welsh, sir.'

A shrug. A rise of one brow. 'Puh.'

You are bristling, Doctor. Do not rise to it. Smile.

Dee gave a small nod. 'Then let me ensure you have all the detail. Yes, the horoscope predicts the Duc d'Anjou will marry and his bride will be young, beautiful and fluent in French.' He ignored Norris looking at him in alarm.

You are thinking of Queen Mary. A sense of satisfaction. The doctor glances at me. A little nod. He knows the bait is taken.

Dee made a heartfelt sigh. 'Yet there is a threat to that fortunate future…'

The Cardinal tensed. 'So, I have heard. What is it?'

'A dark soul, aligned to Mars, the planet of war. If such reputation falls on Mary, she is in danger.'

The Cardinal bristled. 'They would not harm a queen.'

Dee made a milky smile. 'Oh, but the English do not see her as a queen, Your Grace. There is many an Englishman who would see her removed from their worldly realm rather than see her reign in their country realm.'

The Cardinal reddened and stared at Dee.

Alarm. You feel out of control. Panic. See how you press your fingernails into your palms.

The Cardinal clapped his hands and the doors opened. 'Thank you for the message, sirs. If that is all, you may go.'

Norris stood, Dee did not. 'I hoped to ask one question, sir. I understand you have an apothecary gifted in physik. I wondered if I could meet him. He may be able to give me French herbs for Queen Mary's pain.'

Oh, Doctor, you go too far. Norris is gulping his panic. The Cardinal is reddening. He thinks of threat. He is fearful that you know something. We do.

The Cardinal's face darkened into a mask of threat and is voice descended into snarl. 'I barely see him. I know not where he is. And I think you have been warned of meddling with my staff. Go back to England, Doctor Dee, your mission is over.'

You think of the killings. Oh, God.

Dee stood and pointed to Margaretta. 'May she see the sewing now, your Grace?'

A servant was summoned with a clap and instructed in French. The man beckoned to follow and she was taken through another door, along another corridor, and steered into a side room, full of treasures. The servant pointed to the wall, where hung three perfect embroideries. Margaretta clasped her hands together and made a play of sighing her delight and wonderment. Smiling at the servant and making a gesture that they were beautiful. She deliberately pointed at the centre of the first one and made the gesture again to show she was in wonderment of the colours. But she was looking at the borders. And every single one had a border of diamonds and triangles. It was the cypher from Mary's necklace.

Dee was waiting at the palace gates. Norris was nowhere to be seen. 'Well?'

Margaretta spoke their mother tongue. 'He is certainly the older face I saw in the black mirror. He thinks of London, Elizabeth, the apothecary and poison. He is behind this. And Mary speaks to him through her linens – there are three of them on a wall – each with the cypher border. When you asked about his apothecary, he became alarmed. I am frightened.'

Dee nodded slowly. 'As I thought. We have to find Mabelain quickly. I have stirred the hornets' nest and we must flee before they fly and we are stung. Norris is arranging the carriage. We leave at dawn for Wassy, then straight to Calais.'

Chapter Sixty-Six

Like Joinville, Wassy was picturesque with the same red-roofed and cream buildings, gleaming in the dawn light. One church steeple towered to the sky, looking over busy streets full of people, market stalls and animals being driven through by stick wielding drovers. Norris called to the driver to go directly to the weavers' quarter. They rumbled to a stop outside the first house of a long street. Norris alighted, knocked the door and exchanged words with the householder who pointed along the lane. He turned back frowning. 'He knows of no visitors with a limp, but he says to ask the guild leader. He is only a few doors along. We can walk.'

They made their way along the narrow lane, Norris politely greeting passers-by and stepping aside for women. Dee was too interested in getting to the house. The door was answered quickly and a short, bright-eyed man, skin like tanned leather looked out at them. After pleasantries, Norris was evidently asking if Josef Mabelain had come to Wassy. Immediately, the man stepped back, his tone changed to incredulity as he declared, '*Josef Mabelain est mort.*'

Norris gave apologies and asked what had happened, only to be answered in even harder tones with, '*Le Duc de Guise.*' Then he reached behind the door for a coat which he shrugged on quickly and beckoned for them to follow. A short walk in silence and they reached a graveyard. The man marched straight to a group of graves set out in perfect rows and pointed to the third stone.

> Josef Mabelain
> Tisserand
> Envoye au ciel
> Mars, 1562

Oh, my God. What is happening here? Even the doctor is shaken.

The old man and Norris entered rapid conversation, then relayed to Dee: 'Josef Mabelain was one of the first to die in the Massacre of Wassy in 1562; run through as he tried to protect a child. He was a young, fit man, soon to be married. No limp or twisted eye. When they took his body home for laying out, the house had been ransacked and his papers stolen. Also, missing were all the weaving tools that could be carried in a bag. The only thing left was his loom.'

Dee demanded that Norris ask if a man ever lived here who had a squinted eye and a twisted foot. Immediately, the old man's face creased with derision, and he spat at the ground before answering.

'He says the only person with such appearance was Michel Malpied, the mad apothecary. He arrived here in 1559 from Paris to live in the castle. This man is not sure about his eyes as he always wore a leather mask and a long coat to cover…' Norris took a breath. '…metal legs with metal feet, made for him in Paris so that he could walk straight. They called him the medicine horse – or the devil horse – when he smiled beneath the mask.'

Oh my God. He describes the third face in the black mirror. I touch my master's elbow and he nods.

Dee started firing questions. One by one the story emerged. Michel Malpied had been in the pay of the Guise and arrived here after an attempt on the life of the Cardinal of Lorraine had led to banning of long coats and masks in their Paris home.

He lived in the castle and was a true Catholic but befriended the Huguenots. On the morning of March 1st, 1562, he had been passing as they filed into the old barn for their service and offered to ring the bell to summon the worshipers. But he rang the bell for over fifteen minutes, even when all had gathered. The next thing they knew, Guise guards were at the doors, demanding to know why a warning bell was sounding. After hot words, a call had come from the bell tower to 'kill, kill, kill to save the Guise'. And the massacre began. Within twenty minutes, seventy souls were dead. The old man turned back to the graves and wept.

'What happened to Malpied?' demanded Dee.

Through his tears, the man reported that he had never been seen again. The rumour was that he fled back to Paris to hide in the monastery of the monks who raised and trained him as that was the only place he could not be seen.

'Which monks?'

'The Knights Hospitaller, the remains of the Templars in Paris. He is likely still there.'

'No,' muttered Dee. 'He has been hiding in plain sight – in London.'

Chapter Sixty-Seven

John Dee stared at the table in a busy tavern, his forehead creasing as thoughts raced through his mind. Margaretta and Norris sat in tense silence. At last, he looked up. 'Cecil and his spies have been long deceived by the man we know as Josef Mabelain – a name stolen from a dead weaver. The pieces of the puzzle fit. He arrived in London after the massacre of Wassy of which he has strong memories. His is crippled. He works with herbs which he would have learned from the Hospitallers.'

'We also know he could not stitch well when he first arrived. Vicar Tyrwhit mentioned it,' replied Margaretta.

Dee nodded. 'But Cecil is a lawyer and will not want to hear this. It means he has brought danger to Elizabeth. You know what he will say.'

'That it is circumstance. That there could be two men with the same name. If Mabelain is a killer, he would have struck before now.'

'And the Josef Mabelain we know does not walk on metal feet or wear a mask,' added Margaretta.

'We need evidence. Knowing that The Duc d'Anjou and the Cardinal think of him, think of London and think of killing is not sufficient for the cynical mind of Cecil who wants no international discord.'

Norris frowned. 'How do you know their thoughts? They said no such thing.'

And we cannot tell you that I feel it, see it and tell my master after the meetings when you are not listening.

Dee hesitated. 'I just know.'

Norris raised his eyes to heaven and let out a long breath of frustration. 'Dear God, man. You cannot accuse French Royalty of sending an assassin on a whim. This is what you want to think – not truth.'

Dee gulped back his wine. 'I know it. But we will get proof. Mabelain was sent to France days before we left. If he is this apothecary, and he has not been to visit his master the Cardinal in Joinville, then he is waiting in Paris. He will go to a safe place – the Hospitaller Abbey.' Before Norris could object, he stood and made for the door, calling that they needed to set off immediately before the Cardinal leaves for Paris and warns him.

The journey back took just a long day and a half as Dee refused rest and only agreed stops to change the horses. But for Margaretta it was hours in which she could dream of her life with Sam and the Toveys. Norris directed the driver to go directly to the Abbey Hospitaller on the South Bank of the Seine River. Once there, he went in ahead, leaving Dee pacing in the road while Margaretta ensured her paper, pens and ink horn were in the bag.

Eventually, Norris emerged. 'They say he is long gone. But I have stated that this is a matter of importance to the Guise family.' He shook his head. 'You have me lying, Doctor Dee. I hope you know what fire you play with.'

'A scald is worth the saving of our Queen, Norris,' was the barked reply as Dee marched towards the huge carved doors. Inside it was silent, though busy, with monks moving around quietly carrying books, blankets, linens and various bottles. Each one would nod, smile and carry on. Norris led them through to the office of a stern-faced young man, clothed in a white habit, tied at the middle with a gold cord, and around his neck a large square cross. After an exchange of words, they were led through a central yard, surrounded by a cloister walk and through a small door into a narrow arched-stone corridor lit with candles high on the wall in iron holders. Their steps echoed as they trudged towards an oak door that opened onto a laboratory. Silent monks toiled at benches, perfuming the air with herbs. The only sound was the scrape of pestles in mortars. The man who led them walked over to an older monk in the far corner and whispered in his ear. At first, he received a shaking head of refusal. Then more words and eventually a long sigh, as he put down his tools and followed back to the gathered visitors. When he saw Margaretta, he snapped something and wagged his hand to say she should be sent away. Dee stiffened and nudged Norris who announced in French, 'Only our writer. She is pure.'

He would not be saying that if he knew I was thinking of Sam every night.

There was an indignant sniff from the old monk but he beckoned and walked them to a side room where he sat behind a desk and offered two chairs for Norris and Dee. Margaretta was directed towards a low stool where she sat and pulled out her writing materials.

Norris started with a long introduction during which Dee twitched his impatience as he did not understand. Then the first question as dictated by Dee on the journey here. Norris conversed in French and then relayed to Dee.

'We come to learn about a man called Michel Malpied. We are told he was trained here.'

'Yes.'

'When did he arrive?'

'As a child. A foundling.'

Dee began to mutter and turned to Norris. 'This old fool is being obstructive. Tell him that this is a matter of life and death. The death of a queen. And if an English queen dies then a Scottish-French queen is in danger of death by revenge. So, if he thinks he is helping the Guise and their niece by blocking, he is a fool.'

Norris went to translate but the old monk raised a hand. 'I understand your language, sir. What revenge do you report?'

Dee took over. 'Father. You are a man of God, as am I. We have a calling from the Lord to do right. In England our Queen is threatened by a poisoner. If anything happens to Elizabeth, the English will blame Mary of the Scots. We have the lives of two women in our hands. Now please help us.'

The old monk bent his head. 'What has he done now?'

'We think he is the poisoner. Now, I beg you, tell us all you can.'

My, Doctor. Suddenly your gentle side emerges. I think you must have much love for Elizabeth for I have never heard you beg before.

The old monk stared for a whole minute, then sank. 'Very well. Michel arrived with us in 1542 – left in a basket at our door. No name, no gift, no sign of his mother. We could see that he had been harmed at birth. A terrible twisted foot and damage to the side of his face which had pushed his eye out of line. Every sign of a birthing by a poor midwife. We took him in as a charity case and gave him a name that described him – *Malpied* – ill-foot. Our hearts warmed to him for we knew that he would always be crippled, and his face made ugly by his eye. What we did not know is that sometimes, God afflicts the afflicted even more. He failed to grow tall like other children and then when he reached the point at which boys become men, he had such terrible pustules on his face that we had to lance them, making his face even uglier. God knows I used every herbal salve I knew, but only the scalpel would relieve his pain. Slowly the bright, loving child became infected with his own ugliness and he became a bitter, angry young man.'

'We have been told he walks on iron feet.'

The old monk smiled. 'Yes. By the time he was five, he was unable to walk without a terrible twisted gait that hurt his back. We had a blacksmith – a kind and gifted man who fashioned iron frames, padded with sheep's wool, into which we could fit Michel's legs. The frames were attached to metal feet. It took the little boy only a few days to learn and he was walking like any other child. The only difference was that we always knew when he was arriving because of the sound. Chink, chink, chink.' The old man shook his head, his eyes misting as he recalled the past. 'I remember the day the blacksmith made him pattens that were like horse hooves. We all delighted in seeing him gallop around the yard pretending to be a great stallion. Such a sweet child. And so strong.'

The sound of the killer in London. And I think the sweet child used his childhood memories to create Baphomet.

'Was he educated in apothecary skills?' asked Dee.

'Yes. My protégé. He learned fast and was gifted. Though I did have to stop him trying out his physiks on the abbey dogs.' The old man smiled. 'I thought I was creating a great physician.'

Your feeling is growing. Until now your thoughts have been warm. But sadness, fear, worry is rising. You head is bent low and I am not sure the doctor has noticed. I cough. That slight nod.

'And your thoughts of him changed it seems.'

'His fury at life grew. He listened to the stories of Huguenots threatening the Catholics, of eating their children. All the horrors that frightened men speak of each other. Michel began to believe he had been made twisted by a Huguenot midwife who had tried to kill him at birth. He became so inflamed that he wanted to be a defender of the Catholic faith against the heretics as he saw them. He became obsessed with the Knights Templar and the Hospitaller Knights, studying their codes, their prayers, their practices. He even donned a hair shirt that scabbed his body and arms.'

And Josef Mabelain has scabbed arms despite being a physik.

'Did you say codes? A cypher?' Dee asked.

'Yes, the Templar Code. A shape for each letter in the alphabet, made up of the shapes in the Maltese Cross of the Templars and Hospitallers. It is an old code, not used now.'

Dee groaned. 'Yes, it is. It is used to send messages within the Guise family. He must have passed it to them. How did he come into the pay of the Guise?'

'Oh, that is not strange, Doctor. The Guise have a Paris mansion close to us. They are a robust family, but Francios, Duc of Guise, the brother of the Cardinal of Lorraine, had been terribly injured in 1545 when a battle lance went straight through his face. He was always called the scarred one – *Le Balafré* – and was brave – but in the cold, the pain of the scar would be unbearable. Michel had created a salve that numbed his cheeks and gave relief. It was dangerous and if eaten, would kill, but Le Balafré trusted him and he became a regular visitor.'

And the link to poison.

'Did he have good knowledge of poison?'

The old monk bent his head and just nodded, regret flooding his face. 'Michel decided that he must become the apothecary to the Guise family and leave us behind. He rejected his monks clothing and had a long leather coat fashioned to cover his legs, along with a mask to cover his face. He took delight in how he frightened people.'

That must be the long coat on the back of Mabelain's door in London.

The old man continued, 'He moved into the Guise mansion, walking out of here without a word of farewell. Though we heard of his progress – how the Le Balafré became his patron. Then, after an assassination attempt on the Guise in 1560, they banned long coats and masks. We were told Michel had gone to Wassy and we did not expect to see him again.'

But you did. I feel your discomfort. Margaretta leaned forward and whispered. 'Daeth e 'nol.' *He came back.*

That small nod. 'But I think you did see him, Father.'

Silence.

'You must tell us.'

'He arrived suddenly, pounding on our doors early in March 1563. He was maddened. Le Balafré – his patron – had been assassinated in Orléans by a Huguenot the month before and he had watched him bleed to death for five days. The Cardinal of Lorraine, had become his new patron, but this did not quell his grief. Then there had been Wassy.'

'What did he say of Wassy?'

'He had witnessed the massacre there a year before and seemed to be a storm of emotions. One minute he would be rejoicing at the death of heretics and next weeping at the horrors he had seen. He began to insist he was God-sent to save the Catholic faith; that he was infused with the spirit of the Templars and would raise their banner, continue their crusade, and bring about the last curse on any heretic.

'*D'abord la terreur, puis la mort.*' Dee muttered.

A nod.

'And did he ever utter the name Baphomet?'

The old man whimpered and made the sign of the cross as he started to weep. 'He said Baphomet would rise through him, revenge the Templars and protect their faith. That he just needed the sign. We told him to leave and take his madness out of our holy walls.'

And that sign eventually came as the plot of a Cardinal supported by a Papal Bull.

Outside, Dee explained the connections to Norris. It had taken only a few more minutes with the old monk to learn that the Abbey had never seen their one-time protégé after ejecting him, though they had received word that he visited the Cardinal of Lorraine in the Paris mansion every three months. They did not know where he lived.

'It all fits,' said Dee. 'The iron footed apothecary, having created the massacre in Wassy, took the papers of Josef Mabelain. When his patron died a year later, his madness really set in. After his rejection from the Abbey here, he went to London and began his long strategy of becoming a double spy – serving Cecil and the Cardinal of Lorraine. Under the mask of a mild, kind Huguenot, he is a Catholic fanatic, living out the curse of the Templars and using their God Baphomet to create terror then death.'

'Is he here in France?' demanded Norris.

Dee nodded. 'Yes, thank God. Sent here by Cecil the Friday before we journeyed here. But where?'

'Probably hidden by the Cardinal,' growled Norris.

Margaretta grabbed Dee's arm. 'Do not be a fool, master. We have had no sense or sight of Mabelain here. And anyway, his package of physik is somewhere in the palace – delivered by Cecil. Blanche is looking for it.'

Chapter Sixty-Eight

Dee and Margaretta left on horseback at dawn the following morning, Norris having agreed to bring Dee's books when he travelled to London the following month. Margaretta had tried to pack the books in the box but had been shooed away by Dee insisting, 'My books. I will care for them.'

As they turned their horses to the road she challenged, 'You have left poor Ambassador Norris holding that book you stole from Le Louvre, haven't you?'

'I borrowed it... with permission.'

'You lie like truth. Not a twitch on your face. Shame on you,'

'You forget your place, apprentice.'

'Apprentice to a book-magpie. My word, I have achieved much in life.'

Dee had scowled, geed his horse forward and shouted back at her, 'You will be grateful, girl, when your heart is burned. You will need me then.'

Oh, God. He knows my thoughts of Sam. I feel my face reddening. What if he felt my thoughts in the night? Shame. I feel shame. But when I am back all I shall feel is love and I will not care.

The rest of the day was spent in silence until they reached an inn and Dee conversed as if nothing had happened. 'We will eat and then scry. I want confirmation.'

'How?'

He smiled and rummaged under his clothing, finally pulling out his crystal on a silver chain. 'Basic, but we can use it. I have thought of a method by which we can ask the angels.'

Margaretta closed her eyes and groaned.

Dee shut the door of his room and cleared the table. On a paper he drew a pentacle and placed a candle on each point of the star. Within the points he wrote different initials. 'JM for Mabelain, CdM is the French Queen, CL is the Cardinal, DA is that dreadful boy prince and MQS is our captive queen of the Scots. In the centre, he wrote E. We need to prove there is evil connection around Elizabeth.' He handed the crystal to Margaretta, pointing a finger in warning not to argue. 'Hold this above the centre of the star and ask Uriel to show you the connections.'

Reluctantly she stood and dangled the stone, wincing at the shards of light that danced as it swayed within the heat of the flames. 'I ask Uriel to show me a connection between these people.'

Slowly the swaying changed and moved to a distinct swing. Dee jumped up, eyes bright. 'Uriel is speaking. Keep asking for the links.'

The first swing was between CL and MQS, the crystal swinging so wide it was going into the candle flames. Then a shift and it began to swing between CL and DA. All the time, Dee was watching and scribbling his notes.

Margaretta cried out as her hand was suddenly jerked to the right. 'It is hurting, Doctor.'

'Keep asking. We must know all. Look, the crystal is linking DA to MQS. We were right. The Duc d'Anjou seeks to bond to the Scottish Queen. Ask if the Cardinal is assisting.'

As soon as Margaretta whispered the question the stone began a strange triangle between the three.

Her hand began to shake. 'It is hurting. I feel sick.'

'One more. Ask the link to Josef Mabelain.'

She cried out as her hand jerked left, and the pendulum moved between CL and JM, the swing getting strong and stronger. Then it stopped dead and her hand was pulled to the centre where it hung still above E.

'Keep very still,' rasped Dee.

Every facet of the amethyst glinted in the candles and a beam of light shone down onto the E. The paper browned and then a sudden flash and flames. Dee leaped forward, slamming his hands to douse them. He looked at his apprentice though the rising smoke. 'Proof – they plot to kill Elizabeth and clear the path for Mary and that terrible princeling to take the throne.'

'The stone did not swing to Catherine de Medici.'

'The Serpent Queen is not part of this. But we now know who we saw in the cards. The Cardinal is the Hierophant, The Knight of Pentacles is the Duc d'Anjou, recently asked to be the warrior for the Catholic faith, the Queen of Pentacles is Mary Queen of Scots looking down at her evil cypher.'

'So which card was Mabelain?' asked Margaretta.

'Judgement. The signs were all there. Damn. I should have seen it – a terrible deity trumpeting its condemnations. No legs or feet, and on its chest is blazoned a red cross upon a white background – the battle cross of the Templars. Josef Mabelain believes he is a deity bringing the judgement of the Templars and returning Catholic faith to rule us again. He believes he is Baphomet. And the Devil card was trying to warn us of his evil.' Dee slumped on a chair. 'But can we get back in time to save Elizabeth?'

PART FOUR

LONDON

Chapter Sixty-Nine

Margaretta and Dee ran down the gangplank at St Katherine's dock and accosted a passing sailor. 'Is our Queen well?' The sailor frowned and nodded, then shrugged as if he were a madman.

Dee pointed back to the water. 'The river is in flood. Your stomach must suffer another boat trip, Margaretta. And we will have to shoot the London Bridge.' He turned to a young lad and handed him a fist of pennies with instructions to 'run like the wind to Sir Cecil's house and say that Doctor Dee needs him at Westminster'. In minutes, they were heading west, Dee shouting at the surly wherryman to pull straight and pull hard.

The terror of shooting the tide between the pillars of London Bridge behind them, they arrived at the Whitehall stairs and ran into the Palace New Yard and the great hall of Westminster, where a guard was ordered to fetch Mistress Blanche immediately.

Minutes later, Blanche appeared at the top of the steps and Dee ran forward with Margaretta. 'Have you found the package delivered from Cecil's apothecary?'

'Not yet. But I asked only yesterday for the hunt to be increased as Elizabeth is weakening from lack of food. But we have used the salve you sent for her leg.'

Dee sank down on the steps, panting with relief. 'Thank the Lord. For in that package is delivered her certain death.'

Blanche did not wait for questions.

As Dee rose to his feet, there was a shout from the door and Cecil was striding towards them. 'Why have you come here and not to me?'

Dee looked up in fury. 'Because your spymastering has been protecting our Queen's assassin. As I told you weeks ago. Baphomet was hiding in plain sight – and he was hiding in your pocket, William. Send for Walsingham. I will explain all.'

An hour later, Blanche led them to her office. Cecil and Walsingham sat before her desk. Dee stood. Margaretta moved to a seat in the corner. Blanche shut the door tight and sat behind her desk. 'Every inch of the palace is being searched and a ban put on all food and wine entering the privy chamber. Now what is happening?'

Oh. Look how my master rises. He will start to pace now, meting out his wisdom and I will sit as if I had nothing to do with his brilliance. Blanche gives me a little wink. She knows.

'Where is Leicester?' asked Dee. 'Surely he will want to know our evidence.'

Blanche looked grim. 'Elizabeth's fear has made her prickly. A certain lady has been sent from Court and Robert has fled to Greenwich where he is commissioning a suit of armour.'

Dee looked askance. 'Is he planning to go into battle with Baphomet?'

'No, John. He is in a far greater battle – to get back into Elizabeth's favour. The armour is for the tilting he plans to entertain her with at Kenilworth. I will send word to him. Now enough diversion. What have you found?'

Dee clicked his fingers to Margaretta. 'Find the paper where I mapped out the threats to north, south and east.' When it was laid out on Blanche's desk, he tapped on the circle saying north. 'You all thought the threat lies here in the head of Mary Queen of the Scots. You are right… and wrong. You think she still plans to marry a Duke and take Elizabeth's throne. You are right… and wrong. You think she sends coded messages that instructs an assassin called Baphomet. You are right… and wrong.'

Cecil banged his hand on the desk. 'Enough of your riddles, John. What have you found?'

Dee tapped on the circle to the east. 'Here you identified the Court of Catherine de Medici as a potential player in this devilry because she has an interest in pentangles and a penchant for poison. You thought this might be linked to her desire to marry her son to the Queen of England. Again, you are right… and wrong.' He ignored Cecil making a long growl of annoyance and continued. 'You thought the House of Guise, led by the Cardinal of Lorraine were supporting Mary as she is a blood relative, but they were unlikely to be involved. Right… and wrong.'

Cecil could take no more and stood up, shaking with anger to face John Dee. 'Enough of this. You are like a cat taunting a mouse. Now spill what you have found.'

I have never seen you lose control, Sir Cecil. This a mix of fear, shame and anxiety. Terrified you have put Elizabeth in danger and that you will be blamed – you shake to your core. You think of your little boy. Will he lose a father?

Blanche rapped on her desk, snapping at the men with the voice of an angry mother, 'This is no time for male strutting. John – speak all you have found.' She looked to Margaretta and pointed to the crystal decanter on the far table. 'Wine for all of us, my dear.'

A chastened Dee sat and took his glass. 'This terrible story began many years ago when a twisted and disfigured child was left at the door of the Paris Abbey of the Knight Hospitaller – once Templar Knights. The child was taken in, named Michel Malpied, and raised to be a fine apothecary. They braced his legs and made metal feet so that he could run like other children, and as he grew into manhood, he made a coat to cover his legs and a mask to hide the face that made others turn away. They moulded him for success, but they could not control his growing darkness of soul – and his penchant for creating poisons.'

Cecil looked to Walsingham, his face paling.

Dee took a deep quaff of wine and continued. 'Like so many people rejected by society, that young man started to look for reasons and refuge. He became a hater of Huguenots who he believed had caused his disfigurement and became a fanatic of the Catholic faith. Like all religious zealots, he worshipped those who had killed thousands in the name of Catholicism – the Knights Templar and Hospitaller. It did not take long for him to recreate himself as a latter-day knight, invoking the terrible deity behind the Templars and Hospitallers and the curse uttered as the last one died.'

'*D'abord la terreur, puis la mort*,' muttered Walsingham.

'But I cannot see where this is taking us, John,' barked Cecil.

Dee smiled. 'Because we never can see fate, William. Fate took Michel Malpied to the house of Guise in Paris to help the old Duke, also terrible disfigured and pained by a war wound. He gained the trust of the family and left the Abbey – into their patronage. And he took more than his herbal skills. He gave the Templar code to the Guise who eventually passed it to Mary Queen of Scots in a necklace. Then an assassination attempt in their Paris home in 1560 led them to ban long coats and masks. Rather than lose their strange apothecary, they sent him to Wassy. Away from Paris, he could start his own crusade. His first act was to start the Massacre of Wassy by ringing the bell well after all congregants had arrived to worship, bringing the Duke's men to the door, giving him the chance to scream for killing.'

Dee turned to Cecil. 'And here is your link. One of the first to die was a weaver called Josef Mabelain. When they laid him out, they found his house ransacked, his papers and tools stolen. Malpied had disappeared. He would later arrive in London as Josef Mabelain. Dee turned to Margaretta. 'What did the Vicar say about him?'

'His first work would not make a beggar's rag.'

Dee nodded. 'We also found a long leather coat hanging on his door. At the time there was no reason for suspicion. Little did we know this was the long black coat of his other self – Michel Malpied or Baphomet.'

Walsingham's face was creasing with incredulity. 'But Mabelain is a Huguenot.'

'No, he is a fanatical Catholic hiding as a Huguenot, playing a long game, for cover takes time. He had to learn the skills of weaving and sewing; he had to gain trust to become the clothe mender of All Hallows; he had to make Vicar Tyrwhit trust him at a time when foreigners were not welcome in our churches; he had to gain a pattern of going to France to bring back information. Most of all, he had to gain your interest and be sure that you had not suspected him of being a double spy – that you had not uncovered the visits to his patron, the Cardinal of Lorraine, taking information and recently, cyphered embroideries from Mary Queen of Scots.' Dee turned to Walsingham. 'Speaking of which. Did you ever find out what happened to the embroidery taken out of the Tower by young Billy Barker?'

Walsingham shifted in discomfort. 'It was taken to Roberto Ridolfi.'

Dee smirked. 'So, it seems Mabelain has also forged links with your turned informer.'

Walsingham started to bristle, but Dee raised his hand to stop him. 'Something to be investigated. As you will see, there are many holes to be filled in this sorry tale. Back to the plot. The world turned again, fate intervened, and a Guise plot crossed with a Papal Bull. The Cardinal of Lorraine has been scheming to get control of England. What better way than by marrying his niece – Mary Queen of Scots, who he insists has claim to the throne, to the Duc d'Anjou, the defender of Catholic faith?'

'But he has been mentioned as a suitor for Elizabeth,' snapped Blanche.

'And a very reluctant suitor, mistress. The vile little Duc is malign in his speaking of Elizabeth calling her old and unchaste. It was easy to turn his head with the offer of a pretty, French speaking woman already a queen and claiming the throne of England. His mother, Catherine de Medici knows nothing of it. This time, the Serpent Queen is innocent.'

Cecil pinched the bridge of his nose. 'What evidence do you have of this plot between the Cardinal and the Duc d'Anjou?'

Dee faltered. 'Intuition. They leaked.'

Cecil narrowed his eyes. 'You had better not be relying on cards and crystals, Dee. This could be disastrous for our relations with France.' He turned to Margaretta. 'Is it true?'

'Yes, my Lord.' *And this is proof you know of my abilities.*

'What about the Bull?' demanded Walsingham. 'You said it crossed with the marriage plot? Was it arranged by the Cardinal of Lorraine?'

Dee shook his head slowly. 'I cannot say with absolute surety. It is certainly true that The Cardinal would have the ear of the Pope, and a licence to kill Elizabeth, if successful, would clear the path for Mary Queen of Scots to claim our throne. The death of Elizabeth would save an expensive war to get the throne. But it is also possible that it was another twist of fate. But whether fate or factored by the Cardinal, it was the signal for Michel Malpied to start his next crusade as Baphomet. He set out to create terror then death, killing the Huguenots he hated and who had the protection of Elizabeth. His initial attempt at terror failed. When his first victim, old Lucille was found, he pressed for her to be taken to the morgue, but her neighbours refused. Her death went unnoticed. So, the following week, he ensured it was public by terrifying a simple boy and a beggar woman and then leaving a body in the street. While we were searching for Baphomet, he was using his other persona to get death into the palace – his tincture.'

'And he had a perfect, long-made cover,' snarled Walsingham. 'He had the trust of the Huguenots he slaughtered.

He knew who lived alone. He had learned to walk well on his metal feet as a boy. He had the knowledge of poison, the zeal of the Templars, and the madness to believe in their evil deity. But most of all, we could see him so well he did not have to hide himself.'

'Exactly,' said Dee. 'Hiding in plain sight and easily pointing to others. I wager you never found a silversmith called Devereaux, did you?'

Walsingham just shook his head.

The tension was broken by a knock on the door and a servant walked in with a package. 'We have found this, Mistress Blanche.' She pulled back the paper to reveal a bottle of brown liquid, and a note stating that this was a remedy for the stomach, to put five drops into broth.

Dee took the cork from the bottle and sniffed. 'Mushroom. This is it.'

'Where was this found?' demanded Blanche.

'In the office of Master Hemingway, the Royal Apothecary, Mistress Blanche.' The servant gave a wan smile. 'I am told he was much indignant at another man being asked to prepare a physik and so hid it in a chest. He is most sorrowful and begs your forgiveness.'

Blanche tutted. 'It seems that his resentment has been more effective than his remedies. Go tell Apothecary Hemingway that he has probably created the most effective cure of his life.' The confused servant bowed and left.

Relief was short lived as Blanche looked at the three men. 'So, we have the poison but not the assassin. Where is Josef Mabelain – or Michel Malpied as he really is?'

'France,' said Walsingham.

'Maybe not,' said Dee. 'We found no sign of him. I suggest you get to the Pelican Inn and ensure your man left England.'

Chapter Seventy

The carriage arrived in Mortlake long after dark. Dee was dozing, his face still flooded in satisfaction at having jittered Cecil and Walsingham.

And not once did you acknowledge all I had done. Damn you. But my mind moves to more pleasant plots. Tomorrow I will be up at dawn. First The Vintry to check on Huw and then on to the boatyard and Sam. I feel my heart start to beat and flutter at the thought of seeing him. Who thought a woman of my age would be like a flighty girl? But my heart is still that of the girl in a wherry, fifteen years ago, pretending not to like him and every day realising my own lie. But then doubt. Am I being sinful?

'I told you to beware the fire, girl.' Dee's sharp voice jerked her into reality.

'I thought you were asleep.'

'Just thinking. And I can feel you well enough through closed eyes.'

She went to demand if he felt her thoughts, but the carriage rumbled into their yard and the stable boy was already waiting to open the door. Katherine came barrelling out, squawking her delight at having her husband back. He was covered in kisses before he was even on two feet. All was commotion.

Winnie ran to Margaretta with a hug. 'I is pleased to see

you, Mistress. That Bela is a bad one. I've worked me fingers to the bone. And the lies… the nasty words. She's dreadful.'

Margaretta looked up. Lemon-head was in the doorway, hands on hips, and a face that would curdle milk.

I do not need my skills to feel your venom. Poor little Winnie is pulsing with relief. Time to set the trap.

Margaretta was up before dawn and washed in water to ensure she was sweet smelling. Winnie was already in the kitchen, pushing bread into the oven, her face flour-covered and hands red. 'You have been working hard, Winnie.'

The girl rolled her eyes to heaven. 'She will not lift a finger but tells Mistress Katherine that she has done all the cooking. That poor woman has been laid low these past days – weeping one minute for her poor sister and the next for her absent husband. Even Mother Dee has been in to see her and said kind words over a flagon of her good wine.'

'Lordy. Katherine must have been distressed if it has moved Mother Dee to soft words.'

Winnie chattered on, 'Then Lemon-head is in here telling me that she is doubly distressed at the sister's death as she was a good friend of hers. Then her spite about poor Mistress Katherine, saying she is a burden and needing so much of her time. Says she has to spend every minute with the Mistress and that she is not allowed any time alone. Cruel she is.'

Margaretta smiled. 'I think we can make some changes soon. I am away today but will speak to the Mistress this evening.'

It took a few hours to reach The Vintry as the sun was rising. Before she went through the gate, she could hear Huw calling out instructions and the men responding, 'Yes, master.'

I can feel the pride and gladness of these men. Oh, Dada and Mam, you are looking down on my little brother.

Seeing his sister, Huw grinned and, for a second, looked into her eyes. 'Welcome, Margaretta. How was your journey?'

'Interesting, Huw, but how glad I am to be back. Things are going well.'

'Yes. All yellow. Siôn and I have secured two more large orders, and we have agreed terms with a master Burcott in the household of Sir Cecil. We need more hands already. Grace says you know a bottle washer.'

'Alice Burton. I will speak to Mistress Blanche to settle things. Talking of settled, how is our sister?'

Huw groaned. 'She visits nearly every day, wanting to know our sales and our profit. Yesterday she demanded a larger household and new shoes. Grace is patient, but even she needs a glass of good Gascon wine when Susan has left.'

Margaretta patted her brother's arm despite the wincing. 'You deal with the shoes. You can leave the household to me. Now, let me speak with Grace.'

As she turned away, Huw called after her, 'Sister you are pink today. But I see red flames.'

'My pink must be very happy.' But Huw did not smile back.

After discussing Alice's sleeping arrangements with Grace, Margaretta set her horse east. Arriving at the boatyard gate, she smoothed her hair and dress, then breathed deep to stop the pounding of her heart.

I must be respectful of Lottie, not push him too fast. I will visit with Goodwife Tovey first and wait for her to send me to comfort Sam. Oh, but I cannot wait for those strong hands to touch me. Is this love? Yes. It is.

Goodwife looked up from the breeches she was darning. The usual smile of delight was missing, despite a warm greeting. She asked question after question about France, Mortlake, Doctor Dee, Mistress Katherine. Then, she asked about Sir Cecil and filled the room with her memories of working with him.

Why do you look so fretful? Why do you not look me in the eyes or mention Sam? Yet you think of Sam. 'And the family, Goodwife? Are you settling at all?'

Goodwife looked down at the table. 'Our sadness over Lottie and the little ones deepens. Such a hole in our home and our hearts.'

'You are blushing. What is—?'

There was the scrape of the door opening and Sam's voice behind her asking, 'Whose horse is that in the—' A long pause. 'Miss Margaretta. We were not expecting you.'

Margaretta turned with a smile. Sam did not smile back. Instead, he pulled off his hat and turned it round and round in his hands. Goodwife urged, 'Sam, take Margaretta for a walk.'

He nodded with no smile.

They walked to the river in silence.

I feel fear. It is not you, it is me. I thought you would be so glad to see me.

When out of line of sight of the yard, she reached for his hand. 'I have thought of you every day, Sam. Are you well?'

He pulled his hand away and looked out over the river turning the hat again, round and round and round. 'Thing is, Missy, I have realised how wrong I was. I am truly sorry that I was so – so familiar with you. It were the grief you see. Grief and good wine.' He made a weak smile. 'A foolish combination for a man so low in his heart.'

'Sam, I thought—'

'I was so needing the touch of a woman it made my tongue run away with wrong words. Please know you are dear to me, but I cannot love another. Lottie lives in my heart. There can be no other for me.' He paused. 'It were just a kiss anyway.'

My head is spinning. My face is hot. I cannot breathe. The only thing I can hear is my heart, pounding. I hear the words but they seem to be coming down a well into which I am falling, falling. 'Yes, of course. It was just a silly kiss. I had almost forgotten it.'

He reddened. 'Good. I would have been sorry to make you sad.'

I will force myself to smile and shrug. 'Not at all.'

He stopped turning the hat.

I feel your relief. 'Well, I must go Sam. I only called to say hello and give you my best. Tell Goodwife, goodbye.' *For she knows and I feel such shame.*

She stepped past him and walked quickly, biting into her lips to stop the tears. It didn't work.

Susan was sitting before a good fire, a small glass of wine on the table next to her and a book in her hands. The room was warm and cleaned with fresh rushes on the floor and dried lavender in a bowl. She looked up and her face went sour. 'Oh, so you are back at last. We need to talk about Huw. He is not sharing the profit.'

Margaretta crossed the floor and sat on the seat the other side of the fire. 'I have visited Huw. I think he is doing well at the wine yard.'

Susan was looking at her book again and shrugged. 'If he is doing well, then he can be more generous.' Getting no answer she looked up. 'Why are you just staring at the flames like a bobolyne? And your eyes are red.'

'Have you heard of a widower's fire, Susan?'

'No.'

'It burns deep. It pains in a way that I cannot put into words.'

Susan scowled. 'It is cruel of you to speak of such things when you know I will soon be a widow.' She looked back to her book. 'Tell Hugh I need good clothes for the funeral.'

Margaretta arrived home in the late evening.

Dee was in his office, scribbling his notes. He did not look up but pointed at the chair in front of his desk. 'We must be ready to fill the gaps in this investigation. Where are the hooves? The horns? Where does Mabelain – Baphomet – get the poison? What is the connection to Ridolfi, to Norfolk? In fact, is there a connection at all? We will scry.'

'Yes, master.'

He looked up and frowned, then sighed. 'The widower's fire has burned?'

'Yes, master.'

He leaned forward and patted her hand. 'Burns heal, Margaretta. But they hurt like hell until they do. Now get us a glass of wine. Our scrying can wait.'

You confuse me. So selfish, so hard, such a thief. And yet you are kind. The tap of your hand makes me think of – Oh, I want my Dada.

Chapter Seventy-One

Margaretta was woken from a bad dream by banging on her door. 'Get up, Margaretta. We need to be on our way in an hour and we have answers to find.'

She rubbed sore eyes, still puffed from weeping. At some point in the night, pain had turned to fury but that only made her cry harder. Her head throbbed from the wine Dee had poured and her mouth felt sour. What man would want her anyway?

She scrambled into Dee's office, pulling her coif over barely brushed hair. He had created another pentacle with different initials in the star tips. Again, E was in the middle. He tapped around the letters he had written. 'JM for Mabelain, R for Ridolfi, N for Norfolk, MQS for the Scottish queen.'

Margaretta tapped the fifth star tip. 'Why is this empty?'

'We have covered all those we know and established the connections. Norfolk is an obstacle to the Cardinal of Lorraine's plot and Catherine de Medici is not involved. We need to know if there is another threat. Someone we have not yet investigated.'

'I am tired, Doctor. I am not sure I can scry.'

'You must. I moon-washed the crystal last night. It will be quick.' All softness of the previous evening had gone.

She stood, took the crystal and waited for Dee to light the candles placed on the five tips of the pentacle, then stepped forward and held it in the centre. Slowly the amethyst began to sway and the vibration started in her hands.

'Ask about the connections,' commanded Dee.

The crystal made small movements at first but got stronger and stronger until the stone hit the flames again. Then it suddenly moved to swing between Mary and Ridolfi. Then Ridolfi and Norfolk. It changed again and started to move in an oval covering Mary, Norfolk, Ridolfi and the empty star tip. Dee jumped up in excitement. 'So, there is someone else. Put the crystal over the empty star.'

Margaretta did as she was instructed and the crystal went still.

'Ask if this holds the Guise. We must check.'

Stillness.

'Think of the Duc d'Anjou.'

Stillness.

'Ask if the person is known.'

Slowly the crystal began to circle clockwise.

'Yes. Ask if it is more than one.'

The amethyst circled faster.

Margaretta began to sway. 'I think I might be sick. It is like a hum going through me. Please, let me stop.'

'One more. Put the stone over Mabelain. Ask for any connection.'

With a sigh she obeyed. The pendulum was still, then a small movement and it swung towards Ridolfi. Just a few times.

'A connection, but weak. I suspect Ridolfi knows him but does not know what he is.' He tapped on the empty tip. 'We have to know who these are. Get the cards.'

Reluctantly, Margaretta went to the bookshelf, pulled out some volumes and took the casket from its hiding place. Dee put the deck face down on the empty star tip. 'Ask who is in the tip. Cut the deck.'

Margaretta placed her hands on the cards, asking the

question until she had the feeling to split them. She took the top third and turned it over.

'The Five of Wands. Hah.' Dee looked at the card underneath and paled. 'The Tower. Dear God.'

'The Five of Wands is a group of men fighting. This card means a conflict. Two are wearing rich colours of red and blue, the others in poor brown and green. Do you know who they are?'

'Yes,' said Dee. 'It all makes sense. And the Tower gives us their intention. But I think our friends, Cecil and Walsingham, are blind – again. Come we must go to Cecil's. Put these things away and we leave immediately. We have a reputation to build.' He ignored her questions and walked out.

As ever. I do the work and you seek the glory. But what else do I have? Nothing. You are the only one who wants me – and only then for what I give you.

Chapter Seventy-Two

The atmosphere was as cold as ice. Leicester was at the window, his back to the room. Walsingham sat by the fire; his face clouded. Lord Cecil was making notes and looked up, relieved.

Leicester assumed control. 'Thank God you are here, Doctor. I return from Greenwich to learn that Elizabeth has not been protected and is in peril.'

'What news?' demanded Dee.

Cecil glowered at Leicester and then at Walsingham. 'Tell them.'

Walsingham grimaced. 'We have investigated the Pelican Inn. They know Mabelain as the Twistfoot Frenchie – not seen for some months. Captain Wynter did send ashore a boat to collect him on the day agreed, but he was not there.'

Dee looked to Cecil. 'So, Baphomet is still in London.'

Cecil nodded grimly. 'There is more. Go on, Walsingham. There is no covering this.'

'It appears that the embroidered linens from Mary Queen of Scots are taken to Ridolfi by Billy Barker and Ridolfi takes them to the Pelican Inn for collection by Mabelain. But they never meet.'

Dee nodded. 'He likely thinks him only a courier. But maybe this tells you that your belief in Ridolfi being turned to an English spy is false.'

'Incompetence,' shouted Leicester. 'I should have managed this.'

Walsingham opened his mouth to shout, but Cecil cut in. 'No time for argument. The word will soon be out that the poison in the palace is found and Baphomet will restart his campaign. We have to find him.'

Dee walked to the door. 'An assassin needs two things – victims and murder weapons. We start at All Hallows. Then St John's. Robert, bring palace guards to St John's Priory. It is his most likely hiding place. Master Walsingham, go with them and wait at a distance until we arrive. We want no advance warning.'

'Vicar Tyrwhit.' Dee's voice echoed in the arched wooden ceiling of the Church.

There was the creak of a door and Vicar Tyrwhit emerged. 'I have asked you before not to shout in a house of God, Doctor Dee.'

'Even when it is the hiding place of a Catholic assassin who has been murdering your flock?'

Tyrwhit froze. 'What say you?'

Margaretta hissed at Dee to let her speak. 'My master's worry makes him harsh. Josef Mabelain is, in truth, bent on killing our Queen.'

Tyrwhit stared. 'It cannot be. I have known him for years. There is no kinder man.'

I cannot imagine any man is kind. I think you all iron-hearted. 'I think your kindness makes you blind to evil, sir. We are sure. When did you last see him?'

'Two weeks ago. He said he was going on a trade visit to France.'

'Has anything happened we should know about?'

A brief silence and then a cry. 'The clothes of the Patrone.'

'What of them?'

The vicar beckoned and led them to the chest. The lock

was broken. He lifted the lid. Empty. He shuddered. 'I realised they had gone a week ago. Are the Huguenots safe?'

'Not if do not catch him,' growled Dee. 'Have you heard of any deaths?'

'No. But they live in fear. They have stopped meeting on Sunday and do not answer their doors.'

Dee nodded. 'We will go to St John's Priory.'

Vicar Tyrwhit jumped to his feet. 'If I have covered a killer, then I will atone by helping you catch him.'

The palace guards were waiting in Cow Crosse Street. Leicester, followed by Walsingham, urged his horse forward. 'Where do we start?'

Dee pointed towards Clerkenwell Street. 'His house. Bring one guard in case he fights. Margaretta, you come too.'

Walsingham started to complain that 'she is too weak, too likely to scream'.

Dee leaned to Walsingham's ear and his voice went cold. 'Where we come from the women are not born – they are quarried. And this girl of granite has taken us further than you or Cecil in finding this devil. She will see his ending.'

For all my sadness you make my heart soar. For all the times I hate you, there are more times I love you, my friend.

The guards hammered the door down. Inside was cold, the ashes damp and the chairs dusty. Margaretta checked the back of the door. 'No coat, Doctor. He has taken it – or hidden it to look as if he has fled.'

Dee ordered the men to wait outside. 'What do you feel?'

Margaretta looked around, bidding her senses to feel what was in the stones of the wall. 'Anger, fury, hate. Then lust. Not for a woman but for revenge. I see a man before a cross, scratching at his arms. Running and returning. Somewhere dark. Somewhere safe.'

Dee narrowed his eyes and opened the door to the rear room where they had seen all the flasks and bottles. It was empty. 'Dark you say. The crypt. But we will have to move quickly. The talk of soldiers approaching will have him running.'

'He cannot run. He is lame.'

'Oh, yes, he can. He can run on his metal feet.'

They rode, flanked by palace guards, into the yard of St John's Priory, making the weavers and merchants stop and stare. Women came to the doors and called back into others that there was trouble brewing. More gathered to watch. Dee hailed a weaver and asked when he had last seen Josef Mabelain. The man shrugged and called to another who answered it was weeks ago. Dee growled. 'We are not going to find him here.'

Margaretta shook her head. '*Cuddio mewn lle amlwg.*' Hiding in plain sight.

Dark. Running and returning. Who would be out at night? She looked around to see a tavern, where men had clustered by the door to get a view of what was happening. In the window above, two women, brightly dressed in cheap cloth, the waists tight and necklines low. Both were sour looking with dark circles under their eyes. The younger one slugged from a tankard of ale. Margaretta told Dee to wait a few minutes as she dismounted and pushed into the tavern to find the potman. 'I wish to speak to the ladies upstairs.'

He leered through rheumy eyes. 'Well, that will make a pretty change for them, lady.' He made a gormless grin, making beer dribble down his chin and he grabbed his crotch. 'Can we watch if you don't pay?'

'*Twll din.*' Arsehole.

'What you saying?'

'I said, it is on orders of Sir Cecil. Shall I give him your name?'

He faltered. 'I was jesting, lady. I would do nothing to – to gainsay Sir Cecil.'

'Then I suggest you do not gainsay my request and open that door to the stairs.'

The older woman stood and clasped her hands in a sad attempt at dignity. Margaretta made a respectful nod. 'Good morning, ladies. I wonder if you might help us. Have you seen a tall man in a long leather coat walking at night?'

'We ain't on the streets at night,' snapped the older woman in a Devon accent. 'We's respectable whores.'

'I'm sure, mistress. But this man is a threat to our Queen, Elizabeth. We must find him.'

The Devon woman's eyes widened as she looked to the younger. 'Frightens us he do, though he never looks our way,' she whispered.

'What is he doing?'

She shrugged. 'Carrying summat. He goes past, into St John's church yard and back again.'

'And when did you last see him, mistress?'

'Last night.'

Margaretta gave warm thanks and left the two women looking at each other in confusion. *My manners bewilder you – so used are you to a woman like me looking down her nose. But you two may just have saved a queen.*

Outside she pointed at the church. 'He's here.'

Leicester commanded the guards' officer to position his men in a circle ready to catch anyone running. In a minute, they were ready, swords drawn. Walsingham dismounted and started striding towards the church door. Tyrwhit was following.

'Not so fast, sirs,' called Dee and pointed to the right of the building. 'First the physik garden.'

Margaretta trotted after him. 'Do you think he is there?'

'No.' But something bothered me the time we visited.' He stopped at the door in the garden wall and put up his arm to stop his apprentice stepping in. 'What do you see?'

'A physik garden. A yew, herbs, black now and frostbitten. It needs cutting back to let the spring growth come through green.'

'What do you not see? Look down. What would you see if a physik worked here?'

She stared. *What, what, what is missing?* 'Foot tread. No one has walked here.'

Dee nodded. 'It was the same when he showed us the garden. Not touched for weeks, yet he said he was making a tincture for Elizabeth.'

'So, he is collecting his poisonous mushrooms elsewhere.'

'They grow on rotting wood. What did you smell in the crypt?'

'Rotting wood. But there was no wood in there.'

'Hiding in plain sight. But how in a crypt?' He took her arm. 'Come.'

Margaretta lit candles as Dee readied to open the crypt door. Leicester called a guard to stand at the top of the steps and they descended into the pitch black, Vicar Tyrwhit bringing up the rear. Again, the smell of rotting wood hit their noses and Walsingham coughed in disgust. Tyrwhit muttered that this was a terrible place.

'Mabelain. Baphomet. Show yourself,' yelled Dee.

'Josef. If you are here, let us help you. God will guide you,' called the vicar.

Silence. Then, as if coming from a distance, a chink of metal. They raised their candles to get better sight. Nothing. Leicester drew his sword.

'He is close,' whispered Dee. 'When he was here with us

before, he repeated my words. 'He can hear us. But where – where is he?'

Slowly they crept forward and looked in every corner. Something made Margaretta stare up at the bricked-in window. *Why do you bother me?*

Dee led them first to the undercroft to the left, where a door opened into another chamber. The door opened slowly with a dull creak of iron on iron. Empty. He pointed to the undercroft to the right, the shorter chamber. As they rounded the pillar, they could see the altar used as a table. Dee stopped and pointed. 'Six candles. Different heights.'

'So, what?' snapped Walsingham. 'There is nothing strange about candles.'

But Margaretta sighed her horror. 'Each candle is a different height. The one burned down was lit for Old Lucille, the two burned low are Pierre and Lucien. The three still high were for the poor Huguenots found in the wherry at Sheen.'

Dee pulled up the cloth to reveal the altar beneath and pointed to the star. 'This was not a mending table. It was his altar and right in the middle is the Templar code he has been using to carve on his victims. On top the Catholic votive candles by which he recalled his victims. If that is not the sign of a twisted mind, I do not know what is.'

Vicar Tyrwhit put his hands over his face and groaned.

There was a box under the altar. Margaretta pulled it forward, opened it and pulled out a large candle, carved with a triangle pointing left.

'The letter E in the Templar code,' whispered Walsingham.

Somewhere in the void was another chink, then the sound of breaking glass and they froze, Leicester holding his sword ready to fight.

I feel him. I feel fury. Hate. Revenge. But also fear. Trapped. No way out.

Dee took her hand and looked into her face. Then nodded and looked to the other men. 'He is close.'

Walsingham lifted his candle high. 'What are you talking

about? There is no place to conceal himself.' He turned to leave, snarling that this was a waste of time and that they needed to start a thorough search of the city.

'Hiding in plain sight, Walsingham,' called Dee. 'But your spymaster eyes look for the hiding only. The clever think of the plain sight.' He whispered to Margaretta, 'Feel him girl. Where do your eyes go?'

She closed her eyes, breathed deep and tried to calm her pounding heart. *Where are you? You are close. I am drawn to the back of this chamber. I think of that hole.* She moved quickly, pulling Dee by his sleeve. They knelt by the hole made for pouring holy water out of the crypt. A sickly stench of rotting wood came from it. Margaretta leaned close to see if the feeling strengthened. But before she accessed her senses, they jumped as the sound of chink on stone came from the hole.

Dee's brow furrowed. 'How? This leads into solid ground.'

Margaretta shook her head and pulled his sleeve again, walking quickly back into the central chamber of the undercroft. She stopped below the bricked-up window. 'Why is the chamber with the altar half the length of the others? Why would they make a window looking into earth? Why make a hole that only goes into earth when it could clog up?' She looked up at Dee, eyes bright in the candlelight. 'There is something behind that window. That's where the sound comes from… and the smell. But there is no door.'

Vicar Tyrwhit stepped forward. 'Sometimes these old churches had a sealed crypt for the priors. There was no door. You had to climb down.'

Dee froze, then shouted, 'The tents.' He bolted to the steps, taking them two at a time and barreled past the guard. He silenced Walsingham, who was ordering the guards to go back to Westminster. 'No. I want every man.' Dee stopped in front of the tents leaning against the side of the church like striped trees bending in the wind. 'Take them away.'

Leicester shouted orders and men jumped forward. As the

tents were pulled away a void appeared in the middle. When the last few were removed, Dee pointed at the ground and yelled, 'We have it.'

Before them was a wooden trap door with a brass ring. A guard went to open it, but Dee pulled him back. 'I want armed men. God knows what is down there – or what he will do.'

The men positioned and muskets primed. Dee gripped the ring and pulled. There was a harsh scraping and slowly it rose. A terrible stench of rotting wood came out making the guards grimace and turn their heads away. Dee pulled further.

Then, from out of the void came a terrible scream, like a rabbit caught by a fox. They looked down and Margaretta twisted away covering her eyes. Guards shouted their shock and one called out to God. Vicar Tyrwhit fell to his knees.

The void was the size of a small room, lined with old wooden shelves rotting and falling apart. Upon them the ancient oak coffins of the Hospitaller priors, every one mottled with small white mushrooms. Between the caskets were the flasks of brown liquid that had been in Mabelain's back room. Across the floor was broken glass.

In the middle was Baphomet standing on his metal legs, but extended with two metal pattens shaped as cloven hooves. His upturned face was masked and on his head a silver band with two long horns. On the forefinger of his right hand, a bloody metal claw. He raised his arms and screamed again as the leather coat fell open, revealing the clothes of the Patrone of All Hallows. Then a sickening cackle of laughter as he ripped away the ancient cloth and uncovered the terrible bleeding wound he had carved into his own chest – a pentacle with B in the middle.

Leicester yelled at him to show his weapons and then called for a ladder, commanding two men to, 'Haul that devil out.'

Baphomet screamed again and started to laugh like a magpie's cackle. As a ladder was lowered over the side, he lurched sideways and grabbed a handful of mushrooms, stuffing them into his mouth.

When they hauled him up and manacled his arms, he stood still, over six feet tall in his terrible metal hooves. He said nothing – just turned to Dee and smiled with such evil that for a second, they felt Baphomet with among them.

Chapter Seventy-Three

Cecil poured them all a glass of good wine and sat with a sigh. 'Thank God. Elizabeth is safe. You have done well, gentlemen – and mistress. Though Leicester has ridden to Court to break the news and take the glory.'

Burcott entered. 'A messenger from Court requests you all attend the Queen within the hour.'

Cecil nodded. 'Well, for once we go with good news. The threat is gone and Baphomet is in the Tower. He will die a traitor's death.'

Dee took a large quaff of the red liquid and held the glass out for more. 'Foolery.'

Cecil bridled and spilled wine on his papers. 'What do you say?'

'Mabelain – Baphomet – will be dead in exactly two days – by his own poison. You do not even have time to build the scaffold or sign the death warrant. As for Elizabeth being free of threat, you are also a fool.'

Ceil reddened in anger and Walsingham sat forward looking alarmed. 'Explain, sir.'

And here you rise. I can see the satisfaction in your face to instil such worry in these men who think they are in control Your chest puffs with the power you have right now.

Dee took another drink and asked Margaretta to pull out the paper showing the ring of threat around Elizabeth. He spread it slowly on the desk, taking delight in the tension rising around him. He tapped on the North. 'Mary is still there, sending her Templar code messages, still plotting to marry a Duke. She is riding two horses – the Duke of Norfolk and the Duc d'Anjou. Also, in the north are Northern Lords. You think they have fled to the Low Countries and will be silent. Foolery. They plan another rising.'

That was the card you saw with the Tower. The Five of Wands and the warring men both rich and poor.

Dee tapped on the East. 'If you think the Cardinal of Lorraine will drop his ambition to rule England through his niece, Mary Queen of Scots, then you are mad. He will continue his pursuit of our throne.' Then Dee tapped on the South and looked at Walsingham. 'London. You still have the Duke of Norfolk and his inflated sense of importance, a popinjay of a secretary delivering his messages and the malign scheming of a man called Ridolfi, who you were foolish enough to think you had turned. I told you it was not true.'

Walsingham stood, his face darkening. 'You overstep your manners again, sir.'

Dee smiled. 'And again, you under-step your intelligence, master. You are yet to understand scheming of men who seek more than they are ever born to hold. And the scheming of men, and women, who hold more than they should ever have been born to.' He looked to Cecil. 'Being Ambassador of France would be a good schooling.'

Walsingham's fury turned to panic. 'No. I have neither the money nor the time.'

But Cecil smiled.

Dee tapped on the paper again. 'Gentlemen, we have found a terrible plot within a plot. The Northern Lords planned to marry Mary to Norfolk and take the throne – thinking they had the support of France. But all the time, The Cardinal of Lorraine was planning her marriage to another duke – Henri d'Anjou. His apothecary assassin, protected by a Papal Bull that condoned his mission, set about clearing their way to the throne in his own particularly evil way. He failed. But the ambitions of these players remain. Mark my words. Within the year Elizabeth will be living in fear again.'

Chapter Seventy-Four

Blanche was waiting at the top of the steps in the Great Hall of Westminster Palace, clasping her hands in tension. 'Are we safe?'

Cecil bowed. 'For now, Cousin. The immediate threat is passed, but we cannot let down our guard. John and Margaretta have done us proud.'

I am recognised. Sir Cecil has put me side by side with my master. I dare not look to see if he is angry as I cannot feel him. But Blanche looks at me with that wise smile and the little wink.

Blanche nodded to Dee and then to Margaretta. '*Da iawn, y ddau ohonoch chi.*' Very well done, the both of you. '*Bydd Elizabeth yn ddiolchgar iawn.*' Elizabeth will be most grateful. She patted Dee's arm, making him swell with pride and then pointed to the door. 'She waits in the chapel, praying her thanks with Robert.'

They descended into the small chapel to the side of the hall. It was a place of quiet beauty, the walls richly painted in hues of blue, green, red and gold. At the front was Elizabeth, kneeling on a cushion, her head bent in prayer, a bible in her hand. Next to her, Robert Dudley, Earl of Leicester, his hand over hers. After a few minutes she rose and walk up the aisle, the terror was gone from her face and a smile lightening her eyes. She took each by their hand, giving her thanks. Margaretta was last. 'And to you, cariad, a special thanks. I have few women I can trust. It seems both are Welsh blooded – like my Tudor blood.' She squeezed her fingers around Margaretta's and pressed something into her hand. 'It was my father's – the Tudor king for whom your Dada died. When you look at this, remember that a father's spirit lives through his daughter.'

It is a golden brooch in the shape of a dragon, a Tudor Rose in its claw. I want to cry. I have lost the love of my life and yet you remind me of the other love of a great man – the love I will carry to the end of my days. Nothing will ever destroy that. Nothing can steal it away. I feel Blanche's hand on my shoulder, and I hear her say my father's words. 'And all will be well, and all will be well, and all manner of things shall be well.'

Epilogue

The gathered investigators spent an hour in audience with Queen Elizabeth, giving her the terrible details of Baphomet and the remaining threats. When told of the wrongful use of the old St John's Priory, she asked that Vicar Richard Tyrwhit hold a service in the church to expel all evil and make a once holy place peaceful again. Also, that the coffins in the old crypt should be sprinkled with holy water, blessed and the door sealed for ever.

The Queen remembered to thank Dee for the salve that had certainly healed the wound in her leg and smiled as he puffed in delight. She then requested Cecil's attendance to draft a suitable rebuke for the French Ambassador and gave Dee permission to go to the Royal library while they waited for the tides to turn towards Mortlake. For once he did not lose himself in pages and forget Margaretta's presence. He took her to a window overlooking the gardens and sat opposite her.

'We have endured many journeys in the past weeks. Not all on horseback and ship. I think your heart has been on a journey.'

Margaretta turned her face away and nodded, desperately trying to blink back the tears. He leaned over and patted her hand. 'Sometimes the heart must wait. Look at how many years Katherine and I had to play the game of mistress and lodger.'

'Did you always love her? You used to grumble so much.'

Dee made one of his rare, soft smiles. 'I grumble about

you too. But you are my other half in pursuit of truth, just as Katherine is my other half in pursuit of love. We are a good team of the mind, Margaretta, and one day your heart will be whole too. Do not let it harden.'

'Yes, Doctor.'

My voice has gone to that of a mouse again. But I fear this heart is turning to stone.

Dee rose and looked through the glass. 'We have a busy few months ahead, my dear. The Five of Wands shows conflict and strife and I predict it will surface by August. Cecil and Walsingham will now become lax with relief and the players will start their tricks again.'

'How do we stop it?'

A smile spread across Dee's face. 'We don't. We wait. And when the strife strikes, we run to the side of Elizabeth. Her horoscope tells of a long reign. I will remind her and reassure while others regret their foolery in believing Ridolfi.'

Ever the plotting mind. You are shocking.

That evening, Dee and Margaretta were taken home by Royal barge to the delight of Katherine who declared she would open a bottle of her best Gascony wine and get out the crystal glasses given them as a wedding present by Leicester.

Margaretta hugged Winnie and then went to see Mother Dee. She cried in the old woman's arms as she unburdened her heart. Then they made plans to rescue Katherine from Bela's two-faced spite. The following morning, they both sat with Katherine and explained gently that her care was poorly placed. That afternoon, Bela was sent to the house of Susan to work as a kitchen girl and start the extension of Widow McFadden's household.

In the Dee household, Winnie was made house-mistress with a larger salary and a day free a week for her own leisure. On her first day off she went to Holborn and found her Donald. Their courting started the very same day and soon after, on the request of Doctor Dee, he was taken into the household of Robert Dudley, Earl of Leicester, as a groomsman.

By the end of the week, Margaretta had ridden with Grace to Westminster cells where they took into their care, Alice Burton, who walked out in a set of clean clothes, shoes and a warm cloak, plus a purse of twenty pennies to see her through to her first wages – all provided by Blanche ap Harri.

The following month, Ambassador Norris had his pleas answered and was called back to England. His replacement was Francis Walsingham, who had resisted the post for reason of money.

Within the year, Sir Cecil uncovered a long-brewing plot. It involved Mary Queen of Scots, The Duke of Norfolk, his secretary – Billy Barker, the Northern Lords and the leaders of France and Spain. It was organised and bank-rolled by Roberto Ridolfi – the spy that Walsingham thought he had turned. A cypher used by Mary Queen of Scots was found under the carpet in Norfolk's house, though he claimed to not understand it. He was executed anyway.

In France, 1575, the Duc d'Anjou married the beautiful, French-speaking Louise of Lorraine. They had no children. The Cardinal of Lorraine had died just two months before having never achieved his ambition of ruling England through his niece.

In August 1574, Lady Douglas gave birth to Robert, Earl of Leicester's son. He never married her.

Mary Queen of Scots stayed in the household of the Duke and Bess of Shrewsbury, nearly bankrupting them and ruining their marriage. She never stopped plotting or sending messages by cypher.

Historical Facts

Elizabeth and the Papal Bull

In 1570, Elizabeth had been on the throne for twelve years.

In 1568 Mary Queen of Scots had fled to England, and become the focus of the Catholic faction. There was a plot to marry Mary to the Duke of Norfolk. Then began the Northern Rebellion in which thousands of peasants blindly followed the Northern Lords and did storm Durham Cathedral to hear mass. When the rebellion fizzled out, the lords fled to the Low Countries and Elizabeth's men began their bloody revenge. Over 800 were hanged on public roads and it is true that Cecil's son, Thomas, was in the execution party.

In response, Pope Pius V, signed a Papal Bull on February 25th 1570 which excommunicated Elizabeth and gave Catholics licence to kill her without fear of the Church's condemnation. The Bull arrived in England in March but was supressed by Lord Cecil until May of that year.

As in the book, the Northern Lords did not stop plotting. Their scheme bubbled up again as the Ridolfi Plot late in 1570 – and Roberto Ridolfi was at its centre.

Elizabeth, Court and her suitors

The one historical fact I have ignored is that, according to Court records, Elizabeth was in Hampton Court in March 1570. However, the time it would have taken to move back and forth between Cecil's house and Court would have impacted the pace of the book and reduced the threat of the London killings – so I moved her to Westminster.

The depiction of Elizabeth's room and belongings is correct – the shell bed, the unicorn's horn, dishes of sweetmeats, books and the elk horn said to detect poison.

Westminster chapel is as described and still exists – and has been renovated to look as it was in Elizabeth's era – beautiful.

The Medici pearls were indeed a gift to Mary Queen of Scots – and yes, they were purloined by her half-brother and sold to Elizabeth for a below value price. She loved them and wore them often – as pearls were a sign of virginity.

It is true that Elizabeth was prone to anxiety and tears. It was not unusual for her to be pacing through the night and becoming sick. In 1570, she really did have an ulcer on her leg – likely caused by a varicose vein. Master Hemingway was the Royal Apothecary.

By 1570, Elizabeth had spent twelve years resisting an ever-present pressure to marry. By this point, negotiations to marry Charles, King of France, second son of Catherine Medici had been drawn out over years. Elizabeth played the game of hot and cold – though she had absolutely no intention of marrying a boy many years her junior.

Tired of Elizabeth's prevaricating, Catherine de Medici, started negotiations to marry Charles to Elisabeth of Austria, and proposed Henri, Duc d'Anjou as an alternative husband for Elizabeth. See more about Henri under the notes on France.

THE CHARACTERS – ENGLAND

Blanche ap Harri

After Kat Astley's death in 1565, Blanche rose to be the most senior of Elizabeth's gentle women. She was treated as a baroness, though Blanche did not flaunt this.

At Court, Blanche's power was significant – acting as the gateway between Elizabeth and the people who craved her attention and time. By this point she was fond of Robert Dudley and advised him – though her loyalty to Elizabeth would have led to her disapproval of the flirtation with Douglas Sheffield. And yes, Blanche loved reading palms.

Mary Queen of Scots and Tutbury

Mary had Tudor ancestry and, when she was betrothed to the Dauphin of France, the English Royal arms were quartered into her own by her Guise family. She really believed she had a blood-given right to the English throne.

When her husband died of an ear infection, her mother-in-law, Catherine de Medici, was eager to rid herself of a pretty girl who had been appallingly snobbish about Catherine's merchant-class origins. Mary was soon on her way back to Scotland. After a tumultuous few years in which she lost the faith of her people, infuriated her lords, married the dreadful Lord Darnley against advice, and then became implicated in his assassination – she found herself imprisoned. She escaped to England as a royal. She was treated as a prisoner.

Mary was moved many times within months of her arrival in England, and the long lament she gives to John Dee is a true reflection of her experience. It is quite true that she was sent a bundle of poor clothes when she arrived and that she was moved in the cold, making her lady in waiting, Mary Livingston, ill.

In 1569, she was moved to Tutbury Castle and she hated it. As depicted in the novel it was high on a hill and only ever meant as a hunting lodge, but it had fallen into disrepair and was known for the smell of the privies and terrible issues with mould.

Mary saw herself as a queen and was on a constant quest to increase her household to the size of a small court. She did use wine on her face; she did have her own chef and meals of up to thirty-two dishes a sitting. She and Lady Bess spent hours together sewing and gossiping.

It is true that Lord Huntingdon was sent to Tutbury to curb Mary's growing household and caused not only her fury but great hurt to the Shrewsbury's as he was also there to ensure that Mary's charms did not sway the Earl to her side. Research reveals different accounts of when he left Tutbury, one saying January others saying spring. I have opted to keep with the latter as he was a character crying out to be written in.

Mary's complaints of being ill are also true and she did suffer a constant pain in her side which she blamed on her surrounds. She also made frequent accusations of poisoning.

As for the cypher – Mary was always plotting and liaising with anyone she thought sympathetic to her cause. She was well known for writing in cypher, through spies intercepted nearly everything she sent.

In 1570, she had taken to the notion of marrying Norfolk and did call him 'my Norfolk'. She wore a diamond he sent her under her dress, next to her heart.

Her main lady-in-waiting was Mary Seton – one of the four Marys who had left Scotland with her for France. By 1570, only Mary Seton was in constant company and was known for her skill at dressing the royal wigs. She never married and became a nun when Mary Queen of Scots was executed.

The Earl and Lady Bess Shrewsbury

The Earl of Shrewsbury, though immensely rich, was in perpetual angst about Mary being his prisoner. First it brought suspicion, for Mary was indeed a flirtatious woman who charmed men. Secondly, it brought crippling costs. The impact on the family purse was devastating. The constant stress impacted his personality, turning him from a kind man to a neurotic snip-tongue, eventually wrecking his marriage to Bess.

The depiction of Bess, Lady Shrewsbury is accurate. She was a handsome woman who made herself the wealthiest woman in England by marrying an ever-richer line of husbands. She was arrogant and proud, but highly protective of her children. It is true that her son was taken into the household of the Earl of Leicester. She sat for hours sewing with Mary Queen of Scots and was suspected of gossiping with her about Court. It is quite possible that she was playing the strategy of betting on both horses – Elizabeth and Mary – and ensuring she was favoured by both. It is also true that Elizabeth would like her one day and dislike her the next.

The Duke of Norfolk

Norfolk held the highest rank in the realm and was of a wealthy family with influence at Court. It is true that he was called to run the Scots out of England, that he had organised Elizabeth's coronation and had been considered as a worthy king when they feared she would die of smallpox in 1562.

He was also weak. While presiding over the Casket Letter Investigation into Mary, he evidently became enamoured of her, sent her a diamond and agreed to marry her when approached by the Northern Lords. With more money than brains he realised too slowly what treason he had been pulled into. He withdrew his support, wrote to the Northern Lords to say their plot was a folly, and ran to ground in his home. But it was all too late. He was arrested and held in the Bloody Tower, and daily protested his innocence.

Norfolk did have a secretary called William Barker who was certainly a key player in the Ridolfi Plot later in 1570. The depiction of William as a foppish boy in gaudy clothes is fiction. We have no record of his appearance.

As predicted by Dee in the novel, the Ridolfi plot was uncovered late summer 1570 and Norfolk was at its centre. He was found to have a cypher of Mary's under a carpet in his home, he was linked to Ridolfi – the Italian banker who was bank-rolling the plot and William Barker was passing messages. Norfolk was executed for treason.

John Dee

In 1570, John Dee was well established as philosopher to Elizabeth, involved in many strategies and regularly called upon for advice. In 1570, he had married Katherine Constable and was living in Mortlake, his mother's home. Thomas Digges was a star pupil.

By 1570, John Dee was becoming more and more interested in alchemy and the pursuit of the Philosopher's Stone – a pursuit which would grow into an obsession over the following years.

His hatred of John Prestall was another long obsession.

Sir William Cecil

The description of Cecil's house on The Strand is true to the plans. It had a loggia, a bowling alley, a library and an impressive office around a central hallway. The gardens were designed for beauty, including the snail mound. Beyond the boundary were the Covent Gardens. The house was full of treasures including the statues of Roman emperors and a cabinet of gold coins. And, yes – with true Cecilian inverted snobbery – he called it his 'Rude Cottage'.

Cecil was not in the best of health in 1570 and was often plagued by gout. He was also deeply resentful of Robert Dudley, Earl of Leicester, who had plotted against him in 1569 and had been foolishly close to the plot to marry Norfolk to Mary Queen of Scots.

Cecil did indeed receive letters from John Prestall signed Thomas Martinfield and addressed to Lord Conway. Those letters contained warnings of French Royal plots against Elizabeth. In March 1570 he wrote that there was a plot to kill Elizabeth by poison and black magic.

Cecil was also linked to fellow Welshman, Admiral Wynter, and described him as 'a man to be cherished'. Burcott was his trusted household manager.

Mildred Cecil had her own library and yes, she did own a copy of *Medicina* by Johannes Fernelius. The medical book by Girolamo Fracastoro, did exist and contained a poem about a shepherd meeting a Greek king that set out the symptoms of syphilis. She was also adoring and protective of their little boy, Robert, who was either born with a severe spinal deformity or was injured as a baby.

Robert Dudley, Earl of Leicester

In 1570 he was still the Queen's favourite, though the passion of the early years of her reign had subsided. He had also been hurt by her attempt to marry him to Mary Queen of Scots and then live at Court. In 1569 he had plotted against Cecil and had urged Norfolk to marry Mary – only to panic and spill everything to Elizabeth when he realised the folly of his decision.

Around 1570, he began a flirtation with Lady Douglas

Sheffield who looked as described in the novel. She pursued him into a relationship and they had a child – though never married.

In 1570, Dudley commissioned a suit of armour that was made in Greenwich and bears his honours and the bear from the Dudley coat of arms. It was indeed crafted for tilting at Kenilworth. It is now on display in Tournament Gallery, Leeds.

Walsingham

Walsingham had fairly recently joined Cecil's circle in 1570, having warned Cecil of Catholics in 1568. He was called 'The Moor' by Elizabeth who resented his forthright and undiplomatic speaking. However, he was invaluable, promoted by Cecil, and ended up being her main spymaster. He was naturally suspicious and hated Catholics – with a tendency to see conspiracy in every corner and shadow. He did indeed say, 'There is less danger in fearing too much than too little.'

Walsingham was sent to France as ambassador in 1570. He resisted it due to the huge expense – but Cecil and Elizabeth insisted.

Henry Norris, French Ambassador

Norris was ambassador from 1566 to 1570. He was constantly torn between having to maintain diplomatic relations and follow his heart to support the Huguenots. He witnessed much of the horrors of the Religious Wars. He was married to Margery, the daughter of a Welsh Baron.

It is quite true that in March 1570, Henry Norris wrote that a man with one eye and a cut over his face had boarded a ship in France with intent of harming Elizabeth.

The Characters – France

The Court of Le Louvre would have been splendid in every way – but Catherine was indeed having another palace built in 1570.

Catherine de Medici

The depiction of Catherine de Medici is true to her appearance, nature and attitudes. She wore black, a veil and kitten heels which she is said to have invented. She also ate huge amounts – making herself so ill due to gluttony that she was often days in bed. The invention of a fork is also attributed to her. She did own a parrot and had a troupe of perfectly dressed dwarves. She also had a pet bear – but I left him out. The group of women referred to as the Squadron are much written about, though some historians refute that they were used as Court honeypots. The verdict is out – I loved the image of them so wrote them in.

It is true that Nostradamus used to divine the future of Catherine's sons through various means. He once inspected the moles on her youngest son to predict for him a long reign. But he has also coached Catherine in the use of spells. When Catherine's husband, King Henry, died, she was determined to rid the palace of his lover, Diane de Poitiers, who was given a magnificent palace in Chaumont and instruction to never return to Court. When the lady walked in, she found rings of candles, strange symbols and pentacles etched into the floors and the walls. Such was the fear she fled that palace and never returned... nor to Court.

Ruggieri was the replacement for Nostradamus. An Italian soothsayer, he started with horoscopes, but moved onto a different order of knowledge – foretelling the future by studying entrails. He was also an alchemist, fully funded by French coin.

Catherine had worked hard to arrange a marriage between

her second son, Charles and Elizabeth and, in 1570, was frustrated by lack of progress due to Elizabeth's prevarication. In the novel she makes a spiteful barb about Elizabeth being godmother to his child – that did happen.

Even though Catherine was resentful of Mary Queen of Scots, she did petition for her release and for her to be recognised as a successor to Elizabeth.

Her relationship with the Guise family was testy and blew hot and cold. She saw them as dangerous in their persecution of the Huguenots. However, there was a warming of relationships in 1570, and the Cardinal of Lorraine did return to Court.

Catherine adored the Duc d'Anjou above her other children and allowed him many indulgences. Her strategy to marry him to Elizabeth of England started early in 1570.

Henri Duc d'Anjou

The depiction of the Duc d'Anjou is also correct – he loved to wear clothing that was very feminine, and he did have a following of mignons who wore hoop earrings, bore swords and dressed like Henri. However, there is debate as to whether Henri was effeminate or homosexual. He married; there are no records of him having male relationships; and the mignons were fighters. This might have been slander by his many enemies. However, it is true that he was a nasty little bully and was openly offensive about Elizabeth – calling her old and a public whore.

The Cardinal of Lorraine

Charles, Cardinal of Lorraine was as depicted – a handsome man with slightly receding hair, who wore the red clothes of high clergy. A portrait of him in 1572 shows a brightly coloured parrot. He did ask Henri Duc d'Anjou to become protector of the Catholic faith, paying him 200,000 francs as reward. He also created a scheme to marry the Duc to his niece – Mary Queen of Scots.

After an assassination attempt on the Guise in their Paris house 1560, they banned long coats and the wearing of masks.

Le Balafré or Francis Duc of Guise, who is mentioned as Baphomet's patron, was brother to the Cardinal of Lorraine and was indeed terribly scarred by a lance through his cheeks. He was assassinated in February 1563, though the bullet that hit him did not cause instant death. Despite all medical assistance, he bled to death over five days.

SETTINGS, SOCIETY – AND THE MUSHROOM

The churches and other places

All Hallows is sometimes known by the original name of All Hallows Barking as it was owned by the Barking Abbey. It is linked to Erkenwald and Ethelburh who, legend says, healed a cripple. It was the place in which Templars were imprisoned and put on trial and was the resting place of the early Catholic martyrs – John Fisher and Thomas More. The vicar in 1570 was Richard Tyrwhit. It is true that the church had housed a patrone statue which was taken down in 1559 but the clothes, which did look like a Templar, were retained. Their clothe mender, one William Armorer, died in 1560.

St John's Priory really was built by the Knights Hospitaller – the medical and fighting arm of the Templars. It was dissolved by Henry VIII in the dissolution of the abbeys, but loved by his daughter, Mary. Sadly, it was sold to the Dudley family and John Dudley did blow up the church entrance to gather stone for his house on the Strand. By 1570 it was the revels yard and would have held all the paraphernalia – tents, costumes, stages, props. The crypt is exactly as depicted in the novel – the blocked window and the hole for draining holy water are there. However, the Templar altar is not. That is in the crypt of All Hallows. It is true that a long closed and hidden crypt was discovered in an archaeological dig – behind the blocked window and the draining hole.

The Alms-houses at the top of the Anker Lane were real buildings in 1570. Anker Lane, Wirehale Lane and Bretaske Lane all existed and did lead to the river.

The warehouse in Seething Lane did exist on the site of the demolished St Mary Chapel and it was owned by Admiral Wynter.

The Templars

It is quite true that the Templars were accused of worshipping the pagan deity of Baphomet. It is also true that, Jacques de Molay, while burning at the stake, screamed a curse on those who had condemned him. The curse was not *'first terror, then death'*. Though that does describe the deaths of his accusers who both died badly within the year, as described in the novel.

The Huguenots

Huguenots started arriving in London in the early 1560s after the Massacre of Wassy started the religious wars. The depiction of the massacre in the novel is accurate. Huguenots were using a large barn to worship and on the morning of March 1st, 1562, when the Duc of Guise, was en-route to Joinville, the bell was tolled over and over. Thinking it an alarm bell, the Guise soldiers approached the barn and challenged the Huguenots. Conflict started and it ended with the slaughter of fifty unarmed worshipers, including women and children.

The Huguenots in London did set up their own church in Threadneedle Street, but also joined the congregations of other churches. They largely lived around Clerkenwell, Farringdon and Bethnal Green.

It is true that Huguenots carried a Méreaux cross – a small silver coin depicting Jesus on one side and the sun and a biblical tablet on the other. It was used a sign of brotherhood among the Huguenots and they would produce this as a sign of their faith.

The Huguenot Cross. Based on the lily of France it is full of symbolism. The four petals represent the four gospels, the little roundels at the tips of the petals are the eight Beatitudes. Then fleur-de-lys lies between the four petals, each with three petals. That makes another four petals for the twelve apostles.

Destroying Angel

This mushroom does exist and is deadly. As described by Clarissa, it is small, white and grows on rotting wood, especially oak. When ingested there are no symptoms for twenty-four to forty-eight hours and then the patient becomes extremely ill with symptoms of food poisoning as the internal organs fail. Death comes quickly with total liver failure.

Reading List

As ever a historical novel takes months of research. If you want to know more about the characters and history in *The Assassin's Mark*, then a good start would be:

Elizabeth

My bookshelves are now groaning. But for this novel I pulled on my favourite – Alison Weir's *Elizabeth the Queen* and then chapters and snippets from many others.

John Dee

The excellent research by Glynn Parry in *The Arch Conjuror of England* and Benjamin Woolley, *The Queen's Conjuror*, will give you in-depth insights into John Dee, his life and his achievements. Also a much older biography *John Dee 1527-1608* by Charlotte Fell-Smith, which though very much in Edwardian style, is full of rich detail.

Blanche ap Harri

The only book dedicated to this wonderful and important woman is Ruth Elizabeth Richardson's book, *Mistress Blanche: Queen Elizabeth's Confidante*.

The Cecils

So much has been written on the Cecils – maybe because they were so influential. David Loads, *The Cecils* will give a detailed account of their influence; and *Burghley* by Stephen Alford is one of the beset biographies I have read on this great man of the Tudor Court.

Walsingham

Much written about this man focusses on the later years when he was Elizabeth's spymaster and standing in his own right rather than Cecil's helper. *The Queen's Agent* by John Cooper and *Elizabeth's Spymaster* by Robert Hutchison both give insight into the complex character of this man.

Mary Queen of Scots

Again – this woman is an endless enigma and focus of writing. I pulled heavily on *Mary Queen of Scots* by the wonderful Antonia Fraser, and *Mary Queen of Scots* by David Templeman who gives a detailed account of her prisons. I read many more – I can only suggest you go to a bookstore and find a writer whose style you like.

The Shrewsburys

Read *Bess of Hardwick* by Mary S. Lovell for insight into the character of Bess and her husband.

Catherine de Medici

Catherine de Medici by Leonie Frieda gives detail and *Blood, Fire and Gold* by Estelle Paranque explores the two great queens and their rivalry and is a sympathetic analysis of both Elizabeth and Catherine.

The Guise

Trying to distil the complexity and politics of this family into a few characters was helped by the very accessible writing of Stuart Carroll in *Martyrs and Murderers*.

Add to the above various academic papers about the Religious Wars in France, the Northern Rebellion and the Huguenots in London.

and of course, Millie. You make a writer's life better in so many ways.

Finally, my beta readers – the people who give their time and intellect to read, consider, critique and give their honest opinion. They pick up detail, point out mistakes, guide me to be clear and tell me when I need to cut and cut again. This time you not only helped – but you helped in super-quick time. Thank you. This book is better for having had your eyes on it.

Love to all.
GJ

Acknowledgements

I might write the story, but a book takes a team of advisors, friends, guides, challengers, critics, helpers and educators.

This book is in your hands because of the excellent team at Legend Press. Editing by Lauren Wolff-Jones as always sharpened my writing and plotting. Behind her is a team who make everything happen. Copy-editing by Laura Gerrard, and then a gorgeous cover by the very talented Sarah Whittaker are all pulled together and conjured into my novel by the Legend Press dream team. My deep respect and gratitude to you all.

Other experts have made a huge contribution by sharing their wisdom, knowledge and kindness. Adey Grummet, Kathy Taylor, and Clwyd Roberts of All Hallows Church for the help, ideas and sheer fun; Rebecca Raven at St John's Priory for insight and advice; staff at The British Library; Nick Richmond who educated me about Tudor Westminster; Malcolm Mercer who helped with Norfolk in the Tower; and the many gifted teacher historians such as Yvette Reinfor of Hidden Tudor Tours.

I am also blessed by friends who remain interested, positive, uplifting and who are willing to give me a kick when I go into the doldrums of creativity. Nicky, Ceri, Sharon, Liz, Sue, Gabriel, Peter, Rhiannon, Josh, James, Sarah, Nigel, Barbara, Jean, Pat, all 'The Village Damsels'